Living with the Dead

BY THE SAME AUTHOR

Living with the Dead

by
Brian Stableford

A Black Coat Press Book

Visit our website at www.blackcoatpress.com

ISBN 978-1-61227-902-2. First Printing. November 2019.
Published by Black Coat Press, an imprint of Hollywood
Comics.com, LLC, P.O. Box 17270, Encino, CA 91416. All
rights reserved. Except for review purposes, no part of this
book may be reproduced or transmitted in any form or by any
means, electronic or mechanical, including photocopying,
recording, or by any information storage and retrieval system,
without permission in writing from the publisher. The stories
and characters depicted in this novel are entirely fictional.
Printed in the United States of America.

CHAPTER I

The slope of the hill, although still not steep, was beginning to take its toll. Viewed from down below, at the mediocre elevation of the cottage, the climb to the ruins did not seem very intimidating, but it was longer and harder than it seemed. Paul had been living on the mountain for eight years now, and he was an assiduous daily walker, but he rarely went all the way to the top. He was usually content to walk down to the village, or in the woods at much the same altitude, usually to the east of the cottage, because the ancient convent and its extensive grounds, now an eccentric phalanstery, was located to the west, further up the slope. The thought that its inhabitants might be observing him made him strangely uneasy, in spite of the fact that he was on satisfactory, if distant, terms with them. In consequence of his lack of practice, he was now beginning to feel the strain in his legs—but he felt strong, and was determined not to flag.

Although they were both city-dwellers, and hence, in theory, should have been less well-equipped for hill-climbing than Paul was, Victor Marvaud and Gaston Lambrunet both seemed sprightly and vigorous, not at all embarrassed by the slope, and they had drawn a dozen paces ahead, chatting animatedly. Paul remembered that they had done exactly the same thing once before, more than half a lifetime ago for the three of them, who were now comfortably past the age of thirty.

Paul could not help thinking, as he remembered the day they had climbed all the way to the ruins when they were fifteen years old, that the sight of their broad backs moving ahead of him, propelled by energetic legs, had been symbolic and prophetic of their path in life, in which they had seemed always to be ahead of him, forever leaving him behind...except that on that day...

He shivered, suddenly, as if under the shock of a super-natural coincidence, as an arm slid beneath his own.

"I'm being indiscreet, I know, Monsieur Furneret—may I call you Paul?—but my short legs are beginning to protest, and I need a little support. Gaston seems to be engrossed in joyful reminiscences with his friend, and I'm reluctant to tear him away. May I borrow your arm?"

Paul turned to look at Armande Lambrunet, Gaston's new wife, conscious that he must be blushing deeply. Had he blushed as deeply half a lifetime ago when Martine took his arm? Probably, he thought.

"Of course," he said, hesitantly. "But..."

"Oh, Gaston won't mind," she said. "I know that you and he have been friends, almost brothers, forever, so we're prac-tically family...and I ought to make an effort to get to know you. We hardly saw you at the wedding...an introduction and a leave-taking, with barely a few words exchanged in be-tween...and yet I was so curious about you. The famous paint-er of the dead! The mysterious genius! Gaston just talks about you familiarly, as a childhood friend, as if you were an ordi-nary person, and Victor never departs from his customary flippancy, but in society..."

"Surely people in Parisian society don't talk about me?" Paul protested.

"Certainly they do. Absentees usually get short shrift there; living in Provence is the next best thing to non-existence, even for painters whose works appear in the Salon every year, but your name keeps coming up, albeit in whis-pers. Did you really paint your famous portrait of Yvaine de Rochemure after seeing her in a vision induced by animal magnetism?"

"I didn't actually *see* her," Paul murmured, stammering slightly with an embarrassment sharper than any he had felt for at least a dozen years, "but yes, I based the painting on a drawing I had made unconsciously, under a kind of induced hypnosis."

The young woman's gaze was deeply disturbing, although he was not sure why. She was beautiful, of course, with silky dark hair and unusually bright brown eyes flecked with gold, but it was not her beauty that was making his heart pound, nor the fact that she was Gaston's wife, because he knew that if Gaston turned round to see them arm in arm he really would not mind; it was something deeper, which he could not quite fathom...although it obviously had something to do with the echo the situation contained of the day when he had linked arms with Martine, Gaston's sister, in similar circumstances.

"And Baron de Rochemure really begged you to paint it as he lay dying?" Armande added, continuing her interrogation.

"It wasn't as melodramatic as you're making it sound," Paul assured her. "He lived for three months after I completed the painting—long enough, I hope, to derive some...well, I don't know whether consolation is the right word, but..."

"But there was a lot of publicity, wasn't there, when his heirs put it up for sale, along with your other portrait, of a dead medium, and a set of sketches? There was something of a frenzy of interest, more excitement than was generated the Delvilles and the other surrealist paintings, which were more valuable in purely monetary terms?"

"Yes, there was a lot of publicity," Paul admitted. "That was largely Victor's doing, I think. He's always blown my trumpet in Paris as loudly as he could. He's been...a very good friend."

Apprehensive about where the conversation might be heading, Paul was almost relieved when the young woman's next observation was: "But you do portraits of the living too, in Toulouse? Gaston says that you're always in demand there."

"I've been fortunate enough to receive a steady stream of commissions," Paul said, a trifle warily.

"I've suggested to Gaston that he commission you to paint me, while I'm still in the full flower of youth. I thought

7

he'd be delighted, with your being such old friends...practically brothers...but he seemed strangely hesitant. I don't know why."

Armande paused, a trifle provocatively, obviously inviting a speculative explanation.

Paul endeavored to oblige, albeit deceptively. "You're only going to be in Toulouse for a few more days," he pointed out. "Then you'll be settling into your new house in Paris. Gaston knows that I rarely come to Paris, and never do any painting while I'm there, so he probably thinks that there isn't time."

"You did the painting of Rochemure's daughter in Paris, though?"

"Yes, I did, at the baron's request, but that was a rare exception."

"Not the painting of the little medium, then? Or the one hanging in your dining room?"

"No, I did those here, in the cottage," Paul confirmed, again somewhat uneasy about the direction of the conversation—with justification, as it rapidly turned out.

"And the one on your easel at the moment," Gaston's bride queried, "is the woman who died recently? The famous author?" Her tone was level and polite, but Paul knew that she was probing. He had no idea what Gaston and Victor might have told her about his relationship with Jane de La Vaudère, but it was not a subject that he wanted to discuss with a young woman barely into her twenties, who was still at the tail end of her honeymoon voyage, on her way back to Paris to take up her new life.

He looked at Gaston and Victor but they had drawn even further ahead since he had had to match strides with Armande, and they were still deep in excited conversation, Having met up that morning for the first time since the wedding, they had probably moved on from Gaston's impressions of the places that he and his new bride had visited recently to talking about Victor's exploits, especially his recent engagement and his embryonic wedding plans.

Deliberately winding the conversation back to an earlier point, Paul said: "Perhaps Gaston's also a trifle reluctant to have his beautiful young bride painted by a man whose primary reputation in Paris, as you just pointed out, is that of a painter of the spirits of the dead. It might seem..." He paused, not quite sure how to continue

"A little like tempting fate? Armande suggested. "But none of the messieurs and mesdames of Toulouse that you've painted in recent years have died in consequence, have they? And as you say, you have a steady trickle of commissions, so no one here is intimidated. And you've been perfectly willing to accept the commissions, and also to paint your friend Clémence from life, which you surely wouldn't have done if you thought it might imperil her in some way?"

Paul knew that she was still probing, but he supposed that it was understandable. When he had visited Paris to serve as a witness at Gaston's wedding he had barely stayed for a few hours, only long enough to attend the ceremony and pay an obligatory call on Auguste Chazelle, his agent. He simply had not wanted to face the possibility of being asked embarrassing questions—or, even worse, being offered hypocritical condolences—but he could understand that his conduct must have seemed odd to the young bride, making him seem far more a man of mystery than he was...except, he supposed, that he was now making himself even more a man of mystery by being so evasive.

He decided that he had to make an effort. Armande was right; having married Gaston, who was the nearest thing to a brother he had, even closer than Victor, because of...

He cut that thought short, and went on by reminding himself that she really was practically family now, and he ought not to treat her as a stranger. After all, it was not as if he had any secrets...

He almost laughed derisively at that hypocritical thought, and all he eventually said in reply to the young woman's last provocation was: "No, I suppose not."

"Now that Victor's following Gaston's example," Armande said, seemingly feeling that a little more indiscretion was called for, since Paul was being so stubbornly uninformative, "they'll probably be expecting you to follow suit. Gaston's always telling me that the three of you used to do everything together."

"Not everything," Paul objected. "And since we were adolescents we've taken very different paths in life. Victor's a banker, Gaston's a businessman, and I'm a painter. They're both at a point in life when men in their careers typically think of marrying, but painters are notorious Bohemians, who revel in being atypical."

"Are you suggesting that Gaston has only married me because he's at the point in his career when he needs a wife?" she said, teasing him maliciously.

Paul knew that his blush must have turned crimson again. "Of course not," he said. "Gaston has been waiting for years to find the right woman to marry. He's always been the most romantic of the three of us. He would never marry for any reason but a deep and abiding love."

Pompous idiot! he said to himself, secretly.

"Unlike Victor, then?" she said, immediately springing the trap he had accidentally set for himself. "Poor Clorinde!"

Clorinde was Victor's recently acquired fiancée—exactly the kind of fiancée that a socially ambitious young man who was making progress in the profession of playing with other people's money required, in order to create an impression of social stability and respectability.

"Victor loves Clorinde dearly and sincerely," Paul said, hoping that it was true. "His libertine image has always been more show than reality, and if he's engaged in serial flirtations since the days we were at school together, it has mainly been in a spirit of experimentation. Like Gaston, he's been always been looking for the right woman to marry...he's just employed a more active method of enquiry."

"Very delicately put," said Armande, laughing. "So, when Gaston says that Victor would always chase anything in a skirt with predatory fervor, even at the age of fifteen, he's just being malicious, or envious...or both?"

"Victor is a good man," Paul said. "If he's something of a Don Juan, it's not because he's predatory. He doesn't set out to hurt anyone, let alone ruin anyone. He's a handsome man, and he was a handsome boy; girls used to chase him as much as he chased them, and I'll wager that it's still the same in Paris—but once he settles down, he'll be settled. He's doubtless fortunate that Clorinde said yes to him, but she's fortunate too, in my opinion."

"Like me?"

"Of course. There's no better husband on the world than Gaston."

"Absolutely—so you don't agree, then, with the people who tell us that we've got it the wrong way round?"

Paul was startled by that. "I don't know what you mean," he said, honestly.

"I mean that ever since Victor's engagement was announced, people who know us in Paris have apparently been heard to suggest that Clorinde, being so sober and earnest, might have be a better match for the sober and earnest Gaston, whereas I, being so flighty and indiscreet, might have been better suited to a social butterfly and connoisseur of gossip like Victor."

"Even if those descriptions were true," Paul said, "which I don't believe, the judgment would be nonsensical. I've only met Clorinde once, and I don't know you very well either, but in my opinion, the two of you have got it exactly the right way round. A little difference and contrast in a relationship is a good thing. People always used to say of Victor and Gaston that they were chalk and cheese, and that I was neither, but that didn't prevent us being faster friends than anyone else we knew. Quite the opposite."

Armande looked up at Gaston and Victor, who had almost reached the plateau of the ruins, and were evidently making a final surge in order to reach it, perhaps even racing, although Paul was sure that both would deny it if the suggestion were made to them.

"You do seem to be a rather odd trio," the young woman observed. "I can't quite imagine the three of you as friends even at university, let alone school—although I suppose you all passed for intellectuals then, in a company that would hardly have matched the standard of Louis-le-Grand."

Paul, who thought that he, Gaston and Victor could all have held their own very comfortably at the Lycée Louis-le-Grand, refrained carefully from taking offense at that remark.

"We did have plenty of interests in common—literary, artistic, political and scientific," he said, "although you might not think so look at us now, but I think our temperamental differences were as important as any similarities in holding us together. We all had different ambitions and objectives, you see; we were never rivals. Any competition between us was...well, as trivial as the competition that Gaston and Victor are now having to get to the top first. Whichever of them wins, the other won't mind, because it's a matter of no consequence. With regard to serious objectives, we've always been able to support one another wholeheartedly, without any envy, the way that Victor advertises my painting in Paris. It's because we're dissimilar that there's never been any occasion for a serious dispute between us."

"Not even over women?" she asked, malicious again.

"Especially not over women," Paul said.

The young woman seemed to be on the point of following up that issue, but Victor and Gaston had now reached the top of the slope, simultaneously, and were looking down at the laggards.

"Just like last time!" shouted Victor, laughing delightedly. "Paul needed to be helped up then, too!"

Although they were still some distance away, Paul had no difficulty seeing Gaston looking daggers at his friend, casting a slight shadow over his claims regarding their unwavering solidarity.

"What does he mean?" asked Armande, looking at Paul curiously.

"When we climbed the mountain at fifteen," Paul said, "we weren't alone. Gaston's sister Martine was with us. She was only thirteen. Gaston and Victor pressed on ahead, as they did today, and I stayed back in order to help her."

"Ah!" said Armande, as if that answered a question she had wondered about but had not found an opportunity to ask, and said: "Is what when you fell in love with her?"

There was not the slightest reason for Paul to be surprised that Gaston had told her about him and Martine, but even so, he winced. His voice was perfectly level, though, as he replied. "I already loved her—but that was the last time that I was almost alone with her, and it did feel...different. Things between us were never quite the same again.

"But nothing came of it? Gaston says that, so far as he knows, you never even kissed?"

"No," he admitted, "nothing came of it. I never knew whether my feelings were reciprocated, and I was too timid to ask. There always seemed to be plenty of time...but there wasn't."

"Ah!" she said, again—but by then they had caught up with Victor and Gaston.

"Don't look at me like that," Armande said to Gaston, apparently having mistaken the direction of his scowl—or pretending that she had. "I'm just a frail girl, and Paul is a perfect gentleman. You'd have done the same for him, I'm sure, except that he would never have neglected his poor new-lywed wife like that." Her tone was deliberately flippant, emphatically unserious.

Victor laughed again. "It was me he was frowning at," he said. "I shouldn't have made a reference to Martine. I was entirely at fault—it's still a touchy subject, even after eight years. None of us has entirely stopped grieving."

"One of us evidently has," Gaston muttered, darting an apologetic glance at Paul that was apparently intended to convey to the artist that it was not on his own behalf that Gaston had resented Victor's slight gaffe.

"You've painted her portrait too," Armande remembered, addressing Paul again. "I've seen it, in Gaston's house in Toulouse, next to the portrait of their mother..." She stopped. "Now it *is* me you're frowning at," she said to her husband. "Have I said something I shouldn't?"

Gaston opened his mouth, but Paul was quick to interrupt "No, Madame Lambrunet," he said, "you haven't. As you said, I was very fond of Martine, and I was very fond of Amélie too, who was very kind to me after my own mother died. Gaston was generous enough to urge his mother and sister to treat me almost as if I were his brother—which demonstrates what I was saying just now about our being the best of friends. We were both afflicted when they died—but there's absolutely no reason why you should refrain from mentioning them to me."

"Well, then," she said, "if I'm going to be almost a sister to you, I forbid you to refer to me ever again as Madame Lambrunet. I'm Armande—and I won't call you Monsieur Furneret again, or anything but Paul. We can treat one another as family, is that agreed? And do stop frowning, Gaston—the wind might change."

"Actually it hardly ever does up here," Victor put in, trying to lighten the tone. "Always the same updraft. It's a quirk of the local geography—Gaston can tell you all about it, at great length, if he hasn't already."

Gaston raised his eyes to the heavens, which at least wiped the vestiges of the frown from his face.

Armand was already looking around. She scanned the scattered stones that were all that remained of the crude ramparts of the meager fortress that had once occupied the hilltop, but she seemed to decide immediately that they were of little or no interest except as a symbolic marker of the summit—a judgment that Paul had always shared wholeheartedly. The young woman looked westwards then, in the direction of Toulouse, but the city was invisible. Although there were no very high hills in the way, the ground was sufficiently uneven to hide the valley of the Garonne in that direction. She turned to look instead at the slope they had climbed, her gaze inevitably picking out the only substantial building for miles around, which had not been visible from the cottage, or from the road the automobile had followed in bring her up from the village, because it was hidden by trees.

"What's that?" she asked.

"It used to be a Cistercian convent," Victor told her. "Fifteenth century or thereabouts, but built on the site of an older convent destroyed during the so-called Albigensian crusade, which was probably built on the ruins of an early Christian shrine, on what was perhaps a pagan sacred site before that. Nowadays it's leased by a Parisian sect of sapphists run by an old friend of Paul's, although he and she haven't been on speaking terms for four years and she still lives in her Parisian headquarters."

"Is a sapphist something like a Trappist?" Armande asked, apparently in all innocence, even though she was a Parisian.

Victor laughed again. "Gaston can explain that to you too," he sniggered.

"I'm not the only one who can explain things at tedious length," Gaston said. "Victor has only given you the short version of the convent's story. Do tell Armande the rest, Victor."

Victor shrugged. "The Cistercian nuns were only there until the Revolution," he said, "when they were turfed out. The land then associated with the convent was then proclaimed to be national property and broken into lots for sale, but when the Restoration rolled around and committees were set up to enable the return of confiscated estates to their aristocratic owners, mostly émigrés, a Toulousan antiquarian—one of Gaston's many relatives—produced parchments to prove that the sector of the mountain we're looking down on still belonged, rightfully, to the descendants of one of Simon de

Montfort's English cronies, who had been gifted it by the King of France after the Albigensian crusade.

"The descendants in question, the Megister family, had no idea that they owned it, but when they consulted their old family documents, they found the necessary supporting evidence. They started collecting a few meager rents, but didn't really pay any attention to the domain until now, when the most recent heirs have decided to check out their lost estate in the south of France, perhaps because so-called development is all the rage now that the twentieth century is in full swing. They're staying in Toulouse at present, hobnobbing with one of Gaston's many uncles, while investigating their property before going on to tour the Riviera. If it hadn't been for them, my automobile would have been the first ever to set wheels on the mountain, this morning, but their Sunbeam beat my Panhard to it by one day. They're going to drop in again on Thursday, I believe, after consulting the members of the legal fraternity in the city."

"That's right," said Paul, "but I don't anticipate any bad news. I'm a tenant in good standing, and they seemed to be quite pleased during their flying visit yesterday to have a painter of modest reputation living on their mountain. They didn't say what they thought of the convent, but they really ought to be very pleased with the Sisters, who have worked miracles in a mere eight years with the fields, the orchards and the vineyard, without a single male laborer ever setting foot on the terrain."

"You've still left out all the interesting stuff, Victor," said Gaston, maintaining a hint of malice in his tone. "Why don't you explain what those Alpinists are doing in the forest on the far side of Paul's cottage?"

"Alpinists?" said Armande, puzzled, squinting as her gaze followed the direction of her husband's pointing finger to consider a substantial crew of workmen busy in a long but narrow gap in the forest canopy. "You mean mountain-climbers? But we've just walked up the steeper slope of the mountain, haven't we? What on earth do they need those ropes, grapnels and crampons for?"

"You have very good eyes, my dear," Victor complimented her, "but Gaston is being far too modest. All I can tell you is that they're probably looking either for old bones or the Holy Grail, but either way, they're wasting their time. The Great Cleft is said to be bottomless, and even if that's not true, nobody has ever reached the bottom and come up again to tell the tale. Gaston's the one who can explain why there's a fissure there, which requires sophisticated climbing equipment in order to descend into it. Apparently, it dates all the way back to the glory days of the volcanoes of the Auvergne, but Gaston has his own tedious theory about its precise nature. I'm surprised he hasn't told you all about it, but you've only been married for two months and he's probably still afraid of boring you to death if he displays the true colors of his pedantry."

"Oh, you're impossible, both of you," said Armande, laughing. "Do you know what they're talking about, Paul?"

"Oh yes," said Paul, feigning world-weariness. "I've heard it all before, many a time."

"The thing is...," Gaston began, but she silenced him with a gesture.

"I want Paul to tell me," she said. "After all, it's his mountain."

Paul laughed. "If only," he said. "I'm a tenant in good standing, but only of a small cottage, a stable, a well and a vegetable patch. Zosima's acolytes have custody of a hundred times as much land, including an entire farm, fields, pastureland and orchards as well as the vineyard of which they seem to have high hopes. But the short version of the story Victor wanted Gaston to tell is that, however they were caused, there are three deep cracks, or clefts, in the rock of the mountain. People sometimes go down into the shallower ones: paleontologists or archeologists looking for old bones and ancient cultural artifacts, or treasure-hunters, but as Victor says, their chances of finding anything even in the lesser clefts are very slim.

"So far as I know, all the lateral caves are just bare holes, without a trace of paintings or flints reminiscent of the Age of Chipped Stone, and there are several meters of sticky silt at the bottom of the lesser clefts, in which it's impossible to dig without the holes collapsing. The local people sometimes throw shards of pottery and old tin cups down, in order to have a laugh at the expense of the optimistic scholars or grail-hunters, but the joke really isn't very funny, because if it rains—the climate here is very benign, but the weather can be extremely uneven, and when it does rain, it often comes down in torrents—the lesser clefts flood very rapidly, and anyone caught down the hole is in dire danger. Any recoverable bones are likely to be recent, those of treasure-hunters who didn't heed the warning that going down into them in bright sunshine is easy enough, but coming up during or after a rainstorm is well-nigh impossible."

"But why would anyone think that the Holy Grail might be down there?" the young woman asked, mystified.

"Blame a local historian—or a fantasist—called Napoleon Peyrat," Gaston put in, finally grasping the opportunity to display the expertise in matters of local history and legend for which his family was justly renowned. "He published a history of the Albigensians some thirty years ago, which claims that the last whimper of the genocide, when the remaining Cathar refugees were besieged in Montségur, they had custody of an inestimable treasure—probably the Holy Grail—which they smuggled out of the citadel before it fell, hid somewhere within a few days' ride, and which was then lost, because the men who had hidden it were killed. But his whole so-called history is a work of fiction, based on a handful of legends of no great antiquity."

"That's not strictly true," said Victor, competitively. "Obviously, the present population of Toulouse mostly consists of descendants of incomers—by which I mean people who arrived after the twelfth century—and even before the massacre of the Albigensians, the region had had a very troubled history, going beyond Roman times to the fringe of

Massalia, the Phocean colony based in what is now Marseille, but there must be at least a few Occitan families whose ancestry really does to back to the first century A.D. The documentary details of the legend of the three Maries are Medieval, but the evidence of place-names and shrines suggest that the oral tradition must be much older. On the other hand, Gaston is absolutely right that anyone who thinks that the convent down there is built on the site of a shrine raised to one of the three Maries, in the ruins of a temple of Artemis, itself built on the ruins of a temple to a goddess whose name hasn't survived, hasn't a shred of real evidence, and anyone who thinks that the Holy Grail was an actual cup rather than a symbol, which might once have been hidden in or near the absurd fortress in whose runs we're standing, is woefully mistaken."

Armande frowned, as if wondering whether to follow up one or more of the issues raised by that speech, but she was shivering slightly in the updraft that Victor had mentioned earlier, and seemed to make the decision to postpone further discussion of the myth of the Holy Grail until a more relaxed occasion, She could not, however, resist the temptation to take up one issue. She looked around at the scattered stones of the ancient rampart. "Why do you call the fortress absurd?" she asked. "Surely the Midi is full of ruined castles of this sort, built on the top of hills much like this one, as necessary defenses to protect feudal aristocrats from rebellions and invaders?"

"Yes it is," said Gaston, "and most of them are absurd—baronic follies not fit for their imagined purpose. That's why they're almost all in ruins. They were certainly defensible positions, difficult to take by storm, but they're not edifices in which any substantial number of people could actually live, or which could withstand a siege for very long. They were expressions of vanity rather than utility."

"Why couldn't people live in them?" the young woman wanted to know.

"In a word," said her husband, "water. As Paul says, when it rains here, it often rains torrentially, but not for long.

This is a very petty mountain by comparison with those of the Central Massif, whose peaks you can see on the horizon, but it's high enough to accumulate cloud and to become the focal point of sudden violent storms. For long periods in summer, though, it's dry. Doubtless the builders of the fort had cisterns to collect and store water when they could, but not enough to supply a resident population for very long, and if the fort filled up with refugees from an invading force, they would have run out of water in a matter of days."

"There are three springs that open on this face of the mountain," Paul added, "but the only one that hasn't run dry at present is the one that opens in the grounds of the convent. My well has accessible water, but it's a long way down at the moment. Even at the end of winter, though, in the season of the thaw, when all the springs are gushing and the lesser clefts fill up, it wouldn't be possible to supply the fort at the summit if it were under siege."

"And even though we're in the Midi," Gaston resumed, "it sometimes gets very cold in the depths of winter, especially at altitude. The water in the cracks in the rock sometimes freezes—not often, but often enough. And when water freezes in cracks in rock, its expansion sometimes exerts enough pressure to widen the cracks, or split the rock. Over tens of thousands of years, or hundreds of thousands, small cracks can gradually become great or lesser clefts..."

"Theoretically," Victor put in.

"Theoretically," Gaston admitted.

Armande looked at Paul. "Did they argue like this last time they were here?" she asked.

"I can't remember," Paul said.

"I can," said Victor. "No, we didn't—but we were ignorant children then, with no academic expertise to display, and the predominant impression was that of wild nature, inexplicable and in no need of explanation. The convent was just a ruin then, and there weren't any gangs of potholers in sight. The cottage hardly existed. Gaston and his uncle arranged for it to be rebuilt for Paul eight years ago, and even had the road mended, after a fashion—good enough for Paul's horse and a trap. It was improved again, all the way to the convent, when the lesbian nuns moved in, but it's still pretty rough. Are you going to mention that to your landlords on Thursday, Paul?"

"I don't think I'll have to," Paul said. "They brought their automobile up, remember; if their mechanic consents to try it again, he won't leave them in any doubt that it won't be adequate for future purposes. Whether they'll care or not is a different matter. How the sisters get their rickety donkey-carts back and forth from the village half a dozen times a week— more when they go to the big market in Toulouse—I really don't know."

"What you need to do," said Victor, "is to persuade the new owners to have their portraits painted while they're staying in the vicinity, so that you can work your charm on them. They're young, I believe, and the sister's quite pretty?"

"I expect they have plenty of portrait painters in England," Paul observed.

"It's not the same," said Victor. "You're French—and you're the famous painter of spirits, the living proof of the immortality of the human soul. It's a unique opportunity. Have they visited your studio?"

"Yes, very briefly, but they can take a longer look at the paintings on Thursday if they want."

"Not including the one in your bedroom, I hope?"

"No," Paul admitted. "Not including the one my bedroom."

"Why not the one in the bedroom?" Armande wanted to know. She too had seen the studio and the dining room—and for that matter, the kitchen—but not either of the bedrooms in the cottage."

"The best advertisement by far for Paul's work is in the studio," Gaston said, evading the question while pretending to answer it. "The work in progress shows what he's capable of doing for anyone else—although it might be as well not to mention to the pretty landowner that the lady on the easel is dead...oh, damn. Now I'm doing it. Sorry."

"It's all right," said Paul. "Given my reputation, it's a matter that's bound to come up with any and all visitors. If I were sensitive about it, I wouldn't have hung the portrait of Juliette in the dining room, would I?" He knew, though, that the cases were not comparable. Juliette had been dead for nearly six years, Jane only for a matter of months.

Gaston, having spoken thoughtlessly once and repented of it, kept silent, but Victor said: "You really ought to send the picture of Scarab to Chazelle, along with the horror. Let him sell them. It isn't healthy, keeping them at home like that. You are going to send him the La Vaudère picture to him, I hope? That one he can definitely sell, for big money. Méricant still has unpublished books of hers on hand, and the last one she published while she was alive is said to have sold thirty thousand copies, albeit with the aid of the nude photographs. She has a big following. What?" He was looking at Gaston, whose frown was now almost thunderous. "He *said* he doesn't mind." Defensively, Victor added: "I'm only trying to help."

Armande, apparently having given up asking for clarifications that no one provided, looked at each of them in turn. "I can see why you call yourselves the very best of friends," she murmured, sarcastically.

"We are," Paul assured her. "That's why Gaston is being a trifle oversensitive about the possibility that I might be upset by a careless remark, and why Victor really is only trying to help. They care, and I'm grateful to them, but I don't want our conversation to keep stumbling over needless anxieties." He looked at Gaston. "Armande is one of us now, and she needs to be able to ask us anything she wants, just as you and Victor need to be able to say anything you want. Yes, I was deeply distressed by Jane's sudden and unexpected death, as I was eight years ago by Martine's, but I don't need such matters to be surrounded by a *cordon sanitaire*. And yes, I still miss Juliette, even after all these years, and I have absolutely no intention of sending her portrait to Paris to be put up for auction."

Victor raised his hands defensively. "All right," he said. "If that's the way you feel, but in my defense, you have been telling me for years that you and she didn't love one another."

"So I have," Paul agreed. "Perhaps I was wrong, and am only just beginning to understand that. Sometimes, you have to be haunted for a long time before you figure but what the dead actually mean to you. And now, having conquered the mountain, thus proving—or not—that we're still as sprightly as we were at fifteen, and having reminded ourselves that the old stones really are rather uninteresting, whether the fort was a baronial folly or not, perhaps we ought to start back down again. Madame Louvot will be making a special effort for dinner, and I don't want to worry her with the possibility that we might be late."

"We have plenty of time," Gaston assured him. "It's quicker going down than coming up, as long as no one falls and twists an ankle." As if to emphasize the point, or perhaps to redeem himself for his earlier neglect, he offered his arm to his wife. She seemed to be on the point of making a sarcastic remark, but she stopped herself and nodded her head gracefully. She and Gaston took the lead as they all began to make their way back down the mountain.

CHAPTER II

Victor linked arms with Paul, and deliberately held him back for a few seconds, until the married couple had drawn some way ahead. Then he said: "So what do you think of her?"

"Utterly delightful," said Paul. "I think they'll be very happy together."

"You're such a romantic," said Victor. "I'm taking it for granted, of course, that you're going to be a witness at my wedding too?"

"Of course. I wouldn't miss it for the world."

"No, but you might sneak in and out again, hardly saying a word to anyone. I don't want that. I forgave you for Gaston's wedding because Madame de La Vaudère had just died, and I know how fond you were of her, and she of you, even though you lived so far apart and barely saw one another once a year, but at my wedding, I want to show you off. I won't have that many geniuses there, and you're the only one for whose career I can claim the lion's share of the credit."

"The lion's share?" Paul queried. "Really?"

"Well, obviously, you actually painted the pictures, but I've helped to promote them and to guide your first steps on the road to celebrity. I was the one who suggested that you to go to La Pommerat's séance, where you first met the baron, and I was the one who made sure you got to the Observatory for Flammarion's séance. If it weren't for me, remember, you wouldn't have been introduced to Madame de La Vaudère, or to the amazing Zosima. Yes, I think I can fairly claim the lion's share of the making of your reputation. And if you'd only listened to me, you could have made a lot more money and saved yourself a lot of heartache. There's still time for you to make up the lost ground. Paris is full of rich Americans nowadays, all keen to have their wives and daughters painted. The nouveaux riches are a veritable Pactolus, and even a humble painter stands a fair chance of hooking a starry-eyed heiress to a fortune made in the tinned beef or canned tuna trade."

"I'm not looking to trap an American heiress," Paul replied, curtly.

"You don't seem to be looking to hook anyone here," Victor retorted, his tone critical in spite of his obvious effort to keep it light. "I understand that Gaston has introduced you to at least three of his multitudinous female cousins, for whom you'd have been a perfectly eligible suitor, but that you've rejected them all one after another, for no apparent reason, even though they were all manifestly interested. That's bad—not only terribly undiplomatic but bad for you. We're beginning to get seriously worried about you."

"Gaston has been very kind," Paul said, "and the young women in question are perfectly charming, but..." He did not know how to continue.

"But what?" Victor prompted. "Gaston thinks you might be secretly in love with Clémence Sancerre, but that you're no more able to tell her so than you were with Martine before you left for Paris, but I said no...that if you were in love with anyone, it was Jane, even though you hardly ever saw her. Either way, my friend, we're convinced that you're spending far too much time living with the dead and not nearly enough living with the living, if you'll pardon my frankness."

"No pardon is necessary," Paul assured him. "Your frankness has always been one of your most endearing qualities."

"I'm glad you think so. Well, Gaston will be settling in Paris now, to please his wife, and I'll soon be properly settled there too. We both think that you ought to move back there as soon as possible, and that you ought to think very seriously about settling down yourself, with someone like Armande or Clorinde. It's time. I can help, in Paris, just as Gaston has tried to help you here."

"It's very kind of you to take such an interest," Paul said, "but I'm afraid that Gaston's good intentions have all gone to waste. His cousins are delightful, I agree, but the mere fact that they're his cousins makes me feel slightly uneasy. As for the young women you could introduce me to in Paris..."

"All top drawer, I sure you," Victor said "I don't say that all the girls I've had in Paris have been respectable, but I certainly wouldn't introduce you to any that aren't good caliber. Trust me."

"Oh, I do," Paul assured him. "I assume that you stopped hanging around cafés in Montmartre even before you started courting Clorinde, but returning to Paris would be a big step, for which I'm not quite ready yet. I feel that I have plenty of work to do here, with the living as well as the dead."

"I dare say you have," said Victor, "but are you happy?"

Paul stared into space, looking out over the distant plain and the part of the forest below their position. He could see the "Alpinists" setting up their apparatus on the edge of the Great Cleft more distinctly now, and those directing the labor seemed to be men of reasonable maturity, far more likely to be respectable scholars than foolish treasure-hunters—but who could tell, nowadays? The operation was obviously serious, given the efforts they were making to establish secure points of support on the rim for long ropes.

Paul sighed slightly. In nearly eight years, he had been tempted more than once to descend into one or other of the lesser clefts, simply because they were there, just to see what might be at the bottom, but he never had. Rationality had always told him that, on the one hand, there was nothing to be gained, and on the other, that such descents were dangerous. He had always hesitated.

"Happy?" he said in slightly belated reply to Victor's question. "No, I suppose I can't say that I'm happy. I'm glad that you and Gaston are, but I'm not at all sure that the recipes that have worked for you would work for me. And it's not because I'm grieving, over Jane, or Juliette or Martine. As you've often pointed out, my relationships with them could hardly be reckoned satisfactory, for one reason or another...but when I'm painting, I'm at least absorbed, almost in a different world, where happiness isn't really an issue."

"And that's exactly why we're worried. Even as children, we used to worry about you slipping into your little trances, but Amélie always told us not to pay any attention to it, that it was just an aspect of your talent, something you needed, something that ought to be fostered and protected for the sake of your future as an artist. Maybe she was right, given that you have become a marginally famous painter—with my help—and mostly because of paintings based on sketches done in your trances, but I wouldn't want you to get lost wherever it is you go when you leave this world behind. I wouldn't want to stop you going, but you really ought to take an example from those fellows out at the Great Cleft, who are evidently making sure that their ropes are securely anchored in the sunlight, so that they can always be certain of being able to get back up when they're ready to go down. You need an anchorage, Paul, and there's no better anchorage in life than a wife. I understand that you need to be alone when you're actually painting, but you don't have to live alone when you're not."

"I don't live alone," Paul pointed out, politely refraining from drawing attention to Victor's new-found zeal in promoting an institution that he had casually decried for years.

"Baron de Rochemure's old housekeeper doesn't count," his friend persisted, "not so much because she's old, but because she's a constant reminder, a continuing link with the dead. You've never told me what happened to you the night Zosima mesmerized you in Passy, and that's fine, but if nothing else, it bound you to the baron's death-bed long enough to do that painting of his dead daughter, and it seems to me that you haven't been the same since. If you simply must, bring Madame Louvot with you to cook and clean for you in Paris, but at the very least, get yourself a mistress in Toulouse. You must have opportunities, among the women you paint as well as Gaston's cousins."

"I hardly think so. In fact, I think one of the reasons I get so many commissions is that husbands and fathers know that their wives and daughters will be perfectly safe with me."

"Well, I suppose that reputation has its advantages—but one of them might be that it's a perfect cover for clandestine seductions. You ought to spend more time in Toulouse...although there might even be possibilities out here, with an entire colony of madwomen practically on your doorstep, not all of whom are lesbians, by any means, if the refuge in Paris is anything to go by."

Paul laughed, briefly. "I don't think they're even supposed to speak to me," he said, "although they're by no means cloistered. The sisters who come to the back door of the cottage to sell Madame Louvot eggs, vegetables and their experimental liqueurs, always keep their hoods up. When they pass me on the road or encounter me walking in the woods they salute me politely, but they don't speak, and I honestly don't think I'd recognize a single one of them with her hood down."

"Experimental liqueurs?" Victor queried.

"Yes, you can see their little vineyard from here. They pressed the first crops of grapes to make wine, but it was execrable. Zosima's always had an experimental turn of mind, so it didn't surprise me three or four years back to find that she'd set up a distillery to turn the wine into eau-de-vie, which they flavor with the aid of fruits from the orchards. I get the impression that much of the trade they do with us is surreptitious, a matter of the field-workers making a few coins on the side rather than following the orders of the prioresses, but I think they give us occasional bottles of liqueur as a kind of test, to obtain a report on their drinkability."

"And are they drinkable?"

"They've improved a lot over the last couple of years. You can try one after dinner, if you like."

"You don't think it's a little risky?"

"Hardly. They have no reason to want to poison us. If anything, they have a positive effect. I've made some interesting drawings after going to sleep on them."

"Erotic drawings?" Victor immediately asked, in typical fashion.

"A few, but the chimeras are more intriguing. I assume that it's an idiosyncratic effect rather than a fundamental property. Obviously, their principal objective is to produce a product that they can sell in Toulouse with a substantial profit margin. As they seem to have become very mercenary of late. The initiates seem to be increasing their therapeutic practices in Toulouse as well, and their hypnotists seem to be in far greater demand with the women of the city as psychic healers than I am as a portraitist. Perhaps it's because the mental pictures they evoke are far more flattering, but I don't know—nobody talks about it to me, being a male. Madame Louvot says that the word in the village is that there's some kind if internal power struggle going on among the cult leaders, but I haven't seen the slightest sign of it."

"It's the same in Paris," Victor told him. "Zosima's in far greater demand now than she was in the days when she and Talia were doing her double act. Remembering past lives is all the rage, but only among women—and whatever proverbial wisdom says about women being unable to keep a secret, they're very close-mouthed about their explorations of the imaginary past. I'm an expert gossip-collector, as you know, but I can only catch dribs and drabs. It's not surprising, though, that dissent is beginning to break out in the ranks. She and her senior acolytes must have a steady income now, here and in Paris—she has a lot of mouths to feed now that she's taking in so many worn out ex-whores who have nowhere else to go except the dark waters of the Seine—and wherever money begins to accumulate, so do plots to monopolize it. Believe me, I know; I'm a banker."

After a slight pause, Paul said: "In your capacity as an expert gossip-collector, Victor, do you happen to know how Jane died?"

Victor looked at him in astonishment. "Don't you?" he parried,

"I don't know anything except what I read in the newspapers. They didn't say anything about the circumstances."

"No, they didn't," Victor agreed, "and my ear to the ground hasn't picked up any vibration at all. It's the kind of silence that speaks volumes, but exactly what it means, I don't know. Have you seen Zosima?"

"Hardly. Are you trying to match me *non sequitur* for *non sequitur*, or do you think she might know something about Jane that you don't?"

"No, I'm not playing games, and I do happen to know that, even though they haven't been speaking terms for years, Zosima, who is no mean gossip-collector herself, has always been interested in Jane, perhaps because she's always been interested in you. I also happen to know that Zosima is at the convent right now, and even though you're not allowed to cross the threshold, she's been prepared to desert her flock in Paris to talk to you before. You could send your housekeeper up there with a note inviting Zosima to the cottage for a friendly chat."

Paul laughed. "I don't think Jane would approve of me doing that," he said, "and I'm quite certain that Madame Louvot wouldn't. So, although I'd be interested to see Zosima again, especially if her information network has told her something that yours hasn't conveyed to you, it's probably more diplomatic to refrain."

"The story of your life in a nutshell," Victor said. "I'll have it carved on your tombstone: *He always thought it more diplomatic to refrain.*"

"Are you so sure that I'll precede you to the grave?" Paul asked, still laughing.

"Given my bad habits, no—but I'll leave the instruction with Gaston, who'll surely outlive us both. More seriously, though, I know that your distant relationship with La Vaudère has something to do with the reason that you and Zosima haven't had any communication for four years, so I thought that the fact of Jane's death might have had something to do with Zosima coming here—that she might have come here to see you as well as to check up on the black sheep in her tumultuous flock."

"I haven't seen her, and I don't expect to. Even if some of them have adopted the habit of calling regularly at the back door to make little deals with Madame Louvot, and they're always prepared to nod politely in my direction, I think I'm still defined as taboo."

"That probably makes you all the more fascinating to the majority of the junior cult members, most of whom aren't fanatical lesbians, and their mock-monastic rule doesn't seem to be very rigid; it's not just the socialites eager to get in touch with their past incarnations who get out and about in Paris. The only reason that most of the residents stay in the Paris convent, as I said, is that they have nowhere else to go. Madame Z has probably forbidden the members of her flock to speak to you in order to preserve them from temptation—although she must surely have established her succursal here in order to be near you."

Paul shook his head. "I doubt that," he said. "It's probably not a coincidence, and it might well have been what she learned about me when she was making enquiries about me after I returned from Paris that drew her attention to the convent, but I assume that she took a lease on the land simply because it was ideal for her purposes and going cheap. Even so, making the old convent habitable must have involved a lot of expense. Does she really make enough money from her consultations keep the two communities going?"

Victor shrugged his shoulders. "Not personally, obviously, but the organization now has a select band of celebrity hypnotists at its disposal. They're much in demand in certain select circles of Paris society, and rich widows have always been a soft touch for charlatans of all kinds. Now that the renovation's almost complete, though, the community here ought to be nearly self-supporting, even without the help of fancy liqueurs—not so much in terms of producing its own food as generating its own income, while the Three Witches and their intimates replicate the pattern of Parisian social parasitism in Toulouse."

"Who are the Three Witches?" Paul asked.

Victor seem amazed by that question "Don't you know? A trio of would-be enchantresses who came to Paris from Toulouse not long before you and I relocated there; I was vaguely aware of them in my student days, while they were still here and called themselves the Three Maries, but they called themselves the Daughters of Artemis in Paris, which is just as corny. I never paid them much attention in Toulouse—they belonged to an older generation—but you must have run into them. The oldest one, Lilith, was quite thick with Amélie at one time, and they must have known Clémence too."

"Really?" said Paul, genuinely surprised. "No, I don't recall ever having seen a Lilith at Amélie's house, or hearing her mentioned—but Amélie was always close-mouthed about Sorority matters, and so is Clémence. Who are the other two?"

"I think their names are Salome and Justine—calling themselves the Three Maries was purely figurative, as well as hackneyed. Anyway, they seem to have led a checkered career in Parisian lesbian circles before ending up destitute and joining Zosima's cult. Their local connections made them useful in running the succursal, but rumor in Paris says that all is not harmony within the Sapphic Empire, and that the Daughters are on the brink of precipitating the cult's first great schism. Zosima is probably here to calm the waters, or to exert discipline."

"She might also have come to meet with the landowners," Paul suggested. "She and her associates probably have their own development plans for the mountain, or will at least want to know what the Megisters' plans are. As long as everyone leaves my cottage alone, I'll be...content."

"Forgive me for saying so," Victor opined, "but it could be the best thing for you if your landlords did decide to evict you, for one reason or another. If they only forced you to move into Toulouse, that would be a big step in the right direction, even if you keep that old crow Louvot with you."

"I can't imagine what you've got against Madame Louvot? She's an angel."

"She's bad for your image, dear boy. Rumor in Paris says that Rochemure left her and her nephew enough money not to have to continue in service, even if the boy hadn't joined the Republican Guard. The whisper is that she followed you here because she was infatuated with you, like La Pommerat with Lemastur—although he has the excuse that she's rich and he's poor, so it's understandable that he puts up with her. I'm not saying that she really is your mistress, rather than your housekeeper, given her age, but it looks a little fishy, especially when combined with the rumors about you and La Vaudère. You must see that they're beginning to form a pattern in malicious eyes, and if it didn't have malicious eyes, society would be stone blind. Your relationship with Clémence Sancerre, even though she's only ten years older than you instead of twenty-some, extends the pattern further. What you need, my friend, I repeat, is an Armande or a Clorinde. That way, true happiness lies, believe me."

"Oh, I do," said Paul. "But please don't think that you can understand my relationships with Clémence, Jane and Angélique on the basis of ignorant malign rumor. They're much more complicated than rumor could ever understand...or you, for that matter."

"I'm your best friend, Paul, or one of them—practically your brother, like Gaston, even though my mother wasn't best friends with yours, as Amélie was, and I never had a sister. If I don't understand your relationships, it'd because you don't tell me about them."

"There are some things that even brothers don't talk about," Paul told him, "even masters of indiscretion like you. You might have told me more about your sexual conquests than I ever told you about my intimate relationships, but only as a matter of casual boasting, and you always kept at least some of them darkly secret, for one reason or another. That's natural as well as rational. It's with the people to whom we're closest that we have to maintain the most careful censorship."

"Nice paradox—but it doesn't affect the fact that I'm right. You've lapsed into an unhealthy lifestyle and you're too apathetic to haul yourself out of it unless you're spurred. You need a better future, and the only way to build one is on the foundation of a better present. I know you can't help what you draw when you slip into one of your blessed trances. but you can certainly decide rationally what to paint when you're fully conscious. I'll gladly give you a pass on the painting you're working on at the moment, but only if you sell it. Keeping Scarab's portrait forever before your eyes is deliberately augmenting her haunting, and as for the thing in your bedroom, that's just sick...and don't bother to tell me that I don't understand, because I certainly don't. It's one thing to be visited by visions when you can't help it—we all have bad dreams—but deliberately to surround yourself with the most disturbing of those visions during your waking life is something else. You sold your portrait of Talia Cadelan and you painted Yvaine de Rochemure to commission, so you shouldn't have a problem with selling the others. Believe me, Paul, it's what you need to do."

"I notice that you always call Juliette by the nickname that the prostitutes who haunted the local café gave her," Paul observed. "Exactly how well did you know her before she moved into my studio?"

Victor looked at him in astonishment. "*That*'s all you can say?" he queried. "No, I never slept with her. I knew her by sight and by nickname because...well, because I knew a lot of the girls in your neighborhood by sight and by nickname...that's how I found you your studio. We had...mutual acquaintances, but no, I swear on my mother's grave that I never screwed your...whatever she was to you. Would it really matter that much if I had?"

"No," Paul said. "I was just curious...and it's a constant reminder, hearing you always call her that, of an aspect of her life that really wasn't relevant to...whatever she was to me."

"I'm sorry," Victor said. "I never thought...typical me, eh? In future, I'll make every effort only to call her Juliette—

34

which definitely doesn't mean that I think it's a good idea to have her hanging where she is, opposite a sofa on which you must spend a lot of time relaxing, since your exiguous residence doesn't have a separate drawing room. You can't tell me that you haven't put it there deliberately to haunt yourself, maybe even deliberately to hypnotize yourself. It's not healthy...and as for the one in the bedroom..."

"You've made your point, Victor," Paul said. "Leave it now, please. I promise you that I'll think about it. But let's focus on Gaston and Armande for now. Their honeymoon voyage might be technically over and they'll be back in Paris in a few days, but let's try to make things as pleasant as possible for them tonight, shall we? Let's have a dinner that they'll be able to look back on as a pleasant memory."

"Why do you think I'm holding you back so that we can have this conversation in private?" Victor complained...but he could see that Gaston and Armande had stopped, and were waiting for their companions to catch up, to put an end to their secretive conversation.

And as he looked back on what had already been said, on the way up the mountain and on top of it, Paul was sure that Madame Armande Lambrunet's curiosity about him had been stimulated to the point that avoiding thorny questions over dinner might well turn out to be a challenging task.

"Change places," said Gaston, when they drew level with the newlyweds. "Armande's asking me lots of questions about living in Paris as a household, and you're far more able to answer them that I am, Victor—and I also need a quiet word with Paul. All right?"

"Fine by me," said Victor, "I have never in all my life turned down an opportunity to walk down a picturesque hill with a lovely girl on my arm, and I never will."

The exchange was effected, and Gaston dropped back exactly as Victor had.

"Are you sure that's safe?" Paul asked Gaston.

"Certainly," said Gaston. "The days are over when Victor pounced on anything in a skirt, and the two of us have had a code ever since we turned sixteen; we don't infringe on one another's interests."

"Why don't I know anything about this code?" Paul asked.

"Your membership was always tacit; we trusted you far more than we did one another. My cousins asked me to give you their love, by the way—all three of them, separately, of course, and with a certain ironic prejudice. And my uncle also asked me to remind you of him."

"An uncle!" Paul exclaimed. "I can assure you that I haven't debauched any of your cousins, and there's no earthly need for any father to ride out here with a horsewhip to give me a thrashing."

"Not that kind of uncle: more distantly related, older generation, childless—imagine the horror, a childless Lambrunet! No wonder most of the others don't talk to him or mention him. But you know him: I mean Uncle Jean-Bénigne."

Paul did not take the trouble to rack his brains. "Actually, I don't," he said.

"That's just because you can't be bothered to remember all their names—and who can blame you? But you do know him. Even if you don't remember him from the old days, he's the one who helped me to arrange the lease on the cottage and rebuild it. He was still mobile enough in those days to hang around here while the new foundations were being dug, to see whether the diggers turned up any archeological evidence of former habitations. Needless to say, they didn't."

"I was in Paris when the building work as being done, painting my first portrait of Jane," Paul reminded his friend, "so I obviously missed him then; but he must be the one who's entertaining the Megisters with lectures on the fascinating history and legendry of their domain. Isn't he a descendant of the antiquary who identified their family as the rightful owners of the land during the Restoration?"

"Grandson, I think, or perhaps great-grandson—the inheritor, at any rate, of his forebear's mountain of parchment and paper, on the slopes of which another ninety years' worth of rubbish has doubtless accumulated by now. Anyway, he asked me to remind you of him, and invite you to call in some time when you're in Toulouse."

"Why?"

"I think he'd like to see your sketches."

"Again, why?"

"I don't know, but I'll hazard a guess that it's because he's belatedly heard rumor of your ever-growing reputation as a painter of spirits. Since he thinks that you're living on a site that's been inhabited for tens of thousands years, he'd probably like to know whether you've drawn any Mousterians or Magdalenians in your sleep. Have you?"

"I don't think so. How could I be sure?"

"That's probably why he wants to look for himself. On the other hand, he might have more recent inhabitants in mind. I mentioned the drawing you did of a crucified woman, and..."

"*You did what!* I never showed you that picture!" Paul suspected that all the color had suddenly drained from his face. He had no memory of having shown the sketch of Jane crucified to anyone except Jane herself and Camille Flammarion, although Baron de Rochemure had also seen it.

Gaston was alarmed by his reaction. "Yes, you did," he said. "It was ages ago—more than five years, I think. I dropped into see you while I was in the city and it was lying around in the studio. Come to think of it, you did tidy it away rather quickly, but you said it was nothing important. I thought you were just embarrassed because the woman was nude, although I'd seen plenty of other nudes you'd drawn...and what can it possibly matter?"

Paul had pulled himself together. "You're right, of course," he said. "It's just a picture, and I've done many that are stranger...but nothing, I think, that could interest an antiquary."

"Don't be so modest," Gaston said, his voice still a trifle uneasy. "How could all those mythological monsters not interest a folklorist? Perhaps he's after pictures of the sirens of the

Great Cleft...although perhaps I ought to add that I'm not entirely sure that it was on his own account that he was enquiring."

"Whose, then?"

"He's been corresponding with one of the sisters at the convent—only by letter so far, although she's one of those who visits clients in Toulouse, and he remembers her vaguely from the old days, when she and her friends were involved with the floral games."

"The Three Maries?" Paul queried, remembering Victor's remark.

"That's what they called themselves in sorority circles, I believe—a ridiculous affectation, as none of them was actually called Marie, as I remember. Mother used to know them, but I think she was only kind to them because other people weren't, and she was always one to defend underdogs. Apparently, since they were commissioned by your friend Zosima to manage the old convent, they've become even more interested than they were before in local history, prehistory and legendry, and Jean-Bénigne is the local fount of wisdom in such matters. Hence the correspondence. He's probably mentioned the cottage to them, and you...although they must know about you anyway, via Zosima."

Paul was still trying to fit the pieces of the jigsaw together. "And you think he might have mentioned my sketch of a crucified woman to this sister, who has naturally interpreted it as an image of an ancient Christian martyr?"

"Probably. That's their game, after all, isn't it—remembering or imagining the martyrization of their former selves? Jean-Bénigne, typically, inquired about becoming a client himself and recalling his own past incarnations, but his correspondent fed him a line about only women being reincarnated, and only being able to remember female incarnations."

"Damn," murmured Paul, wondering what one of Zosima's wayward sisters might make of some of his other sketches. But what would it matter? Let Uncle Jean-Bénigne look at whatever he wanted. Although the images of Jane...

"Anyway," said Gaston, "that's not what I wanted to talk to you about; I was just being polite in passing on the good wishes. Armande wants me to ask you to paint her portrait."

"So she told me," Paul admitted. "She had the impression that you weren't keen on the idea."

"Well, I couldn't see how we were going to fit it into our schedule, but she said that there was no great hurry. She wants me to invite you to stay with us in Paris once we're installed, so that you can paint the portrait there. She says that if we invite you immediately before or after Victor's wedding you could, as she put it, kill two birds with one stone. She also suggested that I mention that she'd be terribly hurt if you refused, now that you and she have bonded, and that I ought to inform you that I'd consider it a mortal insult."

Paul laughed. "Well, you can tell her that I would no more refuse to paint a truly beautiful woman than Victor would refuse to walk down a hill arm-in-arm with one, and that her sense of timing seems perfect. I wouldn't do it for anyone but you, though."

"Don't be too sure of that—you've met Clorinde, haven't you?"

"Very briefly."

"Well, even without knowing the first thing about her, except that she's agreed to marry Victor, what do you think her reaction will be when she hears that you're coming to Paris especially to paint my wife?"

"You think she's the competitive type?"

"She's a woman—is there any other?"

"There are several hundred not much more than a kilometer away from where we're standing who would presumably deny it, given that they're supposed to be a community of equals living in Fourieresque harmony."

"And would you believe their denials? The word in Toulouse is that the Three Maries have been plotting for at least three years to depose Zosima, take over the convent, and send any renegades back to Paris, conserving their little Eden for what Mother used to call true Marians—that's Marians as in the three Maries, not the Virgin, although there's inevitably some confusion."

"Really? Well, I suppose, as a true anarchist, Zosima will have to submit to the will of the majority. But I take your point about competition: if I paint Armande, I'm bound to have to paint Clorinde. Well, the same principle applies: a beautiful young woman; it will be a pleasure, I'm sure."

"Even if you have to spend several weeks in Paris, including the wedding celebration?"

"Oh, I see—all this is just a plot to bring me back to Paris in order to facilitate to persuading me that it's the best place to be. Like Victor, you think that my present way of life is seriously unhealthy?"

"Not exactly—but I do worry about you a little. A hangover from the old days, I presume, when Mother decided that you needed protection, and made me her auxiliary. I told her back then that you were perfectly capable of looking after yourself, but she just laughed. 'He's a little boy,' she said. 'He won't be able to look after himself until he's at least thirty, and even then he'll need a wife to do the hard work.' Mother was a trifle cynical about the male of the species."

"And is that why you keep trying to throw your cousins at me?"

"I was not *throwing my cousins at you*," Gaston objected. "I was attempting to act in the best interests of all concerned. I know they liked you, although they have to pretend not to now, and I can't for the life of me think why you don't like them."

"I do," said Paul. "It's just..."

"Just what?"

"Too soon."

"After what?"

"After...everything that has happened."

"So far as I can see, hardly anything has happened for at least five years. Your relationship with the author can't have been that serious, given that you hardly ever saw her, and she was old enough to be your mother."

"It's complicated," Paul said.

"Evidently—but you have a life to live, and if you really intend to spend all of it living with the dead...well, it's a pity, that's all. But I can tell Armande that you'll definitely come to stay with us in Paris, and that you'll paint her portrait? She'll want to show you off to her friends, you know. They all know Victor, and even if they don't take him seriously, his publicity has an effect. Anyway, she knows what you're worth—she'd seen your studio, and she loves the two portraits in my house in Toulouse. She says they both have hypnotic eyes."

"That's an effect I strive for," Paul says. "It doesn't always work, but with people I love...or loved..."

"Well, try to love Armande a little...not too much, mind. I know she's safe with you, but we don't want you doting again. Next time you fall in love, let's try to make sure that it's someone accessible, shall we?"

"I can't help what I see when I'm entranced," Paul reminded him. "I suspect that falling in love is similar...if it ever happens again, I won't be able to choose."

Gaston, not being Victor, did not have to ask why Paul had said "again." Instead, he said: "And what shall I tell Uncle Jean-Bénigne, if he asks about you again?"

"Tell him that he's welcome to see the sketches...but don't promise him that I'll show him everything. Some of my work is too personal. The same goes for his correspondent, the mysterious Daughter of Artemis who believes that only women can be reincarnated. She's welcome to look at my sketches...but I'd really rather she didn't know that the picture of Jane crucified exists." He bit his lip, but it was too late.

"Jane?" Gaston queried, instantly. "The crucified naked woman was the author? I never met her. I see what you mean about your relationship being complicated."

"Please don't tell your uncle—or anyone."

Gaston nodded, and Paul was sure that he could be trusted—but the pride of the Lambrunets could not resist adding: "What on earth do you suppose it means that you drew something so weird?"

"I don't know," said Paul. "Neither did she, nor Camille Flammarion. It's a mystery."

"Oh, don't say that around these parts," said Gaston. "If there's one thing the Marian sororities can't resist, it's a mystery. But my lips are sealed. Even Armande will never know. What do you think of *that*?"

They had almost reached the gate to the enclosure of the cottage. Victor and Armande were already there, waiting. *That* was Victor's automobile, a Panhard of the latest model.

"Beautiful," said Paul. "Worthy of having its portrait painted. It's very brave of him to drive it up that hill, though, considering the condition of the road. I hope you'll call in again before to go to Paris, but if you come in the auto, it might be best to leave it in the village and walk the rest of the way."

"You won't be getting one yourself, then?"

"I think I'll stick with the horse for a while longer. The sisters might buy a motor truck, though, or a tractor—their old donkey carts won't last much longer, and when winter comes and they have to buy in supplies from further away to feed however many hundreds of mouths they have in there, they'll need some serious haulage—in which case, the convent will need a serious road. I'll mention it to the Megisters when I see them tomorrow, in case Zosima hasn't already done so."

"Very neighborly of you, if they really aren't even allowed to look you in the face, let alone speak to you."

"Unlike you, they don't know how harmless I am. They probably think that, because I'm a man, I'm the Devil incarnate...especially if your kindly uncle has given their scholarly initiate a distorted impression of my work."

"I'll be sure to tell him to make it clear in any future correspondence that you're the salt of the earth. But if they send a scout to investigate you, for God's sake don't let her into your bedroom."

Paul laughed. "If what Victor says about the pattern of their recruitment is true," he said, "half of them wouldn't know what it is, and the other half wouldn't care—but it's a dead issue, a private matter. It's not for exhibition."

Victor was holding the gate open for them. Armande had already gone into the cottage. The three friends linked arms in order to traverse the short path, with Paul in the middle, but they had to separate again in order to go through the front door.

CHAPTER III

In the interests of keeping the conversation at the dinner table sufficiently general while avoiding excessively technical discussions of local geology and meteorology, Paul prompted Gaston to talk about local legends, and was glad to see that Armande was pleased by the topic, which answered one of the most harmless aspects of her evident curiosity.

"The most obvious relic of the ancient legend of the three Maries," Gaston explained to this wife, "is a twelfth century church dedicated to them in the Camargue. It's now on the sea shore, but when it was first built it was a long way inland. It's built over a spring, and the site is apparently mentioned in documents dated as far back as the fifth century. The connection is slightly speculative, but there was probably a temple of Artemis there, built by the Phocean settlers of Provence who founded Massalia, just like the one that supposedly once existed here on the mountain.

"The church in question is said to be the burial site of two of the three Maries who were bought to Provence by Joseph of Arimathea after discovering Christ's empty tomb, when they brought perfumes to anoint the body. Their identification differs in different versions of the legend, but the most common allegation is that two of them were Marie Jacoby, the mother of James, Christ's brother, and Marie Salome, a close relative of John the Evangelist. The third Marie, Marie Magdalene, is reported by Medieval Christian legend to be buried elsewhere. It was because of the supposed presence of the close relative of the Evangelist and author of the Apocalypse that the church became an important site of Christian pilgrimage.

"It isn't part of the official legend, but associated legends claim that as well as bringing the three Maries from Judea, Joseph also brought the Holy Grail, the cup in which he collected blood from the wound in Christ's side during his death-throes. Several religious Orders eventually laid claim to having had temporary custody of the cup but to have lost it or hidden it mysteriously, but none of those Orders existed during the first millennium of the grail's supposed presence in Provence, and the legend of the grail itself is probably no older than the twelfth century. Because of the timing of that origin, however, it became entangled, inevitably, with the legendry of the Albigensian crusade, and Napoléon Peyrat was by no means the first legend-monger to suggest that the grail might have been in the custody of the Cathars—who, having been exterminated by the crusade, were not in a position either to confirm or deny it."

"Allegedly exterminated," Victor rectified.

"Allegedly exterminated," Gaston agreed, accepting the correction. "The massacres didn't encompass the entire population, obviously. Some of the survivors had probably never subscribed to the Albigensian heresy, whatever it was—because all their documents were destroyed, or allegedly destroyed, we really don't know, and we certainly can't rely on the slanderous accusations leveled by their persecutors—others converted to orthodox Romanism and others, probably, pretended to convert but continued their own rites in secret, perhaps preserving legends from much earlier periods of history, which thus escaped revision or annihilation by the Medieval legend-mongers.

"The notion of secret Albigensian communities having survived the crusade and having passed down their secret lore all the way to the nineteenth century was enormously attractive to Romantic historians, and supposed versions of that secret lore have been bandied about so repeatedly that one can't help drawing the conclusion that it's all fictitious."

"In fact, one can," Victor put in, again. "One can suspect that the accumulation of false lore has merely helped the authentic lore to hide more effectively."

"So effectively that, if it existed, it would be impossible to distinguish it," Gaston argued.

"Impossible for skeptics and scholars," Victor agreed, "but not for the actual inheritors of the lore."

"If they exist," Gaston persisted.

"If they exist," Victor echoed. "But there's no shortage of people in and around Toulouse who believe that they do, and some of them, at least, my dear Armande, have a much more interesting interpretation of the legend of the grail than the one Gaston just gave you."

"Over to you, then, Victor," Gaston said, "but don't expect Armande to believe a word of it. She's a Parisienne."

"I'll make up my own mind about what to believe, thank you, my dear husband," said the young woman. "Go on, Victor."

"Some people believe," Victor said, "and that's all I'm saying—just that it's what some people believe—that the Albigensians had inherited from the descendants of one or more of the three Maries an accurate account of the religious community founded on the shore of the Sea of Galilee by Jesus and his disciples—an account quite different from the one established as official doctrine by the church. They claim that the community in question resembled the modern philosophies of Fourierism and Anarchism, involving the abolition of all kinds of authority, including priestly authority and what Fourierists call 'sexual property'—which is to say, marriage. They claim that the community practiced what is now known as free love. They allege that the reason the Roman Church was so determined to extirpate the heresy in its entirety is that it was the true Christianity, a doctrine whose first principle was the denial of priestly authority...on which, of course the Roman Church was founded.

"In this version of events, what Joseph of Arimathea bought to Provence with the three Maries was the blood of the Galilean community in a purely metaphorical sense: that all three were pregnant with children sired within the community by one or other of its members, but without any of them knowing for sure which one. From this viewpoint, it doesn't really matter, because the rule of the community wasn't invested in a single individual, an authoritarian leader, but in a general principle. The cup containing the blood of the crucified Christ thus became a symbol of the attempted extermination of the entire community—which failed precisely because some of them were enabled to escape by the trader and ship-owner Joseph. The thee Maries might have been symbolic themselves of a larger group, but even if there really were only three of them, the point is, in this version of the story, that they had children, and that those children were the blood of the true Christian community, the true Christian revelation...and the extrapolation of the legend is that there are still, today, descendants of one or other of the three Maries living in or around Toulouse, perhaps severed entirely from the roots of their tradition, not knowing who and what they really are, but perhaps still having the inkling. But you know more about that than I do, don't you, Paul?"

"I don't know anything," Paul said—honestly, in a pedantic sense.

"Come off it," said Victor. "You know full well that there's a substantial sector of the crazy sorority crowd who think that your friend Clémence is a true Marian."

"She makes no such claim," Paul said, laconically.

"Of course she doesn't—the first rule of being a true Marian is to deny it absolutely. But look at her paintings and their symbolism. All those flowers and grails and demure, wistful ladies are blatant Marian symbols for anyone familiar with local mystical traditions. They'd be a complete mystery in Paris, of course, and deliberately so, and the meaning is supposedly concealed even from so-called incomers, like the three of us...or two of the three of us, at least."

That remark jerked Paul out of his laconism. "What's that supposed to mean?" he asked, sharply,

"It's supposed to mean that your behavior over the last five or ten years has begun to stimulate talk in the sorority crowd. How could it not? I doubt that any of the city's obsessive genealogists could connect the Furnerets with any alleged Marian ancestry, any more than they could with the Marvauds or the Lambrunets, but the first rule of legend-mongering is that appearances are always deceptive and secrets always hidden. You're not only Clémence Sancerre's most enthusiastic promoter and best friend, but the legendary painter of the spirits of the dead. You know that the inmates of the lunatic asylum on the hill won't even look you in the face, but nobody else knows that, and even if they did, they'd assume that it was just ostentatious pretence; in the minds of the quasi-Marians you're residents on the same mountain, intimate neighbors."

Paul was now genuinely confused. "But what on earth has Zosima's quasi-Fourierist phalanstery got to do with fantasies about living descendants of the three Maries?" he asked, although he remembered what Gaston had said about the three "Daughters of Artemis" having called themselves "the Three Maries" before they went to Paris, and Victor's suggestion that they were planning to break away from Zosima's mother-convent in order to pursue their own quasi-religious path.

"Probably nothing," Victor said, blithely, "but we're not dealing with rational arguments here. In Paris, hardly anybody can see past the fact that Zosima's cult openly proclaims and practices lesbian free love, but the view from Toulouse is slightly different. The feature that comes into sharper focus in twisted minds here is that they openly and assiduously practice the magical recovery of past lives. Some of the fake nuns up the mountain are transplanted from Paris, but a good many are local women, either returning from exile in Paris or recruited direct from the city. In all probability, they include several suspected Marian descendants...whose recovered memories of anterior existences might link them directly, at least in fantasy, to one or other of the three Maries and to the true origins of Christianity. Thus, your proximity to the nest of mystery might take on an extra significance in the ideas of the sororities."

"But that's preposterous!" Paul said.

"You know that, my dear, and so do I," said Victor, "but do they?"

Paul realized, a trifle belatedly, that Victor was trying slyly to compile another argument as to why he ought to return to Paris. He turned to Gaston. "Have you ever heard any of this nonsense from anyone but Victor?" he asked.

Gaston seemed decidedly uncomfortable. "As a matter to fact," he said, "I have. It's all nonsense, obviously, and I certainly wasn't going to mention it, but it is known in Toulouse that you were magnetized in Paris by Zosima, and that she was the one who enabled you to become a painter of ghosts. They can't see it as a coincidence that she set up her second community here almost immediately after you asked me to renovate this cottage for you. And when these lunacies begin to proliferate, there's no end to them. Nobody in Toulouse— nobody male, at any rate—has any idea what kinds of rites are practiced in Zosima's fake nunnery, so they're free to imagine anything they like. Nobody knows anything about her, either, except that her father was from Marseille. It doesn't take much more than that in these parts to license a suspicion of Marian descent on the part of the crazy people who take that nonsense seriously, and to spark all kinds of speculations about the purpose and the revelations of her magical evocation of ancient lives."

"It's not magical," Paul objected. "It's a hypnotic stimulation of the imagination, which encourages fantasization, with the aid of cryptomnesia. It's basically a kind of experimental psychoanalysis, or psychotherapy."

"To borrow Victor's phrase," Gaston replied "you know that and I know that, and perhaps Zosima knows it too, but I fear that there might be a great many people in Toulouse who don't. Not that that need be any of your concern. We're only talking about a small number of lunatics. Whatever they might think doesn't have any significant consequences for you—or, in fact, for them. Let them imagine what they like, and ignore them."

"You're right, obviously—but I can't help wondering whether Zosima knows about all this. Unfortunately, there's no way to find out."

"Isn't there?" Armande put in. "Now that I know what a sapphist is—no thanks to you—as I understand it, it's only the three of you who can't just knock on the convent door and ask to go in. I could."

Gaston looked at her with evident horror.

"Oh, I'm not saying that I will," she told him, blithely. "Just that I could. We called it something different at school, of course—sapphism, that is—but I'm not unfamiliar with the notion."

The table had fallen completely silent; not a single item of cutlery clinked, and no one reached for a wine-glass.

Armande smiled. "You're all scholars," she observed. "You all think of yourselves as savants and philosophers. What do you think the consequences are of isolating adolescent girls from male company, sending them away to study Latin and die of boredom in convents or secular boarding-schools? Do you think they don't talk to one another? Do you think that they don't teach one another all the things that are far more interesting to them than the curriculum, and not even mentionable in polite society?"

Gaston obviously could not think of any reply to make. Victor, for once, kept his tongue under tight control. Paul did not say a word, but in the privacy of his mind he imagined that he could hear Jane de La Vaudère saying: 'You don't know little girls the way I do,' and he remembered the graphic depiction of the closed society of the dancing girls of the Hindu temple in *Le Mystère de Kama*.

At that moment, Madame Louvot came into the dining-room in order to clear away the dishes of the main course before bringing in the dessert.

"Of course," Armande remarked, "it wouldn't have to be me. If you wanted any questions asked at the convent, Paul, you could always ask Madame Louvot to ask them for you."

The aged housekeeper stopped dead, and looked at Paul, uncertainly.

"It's all right, Angélique," he said. "Just a hypothetical discussion. The *confit* was lovely—a masterpiece."

Madame Louvot—who still played the role of maidservant in company, as assiduously on a voluntary basis as she had when she had been in the employ of Baron de Rochemure de Harvanges—resumed her quiet and expert movements.

In the meantime, Armande's eyes, sparkling with mischief, had gone to the portrait of Juliette hanging on the wall. Paul's heart sank slightly as he wondered what the young woman might be speculating—but he was still caught completely off guard when she turned to him and said: "Would it be terribly indiscreet, do you think, if I were to ask to see the paintings hanging in your bedroom?"

The continued silence must have answered clearly enough in the affirmative, but—silence being merely silence—the young woman clearly felt that she could ignore it.

"It's Victor's fault," she said. "He's the one who whetted my curiosity. But you did say, didn't you, Paul, that I'm one of the family now, and that I can ask anything of you that I might want to."

Paul could not remember having employed those precise terms, but he had to concede that he had, indeed, established the general principle.

"Now?" he queried.

"If you don't mind," said Armande who clearly did not care whether he minded or not. "It will only take a moment. I just want to look at the picture that Victor calls "the horror." Everyone else has seen it, haven't they?"

Everyone else had—which allowed Paul to say: "Perhaps, Gaston, you'd do the honors. It would hardly be decent for me to take another man's wife to my bedroom."

Gaston stood up, and put on as brave a face as he could as he offered his arm to his wife. While they were out of the room, Victor fixed an accusative stare at Paul's face, as if to say "I told you so"—although, in fact, he had not, and it was, as Armande had said, his fault that her curiosity had been whetted to such an extent.

The two absentees had returned to the table before Madame Louvot had brought in the desserts.

"I really don't see what all the fuss was about, Victor," Armande said, as she resumed her seat. "I think it's an interesting work of art, and not a horror at all. Men can be so squeamish, although they've certainly all been there. Who is the woman in the portrait opposite—the one that isn't your work?"

"That's my mother," Paul said, relieved by the swift change of subject. "Painted before I was born, obviously."

"And the drawing on the sketch-pad beside the bed is Gaston's mother—but not a very good likeness, he says?"

The relief vanished instantaneously, as Paul realized that he had neglected to move the sketch that he had made in his sleep the previous night into a drawer in the studio, and had forgotten all about it."

"Yes," he admitted, "that's Amélie, as I remember her. I've drawn her while entranced several times, and the portrait in oils that you've seen was based on one such sketch; obviously, my subconscious was prompted last night by the expectation of Gaston's visit, in the company of his new wife. I'd drawn my own mother a couple of nights previously. Perhaps I'll draw Victor's tomorrow."

"I can understand that," Armande said, nodding her head. "At any rate it's easier to comprehend than why you've hung a picture of a seven-month fetus with a most unrealistic hypnotic stare on the wall of your bedroom."

"Because he daren't hang it anywhere else," muttered Victor.

"I take it, Armande," Paul said, after taking a deep breath, "that Gaston, being the polite and decent good friend that he is, hasn't mentioned to you the stupid joke that I once told in my days as an art student in Paris, in an unguarded moment?"

"No," she said, "he hasn't. But if you're referring to that old slander about you having murdered your sister and your mother before you were born, I fear that it's still doing the rounds of the less scrupulous salons of Paris, every time your name comes up in conversation—which is, not unnaturally, at least every Salon season. Rumor has it that the reason why you paint spirits obsessively is that you're being haunted by the vengeful ghost of your unborn twin, who takes delight in parading your dead lovers before your magnetized gaze in order to torture you."

"Armande!" Gaston complained.

Paul held up his hand in a gesture of pacification. "No, Gaston," he said, "it's entirely understandable and right that, having acquired me as a near-brother by marriage, Armande should want to know the truth about any rumors that are circulating about me, and I thank her for her insight in seeing more in the painting than the horror that is all Victor can find in it. In fact, it's not horrific at all once one understands the symbolism of it, and if people don't, it's entirely my fault for not explaining it—but it's a habit symbolists have, even where their dearest friends are concerned. On the other hand, I wouldn't like Armande to carry away misconceptions, since she's been kind enough to pay me this visit and take an interest in my work."

He took a couple of spoonfuls of dessert and a generous sip of sweet Bourgogne before turning to look directly at the young woman.

"I was very young when I made that stupid joke about having been a double murderer before I was born," he said, "and utterly thoughtless. It never occurred to me that it could possibly have a lifetime of more than a few minutes, let alone that it would still be repeated regularly nearly ten years later by people who have never met me. Presumably, it would have been forgotten had I not lent it new impetus by the direction of my career, although an obliging distraction was provided by Camille Flammarion when he suggested that the rather murky image of the first fetus that I drew under the effect of hypnosis might be a extraterrestrial, which resulted in the daily newspapers reporting that it was a Martian. Only a few interested parties realized what it really was, and established a puzzle that it took me several years to solve, at least to my own satisfaction.

"The story really began, although I didn't realize it at the time, when Victor suggested that I attend a séance at Madame Pommerat's town house, in order to lend myself to an experiment in automatic drawing, under the suggestion of Henri Lemastur. The prospect was intriguing, and while I was in a somnambulistic trance, I drew a picture of a young woman. When a member of the audience whom I don't know identified it as a picture of his daughter, I didn't take the suggestion seriously; I thought it was merely wishful thinking based on a chance resemblance.

"As a result of that experiment, Victor suggested to Camille Flammarion that he ought to subject me to a similar experiment. Monsieur Flammarion invited me to a séance that he had already arranged with Madame Zosima, a hypnotist recently arrived in Paris from the Midi. Victor was unable to go to Juvisy because it was the day that the *Palatine* struck a rock in the Manche, and he became the liaison between the telegraphic reports of the aftermath of the disaster and Gaston's relatives, who were all avid for news. He arranged for one of his neighbors, Antoine Cros, to take me to Juvisy. Antoine was also taking Jane de La Vaudère. It was the first time I had met either of them.

"While entranced by Zosima's hypnosis I produced four images, the sensational reportage of which, exaggerated because of the connection with the search for the Palatine's missing lifeboat, founded my reputation in spiritist circles. I drew portraits of Martine Lambrunet, Charles Cros— Antoine's late brother—and a woman identified by an aged member of the audience as Madame Scrive, Jane's mother, plus a fourth image, which Antoine identified as a human fetus. Zosima's medium, Talia Cadelan, screamed and fainted during the experiment, covering up the fact that Jane was also affected.

"I won't bore you with the details of our attempts to figure out how I had produced those images; suffice it to say that we were all avid to attempt a further experiment, which we did, at Antoine's house. There I drew a compound image of the model I was employing for a painting of the martyrdom of Jeanne d'Arc, which partly reproduced the image in the painting and partly showed her lying dead with multiple stab-wounds. I was unconscious for several hours and Talia suffered a pulmonary crisis that nearly killed her. Again, those two events drew the bulk of the attention, preventing anyone from noticing the extent to which Jane had also been affected.

"Juliette, it turned it, wasn't dead, but she had witnessed a murder, which had precipitated a vision in which she believed herself to be Jeanne d'Arc being burned alive, which prompted her to run to the Pont de Neuf—a distance of nearly three kilometers—and throw herself in the Seine. It became obvious, as a result of that events, that rather than being visited by the spirits of the dead, as conventional spiritist lore represents the typical occurrences of séances, what had actually happened was that in my somnambulistic state, the unconscious part of my mind had somehow made contact with the unconscious parts of the minds of other people present—or, in Juliette's case, absent. Those connections, it turned out, endured, and were seemingly not broken even by the deaths of the people with whom I had been connected, who continued to haunt me, and still do.

"I ought to emphasize that the hauntings in question did not seem to me to be horrific, and still do not. In my experience—though I certainly do not think that it is universally true, the spirits of the dead are not hostile, but affectionate. The intensity of the relationships formed under hypnotism was various, and they were not amorous in any simple sense, but they were nevertheless positive, and it would not be too much of an exaggeration to call them loving.

"I realized very quickly that the small sample of the drawings that I had made at the three séances were selective. Other experiments showed that, as well as the disembodied faces of dead people and fetuses, I often draw wholly imaginary entities, often chimerical, and occasionally draw entire human figures of living people. Four years passed before I plucked up the courage to subject myself to a further experiment, but when I did, at the request of Baron de Rochemure, three of the four images I drew were chimerical, and the fourth was the fetus that provided the basis for the painting in the bedroom—the first one that had open eyes.

"I thought at first that I had failed Rochemure completely; he had specifically requested that I make contact with his daughter, and because I had not drawn her I thought I had failed. I was assured by others, including Madame Louvot, that I had, in fact, succeeded, at least to the baron's satisfaction. I saw him several times after that, and had long discussions with him about what I had drawn; I yielded to his request to paint a picture of his daughter based on one of the sketches I had made.

"As a result of those discussions, I realized that I had been asking the wrong questions about the supposed spirits whose faces I drew. I had been preoccupied with matters of identification, and with the means by which I had perceived images in other people's minds. What I should have wondered was why those images were so starkly present in the minds from which I took them—for example, why was Antoine Cros being haunted by his brother and Jane by her mother. I realized then that all the drawings I was making were, in fact, symbolic: that the real question was, in those instances: what did the image of his brother symbolize for Antoine Cros, and what did the image of her mother symbolize for Jane. The baron and I already knew what his daughter, as I had drawn her—which was not as she had been at the point of her death—symbolized for him. It remained for me to work out what my own obsessively repeated symbol, the fetus, symbolized for me.

"I had assumed, naturally, that the image I had drawn must be the fetus of my sister—but Talia and the baron had both leapt to quite different conclusions, and I realized that the symbol was actually ubiquitous: that it could be, and probably was, any fetus, and that even if I was trying to draw my dead sister, it was not because her spirit was seeking revenge on me for an imagined murder, but because my sister, at the point of death, symbolized something much broader, and much deeper. She was, I concluded, an ambiguous or even paradoxical symbol, as symbols often are, that being part of their utility. And I realized that for me—I make no claim for anyone else, such meanings often being idiosyncratic—the image of the decease of a seven-month fetus, dead before even having lived, was simultaneously a symbol of necessary death and the necessary immortality and reincarnation of the living soul."

"What!" cried Victor, his patience finally exhausted, it seemed, by such a painstaking narrative, which had taken a very roundabout route to reach that destination. "You can't be serious!"

"I can," Paul retorted, "and I am."

"The necessary immortality and reincarnation of the living soul?" Victor protested, pronouncing the words as if they were a blasphemy against his atheistic belief.

"Shut up, Victor," said Gaston. "Let Paul explain what he means. You can tell perfectly well that he's serious, and we know that he doesn't say anything without a solid argument to back it up."

"It all depends" Paul continued, after another dose of sugar and a sip of fortifying wine, "on your point of view. When we think of ourselves we usually think of our individual consciousness, which we think of as our soul, and when we think of the immortality or the reincarnation of the soul we tend to imagine that consciousness somehow floating free of its corporeal envelope, either to pass on to some further phase of its existence or to be reincorporated into anther nascent body—but that's a fantasy. The sense in which human existence is immortal and reiterative is quite different, and the soul of humankind, the soul of life, is something collective rather than individual—which is why the peculiar telepathy, or empathy, of which some individual minds are sometimes capable, is perfectly natural thing, and not supernatural at all.

"We've all heard the expression that a hen is just an egg's way of making more eggs, but we treat it as an item of wordplay. It isn't. It's the fundamental truth of life: organisms, as we perceive them, are simply mechanisms by means of which something very simple—no bigger than a single cell, hardly visible through a microscope, and probably much smaller, perhaps merely a complex atom of some sort within a cell—can reproduce itself prolifically. While reproducing its essence, that simple thing varies some of its offspring subtly, so that while multiplying, its offspring also diversify, gradually, producing the entire spectrum of atoms that are capable of growing into the reproductive systems that we think of as individual organisms. Like a hen, each of the four of us, fundamentally, is just a means for an egg, or an atom, to duplicate itself—to reincarnate itself, if you prefer—and to metamorphose in the process, endlessly, immortally.

"I say each of the four of us, but picking up on something Gaston said earlier, it's worth noting that from this viewpoint, the two sexes aren't equal, and only the females, the producers of new eggs, are endlessly reincarnated. Males are a kind of by-product, useful for variation but a sideline of the main sequence—which adds a curious plausibility to the notion that Zosima's adherents apparently have that only women can truly remember past lives, and only female past lives. If psychic heredity is the prerogative of the egg, to which sperms are irrelevant, that's the simple truth of the matter. At any rate, life is, in essence, reproduction, reincarnation and variation—and death.

"Death, you see, is vital to life. Without death, life wouldn't be what it is, and the immortality and reincarnation of life wouldn't be what they are. Death shapes species by removing from existence the unviable reproductive systems that the atoms life of produce continuously. We think of death, from our individualistic viewpoint, as something that usually happens, and ought to happen, after maturity. But most death occurs long before that; the vast majority of unviable reproductive systems die shortly after formation, long before birth and infancy. And what we call birth and infancy are themselves the products of death. Embryos begin life as invisible specks of plasma, which reproduce and reproduce, doubling and doubling repeatedly, producing masses of cells with slight variations, which are the sculpted by death into shapes and structures—including structures capable of feeling, and even, in humans, of thinking.

"The human brain and human thought are the products of the great sculptor Death. Symbolizing Death as a skull, or as a skeleton wielding a scythe, is a misconception of perception. The true symbol of death is an embryo, gradually taking shape under the refining chisel of the sculptor, until it's finally ready to be born—if it makes it that far. Without death, what we think of as life would be impossible. Without death, the immortality and reincarnation of the human atom would be impossible. Without death there could be no such thing as the human soul: the true human soul, that is; the soul of the species, which is itself merely one a component of a much greater soul, the soul of immortal life. But species, like individuals, eventually die. Only life itself is immortal. What individuals like us think of as our souls are only fractions of something much vaster, and even the soul of humankind entire is only a fraction—a perishable fraction—of the immortal soul of life."

"Mystical nonsense," opined Victor.

"Perhaps so," Paul agreed, equably, "but I think it provides a more plausible account of what the soul is than orthodox religion—or orthodox atheism, which simply gives up on the problem by declaring it unproblematic. At any rate, it seems to me to provide a plausible explanation of *me*—which is, selfishly, what I set out to find. It provides an account of the nature of the unconscious fraction of the mind that offers me a way of understanding how, under certain odd circumstances, the unconscious fraction of my mind can communicate with the unconscious fractions of other human minds, and gives me some inkling of why that communication produces the extremely peculiar effects that it does

"Perhaps, as Victor says, it's all delusion. Perhaps my entire experience of life is a delusion. But if so, it still has to be lived, and understood. Victor accused me a little while ago of living with the dead, implying that that was a bad thing and that I ought to stop doing it. It's true—I do live with the dead. I shared a tomb for two months before I went to be born, leaving a corpse behind me. Now, more than thirty years later, I live with the immediate psychic presence of Juliette Scarran, Talia Cadelan and Jane de La Vaudère, and the slightly more remote psychic presence of a vast host of other dead people—but the latter circumstance isn't a choice, any more than it was a choice for me to spend two months of my life before birth with my poor dead sister. It's not something I could alter by moving to Paris. But it's not a circumstance about which I'm unhappy, for the moment, because the dead who are psychically present most intimately, are the dead with whom I'm comfortable, the dead for whom I have feelings of affection, even a bizarre echo of amour, even though carnal desire is out of the question. Not everyone, I know, would be so lucky."

"If you'll forgive me for pointing it out," said Gaston, a trifle dryly, "your explanation—the part that I haven't heard before, at any rate—seems distinctly incomplete in certain respects. I'm not at all clear what you mean, or could mean, be the notion of a collective soul."

"I know," said Paul. "And I'm sorry, but it's getting very late, and it won't be easy driving back down the hill in the dark. Victor, I know, is a consummate sportsman, and understands his vehicle as well as any expert mechanic, but darkness is darkness and the road, even when bone dry, is treacherous. You'll be in Toulouse for a few more days. If you really want to hear more eccentric metaphysical ramblings, I'll be glad to entertain you with them, but it's been a long day, and I confess that the climb to the mountain top took more out of me than I anticipated. Armande, I think, is having difficulty keeping her eyes open."

"No I'm not!" the young woman protested, unconvincingly—Gaston, at any rate, was suddenly all concern.

Madame Louvot appeared, as if on cue, with a tray containing a coffee pot on cups, plus three brandy glasses and a bottle of liqueur devoid of a label."

"That's the famous liqueur from the convent, is it?" Victor asked.

"One of the samples," said Paul. "Will you try some?"

"Why not?"

Gaston and Armande also agreed to try a little.

"It'll never replace Chartreuse, let alone Benedictine," was Victor's verdict.

"I've tasted worse," was Gaston's opinion—but given that he traveled such a lot, Paul thought, it would have been a great surprise if he had not.

"It's interesting," proffered Armande. "I expect it's an acquired taste."

"I'm sorry about, that," Paul said, as Armande took a swig of coffee, perhaps to take the taste of the liqueur away. "And I'm sorry about going on at such length, after all my good resolutions to keep the occasion light and pleasant. I got carried away, I'm afraid, egomaniac that I am."

"Not at all," said Armande, valiantly. "I asked you a question, and you answered it—and you didn't try to fob me off with something flippant, as practically everyone else I know would have done. People think I'm a fool, but I'm not, as evidenced by the fact that I love Gaston. Thank you, Paul, for taking me seriously—not just now but this afternoon. I wish I had more friends like you...and I can't help regretting the fact that when we return to Paris, we won't see you again. perhaps for months, until you come to paint my portrait. We will come back, won't we Gaston, before we leave for Paris?"

"Certainly, if you want to," said Gaston." If Victor's auto isn't up to the task. I'll hire a two-seater and a couple of post-horses."

"My Panhard," said Victor, proudly, "is superb. I hesitate to trust her to that rotten road too frequently, because she's at least as precious to me as Paul's ghosts are to him, but if I ask her to climb the hill from the village, the hill will be climbed—I guarantee it."

"That's settled, then," said Armande. "And we'll make specific arrangements, Paul, for you to paint my portrait once we're settled in the new house...as soon as possible..." She looked at Victor

"Fine by me," Victor said. "If Paul has to come to Paris twice before the year's end, it can only do him good. And if Clorinde wants a portrait too..."

Paul shook his head, as if wearily, but he smiled, taking the pressure on his time and talent as a compliment.

Once the coffee had been drunk, and the exotic liqueur at least sampled, the leave-taking was inevitably protracted. Paul had already admired Victor's pride and joy once but had to do it again, if only to demonstrate his awe at the power of the headlights that would have to guide the vehicle along the road—which, because it followed the contours of the hill, was far from straight. Paul watched it draw away, until it disappeared from sight, and then went back inside, where Madame Louvot was clearing the dishes from the table.

"Was that wise, my dear?" she asked.

"Was what wise?" Paul queried, although he knew perfectly well.

Knowing that he knew, the housekeeper did not bother to elaborate, but only said: "Your friend Victor is right, you know. Explaining it doesn't really help."

"It shouldn't have to," Paul said. "How was I supposed to know that the girl was going to be so presumptuous as to ask to see my bedroom? One doesn't expect such shocking behavior, even from a Parisienne."

The old woman laughed. "Don't pretend you disapprove of her," she said. "You adored her; she'll be able to wrap you round her little finger from now until your friend catches her in bed with an officer in the guards and somebody shoots somebody."

"That's a terrible thing to say," Paul objected. "Anyone can see at a glance that she's in love."

"She is now," agreed the old woman, cynically.

"Please don't tell me that I don't know little girls he way you do," Paul said. "I didn't believe it when Jane said it, and I certainly won't believe it of you."

"Well, sir," she said, in a sarcastic tone, "It's not my place, as a mere housekeeper, to disagree with anything the young master says, but I had more than one long talk with Madame Jane when she used to visit the old master before he died, and I can tell you for certain that she did know little girls far better than you do. And if she were here, she'd tell you that now she's dead, it's safe for you to return to Paris."

Paul did not bother to point out the paradoxical nature of the remark; he simply said: "The fact that Jane is no longer there could easily be construed one more reason for not going back. But if you want to see more of Fabien there's nothing to prevent you from going."

"Fabien's a guardsman now; he doesn't need an old aunt in his doorstep for his comrades to joke about. But if you want to get rid of me, sir, you only have to say so. I don't want to be an embarrassment to you."

"You're not," Paul said, flatly.

"I wouldn't be, if you had a larger staff, but with just the two of us living here, there's bound to be talk, even with me being so old. We could get a village girl easily—it wouldn't cost much."

"And where would she sleep?" Paul queried. "The grain-loft or the stable?"

"We'd manage."

"We manage now," Paul told her. "If you think the work you do is getting to be too much for you, I'll do more. I'm not really a master, the way the baron used to be."

"Too much? Now you really aren't being serious, my dear. But you're right about not being like the baron—there was a man who knew how to give orders and keep discipline."

"And disembowel anyone who offended him with a bay-onet," murmured Paul, too tired to stop himself.

The old woman stiffened momentarily, but then relaxed, with a contrived sigh. "When you don't want me anymore, *sir*," she said, philosophically, "I'll only have to go up the road to the convent. They take anyone, it's said—even women who've been with men. Of course, if they hadn't been with men they probably wouldn't hate them as much. Do you really think that there are women in there who pretend to have been Marie Magdalene in a past life and to have slept with Jesus?"

"How should I know?" Paul countered.

"Do you want me to find out?"

"No. There's no point. Let them do whatever they do and believe whatever they believe. As Gaston says, it has no consequence for me—or you."

"You're probably right, my dear. I'm losing track—will the Englishman and his sister be coming back tomorrow?"

"No, the day after. It's a busy week, I'm afraid. You'd better take the trap next time you have to lay in supplies; it's a fair way up that hill from the village carrying bags, and the sisters from the convent doesn't seem to have brought us any contraband for several days."

She snorted dismissively, and turned to go, but on the threshold she changed her mind and came back. "They can't throw us out, my dear, can they?"

"I doubt it. I can check the lease if you like—but they don't have any reason to throw us out. I pay the rent. I'm not sure that they can even raise it, but if they can and do, I'll pay it. It seemed to me that they quite liked the idea of having an eccentric painter on their estate—much better than the idea of a lesbian phalanstery, unless I'm mistaken."

"Not much doubt about that, sir, but you know what they say about the English."

"That they can't be trusted?"

"No sir—that's only what they say in Paris. In the provinces, and down here especially, they're a little more graphic. Your two can actually boast about their family going back to the crusades, and but it's the wrong crusade. Vipers in the flower-bed, my dear, vipers in the flower-bed."

"Time will tell," said Paul, philosophically. "Good night, Angélique."

"Good night, my dear," she replied. "Sleep well—and if you draw in your sleep, draw something nice."

"I'll try," Paul promised, although she knew as well as he did that he would have no choice.

CHAPTER IV

The next day dawned as bright and clear as the one before and Paul, who had found an image on the sketch-book
beside the bed of a nude woman in a mildly lascivious pose—
an anonymous nude woman, thankfully—hastened to tidy it
away before Madame Louvot saw it. He was able to resume
work early on his new portrait of Jane de La Vaudère, based
on a sketch drawn from the spirit. He thought that she would
have approved of it, although she might have criticized him
for not having taken a few years off her appearance, recapitu-
lating the image he had formed when he had painted her from
life, in 1901.

He did not slip into a trance while painting, in spite of his
absorption in the work; indeed, it seemed to him that he was
almost hyperconscious, unable to help partial distraction by an
anxious train of thought. When he had started the painting the
only objective he had had in mind was to produce it, to convert the sketch he had made by night, in the dark, into something bright and beautiful, something worthy of its enigmatic
model. It had never even crossed his mind at that point to ask
what he would do with the painting when it was finished. The
possibility of sending it to Paris seemed to be out of the question, but if he kept it in the cottage, where was he going to
hang it? If he put it in the bedroom, where should he place it
relative to his sister? Or should he—could he?—give it pride
of place in the dining room, and move Juliette to another wall,
away from her crucial position relative to the sofa. How would
Juliette react to that? But how would Jane react if he refused
to do it?

He knew, of course, that the last two questions were a trifle lacking in sanity: that the sense he had that Juliette was still
present in his vicinity was a subjective illusion, no matter what
Madame Zosima and others of her ilk would have alleged, but

he also had some sympathy for Baron de Rochemure's idealist formula that if matter was merely the possibility of perception, then perceived phantoms were not only real but could be regarded as material. Either way, Juliette was still in his mind, and although he had been able to separate her from Jane while Jane was alive, now that they shared the same category, and would soon share the same primary form of visual manifestation, a choice would have to be made as to where their portraits would be hung, and what spatial positions they would occupy in his immediate environment.

That they would be jealous, he had no doubt. In another era of his own spiritual evolution—he refused to think of it as the advancement of his insanity—he had sent his painting of Talia to Chazelle, who had sold it to Rochemure, who had employed it as a catalyst in his own haunting, but if he had kept it, and saved himself the regret of no longer having it, what would have happened when he had painted Juliette? There would have been an immediate jealousy and an ensuing conflict: not between the canvases, obviously, since paintings, in themselves, were not entities capable of love, hatred or jealousy, let alone warfare; but pictures, like people could be haunted; they could even be hypnotic; they might not have spirits themselves but they could certainly become a vehicle for spirits. Any battle that had developed between Talia and Juliette at that point would have been fought in his own mind, with his own gaze as heavy artillery, and the only person who could have been a casualty was him, but nevertheless...

He tried to stop the train of thought. It would lead, he feared, to confusion, and for someone like him, confusion was a step in the direction of madness. He had to focus his intelligence on the awareness that it was all metaphor and symbolism, and the idea that, at the end of the argument, they were all simply dead: his sister, Martine, Talia, Juliette, and now Jane. He also had to remind himself that all he was trying to decide was where to hang—or send—a painting; a decision that was really quite trivial.

Except, he thought, that it wasn't. Even Victor, an essentially frivolous intelligence in spite of his decision to quit the libertine life for Clorinde, thought that Paul's decision in regard to hanging his paintings was a serious matter, an important indication of his state of mind.

Might Victor be right? Paul wondered. It was a question he had asked himself many times before, since they were both fifteen years old, and to which he had usually been able to reply with satirical laughter—but not always. Light-minded as he might be, Victor was intelligent, a fine calculator not merely of balance-sheets and risk, as his profession demanded, but of social situations. Victor was successful, Victor had always been happy—far happier than Gaston or Paul, even before the *Palatine* lifeboat disaster had taken away the possibility of their ever being able to compete with him in that regard. Victor could be a trifle insensitive, but he was anything but a fool. Might he be right to suggest that Paul should send all three of the paintings to Chazelle, to be sold to anonymous buyers and hung in locations unknown to him?

Paul asked himself, quite seriously, why that seemed such an unthinkable notion. He could hardly say that they were the only three people that he had very loved. He had stopped insisting that he had never loved Juliette, even though he still thought that it was true, and he was certainly not about to start insisting that he had never loved Jane, because that would be a blatant lie, no matter how peculiar that love might have been, but his sister? Surely twin embryos sharing a womb could not be said to love one another in any meaningful sense...but the painting was not a painting of a dead embryo in a womb; it was the painting of a spirit, and even if that spirit was simply an idea in his mind, it was still the idea of an actual sister, of his closest and most intimate blood relative, whom, if she had not died, he would surely have loved, and who was surely entitled, in consequence, to be loved in spirit...

But that was only one half of the question, Clearly, even if he had loved all three, in one way or another—all peculiar ways, he had to admit—they were certainly not the only three people he had every loved peculiarly. There was Martine, whom he had never kissed, but whom he had certainly loved, perhaps in a purer and finer fashion, precisely because they had never had any more intimate physical contact than they had on the day when they had linked arms climbing the mountain, when he was fifteen and she was only thirteen, and barely nubile.

Who else? Clémence? No, he was certain that that strange fascination did not count as love, and was unlikely to turn into it even if, as was surely highly unlikely by now, she decided that she might love him. Angélique? Definitely not; they both agreed, far more convincingly than it had been agreed with Juliette, that the fact that they sometimes shared the same bed was only evidence of an occasional twinge of physical need, and that it could not qualify as love. That would be almost as ridiculous as adding Yvaine de Rochemure to the list, who had died before he was born, and was a second-hand haunting, borrowed from her father's obsession. He still drew her occasionally, and he had certainly painted her with enormous attention, but that been a commission, a gift for a dying man, a symbol of the forgiveness for which he had been searching for thirty-four years...not her forgiveness of course, since that could always have been taken for granted, but his own.

That kind of forgiveness, Paul suspected, was what the majority of the clients who consulted spiritists wanted and needed. The phantoms from whom they sought formulae of forgiveness were, like priests, only surrogates offering symbolic absolution, just as the phantoms themselves were only symbols...

Which raised the question, Paul observed scrupulously, of exactly what he was seeking by means of his own phantoms. For what was he seeking to forgive himself? For what did he need forgiveness? Of what sin was he guilty?

It was, he knew, a matter of sin and not of crime. Baron de Rochemure had committed crimes—four premeditated and coldly executed murders, to name but a few—but he had not felt the slightest requirement to be forgiven for them. In fact, the sin of omission for which he had been desperate to forgive himself was hardly even a fault, let alone a crime; it had been an accident of circumstance. The reason that he could not be there to protect his daughter when she was savagely raped and effectively murdered, along with the child in her womb, was not that he had failed to do anything practicable or possible, but the fact that he had been shot, and the wounds had become infected, and the Communards had put him in prison. There was nothing he could have done, nothing for which an uncorrupt judge could possibly find him guilty...but the human conscience, as Paul was now well aware, is not an uncorrupt judge.

Baron de Rochemure might qualify as an exception, if he were considered in the context of the human race as a whole, many of whose members felt no apparent need for forgiveness, but in Paul's opinion, that merely demonstrated that the majority were deluded. Within the framework of his own intimate acquaintance, he was certain that Talia and Juliette had felt in dire needed of self-forgiveness, as a result of corrupt judgment. Even if—and Paul still refused to believe it— Talia had actually contrived to abort her own child rather than losing her to an accidental miscarriage, an honest judge would have found countless extenuating circumstances. As for Juliette, the fact that she had been a reluctant prostitute was a matter in which she had had no choice, and in any case, an uncorrupt judge would surely have taken the same view as Antoine Cros in saying that whatever conventional moralists took the liberty of believing, there was no crime or sin in prostitution, and a definite heroism in accepting the necessity. Juliette was Jeanne d'Arc, burned to death by judges who were not merely corrupt but insane, because she was a saint.

Juliette, at least, had found her forgiveness, and her symbolic redemption. She had told him so, on her deathbed. She had even credited him with its achievement. He was the one, she had said—almost in as many words—who had saved her; he was the one who had enabled her to feel that her life had been worth living, that even though they had agreed that neither of them was capable of loving the other, the time they had spent together had redeemed the value of her life, calculated as a pledge to fate, interest included. Paul was not at all sure that he could really count that to his own credit, as the effect had not been premeditated or even intended, but at least it was not a sin in terms of any sane moral calculation...which had not prevented him from being haunted by Juliette, to a greater extent, thus far, than anyone else.

Thus far probably being the operative words.

He was still fully conscious; his gaze was scrutinizing the picture that he was painting, and the steady application of paint by the brush, even while his mind was rambling. Even while he was reminding himself that Juliette was the most frequent and the most insistent of his hauntings, in spite of the fact that an uncorrupt conscience would surely have judged that he had done her nothing but good while she was alive—he had, at least, shown her nothing but kindness, which was surely the same thing—his eyes had been gazing at Jane's face. More than that: his eyes had been watching Jane's face take shape, while his hand had been giving color to the phantom, creating, if not the spirit itself, the symbol of the spirit.

He had been haunted by Juliette more than any other spirit, including his beloved sister, since the day she had died. But from now on...

Had Juliette's spirit—real or illusion, if there was any meaningful difference—been aware all along of that impending treason? Had she been jealous in advance of that inevitable displacement of favoritism? Had she been jealous all along of Jane alive, just as Jane alive had never quite been able to suppress entirely her jealousy of Juliette dead?

Confusion again, surely on the brink of what was nowadays called neurosis, if not insanity.

But if he had no reason to feel that he needed to forgive himself in regard to Juliette, how could he possibly feel that he had any reason to forgive himself for his relationship with Jane—which, he had always insisted, had never done either of them anything but good. Technically, it had been adulterous, but in the same way that Baron de Rochemure felt no guilt whatsoever about his four murders, Paul felt no guilt whatsoever about that.

Unlike Rochemure, however, Jane had never confessed to him exactly why she felt in need of self-forgiveness, of redemption from her own self-criticism. He was convinced, now, that it was her own critical feelings that she had symbolized in her mother's face, that she had only imagined her mother was monitoring her conduct as a psychological stratagem, and a matter of putting a mask on her own corrupt conscience—but as to what that unfair judge had charged her with before delivering an unkind verdict, the only clue he had was the content of her books, which revealed the extent of her distress, but dressed it with such elaborate fictional disguise that it was impossible to see through the clothing to the naked moral flesh beneath. She had never felt able to confess, even to him, the true nature of her self-dissatisfaction.

Even to him? Was that not to overestimate his importance drastically? After all, they hardly ever saw one another; they lived hundreds of kilometers apart, and their relationship had belonged far more to the imagination than the flesh. That the bond between them was strangely strong was undeniable, but, examined objectively, how important could it possibly have been to her, in the context of a rich and busy life? That it had been enormously important to him was surely a reflection of the relative paucity of his other relationships—other relationships with the living, that is—but even in that regard, he had actually spent more time during the last four years in the physical company of Clémence and Gaston than with Jane, and much more time with Angélique. Was it really reasonable of him to have regarded his relationship with Jane as by far and away the most important element of his existence?

After a few moments of reflection, and the application of some delicately blonde paint, with exceedingly delicate brushwork—made slightly difficult by the fact that the light had deteriorated rapidly because of the gathering of clouds over the mountain—to the tresses depicted in the painting, he decided that the answer was affirmative. Yes, it had been completely reasonable for him to regard his relationship with Jane, in spite of its physical distance, as the most important element of his existence. But he could not say the same the other way around. He could not say that he had been the most important element of her existence, or even a more-than-mediocre element. He did not even know how she had died, having received no forewarning of the possibility, and was afraid even to speculate as to why that was.

So, there was no reason why she should have confessed to him exactly what it was from which she was in need of redemption, why she sometimes imagined herself, not being symbolically burned alive like poor Juliette, but being crucified. He was only a minor aspect of her life, probably overshadowed by many other aspects, about whose nature—unindicated, obviously, in her letters—he was afraid even to speculate.

And yet, there had been something highly extraordinary, perhaps even unique, about the bond that had been formed between them, the closeness and tightness of which had not been due entirely to the effect of Zosima's hypnotic suggestion. Zosima had undoubtedly catalyzed the reaction, and perhaps added force to its inherent magnetism, but she had not created it *ex nihilo*. It had existed before he and Jane had arrived at the Juvisy Observatory. It had certainly existed in the two carriages in which the journey to the observatory had been made, and it had been symbolically sealed, in an initial sense, when she had refused Antoine Cros's arm, which convention dictated that she should have taken, and had demanded his instead for the final walk.

But that had not been the true beginning, which had predated the first time that they had seen one another. Paul had known who Jane was when she had been introduced to him, having already read some of her work and found a kinship of ideas therein. She had also recognized his name, and had con-

73

nected it with the painting of Mourgue la Faye that he had exhibited at the previous Salon. When she had complimented him on it at the time, he had thought that it was mere politeness, but he believed now, and she had confirmed it, that she really had been struck by the painting, and that she had felt a similar psychological kinship based on its symbolism.

It would be ridiculous, of course, to suppose that when she had been introduced to him in Antoine Cros's carriage, remembering the painting, she had immediately cast herself, symbolically, as Mourgue la Faye to his Ogier the Dane, that she had seen herself, potentially, as a loving, protective, possessive *femme fatale* whose enchantment could extract him from conventional time and space. She could not possibly have thought that, or meditated any such relationship, even metaphorically...not consciously, at any rate.

But she had, nevertheless, immediately become possessive and protective, and that protection and possession had become instantly manifest when the effects of Zosima's hypnotism—or, more accurately, the shock of Talia's reaction to the mental link forged by Zosima's hypnotism—had caused both of them almost to faint. From that moment on, albeit not consciously, Jane de La Vaudère had cast herself, or had been cast by the collective soul of which they were both fragments, as Paul's Mourgue la Faye: a protective, possessive, peculiarly loving, deeply enigmatic and supernaturally fascinating *femme fatale*.

That role, he now felt sure, had frightened her, by virtue of its inherent paradoxicality, but she had only been partly conscious, to begin with, even of the fear, and she had not known why she was frightened. The second séance, at Antoine's house, had tightened the bond further, and had intensified its confusion along with its paradoxicality, and the third...

Paul found that he was squinting; the light was becoming very poor, and it had suddenly begun to rain. He cocked an ear, to make sure that Angélique had come back from the market in time to avoid the rain, and was instantly reassured by the sound of her working in the kitchen, He put the housekeeper out of his mind, but paused nevertheless to wonder whether he ought to stop work. Then he chided himself for pusillanimity. It was not as if he had to fear the effect of the poor light on the vision of a model. He returned deliberately to the train of his meditation

The séance at Rochemure's house in Passy had taken the telepathy between himself and Jane a stage further. The purpose of that séance had been to forge a link between Paul's unconscious mind and the baron's, and it had achieved that, but the psychic force applied to that purpose was necessarily ubiquitous. All those present had doubtless felt some disturbance, Angélique more intensely than her companions, presumably because of the intensity of her connection with the baron, whose desultory mistress she had been for more than twenty years, but Jane's reaction had inevitably been of a far greater magnitude. Any visions she had experienced during the first two séances had been brief, confused and easily vulnerable to the retrospective censorship of consciousness, but the third had been extended, almost coherent, immune to censorship, and terrifying—and also shared, at least partially. When Paul had been on the brink of waking up after the séance, he had dreamed a fragmentary and blurred version of Jane's dream himself.

Jane, not naturally, had interpreted the significance of the dream as a warning of a great and urgent danger to him; she had forbidden him to allow himself to be magnetized again—ever—and she had taken it for granted, as his Mourgue la Faye, that he would obey the instruction, although it had amazed Zosima that she had even dared to pronounce the sentence, let alone that he would accept it meekly. But Zosima had only catalyzed the psychic link; she had not shared it. She had no idea what had happened, or what kind of bond existed between Jane and Paul, and probably could not have understood it even if she had glimpsed the elements of the dream, as Paul had.

Paul was certain in his own mind that Jane had never decoded the symbolism of that vision, and that she had been afraid even to try, but she had certainly felt its nightmarish emotion very acutely. Her terror of what might happen if the experiment were ever repeated was urgent, and she was entirely sincere in thinking that the person menaced by that danger was Paul, her protégé. Paul, who had only remembered fragments of the vision, which had not been rendered into a coherent narrative by the description of it that Jane had given him subsequently—with all possible honesty, he assumed—had not been able to decipher it to his own satisfaction either, although he had his suspicions about the significance of its principal symbols. Now that Jane had died, unconfessed—at least to him—he did not suppose that he would ever be able to convert those suspicions into solid convictions, but he was not sure that it mattered very much. Life, full of uncertainties, unsolved and insoluble puzzles, had to be lived regardless.

On the other hand, there was a possibility—enough of a possibility to frighten him somewhat—that Jane's vision had been reliable. Even if she had been mistakenly projecting an acute sense of threat to herself, real or illusory, on to him, that did not necessarily mean that he would not be in danger if ever broke her injunction. Indeed, his understanding of psychology suggested to him that his very awareness of the ominous vision might have a deleterious effect if he disobeyed the prohibition, even if there was no objective threat, and Jane's vision had merely been a bad dream, full of sound and fury, but signifying nothing at all...

Confusion, and more confusion...

And the original question still remained, along with its corollaries: What was he going to do with his painting of Jane when it was finished? Could he really bear to send it to Chazelle? If not, would it be necessary for him to displace his portrait of Juliette, or his portrait of his sister, or at the very least to taunt the jealousy of the spirits by providing one or other of their images with a proximate rival?

Life, he remarked again, wryly, *is full of unsolved and insoluble problems.*

There was a sudden vivid flash of lightning outside, undoubtedly striking the summit of the mountain, and belying—by no means for the first time—the old adage that lightning never strikes twice in the same place. Almost immediately, there was a loud crash, coming from the direction of the road that went past the fence of the cottage's enclosure.

Even before he reached a window that gave him a view of the road, Paul had deduced what had happened. One of the donkey-carts from the convent, caught by the rainstorm while returning from the market in the village, had suffered a sudden jerk when the donkey had been frightened by the lightning. Either by virtue of long wear and tear, or because it had been caught by a rut in the road—or, more likely, a combination of the two—one of the wheels of the cart had broken, and the body of the laden cart had fallen heavily and obliquely on to the road.

That rapid mental calculation proved to be optimistic. When he reached the window Paul saw that under the impact of the crash, part of the road had suffered a minor landslide. The slope on the far side was by no means precipitate or very long, but it was a slope nevertheless, and the collapsed cart had been tipped over the edge and had slid down it a little way, spilling its load. The donkey, caught between the shafts of the cart, had been unable to maintain its footing, and had also been dragged over the edge, but only by a few feet. It did not seem to have broken a leg, and it was struggling to free itself from its harness. The driver of the cart, however, had either jumped or had been thrown from the tumbling cart, and appeared to have landed badly amid the brambles of the stony slope. She was now lying on her side, not screaming but clearly in distress.

In a matter of seconds, Paul had emerged from the cottage, traversed the garden and the road and clambered down the slope to the recumbent woman, who was clad in a kind of monastic robe with the hood pulled up, and was gasping in alarm and pain.

Without pausing to make any calculation of the burden, Paul picked the woman up and carried her into the cottage. Fortunately, she was not stout, although far from emaciated. The inmates of the phalanstery, he judged, were certain not starvelings. He deposited the burden on the sofa in the dining-room, and turned to Madame Louvot, who had emerged from the kitchen anxiously. Blood was already pooling on the carpet, having leaked from the left leg, although much of it was retained by the gray woolen stocking that the woman was wearing under her habit.

"Her robe is soaked through," Paul said. "See if you can remove the bloody stocking and cover her up with something dry while I see to the donkey. Then put a kettle on to boil, and find some bandages. I'll try to figure out then how bad the damage is."

Without further ado, and without looking any more closely at the injured woman, whose face was still completely hidden by her capacious hood, he returned to the stricken donkey. Unhitching it from the shafts was not easy, given that it was still panicking and struggling, but he eventually managed to pull it free and help it to its feet. All four legs seemed to be intact, and the animal had no bloody wounds. Paul led it into the stable and tethered it there, somewhat to the apparent disdain of his bay gelding, which found its home thus invaded.

Back in the cottage, he found that the donkey-drover had been stripped of her robe and covered with blankets, but was still covering her face with her hands. Madame Louvot had already filled a bowl with hot water and had armed herself with a block of carbolic soap, but as she bent over the stricken woman Paul knelt down, easing the housekeeper to one side.

"Let me do it," he said. "It doesn't look too bad."

There was more optimism than expertise in the judgment, but once he had wiped away most of the blood he found that it had, in fact, been caused by scratches inflicted by the brambles, which were extensive, but not deep. The soap undoubtedly stung, wringing further gasps from the victim of injury, but she was obviously not given to melodrama, because she did not scream even when Paul began to palpate the badly bruised foot gently, trying to figure out whether any bones had been broken. He thought not, but he could not be sure, and in any case, there was no possibility of the woman walking on the injured foot for some time.

Somewhat to his surprise, his patient's convulsive gasps turned into a series of strange giggles—hysterical laughter, he supposed. Her hands had finally fallen away from her face, rendering her features visible

"What's so funny, damn it?" demanded Madame Louvot, sharply, still standing, with her hands on her hips, looking down at the stricken woman with blatant hostility.

Not surprisingly, the woman did not attempt to answer the question, but she did manage to stammer thanks as Paul bound up the foot and ankle as best he could. It was not until he had pinned the dressing securely that he finally looked at her face. She must have been in her thirties, probably no older than himself but perhaps as old as thirty-five. At any rate, her haggard face, still afflicted by shock and pain, did not seem retain any significant bloom of youth. Her short-cropped black hair was unkempt.

"Don't be unkind, Angélique" Paul said to his house-keeper, surprised at having to issue the admonition. "It was an accident—she certainly didn't do it on purpose."

The housekeeper made no reply, but seemed confused, and took a step back, as if to give Paul more room. To the in-jured woman he said: "The donkey isn't hurt, but I fear that your load will be spoiled by the rain, if it hasn't been by the stones of the slope. I can go and see whether anything can be salvaged..."

"No, you can't," said Madame Louvot, her voice still strained and harsh. "You're soaked to the skin yourself. Go and get changed."

Paul was about to object that it was precisely because he was already soaked that he ought to go out and see whether anything could be done to salvage a part of the convent's sup-plies, but the injured woman interrupted him.

"The lady's right," she said. "No point in catching a chill for a load of potatoes and turnips, and a few sacks of unmilled oats and rye. The sisters won't go hungry, and there's nothing that can't be replaced tomorrow. As long as Tigany's all right."

It took Paul a second or two to see the joke of naming a French donkey Tigany, but when he did, he smiled. From the corner of his eye he saw Madame Louvot raise her eyes to the ceiling, perhaps imagining that she could detect some concupiscence in his smile. He could not imagine why she seemed so angry.

"Can you make some coffee, please Angélique," he said, in a placatory tone. Addressing the injured woman, he added: "There's no point in trying to get help from the convent in this downpour. If it stops while there's still time to get there and back before dusk I'll go up to tell them what's happened, and they can decide what to do, but if darkness falls..."

"She can't stay here," Madame Louvot put in, flatly.

"She'll have to, I'm afraid," Paul told her. "The road's treacherous enough when it's dry—after this deluge it won't be safe to travel in the dark, even if I can set her on the donkey. If the road has a chance to dry out overnight, it might be different in the morning, but..."

"Please don't worry, Madame Louvot," the woman put in, adjusting the blankets that were covering her modesty. "Your friend is in no moral danger from me."

Madame Louvot turned crimson. Paul raised his hand in a gesture of pacification. "The lady won't come to any harm on the sofa," he said. "Hopefully, she'll be able sleep there comfortably enough. Whether I can get to the convent before dark or not, we can't move her before then, but we'll make what arrangements we can to get her home as soon as possible. I'm sure she doesn't want to stay any longer than necessary."

"Oh, certainly not, Monsieur Furneret," said the woman, in a voice that seemed to Paul to be ostentatiously insincere. The tone of her voice was puzzling; he assumed that she was still trying to tease Madame Louvot, having taken offense at her blatant hostility, but he did not understand why there was so much tension between them.

"Since you know our names," he said, in a soothing tone, "may we know your name, Mademoiselle?"

The woman seemed startled by the question, and a trifle confused—perhaps almost offended, but she straightened her expression immediately, and said: "At the convent I'm known as Sister Monique...but Monique will be fine, if you'd rather." Paul found the glance that she darted at him as she spoke, while keeping one eye on Madame Louvot, quite incomprehensible.

"Go and change out of those wet clothes now," Madame Louvot said to Paul, sternly. "I'll make that coffee. Would *Sister* Monique like something to eat?"

"If it's no trouble," said Sister Monique, meekly.

Madame Louvot rolled her eyes, but she had already turned her head away, so the woman on the sofa could not see. Paul followed her into the kitchen rather than going into his bedroom. "What on earth is the matter with you, Angélique?" he asked, in a low voice.

"*That*," said Madame Louvot, "is not a nun, or a lesbian. *That* is a common whore."

"The three aren't incompatible," Paul remarked, "especially if they're successive rather than simultaneous. What does it matter? She's injured. She needs our help. Would the baron have done anything different?"

The housekeeper stared at him for a few moments, and then said: "No, of course not. Go and change now. I'll make the coffee."

Paul did as he was told.

When he returned to the dining room, Madame Louvot brought in a coffee pot, two cups, bread and preserves, and returned to the kitchen ostentatiously, letting the curtain fall with an emphasis suggesting strongly that if there had been a wooden door, she would have slammed it.

"What on earth did you say to her to upset her?" Paul asked, wonderingly.

"Nothing," protested Sister Monique, "until I told her that you were in no moral danger; but by then she'd asked for it five times over, and I couldn't resist. When she recognized me, she pretended at first that she didn't, and I was perfectly prepared to go along with it, but she just couldn't stop looking down her nose, itching to grab me by the neck and strangle me...as if it were all my fault, and not...well, never mind. I'm sorry if I'm causing you embarrassment, but there's nothing I can do about it for the moment except shut up."

"Angélique recognized you?" Paul said, mystified. "You mean that she's met you in the village and something has happened between you?"

His guest looked at him, frowning indecisively, but her mouth was full and they both had to wait until she had chewed and swallowed before she had decided on her reply.

"No," she said, finally, "we met a long time ago. She only saw me a couple of times, and I looked lot better then that I do now, but she has sharp eyes and a good memory—and it was something of a sore point, although it needn't have been. And in a way, it was your fault as much as mine."

Paul's mystification increased by an order of magnitude. "My fault?" he echoed, incredulously.

"Yes. Her nephew came into town looking for you, sent by the baron. Scarab had just been turning some other fellow away—some pushy newspaper reporter—with that old witch of a concierge looking on and laughing, and I was passing, so I stopped talk to her—Scarab, that is, not old Cambourg. Then Fabien turned up, all two meters of him, looking like a demigod. Scarab shooed him away too, said that you were painting and couldn't be disturbed. Poor Fabien didn't know what to do, so I took him to the café, and things went on from there. He didn't pay me, you understand—a lover of the heart, although the heart isn't exactly what was at stake. He used to take me out in the baron's carriage occasionally. The first time the old lady caught us she just gave us an earful, but the second time...anyway, he was a good boy, although he was certainly fully grown, and he only needed telling twice. That was it.

"This was in 1901?" Paul queried, still trying to work out the implications of what he had just heard.

"Probably—I'm not good with dates. A year or so after that, I lost my place, much as Scarab had, for much the same reason. I didn't have a painter to whisk me away to the Midi, and I was reduced to Madame Z's refuge. I left a couple of times, but decided both times that I'd been better off there. A couple more years after that, when we heard that she was opening the colony here, I jumped at it—coming home, practically—and the Three Witches seemed glad to take me aboard. Obviously, I had no idea that you were here, but poor Scarab was long dead by then. I was tempted to talk to you a few times and damn the rule, but when old Louvot came to join you, I gave up on that idea, and kept my hood over my face. She didn't know I was here until you carried me in and dumped me here. Scarab looks beautiful in that picture, by the way—far prettier than I remember her. She must have tidied herself up a lot."

All Paul could think of to say, dazedly, was: "You knew Juliette?"

Not for the first time, Sister Monique looked at him in frank surprise. "You still don't remember me? That's humiliating. You saw me with Scarab at least three times—did you really only have eyes for her? Unbelievable!" She paused momentarily, and then said: "You didn't remember me then, either, did you? I thought you were deliberately ignoring me, but you really didn't remember me. Even more humiliating. My name doesn't ring a bell? Eleven, maybe twelve years ago? Not that Victor ever introduced me, of course. He never even mentioned my name?"

"Victor?" Paul queried, still all at sea. "You knew Victor? In Toulouse?"

"In the Biblical sense, for a while. I wasn't entirely a whore then, but it wasn't him who made me one, and I didn't

83

exactly follow him to Paris. Hang on, though...it's not just Victor who never mentioned me, which is understandable, but Scarab. Damn! I'm beginning to feel like a pariah that nobody wants to admit knowing. Perhaps I ought to be grateful to Fabien's auntie—at least she remembered me.

Paul set down his empty coffee cup. "The rain has stopped," he said. "There's just time for me to get to the convent and back before dark, even with the road turned to mud. They won't be able to do anything this evening, but at least they'll know you're safe."

Monique grunted. "They'll probably be more worried about Tigany than me," she said, not entirely unseriously.

Madam Louvot had emerged from the kitchen, with a swish of the curtain. "Don't go, Paul," she said. "The road will be treacherous, and if you don't make it back before dark..."

"Don't worry, Madame," said Monique. "They won't let him in. He won't be there for five minutes—always a cold welcome, even for messengers bringing good news, all the more so as Madame Z is in brief residence. Even though the two of you are old friends, Monsieur Furneret, she won't be able invite you in. It's the rule, and if the Mother Superior doesn't observe the rule, especially when she's under threat of being within hours of losing her status, who will?"

"I'll be all right," Paul assured his housekeeper, turning away from the garrulous Monique. "I know the mountain...even the sector that I tend to avoid nowadays. I'll be back before dark. Please don't strangle the sister while I'm gone."

Madame Louvot and the invalid exchanged glances that, although by no means friendly, did not seem murderous. Paul put on his heavy boots and picked up a long staff. "We'll resume this conversation when I get back," he said to Monique. "I need some clarifications."

"All you want," the woman assured him. "I'm not one to keep secrets, alas."

CHAPTER V

The slope was slippery, as Paul had anticipated, and the footing more secure off the road than on it, but he made reasonable progress, and by the time he reached the old convent, the sky was cloudless again, having returned all its vaporously suspended water, somewhat selectively, to the region surrounding the mountain. Gaston had explained to him more than once why the mountain seemed to act as a magnet for cloud and why the updraft blowing up the slope on which the cottage stood sometimes provoked sudden deluges, but he had not really paid much attention; he still thought of meteorology as a science more akin to astrology than physics, in spite of his friend's earnest assurances.

The door of the convent had no knocker, but he hammered on it with the rounded end of his staff. After an interval long enough to make him impatient, a judas hole opened, somewhat below the level of his chin, and a female voice said: "What do you want?"

"My name is Paul Furneret," he began, "I live in the cottage down the hill..."

"I know," said the unknown woman, brusquely. "What do you want?"

Paul sighed slightly, but maintained the scrupulously polite tone of his own voice. "You cart broke a wheel outside my cottage and tipped over. Sister Monique has hurt her foot and can't walk, but she's in no danger. The donkey is unharmed but the load's lost, I fear. I believe you have other carriages and other donkeys, so you can send a rig down in the morning, but there isn't time now to get here and back before nightfall, and the road will be too dangerous afterwards. I've got to get back myself."

"Wait there," said the voice, abruptly.

Paul was strongly temped simply to turn away and go, having delivered his message, but he hesitated, uneasily.

He did not have to wait as long this time as he had when he had rapped on the door with the staff before a familiar voice said: "I can't let you in, Paul—regulations—but thank you for coming to tell us. We were worried that something bad might have happened."

"That's all right, Madame Zosima," Paul said. "Do I need to repeat the message."

"Sister Monique is safe?" Zosima said.

"Yes. She can spend the night to the sofa. No harm will come to her, I assure you."

He heard faint derisive laughter. "I know you, Paul," she said. "I know that she'll be safe with you. Can you answer for your guard-dog, though?"

Evidently, Zosima knew that Monique had had dealings with Madame Louvot before—but that was only mildly surprising. "I have to go now," said Paul, offended on Angélique's behalf by the insulting reference. You can send someone down to collect the sister and the donkey in the morning."

"Wait a minute," said Zosima, swiftly. "I need to talk to you."

"There's no point," Paul said. "The prohibition still holds, even though Jane's dead."

"Not about that," the ex-magnetizer said. "It took me some time to work it out, but I understand. I need to talk to you about the English couple. Strictly business."

"It can wait until morning," Paul told her. "I really do have to get back down the hill before nightfall. Come to the cottage—early if you want to get there before the Englishman...although he probably won't be able to get his automobile up the hill this time."

"That's all you have to say? My fault I suppose—I should have led with how good it is to see you again."

"You can't see me," Paul pointed out. "At best you can get a glimpse of my Adam's apple, which doubtless offends you merely by its existence."

He turned to go. Obviously she could see enough of him to be aware of that, because she was in haste to say: "Wait! I'll open the door."

"No," Paul replied. "It can't be that urgent, or you'd have come to see me today. Come to the cottage tomorrow. And if it makes you feel any better, it's good to hear your voice too."

He began to walk away, but as still close enough to hear Zosima shout after him: "I'm not your enemy, you stupid boy!" Obviously, the unctuous politeness she had cultivated in her days as a performing magnetizer had worn away completely now that she was the high priestess of a misandrist cult.

"Nor am I yours!" he called back, carefully refraining from any tactless reference to stupidity on her part.

As soon as he was out of earshot, however, he regretted his intemperate churlishness, even though the glance he cast at the western horizon told him that really did have to make haste in order to get back to the cottage while it was still light, and without committing himself to a reckless urgency that might have catastrophic results.

He should, he thought, have been polite to Zosima, even though she had not made any effort to set an example. He had no intention of ever allowing her to hypnotize him again, and he was not at all certain that he would be entirely safe in her company, even with that determination in mind, but the fact remained that she was more likely than anyone else to be able to help him add more to his understanding of himself and his situation than his correspondence with Camille Flammarion had been able to do.

He knew that, as she had called out to him through the judas-hole, Zosima was not his enemy. She had never intended to do him any harm, nor had she done him any. If she had been selfish in following her own agenda, she was by no means alone in that, and she had never sought to put any pressure on him, or even to put up any argumentative resistance to the prohibition that Jane had imposed upon him. Did she really understand now why Jane had done that, and why he had allowed her to do it? He knew that Zosima had visited Baron de Rochemure more than once during the days following the epoch-making séance, as he and Jane had done, separately and together, and as Henriette Pommerat and Henri Lemastur had doubtless done, separately if not together. There had been opportunities for plentiful exchanges of information in all directions, and he was far from certain that the totality of it had been conveyed to him, even with the aid of Madame Louvot. Perhaps he should, indeed, talk to Zosima, not merely about "the English couple" but about other matters of mutual interest, accepting her temporary presence in the convent as a golden opportunity rather than a potential threat

Jane, he suspected, was not the only phantom who might advise him against that. Talia would surely have done so too. Even if his haunters were products of his own imagination, however, it did not necessary mean that they knew what was best for him. Talia had not known him at all, in spite of her conviction that she had seen into the depths of his soul, and Jane...well, it was not at all clear, in the famous romance that had helped to tie the first knot in their relationship, that Mourgue la Faye had had Ogier the Dane's best interests at heart, and *femmes fatales* had certainly not come by that generic description by accident.

Paul reminded himself sternly, that Jane had never done him anything but good, and that he still owed her loyalty, even though the promise that she had exacted from him four years ago was that he would not have anything further to do with Zosima again while she was alive. In that same melodramatic conversation she had told him that she intended, once dead, to haunt him more relentlessly that his other phantoms, and although her spirit had not yet shown itself to be insistent or demanding in usurping control of his hand, he could not help feeling that she must be watching him, and might take ill any dealings with Zosima that went beyond topics of absentee landlords and their strategies of estate management.

On looking back on the sum of the experience—if he could regard it, even now, as a completed sum—Paul's calculation had to be that Jane had been by far the best thing in his life so far...with apologies to Juliette. And if both of them had kept secrets from him, well, secrecy was one of the primary instincts of the collective soul; if it were not, the protective walls of human individual consciousness would have been blasted away long ago. He could not help wishing, though, that both Juliette and Jane had confided in him a little more than they had.

He got back to the cottage without a serious slip, just as darkness began to close in, which it did quickly once the sun was below the horizon.

Sister Monique was still sprawled on the sofa, dozing, but she woke up as soon as she heard the door-latch click. She was wearing her quasi-monastic habit again, which had evidently been dried out next to the stove, but her ankles were bare, the stockings presumably having been ruined irreparably. Madame Louvot was not with her, but she came out of the kitchen after a few seconds to say, in a slightly sarcastic voice: "Will there be three for dinner, Monsieur?"

"Yes, Angélique, if you wouldn't mind," said Paul, a trifle tiredly.

The housekeeper curtseyed, also sarcastically—thus demonstrating a certain expertise in mime—and went back into the kitchen.

"Did you see Zosima?" Monique asked, a trifle anxiously.

"Not exactly," Paul said. "We exchanged a few words through a tightly closed door."

"Is she angry?"

"With you? I don't think so—why should she be?"

"I'm breaking the rule. I ought to have kept silent, save for strictly necessary exchanges of information."

"I didn't tell her that you'd spoken to me, even to that extent."

Monique laughed briefly. "She knows me too well," she said. "She knows that I wouldn't have been able to keep my mouth shut. She's seen into my soul, in this life and others. She doesn't approve, although it's part of her act to seem to permit everything."

"Act?" Paul queried.

"I'm not saying that the magnetism isn't real," said the woman clad in the absurd robe, "but there's still a lot of theater in the way she goes about it. You must know that, having been through the rigmarole, even though—according to her—you wouldn't be able to remember any of your own past lives, being a man."

Paul had pulled up a chair beside the sofa. "How well did you know Juliette?" he demanded, glancing over his shoulder at the portrait

Monique hesitated slightly, but evidently decidedly that there was no need to feign a reticence that was clearly not in her character. "Pretty well," she said. "A friend, although you might think that I should have been a better one. I was with her in the café on the night she tried to drown herself. I felt guilty about it for a long time. I went to work and left her and Annette together. If I'd stayed and gone up the hill with them...we'll, things might have worked out differently."

"You couldn't have done anything," Paul told her

"Juliette couldn't," Monique agreed. "She didn't carry a weapon. I had a stiletto. Toulousan, remember. Maybe it would have been touch and go, but if the lunatic was concentrating on stabbing Annette, I'll wager that I could have slipped it to him, and I'd have done it gladly, even if I got sent back to Saint-Lazare by the bastard tribunal. Scarab might still have jumped in the river though. She was in a state before—not your fault, though, so don't blame yourself—and she must have changed her mind or she wouldn't have let them fish her out."

"She wasn't trying to kill herself," Paul said. "She had a hallucination that she was burning, and wanted to put the flames out?"

"Is that what she told you? Well, perhaps it's true—but if I thought I was burning on the slope of the Butte I wouldn't have had to run all the way to the Seine to find a fountain. She was in a state all evening, convinced that her life was all over. She was so pleased when you asked her to pose for you—not for the pittance you paid her, obviously, but she took it for granted that you wanted her, and she was at a point when she really wanted to be wanted, if only for a little while longer than a quick squirt. The bastard who was keeping her also took it for granted when she told him she was posing, and he used it as an excuse to throw her out. Then she was convinced that you'd invite her to stay, and she'd have hooked you—but when you permitted her to stay and didn't want to screw her she was devastated.

"She waited up that first night for you to get back from Zosima's séance, more in hope than expectation, but still nothing. Instead, you told her about the girl on the lifeboat, and she thought it was all over for her. If the girl was found, she thought you'd throw her out, and if she wasn't, you'd be so heartbroken as to be beyond consolation, and still wouldn't want her. It didn't make it any easier that people were pestering her all night long with questions about you, after that spiritist rag published a crazy story about the Juvisy séance— questions that she obviously couldn't answer, and forced her to admit that she hadn't slept with you—at which point she knew that everyone else knew that you didn't want her. She was a wreck. I'll give you credit, though; it was kind of you to fetch her out of the hospital and let her stay.

"I didn't see her again until she was pretending to be your secretary, and she was still a wreck because you still hadn't slept with her, even though the girl in the lifeboat was presumed dead. Zosima's so-called medium was hanging around, and some middle-aged society bitch had got her mani-cured hooks into you, so poor Scarab was biting her knuckles to the bone. But again, all credit to you, I would have bet my douche that you wouldn't bring her to Toulouse with you, but you did, and rumor up at the convent has it that you stuck with her until she died. Not many men would have done that. I never met one...except, just maybe, Angélique's Fabien. He might have looked like a fairground Hercules, but he was as gentle as a lamb."

"She wasn't pretending," said Paul, in a low voice.

"Sorry?"

"Juliette wasn't pretending. She was my secretary."

"Well yes, she had to do the job, in order to pretend. She liked turning people away, though—it made her feel powerful, probably for the first time in her life. It was funny watching her give Fabien a flea in is ear—if it had been me, of course, I'd have told him that you were busy, but if he cared to screw me while he waited I'd make sure he didn't get bored, but she was such a little wisp that a prick like his might have disemboweled her."

"You seem to have survived the ordeal," Paul observed, dryly. "And you also knew Victor, when you lived in Toulouse?"

"Oh yes. Lovely boy—a bit shy, but I cured him of that. When I saw him again in Paris, though, he was embarrassed by me. I didn't fit his new image, so he only screwed me on the sly. It's not surprising, on reflection, that he didn't clap you on the shoulder and say: 'Did you know that Monique Magdalen's living a stone's throw from your studio?' Or maybe he didn't want to tell you in case you took advantage—men can be jealous, you know, even of whores. I'm surprised he didn't boast about having me in Toulouse, though—that must have surely have been because he was afraid that you'd take advantage...or that Gaston might, anyway. I liked Gaston...was it his girl-friend you went up the mountain with yesterday, or Victor's? I couldn't really see, from so far away. I knew she couldn't be yours, of course."

Paul was tempted to ask how, but imagined readily enough that Armande had been seen to arrive in Victor's automobile. In any case, his reclusive lifestyle must have caused conclusions to be drawn in the convent, with or without any comment from Zosima. Instead, he queried: "Monique Magdalen?"

"Not my real name, obviously—just a nickname. That's why I couldn't help laughing when you started washing my feet. There are some up there at the convent who think that being a painter of spirits makes you the next best thing to Jesus, although Zosima says no. She might have the magnetism, but she's not as crazy as the Three Witches or some of her other cronies."

"Not crazy enough," Paul wondered aloud, "to think that you might be a descendant of Marie Magdalen?"

His interlocutor's face changed slightly, and he inferred that she regretted having allowed her tongue to run away with her. "Can't talk about that." she said, briefly. "There are rules and rules, and that's a rule. You know why."

Paul wondered whether her simply making that remark might have given away far more than Zosima's "cronies" might have wished, but he did not have the chance to ask any further questions, for the moment, because Madame Louvot returned to the dining room to say: "How would Monsieur like dinner to be served? Will he be lifting Madame up in order to carry her to a dining chair?"

"That would seem to be the most convenient course of action," Paul countered, equably. "After all, we can't ask Madame to eat dinner on the sofa, can we? Will you set a place for yourself too?"

"No thank you, sir," Angélique replied, frostily. "I'll serve you, and eat in the kitchen, as I did yesterday for your other friends."

Without riposting to that thrust, Paul did as he had said, picking Monique up and depositing her in a dining chair. Then he followed Madame Louvot into the kitchen.

"Did she really do your nephew any harm, Angélique?" he asked her, in a low voice. "He must have been of age, and she can't be any older than he is. According to her, it wasn't a...commercial relationship."

"Doesn't alter the fact that she's a whore," the house-keeper snapped, "or that she thinks that I'm one too. You haven't seen her smirking."

"But you're not," Paul said, puzzled by that twist in the pattern of her resentment.

"Nor was I when I was with the baron," she said, "but it didn't stop some people thinking it. There are things you don't know, Paul—things that nobody knows, except Fabien...and perhaps her, if the great wooden-headed lump told her while she was tickling his prick. So when she smirks...I don't know, you see, exactly what she's smirking at. And you fawning all over her turns my stomach."

"I'm not fawning," Paul objected, startled by the vulgarity of her speech, which was most atypical of her. "I'm only being kind—and a little bit selfish, as she appears to know things about matters relevant to me that I never knew before. Not that I'm sure that what she says is entirely reliable."

"Of course it isn't. Whores are liars through and through. Don't tell her anything, by the way. Even if she's not the kind of witch who can command the lightning and cause landslides, and really is here by accident, it won't stop her taking advantage of the opportunity to spy."

"For whom?"

"The madwomen up at the old convent, of course. Do you think that flock of crows hasn't be spying on you for the last four years?"

"The thought had occurred to me that they might be reporting back to Zosima on my activities, but there's really nothing to report, and I decided that I didn't care either way. Anyway, if Zosima wants to spy, she'll be able to do it herself. She's coming to the cottage tomorrow morning to ask about the English couple."

Madame Louvot had suddenly turned pale. "You invited her here? After what you promised Madame Jane?"

It was news to Paul that Angélique knew what he had promised Jane—although he avoided leaping to the conclusion that she knew any more than the fact that he had promised not be magnetized again

"I haven't broken any promises," he said, curtly, "and if we don't carry that tureen through to the dining room, the soup will go cold."

So saying, he picked the tureen up and carried it through to the table. Monique was sitting demurely, giving no indication of impatience.

Without waiting for Madame Louvot to come out of the kitchen—which she showed no immediate intention of doing, and was fully entitled not to do, as she was not really a hired servant—Paul ladled soup into Monique's bowl

"I'm sorry," the unexpected visitor said to her host. "I didn't mean to cause any problems. I loved Fabien, you know. Looking back, I think I really loved him—and he's probably the only one I ever did love.

Paul assumed that she was exaggerating, "You didn't love Victor, then?" he asked, mischievously.

"No, not Victor. Sweet, but too young. I suppose we were much the same age, in years, but girls mature a lot faster than boys. Maybe now...but you never told me whether it was his girl-friend or Gaston's who came in the automobile yesterday."

"That was Armande, Gaston's wife," he said "They've only just returned to France after their honeymoon voyage in Italy. Gaston needs to stay in Toulouse for a few days to catch up on neglected business and make obligatory visits to various members of his multitudinous family, but then he'll be heading for Paris to settle into the marital home."

"In Passy, I suppose?"

"Auteuil."

"Same thing. Well, good for him. Him, maybe I could have loved, although he was no older than Victor, but he wasn't interested. Victor, I presume, is still trying to play Don Juan?"

"Actually, he's just got engaged. A charming young woman, very respectable—the perfect wife for a successful banker. Her name's Clorinde."

Monique sighed. "It would be," she said. "Back then, I laughed at the idea of marriage. 'Why volunteer to be a man's slave,' I used to say, 'when, with a little effort, you can make all of them yours.' What an idiot I was! Now...well, things look very different when you're an old hag, and even the prospect of being the slave of a good-looking man begins to look appealing, even though you know full well that they're all utter bastards...present company excepted, obviously. For God's sake don't tell Zosima I said that, though. In fact, please don't tell her I've said anything, except please and thank you"

"Why? Would she punish you for breaking the rule?"

"Not exactly—they don't use whips or put you on bread and water up at the phalanstery; they just give you the silent treatment and assign you the dirty jobs...unless they decide that you're not fit for paradise and exile you back to the hell of men for good. Only paradise isn't paradise for everyone, some of us having different tastes, if you take my meaning. I've tried, God knows I've tried; I used to enjoy it back in the old days, for a change, with Annette or Scarab, but when it's practically compulsory...oh, perhaps I shouldn't have said that about Scarab...maybe you didn't know?"

"I knew that she had...experience. She didn't name names. It's not important."

"Good. She wouldn't have liked the refuge at all. She wouldn't have gone there, even if she hadn't met you and fallen in love."

"I don't think she did fall in love," Paul said cautiously. "She told me that she was no longer capable of it."

"She told me that too—probably even believed it. I didn't. I don't believe anyone ever becomes incapable—even at Madame Louvot's age. If Scarab didn't love you, she certainly didn't love anyone else—but can you honestly look at that picture up there, and meet those eyes, and think that she didn't love you? Next you'll be telling me that you didn't love her."

Paul, for once, refrained from doing that.

"If you're not happy at the convent," he said, "surely you could go back to Toulouse."

"Oh, don't get me wrong—I'm better off there than I've ever been anywhere else. It isn't paradise, but it isn't even purgatory, let alone hell, in spite of the hard manual labor. As for going back to Toulouse...well, that a lot less easy than you seem to assume. Whoring's a nasty way to make a living, and the constant headache of paying the rent...except that it isn't exactly your head that does the aching." She paused, and said: "I'm actually shocking you, aren't I? Sorry. It's been nearly four years since I last talked to a man, and even though you can't remember me, I still remember you as the friend of a friend...two friends actually...and even though the old days were near enough to hell, stupidly, I can't help thinking of certain aspects of them fondly—Scarab especially, but Victor too. Is he going to come back before he takes his fancy auto back to Paris?"

"Yes, once more, at least. Shall I give him your regards?"

She finished her soup before replying. "Sorry," she said. "Would you believe that my mind is actually racing of its own accord, wondering whether there's any way I could sneak out to say hello to him. Sneaking out would be easy, especially with everything in turmoil—it's the saying hello that might be difficult."

"Turmoil?" Paul queried.

"Can't talk about that—although, to tell you the truth, I don't understand it myself. I'll probably miss the big vote, but that's no bad thing, and I wouldn't know which way to vote, and would be bound to upset someone either way. Don't tell anyone I told you even that much, though. I need to learn to resist crazy temptation, but...well, once I'm out of here, forget that I was ever here, or that I even exist. Sometimes, I think it would be better if I didn't."

"I know the feeling," murmured Paul, absent-mindedly but not entirely dishonestly.

It was her turn to be shocked. "You!" she said. "You're a famous painter—you produced that!" she pointed at the portrait of Juliette. "I know that you were always the sensitive one, the crazy one, back in the day, but you can't possibly think that you're worth less than Victor the banker or Gaston the heir to a choice slice of the vast family business. They're obviously rich and you're obviously not, and you live on your own with a housekeeper whose scowl could curdle milk, but damn it, Paul..."

She stopped, and let a few seconds go by before adding: "Sorry. I've spent my whole life thinking that everyone else is having a better time than me... even the poor sluts up at the phalanstery who spend their time fantasizing about being hussies at the courts of Charlemagne and mistresses of all the Louis, not to mention riding into battle with Penthesilea, sailing the seas with Joe of Arimathea and offering bloody sacrifices of hearts and balls to the Triple Goddess...I forget that they have problems too. It's not just Scarab that you've lost, is it? Gossip at the convent says that you were fond of someone else who died a few weeks ago...although that may be hot air, because for years rumor up there has been linking you in alchemical marriage with Clémence Sancerre."

"Really?" Paul said. "There are Rosicrucians up at the convent too? Not surprising, I suppose, given their recruitment pool. But I thought that the so-called alchemical marriage was a spiritual thing, not an actually marriage?"

"I wouldn't know. Some of the initiates talk in gobble-dygook that I can't make head nor tail of, being just a poor penitent."

"But there's been gossip at the convent for years? Gossip linking me with Clémence? About me I can understand, given that I'm the only person of any note visible on your literal horizon, but Clémence? I suppose you remember her from the old days, when she was already an artist of some note, but why should what passes for scandal up the mountain link my name with hers?"

"We're not cut off from the world, you know. Well, I am, and so are most of the other penitents, but it isn't just the Three Witches who get to go into Toulouse to see...clients. It's all secret, obviously, but there are leaks."

Madame Louvot came to clear away the soup dishes, and brought in a large trout, cooked whole in a delicately seasoned butter sauce, but she did not volunteer to being another bottle of wine, perhaps because Paul and Monique had not yet made significant inroads into the first and perhaps because she was inflicting a subtle punishment on her supposed employer and his unwelcome guest. Paul considered demanding that she join them at table, but decided that it would simply be humiliating if she refused, as she well might.

When she had returned to the kitchen, Paul said to Monique: "So, I'm a consistent topic of gossip at the convent?"

"Of course you are," Monique said. "We're all women, and you're our only near neighbor. We know you steer clear of the place, but that only makes you more interesting. As I said before, there are some who consider you to be a kind of saint...we're not short of mystics of our own, but that only makes the crazy ones more interested in imaginary kin. Zosima always asks about you when she visits, and the Three Witches seem to be very interested in any bits of information they can collect about you."

"The women you call the Three Witches are the ones who used to call themselves the Three Maries in Toulouse and the Daughters of Artemis in Paris?" Paul queried, just to make sure.

"That's right. You knew them back in the old days, then? And in Paris too?"

"Not really. And now they're the leaders of the phalanstery, at least while Zosima is in Paris?"

"Theoretically, we're not supposed to have leaders— even Zosima pretends not to be one—but that's just pretence.

Obviously, someone has to determine how things are organized, who does what and what it's all for. Anyway, we're supposed to be a secret society, so there are initiates and inner circles, and the innermost one of all, here on the mountain, is the Three Witches. But you're not supposed to know that, and if you tell Zosima that I told you...well, I'd say that I'd be expelled for sure, if I hadn't already broken more than enough rules back in Paris, and even here, to get thrown out, without actually being expelled. The sisters really are very tolerant to a wretched sinner like me, and I suppose I'm just an ungrateful bitch. But no more about that, please. Talk about something else"

"All right. Why does my supposed relationship with Clémence Sancerre figure in gossip at the convent?"

She made an exasperated gesture. "That's not changing the subject! Please, for the sake of mercy, stop interrogating me about things I couldn't tell you even if I knew them, which I don't. It must be my turn by now. How on earth did Fabien's aunt end up working for you after old Rochemure?"

"Pure kindness on her part," Paul told her. "We met when the baron was dying. He left Angélique a little money— enough to get by—but she's been a housekeeper all her life, and she wanted to continue being one. The baron thought that I was something of a saint too, and that had I had done him a huge favor, although I hadn't actually done anything significant, or even comprehensible. His gratitude made a big impression on Madame Louvot, and she knew what my circumstances were down here, so she wrote to me when Rochemure died and asked if she could come and work as my housekeeper. I was grateful. She's been a godsend, far better than the woman from the village who used to come on a daily basis to do the laundry and various tiresome domestic jobs."

"This huge favor you did the baron," she said, "wouldn't have had anything to do with his dead daughter, would it?"

"Yes. What did Fabien to tell you?"

"You're doing it again—but no matter. Just that the old man was still mourning his beloved daughter, even after thirty years, trying to get in touch with her through spiritists because he wanted to be forgiven. Fabien didn't know exactly why, but he was insistent that the baron hadn't done anything to feel guilty about. Fabien idolized the baron, and wanted to be like him—he wanted to be a soldier himself, but the baron had forbidden that absolutely, so Fabien said that he'd have to wait until he was dead. Some people thought that the baron was Fabien's father, but Fabien said no, that his real father was a man named..."

Madame Louvot had appeared by Paul's side as if by magic, and she interrupted vehemently: "Shut up! You have no right! Whatever he told you, you have no right to repeat it, not here and not in that nest of vipers up the hill!" Her eyes were positively blazing.

"I'm sorry!" yelped Monique. "I didn't know it was a secret! I'm sorry. I'm not your enemy, Madame Louvot. I was upset when you stopped Fabien seeing me, because he was a grown man, and even if I wasn't good enough for him...well, it was a long time ago. It's forgotten. It can't possibly matter anymore. There isn't any need for you to hate me."

Madame Louvot made a visible effort to pull herself together, and apparently succeeded. "I'm sorry, Paul," she said, finally. "And to you, Mademoiselle. But please, for the sake of kindness, don't say any more about what Fabien might have told you. I can understand why you think that the name you were about to pronounce is of no consequence, but it is to me. Please, don't speak it—not while I'm alive." She collapsed, then into one of the vacant dining chairs.

Stunned, Paul did not know what to say, and Monique's lips were temporarily sealed tight. After a lapse of more than a minute it was Madame Louvot who broke the silence. "And for what it may be worth, Paul," she said, "you don't know the whole story of why I wanted to come and work for you. You don't even know the full story of what happened the night he worked his miracle—which was, believe me, a miracle. You brought the baron and his daughter together again, after years of pain. You completed the haunting—and it nearly cost you your life. So, Sister Monique, I don't know about your mystics at the old abbey, but I do know that having visions is dangerous—it can kill. I've told Madame Zosima to stay away from Paul, but she obviously isn't taking any notice. If, if you really cared about my Fabien, and Monsieur Paul's Juliette, and his friend Victor, then help me to keep them away from him."

"Forgive me for asking, Angélique" Paul said, in a tone as mild as he could contrive, "but exactly when did you tell Zosima to keep away from me?" The fact that Zosima had referred to Angélique as his guard-dog had ceased to seem like a gratuitous and casual insult.

"Four years ago, when she came back to pester the baron after the séance," he housekeeper replied. "I had talked to Madame Jane by then, and we'd agreed that...well, that it wasn't in your interests to have any further contact with Madame Zosima. The way things are going...your friend Victor might be right, and you'd be better off in Paris....although Zosima will be going back there soon, won't she? This is all too complicated."

It certainly is, Paul thought.

"They're going to think this is all my fault, and it's not," Monique lamented. "It really isn't. I couldn't help Tigany jumping at the lightning. But they don't believe in chance—they'll see the lightning as an act of the goddess, an omen. And they'll blame me for opening my mouth, and telling you both what you aren't supposed to know..."

Paul's patience snapped. "You haven't told me anything at all, damn it!" he snapped. "In any case, Zosima has always said, and she repeated it today, that she isn't my enemy, and I have no reason to disbelieve her. Nor do I have any reason to disbelieve her when she says that she wants to talk to me because we're both tenants of the new owners of the domain on which we lodge, and they're temporarily available for consultation about the urgent need for repair that the road we both use has—which is even more urgent now that a slice of it directly opposite the cottage has crumbled away. So there isn't any need for hysteria, is there? Do we, by any chance, have anything left for dessert, Angélique, or should we just move on to the coffee now that we seem to have demolished as much of the trout as we can accommodate for the moment?"

There was no verbal reply to that, but Madame Louvot got to her feet, silently gathered the debris of the main course, and returned to the kitchen.

After a few seconds, Monique said; "This isn't exactly how I used to imagine this meeting going."

"You imagined meeting me?" Paul queried.

"Couldn't help it. Not a natural amazon, remember, and you're the only man for miles around. I assumed, naturally, that you'd remember me, as the mysterious beauty who had slipped away from you twice, but whom you'd always thought of lustfully. I knew you weren't a Fabien, or even a Victor, but at least...anyway, it wasn't supposed to go like this. I assume that when the sisters come to collect me in the morning, you won't be slipping me any notes saying that you can't wait to see me again."

"I hadn't made any such plan," Paul said, wryly.

"And if you had, Auntie would slap your wrist and forbid it. You wouldn't consider sacking her, I suppose, and hiring me as your housekeeper? I'd keep your bed warm as well as doing everything she does, and God help me, I'm ready for it now. Not much more than thirty, and already prepared to settle for being a household slave. Sometimes, I hate myself—and please don't murmur that you know the feeling. Nobody who can do *that* can possibly hate themselves"—again she pointed at the portrait of Juliette—"not the way I do, anyway. But I suppose I ought to warn you, just in case...you're seeing Zosima tomorrow?"

"In spite of pleas and warnings, I can't avoid it now."

"Well, when Zosima visits she always hypnotizes some of us, and it was my turn this time around. She hypnotized me two days ago. I never remember what I tell her under hypnosis. She usually reports back what we've supposedly remembered, in some detail, but this time she just said that it was the usual. She wasn't critical—she never is—and I'm not the only one who remembers, or imagines, sexual experiences, and even the hardened amazons sometimes remember being screwed by men in past lives, but I...well, on past occasions, I've mentioned you by name, and I might have done it again. As I say, you're the only man for miles, and I remember you, even if you don't remember me...so if Zosima says something, or sniggers, that might be why. I'm sorry."

"I suppose I ought to be flattered," Paul said.

"Yes, you ought—but I'm not sure she'll see it that way. I'll bet that I'm not the only one, though. I know you avoid the convent, but you're still the only man that some of the sisters ever see. We don't all go to market, let alone make secret deliveries of Salome's magic brew. I only have pleasant fantasies, but some of the others don't—you'd be surprised what nasty fantasies lurk deep down in the meekest of them. And to stimulate ideas, you went up the top of the mountain yesterday, clearly visible to everyone. I don't think even the locals would have recognized Victor—at least, I hope not—but they all know who you are, and some of them know the antiquary's cousin, too."

"The antiquary?"

"Gaston's cousin, or uncle, or whatever—Jean-Bénigne Lambrunet. Lilith writes to him, about the temple of Artemis, the Albigensians and all that stuff. He's supposed to be the local expert."

"I gather that he is, although I was only reminded yesterday that he helped negotiate the lease for this cottage, and for the convent. Lilith, I presume, is the mastermind who's plotting to wrest control of the convent from Zosima?"

"That's right. But..."

"But you can't talk about that. Can you talk about Jean-Bénigne?"

"Not really. I heard of him vaguely, back in the old days—great local historian and all that. Didn't interest me then."

"Apparently, he's the grandson or great-grandson of the busybody who told the Megisters that they owned the mountain, back in 1816 or whenever."

"Really? You'd think that, as a Toulousan, the last thing he'd want to do is help descendants of Simon de Montfort's cronies recover domains in France they'd forgotten about—but the Lambrunets aren't real Toulousans, are they? Probably descended from Montfort's cronies themselves, or Norman bastards."

"Unlike you, as a descendant of Marie Magdalen, at least by nickname?" Paul suggested, sarcastically. "Which would make you remotely Judean, possibly even descended from Christ, I suppose. Well, thanks to the brambles on the hillside, you now have a few stigmata. How are your hands?—I didn't check."

She blushed, closed her fists, and said nothing. Paul decided that it might be diplomatic not to pursue the point.

"Richard Megister said that he was intending to do some genealogical research while he and Ellen are in Toulouse," Paul mused. "Evidently, Gaston's cousin will be helping him with that, as he's their principal contact in the city. He's presumably involved in the property sector of the family business. If the Megisters want to sell the domain...or to develop it in some way...he'd doubtless be involved. Gaston didn't seem to know anything about it yesterday, but he's been away for a month and he was in Paris for some while before that, so he's probably completely out of touch."

"The important thing," Monique reminded him—speaking, of course, from her own point of view—"is that if Zosima makes any nasty remarks about me tomorrow, it's not my fault. I can't help my dreams or what I remember under hypnosis—and just between you and me, I think Zosima goes out of her way to stimulate fantasies of that sort. She gets a kick out of it. She's...well, it's not for me, as an ex-whore living in an amazon phalanstery, to call anyone perverse, but with all due respect to Her Holiness, and strictly between the two of us, she's more than a bit weird. Don't you think so?

Given the semi-serious offer that the ex-whore had just made him to become his mistress and housekeeper, Paul felt that it was a trifle disingenuous of her to claim that she could not help the fantasies that she revealed under hypnosis, but he did not pursue the point. Instead, he replied to the question posed, saying; "I suppose I should, given that she's been thoroughly demonized by people close to me. Jane loathed her, and even Talia, who loved her, warned me against her, but she's always been straight with me, so far as I know, and even her constant sarcasm has been good-humored. She annoyed me today, but that was as much my fault as hers...I have to admit that I've always quite liked her, and I don't believe that she's insane...or, for that matter, perverted."

Sister Monique uttered an oath of which he fellow amazons could not have approved, and added: "There's such a thing as being too kind. We're never going to get any dessert, are we? Or coffee. Do you think the old lady's died in there?"

Paul frowned. "I'll go and see," he said.

Madame Louvot had not died, but it was evident that Monique's pessimism s regard to the dessert was justified. The housekeeper was sitting in a corner of the kitchen, in the armchair positioned in the nook beside the stove, weeping gently but relentlessly, in what seemed to be a state of utter collapse.

He placed his hand on her shoulder. "What's wrong Angélique?" he asked.

"Of all the people to turn up on your doorstep," she said, "with a bad foot that made it impossible to kick her out, it had to be *her*. A trick of the Devil, sent to doom us all."

"She'll be gone in the morning," Paul said, "and she hasn't said anything."

"I'm a fool," said Angélique. "If I'd just pretended that I didn't recognize her, she'd have done the same, and Fabien's name would never have come up."

"I doubt that she'd have been able to keep quiet," Paul told her. "I've encountered some loose mouths in my time, but she's a real torrent: a compulsive bean-spiller, even when she stops herself mid-sentence."

Angélique looked up at him, sharply. "You *know?*" she said. "I knew I'd have to tell you, now—but you already know. She told you!"

"In fact," Paul confessed, "it was your reaction to the fact that she was about to pronounce the name that enabled me to guess. I know that Monsieur Louvot was in the baron's regiment, killed in one of the Tonkin campaigns before Fabien was conceived, and I know that your sister was an unmarried woman in service on the Baron's estate, so there's only one name of whose pronunciation you could have been so fearful—although I really can't understand why it would have terrified you."

"What name?" she demanded, grimly.

"Ignatz Fell, the estate steward—the man that the baron ordered to find and castrate his daughter's lover, in a fit of delirious rage—which he didn't do, so I can't see..." He stopped, abruptly, remembering that that was not the only thing that he baron had revealed about Ignatz Fell during his strange confession on the night of the séance, when both Fabien and Angélique had been listening to every word. Fabien had said afterwards that the confession was unfamiliar to him...but that did not mean that he had not asked the baron previously who his father might have been, perhaps in association with another, associated secret.

"It doesn't matter," he said, swiftly. "You don't have to tell me anything. All I need to know is that you were the baron's housekeeper for twenty years and more, and that he approved of you."

He could tell, however, that she knew that he had guessed the further secret. The baron had included in his confession the remark that when he discovered who had murdered Ignatz Fell he had not denounced that person to the police, presumably because he did not disapprove of what she had done. He might, however, have revealed her identity to the child of one of Ignatz Fell's rapes, as a matter of perceived duty, while demanding the child's understanding and forgiveness."

"Yes, I killed him," Angélique whispered. "I couldn't disembowel him with a bayonet, but I killed him, and I told the master why. The baron told Fabien, long after, that it had been the right thing to do: a matter of justice and duty—but he would think that, wouldn't he? Fabien believed him; he idolized the baron. I never idolized him...but I did love him. He didn't throw me out. You can, if you want to. I wouldn't blame you."

"There's no possibility of that," said Paul. "This is your home, for as long as you care to make it so. Go to bed now—it's late. Try to sleep. We can talk about it tomorrow, if you like, when Monique has gone, but there's to need. It really doesn't make any difference to me."

She was still staring at him. "If Zosima knows...," she whispered.

"I'm not sure that Monique knows, let alone Zosima," Paul told her. "And even if she did, it wouldn't make any difference. Nobody is going to denounce you. Everything is fine. Go to bed."

There was rebellion in the housekeeper's gaze, but she knew full well that the only rational course available to her was retreat. Before she went, however, she whispered very softly, as if to herself: "I couldn't let him get away with it again."

Paul made a pot of coffee before returning to the dining room.

"You were right about the dessert," he said

"Is the old lady all right?" the ex-whore asked, uneasily.

"Yes. A little indisposed...your arrival took her by surprise, and upset her a little."

""Well, tell her I'm sorry, if I don't see her again. And she has nothing to worry about. I didn't tell anyone what that blockhead Fabien told me eight years ago, and I won't now. All prick and no brains, that boy. I had to explain to him that just because he was proud of what Auntie might have done in the past, that didn't make it a good idea to boast about it to girls he slept with, especially girls like me. I forbade him ever to mention it again to anyone, and I hope he took it seriously, because he's in the Republican Guard now, and if he brags about it in barracks...she might have reason to thank God that she's here. And she needn't worry about me talking in my sleep; if I ever dream about Fabien, it isn't what comes out of his mouth that I dream about. This coffee's going to keep me awake, you know—but perhaps you planned that. Are you going to carry me off to your bed now that your chaperone's out of the way?"

"No," said Paul, softly.

"Pity," she said, "but only to be expected, and perhaps for the best, if Scarab's ghost is still haunting you. I'll tell myself that you only refused out of loyalty to her, and not because I look like a scarecrow. If you ever change your mind, plant a white flag on top of the mountain. I'll know what it means."

"I'll do that," Paul promised, "if I ever do."

CHAPTER VI

Paul woke up the next morning at first light and knew even before he had opened his eyes that he had had an active night; the after-effects of episodes of somnifabrication had long ago become recognizable. He got dressed in haste while the light was still poor, but as soon as the sun had begun to appear over the horizon he unhooked the curtain from the window in order to study the drawing pad that he kept on the table beside the bed.

He had been hoping for something clear and simple—for a recognizable face, perhaps a new image of Jane, which he could have considered as a visitation—but the image was blurred as well as chimerical. It seemed to be a kind of winged dragon, with a long body, clawed feet and strange quasi-insectile wings. It had a human face, as most of his monsters did, but the face was not one he knew, as was almost invariably the case. As always, he searched it for suggestive "family resemblances" but could not find any, and could not even be certain that the face was female, although the pattern of his productions favored that probability.

The feeling of frustration that he felt as he looked at the picture was all too familiar. Although he knew perfectly well how ridiculous and futile it was for the conscious part of his mind to curse the unconscious part for its inability to make more comprehensible use of the facility of dreaming to communicate imagery to his uncannily skilled hand, he could not help it.

Unusually, Madame Louvot had not yet emerged from her bedroom, and Sister Monique was fast asleep on the sofa. Paul made every effort not to make any noise as he went outside to the privy and then washed in the kitchen, but no one had stirred by the time that he returned to the bedroom and took the drawing through to the studio. There, however, he simply put it down on a table, because he could see from one of the studio windows a donkey cart making its way along the road that led to the invisible convent, accompanied by a dozen "amazons" in their hooded robes. Still making every effort to be quiet, Paul unbolted the door of the cottage and went out to the road to await their rival, steeling himself for the confrontation with Zosima.

It was, in fact, a confrontation of sorts, because of the ceremonious way in which she pushed back her hood to leave her head bare. Her short-cropped hair had considerably more gray in it than he remembered, and her face had a few more wrinkles as well as being thinner—as, in fact, was her whole figure, although it still gave the impression of being vigorous. She was not unhandsome, and her eyes, although calm, communicated a definite expression of force.

"Good morning, Monsieur Furneret," she said, with studied politeness, with only the slightest inclination of her head by way of a salutation. "We've come to collect our sister and our property, with your permission."

"Of course," Paul said, trying to mimic her artificial formality. "Monique is on the sofa in the dining room, still asleep—feel free to go in and collect her. The donkey is in the stable over there. You can see everything else."

Two of the sisters immediately went into the cottage, and collected Monique from the sofa. They carried her out to the cart, although Paul suspected that she could have walked if she had wanted to. Still half-asleep, she seemed resentful of the fact that the women carrying her gave Paul a conspicuously wide berth as they transported her to their own cart, but the faint expression of gratitude and regret that she showed him gave evidence of her intimidation. He was tempted to go to the cart in order to bid her farewell, but he was well aware that he was under observation, and not merely by Zosima. Instead, he watched the other sisters scrambling down the slope to examine the debris of the broken wheel and the spilled load.

"They won't be able to salvage much, I'm afraid, Madame." Paul said to Zosima, still speaking in a rather stilted manner, "and you won't be able to rebuild the wheel or make a replacement. That will need a good wheelwright—better, I suspect, than the village smith."

"The fundamental principle of a phalanstery," said Zosima, equably, loudly enough to be overheard by all of her companions, "is self-sufficiency. Don't underestimate our capabilities, Monsieur Furneret."

"I apologize," Paul said. He added: "You really are Fourierists, then?"

"We're the *only* true Fourierists, Monsieur Furneret," Zosima informed him, loftily. "None of the others, least of all Prosper Enfantin, have so far understood that the abolition of sexual property requires the abolition, or at least the expropriation, of its self-appointed owners."

"That might make the reproduction of the workforce a trifle difficult," Paul suggested, relaxing into sarcasm.

"Do you think so?" Zosima retorted. "Ours isn't a cloistered order; when pregnancies are required, they can be arranged. But the phalanstery is a very much a work in progress, not ready as yet for independent functioning—as evidenced by the fact that we still make abundant purchases from markets. May I talk seriously to you, Monsieur Furneret? I need to have a word with you about the English couple. As fellow tenants, we have certain interests in common, including the road on which the convent and the cottage both depend. I know that you don't like me and don't approve of me, but in this matter, we need to put our differences aside. It's strictly a matter of business. Please?" She was moving away as she spoke.

Startled, Paul paraded his glance around the sisters, who were obviously the people that Zosima wanted to exclude from their private conversation, there being no one else in the vicinity except Madame Louvot, who was still in bed. Then he nodded his head and followed her meekly, not having to make any effort to seem more than a little uneasy and reluctant— even more so when she veered off the road as soon as it entered a clump of trees and took him into the thicket.

She did not take him far, but she made sure that they had not been followed before moving closer to him than he found entirely comfortable and speaking to him in a low and confidential voice.

"I apologize for that Paul, and for my rudeness yesterday," she said. "My situation in regard to my so-called sisters is awkward at present...but that's not your concern. How are you?"

"Perfectly healthy, as you can see," he told her, guardedly.

She sighed. "You know that's not what I mean. Jane's unexpected death must have hit you hard—or did you have prior notice no one else had?"

Still guarded, but seeing no reason to lie, he said: "No, I didn't. I don't know anything about it, except what I read in the newspapers. I sent condolences to her husband and son, but I didn't dare ask questions."

"I can probably find out more than the papers reported, if you wish."

"I'd rather you didn't. I don't think Jane would approve of your investigating her death, for whatever reason."

"I'm sure she wouldn't, and I'm sure that you still intend to honor the promise she extorted from you, even though she's passed on. Do stop looking at me like a finch contemplating a viper; I have no intention of attempting to magnetize you without your consent. How did Sister Monique behave while she was your guest?"

"With perfect discretion and decorum."

"It's too late in life to embark up a career as a liar, Paul—I've seen the depths of her soul, remember. Well, for what it may be worth, any offer she made you would have been sincere. She's utterly egotistical, but honest in her slutty fashion. She'd probably have offered herself anyway, but the fact that she knew Juliette will have piqued her...let's call it a spirit of emulation. But I know you, too, so I know you'd have turned her down even if La Louvot and Jane's ghost hadn't been watching you. Can we please be straight with one another? With the possible exception of Madame Louvot, I might be the only resident of this entire region that you can trust."

Paul frowned, but he raised no objection to her qualification of Angélique as only a possible exception. "Go on," he said.

"The only reason you don't trust me is because Jane didn't,'" she said, speaking rapidly. "I don't blame you for that, and I don't blame her. I don't know what the exact substance was of the vision I induced that night, but it obviously scared her very badly, and I now have some inkling of why. Apart from the baron and Jane, the only other participant in the séance who seems to have obtained a significant hint of the collaborative enterprise is Madame Louvot, but Madame de La Vaudère got to her before I did, and seems to have recruited her support, perhaps even to the extent of planting her in your kitchen. I can't help admiring Jane—once having decided to become a disruptive presence in our relationship, she certainly took her disruption to an extravagant extreme. You trusted her, and she'll probably haunt you until you die. I can't fight that—but all I'm asking is that you remember the circumstances in which our...arrangement developed. I have never done anything to you without your consent, as fully informed as possible. I can't claim that I've always been as scrupulous in my dealings with others, but I now regret the excesses of my youth, and I try hard not to renew them—as evidenced, I hope by the dramatic change in my career, although that has not, I fear, been without dire complication. Not only am I not your enemy, Paul, but if you ever want or need my help, you can rely on me."

Fearful of falling into error by virtue of subtle suggestion, Paul refused to meet his interlocutor's eye, and said: "What did you want so say to me about the Megisters?"

This time, she did not bother to sigh, but merely shrugged her shoulders. "Has Richard Megister told you anything about any plans he might have for the estate?"

"Not yet. I'm meeting him later today. He's coming out from Toulouse again in his automobile. Unlike Victor, though, he doesn't appear to drive it himself—which seems like cheating to me. Not true sportsmen, the English."

Zosima did not contrive the slightest hint of a smile. "Well," she said, "if you can get anything out of him, I'd be obliged if you could let me know, if only because there are people at the convent who would rather I were uninformed. In any case, it would be to your advantage as well as mine, if he asks you for your opinions, to put a damper on any schemes that Jean-Bénigne Lambrunet might have helped to insinuate into his mind. Megister practically backed away holding up a cross when I was introduced to him in Toulouse, but you can talk to him man to man and scholar to scholar—preferably in English, because his French is terrible."

"I can speak English well enough," Paul assured her, hoping that he was not exaggerating his linguistic skills, although he had not had any difficulty when the Megisters had left the automobile at the cottage two days before.

"Good. If my brief impression can be trusted, that little goose of a sister might be easy pickings for a man as handsome as you, with a conveniently Byronic reputation, if you didn't have scruples, but we don't have time for roundabout routes anyway. Try to find out from the brother whether anyone has been trying to pull his strings via the antiquary."

"Do you have a particular anyone in mind?"

"Sister Lilith," said Zosima, tersely, her eyes sharp as she watched for Paul's reaction to the name.

"Victor told me that the word in Paris is that she's trying to take over the convent," Paul said, mainly in order that Monique would not get the blame for talking too much, "and I know that she's been corresponding with Jean-Bénigne Lambrunet about antiquarian matters, but I can't imagine what kind of strings you might have in mind."

"I suspect that Lambrunet has been trying to interest the Megisters in archaeological and geological investigations. Have you, by any chance, talked to the fellows who were preparing climbing equipment for a descent into the Great Cleft two days ago, before the storm sent then scurrying away?"

"No, they didn't come to the cottage, so I just ignored them. They're not the first people I've seen poking around in one or other of the clefts, and they surely won't be the last. Why would an interest in archeological or geological investigations on Richard Megister's part be problematic for you?"

"Don't you think it might be problematic for you?" she countered. "Your cottage is rumored to stand on a site where there was once a shrine erected to Marie Salome—about which my Sister Salome claims to remember far more than a rational man like you would find plausible. The convent stands on a site that might not only have been a place of serious Albigensian worship but the location of a temple of Artemis. Do you have the slightest idea what has happened to the Puy de Dôme since the remains of a temple of Mercury were found there in the seventies, at the height of the fad for native archeology? Do you have any idea what has happened to the once-pleasant corner of the countryside that is nowadays called Lourdes since that little shepherdess had visions of the Virgin Mary there?"

Paul had no difficulty taking the implication. "I know there are Marians in your convent—our Marians, that is, not the Roman Church's Marians—and the supposed memories of past lives you've been helping them to receiver doubtless include memories, or visions, of the three Maries. It would be amazing if they didn't. But you can't liken their delusions to the one experienced by little Bernadette Soubirous. She had an entire Catholic country primed to take her visions of the mother of Christ seriously, and motives for so doing. Who, outside your phalanstery, apart from a handful of eccentric members of the Toulousan sororities, could have the slightest interest in Sister Salome's recovered memories seriously, even if they include inside information about the prophet of the Apocalypse?"

"Don't forget John the Baptist," Zosima countered, sarcastically. "Our Salome is a trifle generous in her conflation of the various Biblical characters who share her name, with a blithe disregard for chronology. And let's not forget her visions of the Sapphic bacchanals of the worship of Artemis, or the older goddess that Artemis replaced, which might have come straight out of one of La Vaudère's fanciful novels. In private, I approve entirely—mine is a very broad church—and I consider dreaming to be mentally healthy, but it wouldn't make for wise publicity."

"My point exactly," Paul retorted. "Your chances of re-paganizing France are exactly zero. Better charlatans than you have tried."

"I'm not a charlatan, Paul—you know that, and you know full well how limited my ambitions are. Lilith and her cabal aren't charlatans either...but I wonder sometimes... Let's not leave out of account, either, the possibility that there might be authentic visions of the past to be recovered. A great many people would deny that *a priori*, but you can't seriously be one of them. All I know for sure is that Lilith has been taking a strong interest recently, with Jean-Bénigne Lambrunet's aid, in the archeology and geology of the mountain. I'd like to know whether she's been trying to communicate that interest to the Megisters. If they have any plans of that sort, I'd like you to tell me, in order that I can figure out the strategy of the annoying game that's being played in the convent."

Paul shrugged his shoulders. "All right," he said, "I suppose, if our moral accounts were added up scrupulously, it could be argued that I owe you a favor or two. But I really can't see that it matters in the slightest. Gaston has always had a certain fascination with local geology, which he doubtless shares with Jean-Bénigne, but I can't see any practical relevance in it."

"Think about it, Paul. Thanks to my careful design and management of our agricultural and artisanal resources, my phalanstery can get most of the things we can't produce for ourselves from the markets in the village and Toulouse, just as you can buy all the supplies you need there—but what's the one thing you and the convent can only acquire at the whim of the mountain?"

Partly thanks to Gaston, Paul knew the answer to that one. "Water," he said.

"Exactly. And do you know how many people the current water supplies to the convent can support for any length of time?"

"At a guess, you're going to tell me that it's exactly the number that are presently living on the mountain...that your little colony can't expand any further...unless something could be done to retain water that normally flows away, or to divert the pattern of flow. And it's not just the convent's land. If Richard Megister has any plans to develop the rest of his land, irrigation would be a vital issue. And for several years now, you've been trying to develop your scrawny little vineyard into a commercial proposition."

"There you are," she said. "All it takes is a little imagination. Except that the vineyard and the distillery were Sister Salome's idea, not mine...and any entitlement I had to direct their future development is fast disappearing, and probably already beyond repair. I still care, though—just as I still care about you, and the interesting enigma that you pose. That's something else in which Lilith has become increasingly interested recently...which is another reason why my problems and your potential problems are connected. Perhaps I shouldn't care about that, but I do, and it isn't just my pride at stake. I've put my heart and soul into this endeavor, and it's bad enough having to see Lilith, Salome and Justine take it away from me without seeing them add insult to injury by taking you along with it. So, I'd like to find out what's happening on both fronts, if I can, and I'd like you to help me, if you will."

"All right," Paul promised. "I'll try to find out from Richard Megister what plans he has for the domain, but I doubt that he'll be very forthcoming. In his eyes, I'm just a crazy painter."

"And work on the sister as well, if you get the chance—I know your intentions would be totally honorable, but a smile or two wouldn't hurt. If they decide to stay in Toulouse for any length of time, it might be to your advantage to cultivate her acquaintance...and mine."

"You want to magnetize them!" Paul was already beginning to have second thoughts about the wisdom of volunteering to act on Zosima's behalf with regard to the Megisters.

"Only if they're willing," she emphasized scrupulously—and then, after a moment's hesitation, she added: "but primarily, I want to make sure, if I can, that no one else has magnetized them, or will."

"You mean Lilith?"

"Obviously. The internal politics of my little cult are complicated, but you probably have some idea of how these things work: as soon as an organization of that sort reaches a certain size, there's always an eel under the rock, always a schism waiting to happen. Lilith doesn't have my psychic force, but she's a skilled hypnotist, with a particular talent for inducing mystical crises. I no longer have the notional authority here, but I still have the committed loyalty of a minority. I can't send more people down from Paris because the convent is effectively full, but I'm not entirely helpless. That needn't be your concern, of course, except..."

Well aware of his probable resemblance to a fish looking at a baited hook, Paul simply said: "Except what?"

"Lilith isn't just trying to cultivate influence within the cult but without, and you know what rich ground Toulouse is for the recruitment of mystics. I don't know what her long-term plans are, and most of the strings she pulls in the city are invisible to me, but one thing I do know is that she's trying hard to recruit Clémence Sancerre, possibly as a prize in her own right, but more probably with the objective of trying to get to you through her. She knows a great deal about you, Paul, including a lot of information I gave her, perhaps carelessly, when I was training her. I've been able to reciprocate, and I now know most of what she knows, but not all. The point is, however, that she and I both know more about you than you do, and although I don't know exactly what her plans are, I am sure that they concern you, and that she's more dangerous to you than I am. She wants to use you, Paul."

Paul was skeptical about all of that, and not a little annoyed about the manner in which he was being teased and manipulated. "For what purpose?" he snapped.

"To induce visions, of course. What else are you good for?"

"She's not like you, then?" he retorted, sarcastically.

"In some ways, she's very much like me; in others, not. I work entirely with my collaborators' consent, as you know. Lilith might not be as scrupulous. I would never expose you to a danger that you didn't want to face, even if your reasons for not wanting to face it were puerile or misguided. I fear that Lilith not only wouldn't care, but might relish the opportunity. I know that you don't trust me, but for the moment, our interests coincide. Neither of us wants Lilith to send you forth in search of her imaginary holy grail, on a pointless journey into imaginary space from which you might not return. And if anyone is to assist Ellen Megister to remember her previous incarnations, please believe that it's in your interests as well as mine to persuade her to let me do it before someone else persuades her to allow Lilith to do it."

"Why," Paul queried, sarcastically, "if they'd be the same previous incarnations?"

"Don't be deliberately obtuse, Paul. For one thing, even in the most naïve version of the theory, there are a large number of previous incarnations from which a selection might be made. For another, I remember very clearly explaining to you why even honest practitioners cheat. I cheat, and Lilith cheats; but what I do, by means of cheating, is a form of psychotherapy intended to help patients to get to know themselves a little better, to help them to be a little more content with themselves. I can't make people happy, but given time, I can usually help then to be a little less unhappy, resigned if not content. What Lilith seems to be doing, both within and without the phalanstery, is cultivating her peculiar madness in others. In the short term, that sort of intervention can produce spectacular results; it can hit people with the force of a revelation, make them blissful, or at least more self-satisfied; it conveys rewards. In the longer run, though, it often harms them, sometimes badly."

"You seriously think that I might be in danger from the wiles of a crazy Marian who thinks I can be pressed into some kind of saintly role in her cult, even though I'm a man?"

"As a matter of fact, I do. If you doubt it, consult your phantoms. Consult Jane and Juliette, and Talia if you can still reach her. If you don't trust the dead, consult Camille Flammarion, or Henri Lemastur, or Gabriel de Lautrec. Any one of them can tell you that the kind of danger I'm talking about is real, and that you're far too sensitive for your own good. But don't worry too much—you have a powerful ally in me. I don't know for sure what the left hand of my own organization has been doing since I was persuaded to institute this succursal, and now it has succeeded in taking over the reins of this fraction of the organization and reducing me to a mere figurehead, my chances of finding out might be slim—but your Toulousans don't know who they're dealing with. I've lived in Naples; I know how Camorras work...but this conversation has already gone on far too long. We'd better get back to the cart, so that I can get Monique safely back to her own narrow bed and see what can be done about fixing the cart. I'll come to see you again soon to give you a fuller explanation, probably by night so as to attract less attention. Have I given you enough food for thought for the time being?"

"You know you have—and you planned your effects like the skilled performer you are. But I'm not convinced that it's anything more than hot air."

"Because I'm your friend, Paul, I'm prepared to hope that you never find out otherwise, but be careful, please. You're an asset to the world, and need to be treated preciously. And whatever your protectors, living or dead, can do, the day will eventually come when someone as desperately in need of the illusion of redemption as Baron de Rochemure de Harvanges was will approach you and ask for the loan of your gifted or afflicted soul—and because you have SOFT TOUCH branded on your forehead in capital letters, you'll consent."

And with that, Zosima turned away abruptly and strode back to the section of broken road where her acolytes were waiting for her, with a patient calm that was probably faked.

CHAPTER VII

When Paul arrived back at the house, all the members of Zosima's strange organization, including Sister Monique, were disappearing round a bend in the path. Madame Louvot was just about to set forth for the village. It seemed to Paul that she almost rushed away, without even bothering to offer the excuse that she was a hurry, because they had yet more guests due, perhaps the most important ones of all, but she could not resist the temptation to pause in order to say, accusatively: "You've been with *her* all this time?"

"It was only a matter of minutes," Paul told her, "and no harm came to me. She told me some things that I probably need to know, so it wasn't a waste of time."

"What did she want from you in return?"

"She wants me to find out what the Megisters' plans for the estate are, if they have any—but I wanted to know that anyway—and she wants my help to figure out what Lilith might intend to do with me...and, at the very least, she wanted to frighten me."

"And she wants you to tell her whatever you find out from the Megisters?"

"Yes. It's a reasonable request, I suppose."

"Why can't she ask the Megisters herself? And how can she possibly need you to figure out what Lilith's plans are?"

"I think she tried to talk to the Megisters when she was introduced to them in Toulouse earlier in the week, but it didn't go well. She thinks that they might feel more comfortable talking to me, and more forthcoming—and she's probably right. But that's a minor issue. As to the matter of Lilith, I can't make head nor tail of that yet, but I really don't care about their squabble over control of the convent. I doubt that there's any need for either of us to worry about it."

123

"Don't be ridiculous," she said. "It's easy enough stop worrying about myself—seeing the whore like that just took me by surprise, and I'm over it now, although knowing that the nasty little slut must have told Zosima everything sends a slight chill into my heart—but it's not so easy to stop worrying about you, now that the Egyptian has wormed her way back into your life."

"Actually," said Paul, "I think 'nasty little slut' is a trifle unfair. She's certainly something of a slut, but Monique's not so little, and I don't believe that she's nasty. She convinced me that she was genuinely fond of Fabien, and really didn't do him any harm. She was able to tell me some things about Juliette that I didn't know, and for which I'm grateful to her. I'd be obliged if, as a favor to me, you could forgive her."

"You mean that she's going to come back too?" the housekeeper snapped. "And that you're going to sleep with her?"

"I can't guarantee that she won't come back," Paul told her, "but I can guarantee that I won't sleep with her. Apart from anything else, Juliette would never forgive me. And please don't tell me again that I don't know little girls the way you do, or that I have SOFT TOUCH branded on my forehead in capital letters. I'm not as naïve as I used to be."

For a moment, it seemed as if Angélique might argue that point, but in the end, since she really was in a hurry, she picked up her basket and set off for the village. Paul went into the studio and immediately resumed work on the painting of Jane, hoping that it would absorb him and help him to clear his mind of all the confusion that had accumulated there so rapidly.

He succeeded in that, without abandoning himself to the extent that he slipped into a quasi-somnambulistic state. While he was in company with Jane's image—twice over, as he had the sketch on which he had based the oil panting pinned to a board a few feet away, similarly posed on an easel—he felt that his consciousness and his will were protected. It was an illusion, obviously, but it was an illusion he cherished.

Even though the questions were relegated to be that back of his mind, though, he couldn't help being aware of them. He resented the fact that everyone seemed to know more about what was going on behind the peaceful scenery of the mountain than he did. Even Angélique, it seemed, was familiar with the name of the mysterious Lilith and she too feared that she might pose some kind of threat to him—which presumably meant that there was gossip about him in the village. There, as in the convent, he was a prominent figure on the local horizon, and it was perfectly understandable that the villagers should be exceedingly curious about him as well as about what went on in the convent. He could hardly complain about being uninformed of what that gossip contained, since he had always made every attempt to avoid listening to it—but that was when he thought that it could not have any real relevance to him. Evidently, Zosima thought it had, and so did Angélique.

Eventually, the nagging itch of those questions brought him back from his attempted self-absorption.

Damn it, Jane, he said, silently addressing the sketch rather than the evolving oil painting, *what's the point of haunting me if, like all the others, you're going to do it silently? You didn't want to tell me while you were alive exactly why you were so afraid that I'm in danger, or exactly why you cared, but now that you're dead you could surely loosen up a little? You do realize, I suppose, that I'll have to get the rest of the story from Zosima, whether you like it or not?*

There was, inevitably, no answer.

What Monique had said about an "alchemical marriage" also haunted him. When he had first arrived in Paris at the very end of the fin-de-siècle the neo-Rosicrucian cults had already begun to decline, and he had paid little or no attention to the "hot air" of their assertions, but so far as he knew, the royal "chymical wedding" of the fictitious Christian Rosenkreutz was a purely symbolic one, a spiritual union rather than carnal sexual congress. In any case, given the nature of their cult, Zosima and Lilith were hardly likely to represent their Ideal, even metaphorically, in terms of a union between a symbolic king and a symbolic queen...except, as Zosima had remarked when he had made a snide remark about renewing the phalanstery's workforce, that that some kind of comprise with the process of fecundation could easily be obtained...

He shook his head, and concentrated on Jane's eyes—always the most vital part of any oil painting, always the focal point of the hypnotic power of Art.

Give me a clue, he pleaded—and then remembered that she already had, in the strange vision that they had shared, and also shared with Baron de Rochemure and Madame Louvot, on the night of the séance in Passy. The voice that had spoken to him in that vision had mentioned both Clémence and the Holy Grail. And it occurred to him that Jane, who had long been familiar with the occult underworld of Paris when he first met her, and had surely maintained connections within it during the eight years of their strange relationship, might well have been in contact with the Daughters of Artemis during that time.

He remembered that when he had first mentioned Clémence's name to Jane, it had not seemed to be familiar to her, but that even before he had mentioned the name, Jane had asked him whether his new female friend had any connection with the floral games. He had thought at the time that it was a natural guess, on the part of a writer, but now he could not help wondering whether there might have been more to it than that.

When he had left Paris to return to Toulouse with Juliette in 1901, he knew, the three Daughters of Artemis must still have been in Paris and had not yet joined Zosima's cult. At that point in time, Jane had been intensely curious about him, and had not been able to comprehend the rapid attachment that she had formed with him. Of all the people in Paris available for consultation on the subject, it was not improbable that the Daughters of Artemis might have come to mind. The mysterious Lilith had not yet been trained by Zosima in the art of re-covering or inducing visions of past lives by hypnosis, but that did not mean that she had no interest in such matters...and if she and Jane had exchanged information...

Monique had not mentioned having had any substantial contact with the Daughters of Artemis while she was in Paris, but as Lilith was a topic that she had been avoiding—far too conspicuously—it was not improbable that she had, and that Lilith could therefore have obtained information from her about Victor, and about him...

But how could it matter, even if Lilith, fueled by information regarding him gained from various sources—including, of course, the infamous *Mercaba* article—had singled him out as a person of potential interest, and perhaps even potential utility? Clearly, she had not done anything about it for eight years, for more than half of which time she had been living almost with a stone's throw of him, and even if she had decided to do something about it now, what could she actually do? And why would she?

His train of thought was at that point in when the bell at the gate rang. He broke off his work and stood back, appraising his progress. He felt that the painting was ninety per cent finished. He was satisfied with the likeness, and thought that Jane would be pleased if she could see it—as Zosima, of course, would have assured him that she could.

He was still cleaning his brushes and had not yet removed his smock when the door of the studio opened and Ellen Megister came in.

"Please excuse my rudeness, Monsieur Furneret," she said, in English, with the blithe confidence of a young woman who had already discovered that a pretty face will always obtain forgiveness from impressionable men, for sins far worse than rudeness. "I should have waited to ask your permission, I know, but I wanted to see your picture again, having only had a brief glance the other day, and knowing that it ought to be nearly finished by now. Please forgive me?"

"No forgiveness is necessary," Paul assured her, automatically, answering in the same language. "I'm flattered by your interest."

Richard Megister had come in behind his sister, but he stood aside after sketching a salute, allowing the young woman to take the floor and continue the conversation.

Ellen Magister was robust and vigorous, perhaps pretty rather than truly beautiful, but more than pretty enough, with dark hair and dark eyes, which contrasted pleasantly with a complexion that was pale without looking in the least unhealthy. She had an ingenuous exuberance that supported her ready smile and made it seem quite charming. Her brother, who must have been three or four years older than her, in his mid or late twenties, was even more robust, but his eyes and hair were a lighter shade of brown, and his complexion was sun-tanned, which gave his rather delicate features a hint of fortitude that suited him very well.

"It's beautiful," said Ellen, standing in front of the painting, carefully keeping a respectful distance because she knew that it was not dry. "A beautiful woman—she must have been stunning when she was young. I tried to read one of her books, but it was too difficult. My French isn't good enough. I'll have to practice hard, though, now that Richard is a French landowner. Is the sketch you're working from one of the famous ones that you draw in your sleep?"

"Yes," said Paul, warily.

"And this one?" she asked, moving to the table where he had placed the sketch that he had made during the night. "I probably shouldn't ask, but what on earth is it supposed to be?"

"I wish I knew," Paul said. "I can never remember the dreams in which I make my automatic sketches, or even whether there actually was a dream."

"It's a dragon," she announced, apparently feeling free to offer the opinion, in view of his confession of ignorance. "Like of one the beasts of the Apocalypse—don't you think so, Richard?"

"I don't know," her brother replied. "I've never seen the beasts of the Apocalypse, mercifully."

Ellen began moving around the studio, then, looking at the other visible canvases with an evident curiosity, although she had already visited the studio briefly once before, and there will little visible now apart from the new sketch and the nearly-complete painting that had not been visible then.

"Your road seems to have suffered a small landslip," Richard Megister observed, clearly not sharing his sister's fascination with Paul's art-work. Paul had removed his smock and belatedly shaken his guest's hand before the latter added added: "I hope that wasn't my fault," presumably meaning the landslip

"No, of course not," said Paul. "How could it be?"

"The old girl is a little heavy, I'm afraid," said the Englishman, evidently referring to his automobile, "and country roads like that one weren't designed to carry such vehicles. I'll talk to the notary about having it repaired. I don't think you're in any danger of being cut off here, but the...ladies who live up the hill could be in difficulties if more of the road surface slides down the slope."

Grateful that that was one topic that he would not have to bring up with the air of a solicitor of favors, Paul ushered his guests into the dining room, where Madame Louvot had already set a samovar and cups on the small able.

"Did you have a productive day yesterday in your genealogical research?" Paul asked, when they were all settled in armchairs holding teacups. He noticed that Ellen was gripping her cup in a slightly precious fashion, with the extended little finger that English etiquette demanded, but that Richard was displaying no such affectation.

"Oh, yes," said Richard, but without any marked enthusiasm. "Monsieur Lambrunet is a marvel. He knows so much, and it's very interesting. English history is dull by comparison—so dull, apparently, that the Normans had to make most of it up. He has documents and artifacts too. We could probably have spent another day at his home without running out of conversation." His observation did not give the impression that he would have relished the extended conversation particu-

129

larly. "You must be quite familiar with his collection, I suppose?"

"No," Paul confessed. "I don't really know Monsieur Lambrunet very well—hardly at all, in fact."

"But he said that you were practically one of the family—almost adopted, he said, by the poor woman who was lost in the shipwreck in the Channel in 1901?"

"Yes, that's true," Paul admitted, "Amélie's son, Gaston, was a close friend throughout my childhood, and still is. I must have met Jean-Bénigne at Amélie's house more than once, but the Lambrunets are a big family, and as a boy I found it impossible to keep up with all the names of the adults that drifted past, who were paying little or no intention to the various children who were around. Our friend Victor was usually with us, and Gaston's sister Martine. The societies of adults and children can exist in parallel in overlapping spaces without either taking much notice of the other. But Jean-Bénigne also helped with the leasing and the renovation of this cottage, for which I'm very grateful. It was a strange whim on my part, I suppose, to want to live out here, such a long way from the city, but I remembered visiting the mountain as an adolescent and climbing it, and that day had stuck in my memory as a particularly pleasant one. It all came back to me vividly two days ago, when Gaston, Victor and I climbed it again."

"Monsieur Lambrunet told us yesterday that the cottage is built on the site of an old shrine," Richard said offhandedly. "He told us that when the renovation was being done he came out to inspect the new foundations, and searched for artifacts, but couldn't find anything. Far too much time had elapsed, he said. He was sorry that no such work had to be done on the old convent, which would have allowed him to look for artifacts from several interesting eras, going back to a temple that was on the site more than two thousand years ago. What was the name of the goddess, El?"

"Artemis," she said. "The goddess of the hunt...and chastity. The protector of virgins—not inappropriate, it seems to the present usage of the site."

Paul was careful not to hazard a guess as to how many of Zosima's "amazons" were actually virgins, but he took leave privately to hope that Artemis, if her phantom was still in the vicinity and not too attenuated by time, might protect them nevertheless.

Richard was quick to take up a different aspect of the goddess's attributes. "Was the hunting good in these parts back then, do you think?" he asked Paul. "Monsieur Lambrunet said, apologetically, that it isn't nowadays. He seemed to think that because we're English, we might want to hunt foxes here, but I fear that I've never done that. I ride tolerably well, of course, but only for everyday purposes. In sporting terms, I've only ever played polo, rather badly."

"It wouldn't be possible to hunt in the forest," Paul said. "Far too dangerous, because of the clefts. Do you know about the clefts?"

"Oh yes—one of the lawyers asked me to give my permission for some people from the university to go exploring there, although they had to suspend the expedition temporarily after the first day because there was a bad rainstorm. I hope you don't mind—perhaps it's your permission rather than mine they should have been asking for."

"Not at all," said Paul; it's your land—but do you mind if I ask what they're looking for?"

"One of them said something about strata and fossils, and another went on about seismic activity and metamorphic rocks. They were speaking French, and I got completely lost, I'm afraid."

"I didn't believe them," Ellen opined. "I think that was just a cover story."

Richard laughed. "For what?"

"I don't know—but you heard what Monsieur Lambrunet said...or perhaps you didn't, because he had to keep slipping back into French when he didn't know the English terms. But you must have got the gist of what he was saying about the Cathars having passed on custody of the Holy Grail to the Knights Templar when they were massacred by our ancestors, and the Templar Order being broken up in its turn, but hiding all their treasures to save them from the predatory king."

"I heard it," Richard admitted, "but I didn't pay much attention. Fairy stories. You can't think that even French university professors might go potholing looking for Templar treasure or the Holy Grail?"

Paul did not take exception to the Englishman's derision of French universitarians, and left it to Ellen Megister to reply to the provocation.

"Who can tell?" she countered. "Even if they weren't, Monsieur Lambrunet might have been hoping that they would find something more relevant to his interests than theirs. He'd probably have gone down with them if he'd been thirty years younger."

Richard laughed again. "He's had an entire lifetime to try," he said.

"But when he was young he hadn't read all the documents he had inherited, and he hadn't acquired more. My impression was that his recent correspondence with the abbess of the convent, although she refused to let him on to the land her order had leased, had provoked new interest in his part. Didn't he show you some artifacts that she's sent him?"

"Probably," Richard said, "but it's difficult to muster any interest in fragments of old pottery and the occasional piece of tarnished metal. It seems to me that you can make up any story you like about rubbish like that, and so-called archeology is mostly fantasy, even when it's sanctified by the British Museum. Have you ever visited the British Museum, Monsieur Furneret?"

"I'm afraid I've never visited London," Paul admitted.

"Well, if you ever do, don't bother with the British Museum. Or the Tower. Ludicrously over-rated. Hampton Court is much more interesting. Presumably, you've been down into these clefts yourself?"

"In fact, no," Paul said. "Even the lesser clefts are dangerous, and the Great Cleft is especially so."

"We have scores of so-called bottomless pits in England, too," said Richard dismissively. "All nonsense, logically. As for the legend about sirens living in it that lure people into the depths with mysterious hypnotic songs...crude superstition, and far from original. Don't you agree?"

"Certainly. My friend Gaston assures me that the strange sounds that are sometimes heard emerging from the Cleft are caused by water leaking into it and producing tiny waterfalls after heavy rainfall. He says that the bottom of the Great Cleft, like the bottom of the other two, will be a slow-moving stream of muddy water, which carries away the debris that falls into the hole, but that we don't have any rope long enough to take anyone down far enough to perceive the splash if a stone is dropped—or didn't, at any rate, the last time a descent was attempted. But that was more than a hundred years ago, I believe. With modern equipment, and determination, who can tell? It might not be wise, though, to grant too many permissions for exploration, if you don't want to be the unwitting cause of someone being killed."

"It's not for me to stop fools rushing in where angels fear to tread," the Englishman opined. "Anyway, those fellows from the university probably know what they're doing."

Paul seriously doubted that, but he was an alumnus of the institution in question, and did not want to cast aspersions on it. Instead, he said: "I'm afraid your domain isn't exactly ripe for development, which is probably why your grandfather or great-grandfather took one look back in 1820 or thereabouts and decided to forget it all over again."

"So I've observed for myself," said Richard, with a slight sigh of regret. "The new tenants of the convent are planting crops and raising livestock, and they've been in contact with the agents about leasing more land and trying to improve the irrigation, with a view to expanding their viticulture, but at a distance, theirs looks like a very marginal operation, and the prospect of attempting something similar specially if it would necessitate damming or diverting springs seems to me like a big risk for a meager potential reward.

"I've taken a look at the woodland, and the timber seems to be third-rate at best, but I'm no expert. Grandfather might have been able to make a better estimate—but as you say, Monsieur Furneret, he and his own father probably did, and couldn't see any economic potential. The world is different now, but modern agricultural machinery couldn't do anything on slopes like those, even without your famous clefts. One hears stories about people making money nowadays bottling spring water, but Monsieur Lambrunet says that most of the local ones dry up in summer, so even if the mineral content made it marketable, there isn't sufficient volume to make it exploitable.

"In sum, the local geology is unhelpful for any economic development, apparently—nothing like the Pyrenees or the Jura, too far away from the Central Massif. The domain was much bigger, according to Monsieur Lambrunet, when it was first gifted to our remoter ancestors, but their later descendants sold off the good land bit by bit, and abandoned the rump long before the Revolutionaries came along to claim it for the State. It was effectively worthless by then, and it's still worthless now. The few rents we collect are all that we're ever going to get—meaning no disrespect to you, Monsieur Furneret; as tenants go, you're one from whom we can borrow some pride, whereas the so-called convent higher up the slope might easily be reckoned more of an embarrassment."

Paul was carefully storing that information away, not knowing whether or not Zosima would probably be glad to hear it, when the bell at the gate rang. Madame Louvot headed for the door in order to answer it.

Astonished, and unable to imagine who it might be, Paul called after her: "Apologize, please, and say that I can't receive anyone at the moment."

The housekeeper returned after a few seconds and came to whisper in Paul's ear. He had to put his teacup down abruptly, afraid that his hand might begin to shake.

"I'm sorry," he said to Richard Megister, "But it appears that my visitor would like a word with you. It's one of the sisters from the convent: a Sister Lilith."

"With us?" Richard Megister queried. "I thought...but I suppose they don't get around much, and their rule wouldn't let them invite me there, so this must seem like convenient neutral ground. Would you mind, Monsieur Furneret, if we hear what the...lady has to say."

"Not at all," said Paul. Addressing Madame Louvot, he said: "Please show the lady in."

Having heard Sister Monique refer several time to "three witches," Paul was vaguely expecting a crone out of *Macbeth*, although the approximate account of their lives that he had been able to piece together did not support that image at all. In fact, Sister Lilith was younger than Zosima, certainly no older than her mid-forties. When she came into the dining room she immediately pushed back her hood to reveal jet black hair with not a hint of gray, but her eyes were green—a combination sometimes seen in Bretons, but rare in the Midi. Her complexion was smooth, a little darker than Richard Megister's suntan, but by no means Moorish, and her lips were red and full. She was smiling and did not give the impression of being in the least malevolent

Paul and Richard had both stood up, and they each bowed, a trifle awkwardly.

"I'm terribly sorry to intrude like this, Monsieur Megister" said Zosima's unlikely *bête noire*, speaking English for the benefit of the visitors, "but I have been wanting to talking to Monsieur Furneret for some time, and I was also eager to speak to you, so when I learned that you were both here—your automobile is rather conspicuous—I thought that I ought to take advantage of the double opportunity. I know that you were introduced to our former Mother Superior in Toulouse the other day, but she is only making a brief visit, and spends almost all her time in our community in Paris, and there is abundant information that I can give you about the geography and history of your domain that she could not. I wish I could invite you to the convent to show you what we have accomplished there over the last five years, but I have not yet had time to modify the rule imposed on us by our founder. Mademoiselle Ellen would be very welcome there, but I can understand why you, as her brother, might not allow her to visit such a location. May I sit down?"

Paul brought a chair forward in order that she could join their circle, while Madame Louvot fetched an extra tea-cup, and shot Sister Lilith a glance almost as hostile as those she had addressed to Sister Monique, with similar obliquity, some twenty-four hours before.

In spite of the declared purpose of her visit, it was to Paul that Sister Lilith turned first, although she spoke in English, for the sake of politeness to the visitors. "I want to thank you, Monsieur Furneret, for your enormous kindness in rescuing Sister Monique after her fall, binding the wound and allowing her to stay until we were able to send a cart to collect her," Without waiting for a response, she turned to Richard Megister. "Your tenant is quite a hero, Monsieur Megister, as well as a great artist. You must know of his reputation, I presume, as a painter of spirits?"

"Yes, of course," said Richard uneasily, seemingly having no idea what to make of the unexpected intruder.

"He paints the living as well, of course," Sister Lilith said. "You must already have seen his work while you have been in Toulouse. He's much in demand there as a portraitist. If you're staying in the vicinity for any length of time, you must ask him to paint your lovely sister, while she is at the first peak of her perfection...if I'm not being too presumptuous."

"I don't think we'll be here long enough," Richard replied, presumably supplying the point of information for which the sister had been fishing. "We're planning to tour the Riviera before returning to England, and we'll probably take a different route northwards, after visiting Monte Carlo. To tell the truth, making the journey here was as much as matter of testing the capabilities of my automobile as discovering more about my family's remoter history, although if I had realized how difficult it would be to transport the machine over the Channel I would have thought twice about the whole trip."

"I saw your mechanic outside," Lilith commented. "He was kind enough to move the vehicle in order to let our cart through—it's necessary to replace the supplies that were unfortunately ruined by yesterday's rainstorm. It doesn't often rain here, but when it does, it tends to be torrential. Poor Sister Monique had the bad luck to suffer an injury when the wheel of the cart broke, and if it hadn't been for Monsieur Furneret, she might have suffered badly from exposure to the elements."

Before Paul or Richard could formulate a response to that remark, Ellen—whose eyes were fixed on the portrait of Juliette hanging on the wall, said: "Actually Richard, I wonder whether we might extend our stay in Toulouse for a day or two longer. Monsieur Furneret has almost finished his painting of Madame de La Vaudère, as you just saw, and I rather like the idea of being painted by a famous French artist while I'm at what Sister Lilith describes, far too kindly, as my first peak of perfection. You wouldn't mind asking Bernard to drive me here for sittings, I'm sure—and perhaps I could even take the opportunity to visit the convent, as Sister Lilith suggests...with your permission, of course."

That bombshell apparently left Richard Megister speechless. Paul was still struggling to find words himself, in English or French, when the young woman went on: "If Monsieur Furneret could make me look half as fascinating as that young woman on the wall there, I'd be very satisfied. She has such a hypnotic gaze, don't you think, Richard?"

"Sister Monique was very struck by that portrait too," Sister Lilith put in, "and I'm interested to see it myself. Sister Monique knew the model well, apparently, but she died, alas, before I had a chance to meet her. You loved her very dearly, I believe, Monsieur Furneret."

"Not well enough, alas," said Paul, after almost gasping at the blatant impertinence of the remark. "But you came in order to say something to Monsieur Megister, did you not?"

"That's true," said Lilith. "I can always come back another time, can I not, to discuss matters of mutual concern with you, Monsieur Furneret? After all, the precedent has been set now, thanks to Monique's accident, and, in my opinion, the rule of non-communication has been construed far too narrowly during these last five years, given that you have so many interests in common with us. So, Monsieur Megister, firstly, may I ask you what plans you have for the domain that might affect the convent? I hope you'll agree that it isn't unreasonable for me to ask?"

That simple, Paul thought, wondering belatedly why he had beaten around the bush so tentatively.

"No, not at all," said Richard, having found his tongue, "although, to tell you the truth, as I was just explaining to Monsieur Furneret, I don't really have any plans. Monsieur Lambrunet, who has been entertaining us so richly during our visit, has waxed lyrical about the archeological discoveries that might be made on the land, and I've given my permission for him and anyone else to carry out any investigations he wishes—although that might have been hasty and I'll probably have to add provisos specifying that the tenants aren't to be disturbed or inconvenienced—but I'm certainly not about to finance any investigation of that sort. Fanciful legendary associations between the mountain and the Cathars, or ancient Christian saints, are amusing, but..." He paused, searching for words even though he was still speaking his native language

"If you'll forgive me saying so," Sister Lilith interjected, smoothly, "the associations are not fanciful. There really was a Cathar church on the site of the phalanstery, and, long before that, a temple of Artemis, which itself replaced a temple of the primal goddess that some modern antiquarians call the Triple Goddess. In fact, our community is attempting to carry forward the true Christianity practiced by the Cathar perfecti and by the associates of Marie Salome, to whom the shrine that Monsieur Furneret's cottage has now replaced was consecrated."

"I know that Jean-Bénigne Lambrunet has archeological evidence to support those allegations in his collection," Richard Megister said, very uneasily, "including some that you have supplied, but to be perfectly honest, his collection also includes a blatantly fake mermaid of the kind that used to be mass-produced in Antwerp, specifically for sale to antiquarian collectors, so I can't help feeling that his standards of evidence might be a trifle low, and some of his interpretations rather optimistic."

"That may be so," said Sister Lilith, calmly, "and you might be skeptical, too, about the evidence on which my own convictions are based—but I believe that, if given the opportunity, I could convince you. With Monsieur Furneret's help, if he were willing to lend it, I could certainly convince you. He is a uniquely talented medium, as you must be aware if he has shown you his art-work."

"Publicity," said Richard Megister succinctly. "He paints dead people from memory, but so what?—if you'll forgive me for saying so, Monsieur Furneret. And again, if you'll forgive me for saying so: you draw in your sleep, but so what? It doesn't make your talent supernatural."

"I agree," said Paul. "It happens, therefore it must be natural. Unfortunately, I've never been able to figure out exactly what that nature is, and what its corollaries are."

"I had gathered that you had a problem of that sort, Monsieur Furneret," commented Lilith, "and I can understand your reluctance to experiment. Monsieur Megister on the other hand, is a skeptic, who has nothing to lose by lending himself to experimentation, except his skepticism. Don't you agree, Mademoiselle Megister?"

What experimentation? Paul wondered, suspecting that the comment might have been aimed Ellen rather than her brother, and remembering what Zosima had said about her desire to make sure that no one else but her hypnotized the landowner and his sister.

All that Ellen had to say in order to avoid the matter, Paul knew, was that she did not agree with the vague judgment, or that she did not even understand it. The problem was, however, that she did appear to agree, even without knowing what she was agreeing to. Was that because Lilith had planted the suggestion in her mind by telling her a few minutes ago what she "must" do? Paul had already observed the interplay of the siblings' relationship long enough to understand that Ellen was more than a little resentful of her brother's casual assumption of authority over her, and would like to break free of what she saw as a tyranny. From that viewpoint, Lilith was simply offering her an opportunity to assert her independence harmlessly.

All that Ellen was prepared to say explicitly, for the moment, was: "Perhaps you're right, Sister," but she immediately followed up the carefully neutral judgment by saying to Lilith: "Why do you say that you understand Monsieur Furneret's reluctance to experiment?"

Lilith smiled, seemingly glad to be asked, but she looked at Paul. "May I answer that question, Monsieur Furneret—at the risk of being indiscreet?"

At least as curious as his visitor to hear the answer in question, Paul had no difficulty in relying: "Please do."

Turning back to Ellen Megister, the strange sister said: "I'm told that Monsieur Furneret has had some unfortunate experiences as a result of induced hypnotic trances, including some provoked by one of my sisters. In his position, I would be equally wary of allowing myself to be hypnotized again, especially by her, all the more so because he apparently has a tendency to slip into somnambulistic states spontaneously, even while awake. His strange ability has evidently enabled him to produce some superb works of art—although I had not seen his very best work until today—but such abilities are often costly, one way or another. I have every sympathy with Monsieur Furneret's anxieties, as you should too—but that need not prevent you from taking advantage of his talent while you can. The portraits of the living he has done in Toulouse are not as brilliant as that portrait on the wall, but the one he has done of Clémence Sancerre is very nearly up to that standard, and I believe that you have everything necessary to inspire him to do at least as well, if not better."

"Who is Clémence Sancerre?" Ellen Megister asked, reflexively.

"An artist, like Monsieur Furneret. You must visit her studio while you're in Toulouse—she does beautiful work, and I believe that her Marian ideals have a good deal in common with our true Christianity and our reverence for the primal goddess."

Richard Megister made a slight sound of disgust, apparently unworried that the rudeness would be evident, but Paul did not give him a chance to make any further comment. "If what I've been told about them is accurate," he put in, swiftly, "true Christianity and the worship of the primal goddess don't seem to be compatible."

"Perhaps that's because what you've been told is inaccurate," Lilith informed him, flatly. "I could easily clear up any misconceptions you might have, over time—without the need for any hypnosis."

Richard Megister was plainly out of his intellectual depth, but he was no fool, and he understood perfectly well that there was some kind of contest going on between Lilith and Paul, in which his sister had somehow become an unwitting pawn. "If you'll forgive me for saying so, Madame," he said, that having apparently become his favorite phrase, "isn't Lilith a rather curious pseudonym for someone who claims to be a true Christian? It's the name of a demon, after all."

"There are no demons, Monsieur Magister," the alleged sorceress retorted, "except the ones that men invent for the purposes of moral terrorism. In the legend, Lilith's only crime was to refuse to accept arbitrary male domination. In true Christian belief, she is a heroine, and I am proud to wear her name, although it is not a pseudonym; it was given to me by my mother at birth."

Richard Megister was plainly unimpressed by that argument, but he was not given the opportunity to debate the matter further; Sister Lilith had other things to say. She went on:

141

"Perhaps we should set aside spiritual matters for the time being, Monsieur Megister, "in order to concentrate on the material. I have made a study of the matter, and I believe that the value of your domain, including the sector of it leased by our community might be increased considerably by means of a few relatively inexpensive amendments to its irrigation. I have an appointment to see your agents in Toulouse tomorrow morning, in order to discuss some technical issues involving the lease. Your presence is not strictly necessary with regard to that matter, but it might be a good opportunity to discuss wider issues. May I hope that you will come along to the meeting?"

Richard Megister was scowling. "The question of the irrigation of the lower slopes of the mountain has already been mentioned to me by Monsieur Lambrunet," he said, "but it all seems to me to be rather fanciful. I'll certainly refer it to my advisers in England, but I suspect that they'll counsel against any substantial investment in such a scheme."

Paul shared that suspicion, for numerous reasons—not least the fact that Richard Megister's promise to refer it to advisers was a blatant evasion, sparing him the impoliteness of a blunt refusal. All Sister Lilith said, however, was: "That's very wise. In order that you can inform yourself, and them, more fully about the issues at stake, I'll bring the relevant documentation to the notary's etude tomorrow. My appointment is at ten o'clock, and I'll be delighted to see you there—and Mademoiselle Ellen, of course—if you care to come along. For now, though, I shouldn't intrude any further. Thank you for the tea, Monsieur Furneret; I hope that we shall have an opportunity in the near future to talk at length about matters that are of no interest to Monsieur Megister, but of intimate concern to us. I am particularly glad to have met you, Mademoiselle Megister, and I hope that we shall meet again. If I or my sisters can be of any service to you, please don't hesitate to ask tomorrow. *Au revoir*."

As a dutiful host, Paul escorted her to the door, and then to the gate. "Please give my best wishes to Sister Monique," he said. "I hope that her foot doesn't inconvenience her for long."

"I will," Lilith promised. "Would you like me to pass your good wishes on to the Mother Superior as well? I know that you have been at odds for some while, but I can assure you that she never meant you any harm, and if I can help to make peace between you, I would be glad."

"That's very kind," said Paul. "Yes, please do that, and assure her that I have never considered her as anything but a friend."

As the strange guest walked away, watched by the idle eyes of the Megisters' chauffeur, who was sitting patiently behind his steering wheel, Paul returned to the dining room, pensively.

"I'm sorry about that interruption," he told his guests. "It was quite unexpected."

"That's perfectly all right," said Richard Megister. "It's understandable that the residents of the convent might be anxious about any plans I might have had to introduce changes at the estate. I ought to have made my intentions, or lack of them, clear the other day to her Mother Superior, but to be honest, I didn't like the woman and didn't care to get into a discussion with her. I should probably apologize to you, for creating a station in which she thought it politic to send her associate to speak to me here, although why she didn't have the notary invite me to this meeting directly, I have no idea. What on earth did she mean about technical issues to do with the lease?"

"I don't know," said Paul—although he had strong suspicions—"but she probably left it unexplained in the hope that you would come to the notary's office tomorrow in order to inform yourself."

"I rather liked her," said Ellen. "Much more than the other one, at any rate. I don't mind going to this meeting to-morrow, Richard." Without a pause, she changed the subject, addressing Paul: "Would you be willing to paint my portrait,

Monsieur Furneret, if Richard were to commission you to do it?"

Paul looked at Richard, whose expression declared clearly enough that he was now utterly confused and perched on the horns of a dilemma. The Englishman said nothing.

"It would be a privilege, Mademoiselle," Paul said, with scrupulous politeness, "but I wouldn't want to disrupt your plans to tour the Riviera."

"Oh, don't worry about that," said Ellen. "They're vague, at best—no determined itinerary and no fixed timetable. There's no reason at all why we can't stay in Toulouse a little longer, and the automobile makes it very easy for Bernard to bring me here for sittings."

Paul could see that Richard did not like the implication that he need not accompany her on such any excursion, and he interjected: "I wouldn't want to put you to the inconvenience of driving out here repeatedly, Mademoiselle, especially with the road in such a dreadful state. If your brother were to decide that he would like to commission a portrait, I wouldn't mind riding into Toulouse for the sittings."

"You can't possibly do the painting in the hotel," Ellen objected. "It isn't suitable at all."

Richard seemed to be on the point of issuing a flat refusal, and Paul thought it diplomatic to intervene again. "There's a studio in the city where I'm sometimes permitted to paint clients whose homes are unsuitable," he said. "I've done portraits there before. If you wish, I can go to see Clémence tomorrow and ask her whether it would be convenient, if Monsieur Megister were to decide in favor of your request."

"Clémence Sancerre?" asked Ellen.

"That's right. If she's agreeable, you'd be able to look at her work as well, which really is very interesting—and she also knows a great deal about the history of the floral games, with which she'd been involved for many years. You'll probably find that interesting." He kept his eyes on Ellen, knowing perfectly well that Richard would not find the floral games interesting at all

"I'm very apprehensive about the time such a project might take," Richard put in, shaking his head dubiously.

"Don't be, dear," said Ellen. Without giving her brother time to raise any further objection she turned back to Paul and said: "Did the Sister say that this cottage is built on the site of a shrine to Marie Salome? Monsieur Lambrunet mentioned that, but he said so many things that I became rather confused."

Paul accepted the obvious invitation to change the subject in order to give her time to bring her brother round to her way of thinking with regard to the possible portrait. He gave the Megisters a brief reminder of the basic legend of the three Maries, and then added: "Marie Salome is credited in some apocryphal references with a close relationship with the Evangelist John, represented as either his mother or sister. Monsieur Lambrunet knows a lot more about such matters than I do. I have no idea at all what kind of syncretic mysticism has been cooked up by Zosima for the purposes of her cult and modified by Lilith and her own Sister Salome for their Toulousan variant."

"It's all pure fantasy," Richard opined. "London is full of these bizarre little sects, which have their own variant religions based of supposed revelations, dreamed or faked—or both, if hypnotism's involved. Fortunately, Ellen and I are both strong minds, immune to that kind of trickery."

Ellen said nothing, but she was looking at Paul curiously, evidently interested in his reaction, in view of what Lilith had said in response to her previous enquiry.

"I'm certainly not immune to hypnotism myself," Paul admitted. "Far too sensitive, in fact—but I'm not entirely sure that that makes me weak-minded, or that strong minds, in the sense that the term is usually employed, are necessarily immune to the power of suggestion."

"But you know, don't you," said Richard, continuing in the same undiplomatic vein, "that things like the dragon you showed us his morning are just phantoms of your imagination?"

"I do," Paul agreed. "The problem is that I'm not sure that my imagination is entirely my own. I'm not sure that anyone's is, but most people are adept at protecting the conscious part of the mind, surrounding it with figurative ramparts, able to withstand siege and invasion. The isolation is never absolute, but the leakage can be sometimes be reduced to a trickle of dreams, without the penetration of more elaborate delusions, obsessions and other hauntings. The psychically blind either can't see, or refuse to see, disturbing input from the unconscious mind, whereas the psychically sighted are sometimes overwhelmed by such intrusions, and are then considered, probably rightly, to be mad. I seem to be caught in the middle, able not to see, but unable not to draw. I live with the constant anxiety that the balance might tip, but in the meantime, I try to make the most of what invades my mind in my art, just as many other artists do. I try to do so moderately, because I fear that stimulating or encouraging the intrusions by means of hypnotism, drugs or even excessive emotion might be catastrophic. Perhaps it's a ridiculous fear, and I'm just a coward, but perhaps not."

After a slight pause, Ellen, evidently feeling that if her brother could be flagrantly impertinent, so could she, said: "Excessive emotion? Do you mean anger, or lust?"

"Any," replied Paul, shortly, pretending that he had not seen Richard's grim frown, provoked by the blatant indelicacy of the question.

Ellen looked at the portrait of Juliette, doubtless remembering what he had said to Lilith when asked an impertinent question about her, but she did not say anything more.

"If you think that hypnotism is potentially dangerous to you," Richard Megister asked, curiously, "why do you live in such close proximity with a convent that's allegedly full of hypnotists?"

"Until this morning," Paul told him, frankly, "I thought I was more isolated here than I might be in Paris, because the way they interpreted their quasi-monastic rule meant that they were wary of even looking at me, let alone speaking to me. In the space of twenty-four hours, that has changed, drastically. I don't know why, but there's nothing I can do about it, except run away, and I'm not sure there would be any point in that. It seems to me that, as they say in Boulevard du Temple melodramas, I can run, but I can't hide...in which case, I might as well stay, and carry on."

Paul could see that Richard Megister, who was not good at hiding his thoughts, was now looking at him as if he were mad, and feeing a trifle apprehensive in consequence, perhaps fearing some sort of contagion. Ellen, on the other hand, seemed intrigued, and curious. Richard had obviously noticed that too, and it increased his apprehension; he was beginning to fidget, and when Ellen leaned forward, poised to ask another question, he interrupted her brusquely.

"I think perhaps we ought to drive back to Toulouse now, Ellen" he said. Without giving her time for a response, he turned to Paul and said: "I'll give some thought to the possibility of commissioning a portrait, Monsieur Furneret, and the question of whether I can stay long enough in Toulouse to make it practicable, but for the moment, I can't promise you an affirmative answer. I'll let you know when my sister and I have reached a final decision."

Ellen's expression looked thunderous for a moment, but she was far more skilled at hiding her feelings than her brother, and she evidently decided that if there was to be a contest between the two of them, it would be better to work it out in private; her face swiftly became serene again.

Richard Megister stood up, positively, and extended his hand to be shaken. Paul took it meekly. "Thank you for visiting," he said. "It's rare for us to see anyone, and the last few days have been unprecedentedly hectic, but it's been a particular privilege for me to meet the owners of the land, and to discover that they have such an interest in its colorful history. Do drop in again before you continue touring, if you have the time."

"I will," said Richard, reflexively. "Thank you for entertaining us. If we don't meet again...."

"We'll let you know about the portrait as soon as possible," said Ellen, as she shook Paul's hand in the same brisk fashion. She clearly had no doubt what the message in question would be.

Paul escorted his guests to the gate of the property and watched them climb into the Sunbeam. The mechanic had turned the vehicle around while moving it out of the way of the convent cart, and the nose of the auto as already pointing downhill. It only had to draw away.

Paul looked around, half-expecting to see Zosima to emerge from hiding somewhere along the road, but by the time the automobile had dwindled to a distant dot on the plain, the mountain-side was peaceful and almost silent in the warmth of the late afternoon sun.

When he went back into the cottage, Madame Louvot said: "You could have made up an excuse in order to refuse that commission."

"And side with the arrogant know-it-all at the expense of the pretty girl he has in his power because he holds the purse-strings?" Paul objected. "What kind of hero would I be then? And what kind of professional painter?"

"The women at the convent aren't going to let you alone anymore," the housekeeper opined. "Not now. That taboo is well and truly broken. Zosima will be back, as dangerous as ever.

"She'll certainly be back," Paul agreed. "Before dawn, I'm sure, if not before nightfall. I don't know if she's been swiftly outmaneuvered, or whether she only came to see me this morning because she knew that Lilith would come to see me this afternoon, but it doesn't matter in the slightest. They're welcome to play their games—I really don't care who wins. It might even be amusing, if they're both determined to involve me somehow. But for now, I'm going back to work while there's still a little light left."

"Make the most of it, my dear" said Angélique, ominously. "It might not last long."

CHAPTER VIII

Paul and Angélique had almost finished dinner, and darkness had fallen some time before when a discreet three raps sounded on the cottage door, which Madame Louvot had already bolted. As she stood up to go and answer it, Paul gestured to her to sit down again, and went to draw the bolt and turn the key himself.

As he had anticipated, it was Zosima.

"May I come in?" she asked, "or am I *persona non grata*?"

"Come in," said Paul, neutrally. "We've finished the food prepared for dinner, but there's a little wine left, and Madame Louvot can doubtless find you something to eat if you're hungry."

Zosima had already made her way through to the dining room. "Please don't go," she said to Madame Louvot, as the latter stood up and made as if to leave. "I need to talk to both of you. I should have done it a long time ago, but I was hesitant, for various reasons; now, it can't be put off any longer. I need information that only the two of you have, thanks to Madame de La Vaudère's unexpected death, and you both need information that I have. We ought to exchange that information, compare notes, and decide how to go forward. You and I, Madame Louvet, need to know exactly what has happened in the past and what's going on now, if we're to continue trying to protect Paul. Can we declare a truce?"

"Ask Paul," said Madame Louvot, curtly.

"Zosima and I have never been at odds," said Paul. "And to tell the truth, Angélique, I'm not at all sure why you and she perceive that you're in conflict."

"May I sit down?" Zosima asked, again addressing Madame Louvot. The housekeeper nodded, and then resumed her own seat.

"Thank you," said Zosima. "I will take that glass of wine, if it's no trouble "Temperance still rules at the phalanstery, in spite of the fact that the initiates have taken to distilling exotic liqueurs from the unimpressive product of our vines...although so many other rules have been broken there of late that, for all I know, the Three Maries might be having a drunken orgy as we speak."

"Are we calling them the Three Maries now?" Paul queried as he poured Zosima a glass of Blanquette de Veau and then shared what was left in the bottle between Angélique's glass and his own. "Rather than the Three Witches, or the Daughters of Artemis, that is?"

"They used to call themselves the Three Maries in Toulouse before they came to Paris," Zosima explained, "and I suspect that it's how they still think of themselves in those terms, even though they're now Sisters Lilith, Salome and Justine, and they're no longer a joke, in Paris or Toulouse. Ours is notionally an anarchist organization, so they're supposed to be a trio of equals, but Lilith is their guiding intelligence and the shaper of their ambitions. Those ambitions have only had a peripheral bearing on you for most of the last decade, Paul, but recently..."

"Just a moment," said Paul. "I have a couple of questions to ask. When you came to see me his morning, did you know that Lilith was going to drop in on me this afternoon."

"No—I think that was a hasty improvisation on her part. Lilith was certainly intending to make contact with the Megisters, but I presume that she was planning to do it quietly and mysteriously, in Toulouse, and she was certainly planning to contact you as well, probably as soon as they had left Toulouse, and I had returned to Paris, but when she heard that you and I had talked for a while this morning, she presumably decided to make her first move right away. What did Richard Megister tell her about his plans?"

"That he doesn't have any. Jean-Bénigne Lambrunet had obviously passed on some scheme of Lilith's to obtain better irrigation for her crops and vines, but his instinctive reaction was to recoil. I got the impression that, in spite of the fancy automobile, he might not be as rich as he pretends. I suspect that he was a trifle disappointed to have confirmed by his own observations that the prospects of selling the domain are remote, and that he's fortunate to have any tenants at all. Lilith's going to give him the documentation of her project, but I doubt that he'll even glance at it"

"Good," said Zosima, although she did not seem to be entirely delighted. "But she's going to see him again, then?"

"She has an appointment tomorrow morning with a notary in Toulouse to discuss what she called technical issues to do with the lease. She suggested that he and Ellen might like to be present."

Zosima sighed. "The war is effectively over in legal terms, alas, and it's just a matter of mopping up. I don't suppose, knowing you, that you made eyes at the girl, as I suggested?"

"No, I didn't," said Paul, "but with a little unsubtle prompting from Lilith, she asked whether I'd be prepared to paint her portrait. That took Richard by surprise, and he didn't like the idea at all, but I think she might win the argument. I gave her a provisional yes, but suggested that I do it in Toulouse."

Zosima frowned. "Why?" she said. "It would be much more convenient to do the sittings here. Their hotelier isn't going to look kindly on your setting up your equipment there."

"I told her that I could borrow a corner of Clémence Sancerre's studio, as I have for a few other portraits I've done in Toulouse. I thought that might help to ease Richard's anxieties."

Zosima raised her eyes to the ceiling. "Idiot," she said. "That's a complication you could do without—but I suppose that Lilith took the opportunity to recommend that they visit her studio anyway?"

"Yes, she did," said Paul, "but I don't see..."

"I know," said Zosima cutting him off. "There's probably no harm done, and we have more important things to discuss. As I said, we need to trade all our information, but the most significant thing that I still need to discover is what it was that scared Jane de La Vaudère so much four years ago at Rochemure's house. Doubtless she told you what she was prepared to tell you, Paul, but first of all, I need to hear what the only other informed witness saw. I'm not wrong, am I, Madame Zosima, in thinking that you shared the vision too, and that you had abundant opportunity to discuss it with the baron before he died?"

Angélique looked profoundly uncomfortable, and Paul had no difficulty deducing—as he had suspected for a long time—that his volunteer housekeeper knew more about what had happened that night that she had ever confessed to him. He thought it diplomatic as well as reasonable to intervene.

"Just a minute, Madame Zosima," he said. "If you've come here to request that we trade information, don't you think that it's up to you to start by telling us what you know about any possible threat to me?"

Zosima raised her eyes again, but said: "There's no point arguing about it, so I'll summarize what I know. How much do you know about the Toulousan sororities associated with the floral games?"

"Only what's common knowledge," said Paul. "It's mainly a matter of social circles, not much different from Parisian five-o'clock teas or restricted salons—the society we live in tends to provide men with great many activities from which women are excluded or in which their role is marginalized, so it's only reasonable that they should form parallel societies of their own, from which men are largely excluded or in which they only play a marginal role. In Toulouse, the floral games, and their employment of Clémence Isaure as a symbolic figurehead, are a useful focal point for their concerns, and for the recruitment of an element of mystery. Obviously, I've never been involved."

"Yes you have, unwittingly," said Zosima, "and it was within the context of that social network that your psychic sensitivity was first remarked, and first influenced."

Paul was astonished. "By whom?" he demanded.

"Amélie Lambrunet. Don't look at me like that; I'm not accusing her of wanting to harm you in any way—quite the reverse—but she was the first person to detect your sensitivity, when you were still a small boy, and to inform other members of her sorority, merely as an interesting datum. None of them, I believe, wanted to do you any harm, but they were interested. It's probable that Amélie attempted some hypnotic influence at an early stage, and played a minor role in stimulating your spontaneous lapses into somnambulism and the drawings that you produced, but whatever she did, I'm sure her purpose would only have been to help encourage your artistic talent. I think it more likely that the first time she actually hypnotized you in order deliberately to plant a specific post-hypnotic suggestion was when you were thirteen or fourteen years old."

"Are you saying that Amélie caused me to fall in love with Martine?" Paul said, incredulously.

"No, the logic of the situation did that, as Amélie must have understood very well, and she must have thought it potentially problematic. The suggestion that she wanted to impose upon you, and apparently succeeded in so doing, was to make sure that you respected Martine, and that your infatuation with her wouldn't lead to any unfortunate consequences."

"And what evidence do you have for that assertion?" Paul snapped.

"Primarily, reports of rumors circulated through the sorority circuit, to which the Three Maries were party as well as others."

"How many others?" Paul asked, aghast

"Who knows? What matters at present is that they reached as far as the Three Maries, who presumably regarded it, at the time, merely as an anecdote—almost a joke—of no particular interest, and continued to do so at least until 1901, when the newspapers published accounts of the Juvisy séance, and Jane de La Vaudère consulted them for information about you. Even then, Lilith probably thought it a mere datum, of no particular relevance to her."

"That's not evidence!" Paul scoffed. "It's just gossip. I don't believe it."

"An understandable initial reaction," Zosima conceded, "but I think that if you interrogate your own history, you'll find it the argument convincing. I won't say that the suggestion in question has blighted your life, and you might argue that its effects have been at least partly benign, but that it has had an influence, I have no doubt. Amélie Lambrunet presumably had no idea that the suggestion would prove so powerful, so broad in its effect, or so long-lasting—but you really are extraordinarily vulnerable to hypnotic suggestion."

"Respecting Martine hasn't been a problem for the last eight years," Paul pointed out, stonily.

"No, it hasn't—but the side-effects of the instruction might have been. Whether those side effects were due to Madame Lambrunet's careless phrasing of the suggestion, or the manner in which your unconscious mind construed the edict, I don't know, but again, I have no doubt that it affected your attitude not merely to Martine but to women in general. In all that time, so far as I know, you have only had two substantial relationships with women, and you appear to have insisted, not only for the two years that you lived with Juliette but long after, that you did not and could not love her. As for Jane de La Vaudère, you have hardly seen her half a dozen times since the night that the two of you got rid of me so unceremoniously from the baron's carriage. Interrogate yourself, Paul, as to whether you have ever felt capable of loving anyone, and how, if you have felt capable of it, the relationships in question have worked out. Don't tell me—just ask yourself. May I go on?"

Paul looked at Angélique. "You knew about this, didn't you?" he said, accusatively.

The housekeeper nodded her head.

"You've known about it for four years? Jane told you, before the baron died?"

"I didn't believe it either, at first," she said, defensively. "Madame Jane wasn't certain...but..."

"And neither of you ever thought to mention it to me? Even though, apparently half the population of Toulouse knows about it?"

"Don't be too hard on either of them," Zosima put in, "or anyone else. I haven't known for quite as long, and I always intended to tell you, when I realized the effects it had had on you and was still having, but even I hesitated. There's more, but it's probably best to take things in a slow and orderly manner—there's a lot to take in, and I still need a piece of the puzzle that Madame Louvot might be able to provide. May I continue?"

Paul looked down regretfully at his empty glass, and thought about going to the larder to fetch another bottle of wine, or the open bottle of convent liqueur, but in the end he simply said: "Go on."

"The second time that you were definitely hypnotized was by Henri Lemastur, at Madame Pommerat's séance. Lemastur didn't impose any deliberate post-hypnotic sugges-tion on you that the witnesses were able to perceive, but in inviting you to make contact with a dead person who had a significant connection with someone present in the room, he evidently provided the stimulus that established a telepathic link between your unconscious mind and Baron de Rochemure's. Why Rochemure rather than someone else? I don't know for sure, but I think it highly likely that the crucial point of contact was the great significance that both of your unconscious minds attached to the notion of the death of a seven-month fetus.

"I'm inclined to wonder, however, how you came to be at that séance in the first place. I know that your friend Victor Marvaud suggested that you go, and it might well have been a spontaneous idea on his part, but it might not. Monique says that she made no such suggestion, although she was seeing Victor at the time and was slightly aggrieved by the fact that you appeared to be refusing to acknowledge her existence, even though you had seen her more than once in Montmartre. She and Victor probably talked about you. She didn't know until last night that you didn't even remember her, and she's still reluctant to believe that you didn't. I think, however, that the fact that you didn't might not be unconnected with the effects on your unconscious mind of Amélie Lambrunet's post-hypnotic suggestion.

"A week later, I hypnotized you at Juvisy, and the serious complications set in. It probably wasn't at the actual moment of her death, as Talia claimed, but there is no doubt in my mind now that you formed a mental link with Martine, in spite of the enormous distance between Juvisy and the Manche, the groundwork for which had been laid long before by her mother. You were in such a heightened state of sensitivity that you also formed links with the two people with whom you had traveled to Juvisy, one of which immediately became extraordinarily intimate, although neither of you realized it consciously at the time. Perhaps that was a simple matter of spontaneous erotic attraction, complicated by the fact that the attraction immediately generated a reaction, not only in your unconscious mind, because of Amélie's suggestion, but in hers as well, for different reasons. The bond, of which you were only vaguely conscious, was not only firm but extraordinarily convoluted, and must have been very difficult to interpret on either side.

"Interpretation of the fourth sketch that you produced at Juvisy is more problematic, but I now think that Talia was correct in her belief that it arose from the link you formed with her under her force of the instruction that I had given you, directly and explicitly, to focus your attention on her. I had no idea, at the time, how powerful that focusing might be. The significance of what your unconscious mind detected in Talia's was, of course, dictated by the same factor that had caused you to form a bond with Rochemure a week earlier.

"The complications of the bonds formed at Juvisy became even more entangled when they were reinforced at Antoine Cros's house, by which time—perhaps still under the influence of my magnetic force—you had also formed an intimate bond with Juliette, which became the dominant factor in occasioning the drawing you made that night. Again, you formed a link with her in spite of the distance separating you, and as well as drawing her illusion of being consumed by fire, you also drew her terror of being stabbed to death, triggered by what she had just witnessed. The combination drove her out of her mind temporarily, and plunged you into a protective slumber. The links that you had already formed with Talia and Jane caused them to feel the psychic explosion too, with near-disastrous effects in Talia's case."

"Antoine and Camille were there too," Paul pointed out. "I know Camille had a vision of sorts, but Antoine was completely unaffected."

"Perhaps not completely," Zosima suggested, "but the main point of difference, obviously, is that they were men. I've pointed out to you before, if you recall, that your unconscious mind is blatantly discriminatory in the links it forms, probably because of your innate heterosexuality, complicated by the fact that Amélie Lambrunet's post-hypnotic suggestion, although intended to apply specifically to her daughter, was evidently applied by you, unconsciously, to any woman to whom you could be carnally attracted."

"Excuse me for a moment," said Paul, and went to the larder, as much to obtain a pause for thought as to fetch something else to drink. He seized the bottle of liqueur and brought it back. He poured a moderate measure into his wine-glass and offered to do the same for Angélique, who refused. Zosima still had some Blanquette de Veau in her glass, although it had probably gone flat.

"Go on," Paul said, again, to his tormentor.

"Which brings us, after a four year interval, to the séance at Rochemure's house," Zosima continued, "which caught me by surprise, I must admit. I received his invitation at short notice, and then things moved very rapidly. When I hypnotized you, my hope and expectation were that I might enable you to draw Yvaine, as the baron wanted, although I did complicate the matter, under the spur of temptation, by asking you again to focus on Talia, via the painting you had made. I assumed that if you formed any intimate contact with anyone other than the baron, it would be with her. I was greatly mistaken. The contact you made with the baron was remarkably intimate—far more than it should have been, given that you were both heterosexual males, and I strongly suspect that you were only able to contrive it by employing Madame Louvot as a kind of psychic bridge.

"Jane de La Vaudère was also present, and already bound to you in an intimate and complex fashion. She had an intense vision as a result of the contact, much as Juliette had done four years earlier—which did not, fortunately, impart any impulse to run and throw herself in the Seine, but was nevertheless powerful. It enabled her to witness, in symbolic terms, the psychic fusion achieved by you and the baron, with the intermediary of Madame Louvot, and what she saw must have frightened her badly—not on her own behalf, but on yours. I'll return to that matter in a moment, in order to add another supposition, but hopefully, you can now understand why. if we're understand fully what happened, and what alarmed Madame de La Vaudère, we need to know what Madame Louvot can remember of the vision, if she saw anything it all, and, at a very minimum, what Baron de Rochemure and Jane de La Vaudère told her about it. Will you tell us that, please, Madame Louvot, as fully as you can?"

Angélique Louvot looked at Paul.

"Please, Angélique," he said. He did not add that after four years of stubborn silence, she certainly owed it to him finally to tell him everything she knew.

"I thought it was just a dream," Madame Louvot said, defensively. "Even after Madame de La Vaudère told me that she had had a dream too, and we had compared notes, I still didn't believe that it was anything but a dream. You hear anecdotes, don't you about people having the same dream? But then I told the baron, and he told me what he had seen and felt, and we realized that even if it had been a dream, it meant something. The baron said that it was symbolic, but that it was nevertheless real. He asked me not to tell anyone else about it, at least while he was still alive, and Madame Jane also asked me not to tell anyone else, while she was still alive, and...well, I haven't. I know they're both dead, but...well, not in my mind. I still feel the baron's presence, and I know that Paul still feels Madame Jane's, and he has all these theories about life and death, immortality and reincarnation, and I really don't know any more exactly what those words ought to mean. Still, they are both dead, so I hope they'll forgive me for breaking my promise now, or for not breaking it before, whichever they think appropriate."

She paused for breath, and Zosima took the opportunity to say: "Did the baron tell you to come you work for Paul after his death?"

Madame Louvot shook her head, but the negation seemed slightly dubious. "It wasn't an order...but he did say that, although he'd left me enough money not to have to work again, he thought that I might not be happy living on my own, and he said that Paul was unmarried, that he would probably benefit from the assistance a housekeeper could give him, and that no one he might hire could possibly look after him as well as I could. He was very grateful to Paul for...what he did for him. It was far better he said, than he could have hoped for. He was only expecting drawings, I think—he appreciated those too, he said, but the other was...well, he called it his miracle, his redemption."

"That's what we need to know about," Zosima said.

"But you were there," Angélique objected. "You did it. How can you not know?"

"I didn't see anything," Zosima told her. "I never do. I always had to rely on Talia to tell me what I'd enabled her see or do, and I wasn't always able or willing to trust her account, which often seemed to be distorted, and sometimes she deliberately held things back—which was extremely frustrating."

"But if it was your magnetism that produced the psychic fusion," Paul said, "how can you not know what it contained."

"How can you?" Zosima countered. "You forget everything. You don't even understand the drawings you make when you look at them afterwards. Think of yourself, if you like, as an automobile, like Richard Megister's Sunbeam. All I do, in helping to set you in psychic motion, is fill up your fuel tank with gasoline. You can't go anywhere without it, but how you function when the fuel renders you operational depends entirely on the design and condition of your engine—and where you go depends entirely on who, if anyone, is in the driving seat. That's what I didn't understand for a long time. I thought that the spirits of the dead had to take the wheel, one by one. I didn't realize how much more complicated it was, or could be, until I began to see a pattern in the sketches you had made, and even then, interpreting what happened at Passy...well, that's why I need to know what Madame Louvot, Madame de La Vaudère and Baron de Rochemure saw and felt, from different viewpoints. It took me some time to figure out that Madame Louvot must have been the bridge, or the glue, that enabled Paul and the baron not merely to make contact but to achieve a kind of fusion, but I'm not wrong, am I, Madame Louvot? Not am I wrong in assuming that you loved the baron?"

Madame Louvot's head was bowed, but she murmured, resignedly. "Of course I did—but it wasn't reciprocated. The baron..."

"You don't have to explain, Angélique," said Paul, gently. "We understand how these things are."

"I'm not sure you do, Paul," Zosima said, "and I'm sure that I don't—but again, it doesn't matter. Please, Madame Louvot, tell us what you saw in the dream you had under the effect of my magnetism."

Still hesitant, Angélique looked to Paul for support yet again.

"Please," Paul repeated. "I need to understand too. Sometimes, promises of secrecy need to be broken, if new circumstances require it. I honestly think that if the baron were here, he would release you from the promise he asked you to make."

"He is here," Zosima supplied, "and if you ask him, I believe that he'll do what he can to let you know that Paul is right. Trust him."

Whether that argument had any effect or not, Paul had no idea, but in the end, his housekeeper said: "It was only a dream, so where's the harm?

"There was a battlefield, but the battle seemed to be over, except that there were a lot of people wounded and dying, including woman and children, and bands of soldiers moving among them, not helping them but finishing them off with bayonets. It was horrible—far more horrible than I can describe. And on the horizon there was a vast line of crosses, and on the crosses, people were crucified, again including women and children. And I knew, even though I don't really understand symbolism, although the baron tried hard to educate me, that the battlefield was the world.

"Moving across the battlefield was a kind of carriage not much bigger than a fiacre, driven by a coachman who was a kind of monstrous ape. Inside the carriage, the baron and Paul were sitting side by side. There ought to have been room enough for them to do that, but there wasn't. That was partly because I was there too, wedged between them, although they couldn't see me, because I was invisible. There were other things in the carriage, phantoms of some kind, also invisible, who were jostling and fighting to make room, even though they were so thin that they hardly took up any space at all. I think they were dead—most of them, at least. I'm sorry if that doesn't make much sense. Anyway, the baron and Paul were very uncomfortable, and so was I—me most of all, I think, because I was in the middle, and they couldn't see me, so they kept on squeezing me,

"The baron and Paul weren't speaking, although I think they wanted to. I think they were partly dead themselves. The baron didn't want Paul to get out of the carriage, but he was afraid for him, because he knew that if he stayed until it reached its destination, he would be in danger. The baron didn't care about the danger to himself—in fact, that was the

161

whole reason that he was in the carriage, going back into his past. I don't know how I knew that, in the dream, but I did—and it was true, because the baron told me later, when I described it to him, that that was exactly what he was thinking and feeling.

"I didn't want the baron to go on, but I couldn't make myself heard, and I could only make myself felt in pushes and nudges that simply annoyed him. At first, I didn't know where—or when—we were going, but I realized that there was only one place, or time, that it could be. He was going to his daughter, to the time when she was attacked and murdered, and I knew, partly because I'd heard him say it more than once, that what he wanted to do there wasn't to try and save her, because it had happened and there wasn't anything that could be done about that, but because he wanted to feel her pain, her humiliation, and her horror.

"He wanted to feel his daughter's life, her future and her hopes being smashed and torn apart. He knew, because he'd talked to her later, as she was dying, that he couldn't stop her feeling the terror and the pain, but he thought that if he could share it with her, mentally and spiritually, if he could sacrifice himself to it, then she would know, while it was happening, that she wasn't alone, that there was someone with her who loved her enough to go through it with her, and that even if that knowledge wouldn't make the physical pain any less, it would change the significance and meaning of the pain, and thus provide a kind of compensation.

"I knew, though, that he was frightened for Paul. He couldn't get to where he wanted to go without Paul, because it was Paul's carriage, but he thought that, even though he wanted to take all Yvaine's pain into himself, and bear it, even if it killed him, he had an obligation not to drag someone else down with him—because he was sure, in his own mind, that Paul wouldn't be able to take it, that it would destroy him, probably not in his body, but in his mind. I knew all that in my dream, and the baron confirmed it all later, so it was all true, and I really was reading the baron's mind.

"The baron didn't want to turn back. He couldn't turn back. But he didn't want Paul to suffer with him. So he began to pray for help. He began to pray for someone or something to come to snatch Paul out of the fusion that bound them together, at the last possible moment, so that he could be with Yvaine but Paul didn't have to be. I wanted to do that, but I couldn't. In fact, I wanted to stay with the baron anyway, to take Paul's place, but I couldn't do that either. I could make myself felt but not heeded. I loved him enough, you see—more than enough—but he didn't love me. It wasn't his fault; he would have loved me I think, if he could have done, in spite of what he knew about what Ignatz Fell had done to me, and what I had done to Fell when I found out that he's also done it to my sister, and left her pregnant, but he just couldn't. His daughter's death had taken that ability out of his soul. He couldn't love anyone any more, least of all himself.

"But I did help, I think. As you said, Madame Zosima, it was partly because I was there, wedged between them, that they were bound together, but it wasn't just that. There was something else. Again, as you said before, I think it was because they were both haunted by the thing that Paul drew, and painted, and hung in his bedroom: the thing that looks like a fetus, but which Paul says is really a symbol of death and life. Paul and the baron shared that haunting, and that was a cord binding them. But I did help; I think my presence was necessary too, even though they only perceived me as an annoyance, and couldn't sense that I wanted to help, that I was desperate to help,

"Madame Jane told me later that she wanted, desperately, to help as well, but that she was nailed to one of the crosses on the horizon, and couldn't do anything. The baron told me afterwards, although I didn't know it in my dream, that he had decided, as a matter of duty, that if his prayer wasn't answered, and no angel came, then he would give up his own plan and save Paul, but that it wasn't necessary. When the carriage arrived at its destination, and I saw those rifle-butts smashing into that poor girl's belly, trying to kill the child in her womb, I shut my eyes and I screamed, but no sound came out—and even though my eyes were shut I imagined that something swooped down from the sky and seized Paul, and carried him away, at exactly the same instant that the baron fell into his daughter...or dissolved, or whatever he did. I can't be sure. My eyes were shut.

I fell out of the carriage then, which had vanished, by magic, and left me lying on the ground, alone. Then I woke up. And when I had pulled myself together, I went to sit with Paul, because I thought that that was what the baron would have wanted me to do. And I'm still here, because I think that was what the baron would have wanted me to do.

"Madame Jane told me later that it had been much more complicated than I imagined; that if I'd kept my eyes open, I would have seen it quite differently. She seemed annoyed because I hadn't, but how could I help it? I was dreaming. I wasn't thinking rationally. I wasn't in control...and it was too horrible...much more horrible than what had happened to me when I was raped, although I'd thought that was bad at the time.

"Madame Jane told me that Paul had still been with the baron when they jumped out of the carriage, and while the baron tried to share his daughter's agony. She said that when they separated, Paul had tried to share with the unborn child, who might have been already dead, but that he couldn't do it, or wasn't allowed to do it, and that it wasn't until he realized that he wasn't helping that something pulled him away. She said that I was wrong about it swooping down from the sky, that it was something that had been in the carriage with us, but that's not what I imagined. I had my eyes shut, so I suppose she was probably right, but when I asked her what the face of the winged creature look like, she had to admit that she didn't know, so I suspect that either she had shut her eyes too, or that she was partly blinded by tears.

"The baron told me that after he jumped out of the carriage there was a split second before he threw himself over his daughter, when he knew that something with wings—an an-

164

gel, he assumed—had snatched Paul away, and that he already knew when he threw himself down that his prayer had been answered, and that he was free to share Yvaine's pain and horror. He said that it was terrible, more terrible than he had been able to imagine, and that if he hadn't been three-quarters dead already, it would surely have destroyed him, but being so nearly dead gave him strength. And he thought—he was absolutely convinced—that his sacrifice, his martyrdom, hadn't been in vain, that he had enabled Yvaine to feel loved even as she was enduring what she went through, and that awareness had allowed her, when she was overwhelmed by the humiliation, to turn aside the thrust that she had aimed at her navel, so that it only gashed the epidermis, and didn't penetrate any of the organs.

"He said that, in a way, that had prolonged the pain, and had made her death more protracted, but that it had also prolonged the love, and enabled her to know, at the end, that her father was not only beside her bed, clutching her hand, but that he was with her completely, heart and soul, and that they would always be together, even after she was dead: that she would be able to haunt him, and feel him, and know that all his love was for her. And he said that he knew that it had worked out that way, because she had always been with him from that moment on, and although she had never been able to speak to him, he now knew, beyond a shadow of a doubt, what she had felt while she haunted him, and why, when Paul had drawn her, twice, she had been beautiful, and not racked by pain and shame in the slightest. And he wanted Paul to paint her that way for him, which Paul did. And that's all I know."

Zosima sighed, deeply. The sigh was full of disappointment and frustration, but all that she said way: "Thank you"

"You don't sound as if you mean that," said Madame Louvot, resentfully.

"I do," Zosima assured her. "I can't help admitting that I had hoped for something more, but I hadn't dared to expect it. I'd hoped that you or Madame de La Vaudère had recognized the face of the entity that snatched Paul from the jaws of death—but I can't say that I'm entirely surprised that you didn't. If that's all we have, then that's what we'll have to work with.

"Don't forget the voice," said Madame Louvot.

"You and Jane heard a voice?" Zosima queried.

"No," said Madame Louvot, "but Paul did."

Zosima turned to Paul. "I thought you didn't remember anything of your somnambulistic experiences," she said.

"I don't retain anything of what I experience directly," Paul told her, "but I caught a kind of echo of Jane's dream—the whole thing, I think, was more Jane's dream than anyone else's, even though the baron and Angélique shared it. I don't think I saw anything that Jane and Madame Louvot didn't, but I had a long silent dialogue with a voice. I thought it was just my imagination playing tricks, some kind of personal reflection. The voice told me that dreaming was a mistake, and that I ought to stick to drawing, but when I asked it what I ought to draw it only said 'Water from a well. What else is there?' I suggested oil, but it accused me of joking. Then it asked me if I wanted some advice, and I said yes."

"And what advice did it give you?"

"It told me to go home. It said that I might have to wait a long time for Clémence or someone else to love me, but in the meantime, I could still paint. It told me that there's no better prison than paint. If I can remember its exact words, it said: *Paint, and hope. It's the best you can do. And if you want to call it redemption, do so. It's only wordplay, but there's no other game in time. Believe me, I know. The odds are against you, because the universe cheats, but there isn't any alternative. Go home, my love.* And I said that it wasn't safe—that Yvaine had been going home, with someone to watch over her, and look what had happened to her. Then I woke up."

"You didn't recognize the voce?"

"No, I asked it several times who it was, and made suggestions, but the only answer I got was a straightforward denial that it was Talia Cadelan. As soon as I recalled it to mind consciously, I concluded that I had only been talking to myself, imagining the voice as a kind of rhetorical strategy—and I wondered whether the anonymous winged creature that had saved me from sharing the baron's martyrdom and redemption might have been a similar rhetorical device, not a person at all but a symbol."

"You might be right," Zosima conceded. "Unfortunately, it's just an extra complication, which doesn't make the problem any clearer, at least for the moment. And that's everything is it? There's nothing left to add?"

"Not by me," Paul said. "But you told us that you had one more supplementary datum to add."

"More of a conjecture than an item of information, I fear, but it might help to explain some things that are still slightly puzzling."

"What things?"

"Talia's reaction to forming a sudden and unexpected bond with you, and the similar reactions of Juliette, Jane de La Vaudère and Madame Louvot. To every action there is a reaction, isn't that that law of physics? Perhaps it has a psychic parallel. The effect that the formation of the bonds had on you was ambivalent, perhaps paradoxical, compounded out of natural carnal attraction and the simultaneous withdrawal planted by Amélie Lambrunet's posthypnotic suggestion. I suspect that the reaction to that confusion within the bonds you formed with other was a protective impulse, perhaps an echo of Amélie Lambrunet's attitude and motivation when she planted the suggestion. Naturally, the people with whom you bond explain that protective impulse themselves as a perception of danger to you, and a desire to shield you from it, but I suspect that that's just a rationalization."

"You don't think I'm really in any danger, then?"

"Oh, I know that you're in danger now—but I don't think that's the explanation of why Jane de La Vaudère and Madame Louvot were suddenly seized by such a strong desire to protect you, to the extent that they could. Talia and Juliette probably didn't even know that Lilith existed, and Jane felt the desire to protect you long before she identified Lilith as a possible source of threat, and presumably warned Madame Louvot against her. Before doing that, Jane focused her attention on me—but we know, don't we, that I'm not your enemy?"

"So you say," Paul agreed. "But you say that Lilith is. Presumably, she would tell a different story."

"Indeed she would," Zosima concluded, "and she doubtless will. You'll have to make up your own mind as to which of us is telling the truth—but if you want a hint, it's me, and if you don't believe me, it might cost you your sanity, and perhaps your life."

"But you want to protect me," Paul said, slowly, "because we've formed a bond, and you can't help yourself. That's the real reason why you're here now."

"Succinctly put."

"But, extrapolating your own argument," Paul said, "if your desire to protect me is simply a reaction of your unconscious mind to its contact with the confusions of mine, the danger you perceive in Lilith might be as phantasmal as the danger Jane saw in you: a rationalization, devoid of any real basis."

"Very good," said Zosima, with apparent equanimity. "Hoist by my own petard, as they say—but the fact remains that I can perceive a grave danger in Lilith's present maneuvers, to you rather than to me, which you might ignore at your cost. At the very least, you need to listen to my explanation, so that when Lilith comes to see you again, as she certainly will, you'll have a little mental ammunition with which to oppose her assault."

"I'm listening," said Paul, taking a fortifying swig of brandy. "Fire away."

CHAPTER IX

"When Lilith, Salome and Justine began calling themselves the Three Maries they were adolescents and it was just
a silly affectation," Zosima said. "It was a cliché, in fact, given
that even in the nineteenth century the Midi was still so full of
reminders of the myth that you didn't have to be an antiquarian to be familiar with the bare bones of the legend. It was also
fashionably irreverent, perhaps even slightly blasphemous—
but they could hardly help perceiving themselves as outcasts
of a sort, considered by their heterosexual peers as wicked,
abnormal, unnatural, and all the other adjectives routinely applied by the censorious to women like me. The fact that there
were three of them enabled them to form a conspiracy of sorts
against a world that was at least suspicious of them, and
shunned them to some extent, even though they didn't declare
the sexual nature of their relationship openly, and no one accused them overtly of something essentially unmentionable.

"Inevitably, they gravitated toward the mystical aspects
of sorority culture, and the symbolic aspects of the floral
games. They became intensely interested not merely in the
Medieval legends of the three Maries who had been supposedly brought to Gaul by Joseph of Arimathea, along with the
Holy Grail, but other aspects of local history and myth. Un-
derstandably, they always preferred unorthodox pseudohistory
to orthodox and official accounts. They loved Napoléon
Peyrat, and Jules Michelet's heretical account of the witch
craze, which made witches into heroic defenders of an ancient
egalitarian faith attempting to maintain virtuous feminist ideals in secret while being persecuted by the evil hierarchies of
church and state. In the matter of the Albigensian crusade,
they sympathized entirely with the Cathars. When people
started calling them the Three Witches it was probably intended as an insult, but they doubtless relished it, and they set out

actually to be witches, but witches of their own design, with a set of heretical beliefs made to measure. Doubtless they all contributed to that design, but the powerhouse of their collective imagination was always Lilith, the oldest of the three.

"All three of them were from respectable families, who doubtless attempted to marry them off, as respectability prescribed, but as their refusal of comply with that expectation became more obvious, and hence more problematic, their relationship with their families became increasingly fraught, and led to threats of disinheritance and withdrawal of financial support. They thought of themselves as artists—poets, singers and dancers—as well as magiciennes of a sort, and when they left Toulouse for Paris in order to seek their fortune they undoubtedly hoped to build a career of that sort, in order to save themselves from the Hell of marriage or prostitution, but they were still largely supported by money provided by their families.

"Now calling themselves the Daughters of Artemis, the three made contact in Paris with various salon coteries, lesbian, occult and Bohemian, but they always remand marginal to the communities they attempted to join, never attaining much success in their various endeavors—which only bound them more tightly together, and involved them more intensively in their private fantasies.

"You seem to have been blithely oblivious to their existence, Paul, as you were of Monique's, but, just as Monique was aware of you, so were they. They probably appreciated your Mourgue la Faye when it won a minor medal at the Salon, and boasted about knowing you...and probably spread the old anecdotes about your adoptive mother hypnotizing you in order to protect her daughter, as an a item of light gossip. They were inevitably interested to read the newspaper accounts of the Juvisy séance, and had an intense interest in the *Palatine* lifeboat disaster because they really did know Amélie and Martine Lambrunet. When Jane de La Vaudère actually sought them out, while collecting information about you, that must have seemed particularly rewarding, given her social status and the fact that she was not only a best-selling author but a rather scandalous figure, unafraid to mention the previously-unmentionable in her work.

"They had undoubtedly been experimenting with hypnotism for some time, with only a little more success than their other various endeavors, but Lilith proved to have a knack for it. When I founded my community in Paris in 1902, they were immediately drawn to it for several reasons, and it might be too cynical to believe that the most important was the fact that they found themselves almost completely destitute. They had a genuine sympathy with many of my ideals, and were easily able to put on a show of complete support even while remaining a distinct party of three within the organization, with their own idiosyncratic concerns and ideas. I didn't mind that at all; mine was always intended to be a broad church. They had been interested in ideas of reincarnation for some time—such notions were still very fashionable, although Madame Blavatsky's heirs and followers had lost their brief impetus—but it wasn't until they joined my community that it became the central and obsessive focus of their attention.

"It was the force of my magnetization that enabled them to begin to recover memories of anterior lives much more prolifically and much more intensely—and also to be much better able to bring such memories to the surface in others. They soon became important members of my inner circle of initiates, the most spectacular successes of my method, my pride and my joy, and my most valuable collaborators...the women most likely, and most able, eventually to stab me in the back and take my place here in the Midi. I can't really hold that against them; it's the logic of the situation, the way of the world...which doesn't make it any more comfortable.

"Between the three of them, they built a complicated pseudohistory in which they had been associated for centuries, never separated for long by the whims of fate. They quickly remembered, or imagined, that they had all been priestess of Artemis in Massalia, the Phocean colony in southern Gaul; and more recently, they've begun to recover memories of be-

171

ing ardent worshipers of the primal goddess of whom Artemis, along with Isis, Inanna, Ishtar and so on are all watered-down versions. Obviously, they remembered under hypnosis in much more elaborate detail that they had been members of the Christian community founded in the region when Joseph of Arimathea transported the nucleus of the Galilean community from Judea. They became convinced that their trinity, as they called it, had enjoyed a whole series of rebirths, extending all the way from their origin as priestesses of the primal Triple Goddess through their service as Daughters of Artemis to multiple descendants of the original three Maries, so their remembrance of their psychic heredity gradually hybridized their version of the veneration of the Triple Goddess and Artemis with the later veneration of the Virgin, the mother of Jesus, which they construed in a typically unorthodox fashion.

"In their view—which, in their minds, is not a speculative scholarly hypothesis but something they have been enabled to remember as if they had actually lived it—the community founded on the shore of the Sea of Galilee, whose primary deity was the Virgin rather than her son, was essentially an egalitarian one, in which all property was held in common, including what modern Anarchists and Fourierists call sexual property. The members of the community, echoing various earlier phases of the worship of the Triple Goddess, but evolving continually, allegedly practiced and celebrated erotic freedom, not only licensing but encouraging homosexual relationships. In Lilith's memories, the original three Maries were lovers, and they were exclusive lovers, exactly as their predecessors in the worship of earlier versions of the goddess had been, and as their modern counterparts are.

"This morning, Paul, in a slightly atypical burst of sarcasm, you made the observation that a community like the one further up the mountain might have difficulty renewing its workforce, and I replied, in a rather more typical sarcastic spirit, that when pregnancies are required, they can be procured. Legend-mongers have long ago taken account of the problem in their representations of the Greek amazons. In the memories recovered by Lilith, Salome and Justine, the Galilean community was predominantly homosexual—logically, since it was a community composed of outcasts and social pariahs—and predominantly female, but there was still a necessary role for at least one male to play with regard to the lesbian fraction of the community, and in their memories, that role was, in fact, attributed to a single male—the male mistakenly seen by later commentators as the leader of the community..."

Paul could not remain silent any longer. "You're saying that in Lilith's interpretation of history, Jesus wasn't a prophet but an item of breeding stock: a bull, a ram or a rooster?"

"In vulgar terms, yes...but Lilith, not unnaturally, doesn't represent it in vulgar terms, and she doesn't put the same emphasis on the brutal and strutting aspects of masculinity that animal breeders tend to do. And in Lilith's view, Jesus was also an instrument of the goddess—the Virgin, in Christian parlance—who was the real architect of his career as well as his birth, and her maternal role was only one aspect of a symbolic trinity."

Paul's glass was empty again, but this time, he deliberately refrained from reaching for the bottle of brandy. He was already a little intoxicated, and he thought that it might be a good idea to retain as clear a head as he could in order to follow through the multitudinous implications of what Zosima had just told him.

"You're implying that Lilith's new interest in me is because she's cast me in her schemes as a supplier of sperm?" he interrogated

"If only it were that simple," Zosima said, "it would be a rather amusing irony, don't you think, in view of the psychological history that I've just mapped out? But it's not. It's much more complicated than that."

"Alchemical marriage?" Paul queried.

Zosima laughed. "It had to be Monique, didn't it, who was tipped out of the vegetable-cart outside your door? The rain and the lightning obviously played their part, but if I had

173

to wager, I'd bet that the real cause of the accent was her inattention to what she was doing, and that the reason she was distracted at the precise moment that she was steering Tigany past your cottage was that she was, quite naturally, thinking about you. So she's overheard mention of alchemical marriage, has she? But she has no idea what it means, because she's the last person that Lilith and her sisters would include in their convoluted conspiracy. Can I continue with the story now?"

Paul exchanged a glance with Angélique, who seemed amused, obviously appreciative of the irony that Zosima had pointed out, no matter how much she might disapprove of its implications.

"Go on," he said.

"In Lilith's remembrance, as might be expected, the Albigensians were the inheritors of the ideas and the ideals of the Galilean community, but not in the fashion that other fantasists thinking along similar lines imagine. Antiquarians like Jean-Bénigne Lambrunet routinely imagine little pockets of Occitan culture in which particular families have been handing down old beliefs and practices from one generation to the next, secretly, because that kind of transmission is the only one that their way of thinking permits. Believers in reincarnation, however, have an alternative. In their thinking, beliefs and practices can be extirpated completely, and disappear from the world for generations, only to be revived when the relevant memories are recovered in particular circumstances, when they reappear as literal revelations.

"Necessarily, Lilith, Salome and Justine suppose that the particular circumstance that permitted and produced their revelation is precisely the fact that there are three of them, a crucial trio of predestined lovers and visionaries, whose mission is to reconstitute, not a replicated quasi-Cathar commune or an echo of the Galilean community that the Albigensians were striving to replicate but a new, evolved version of an ideal community whose ultimate origins lie even further back in time than the priestesses of Artemis, in the worship of the primal Triple Goddess..."

"Which are also echoed by the Roman vestal virgins," Paul put in, "and various other select communities...like those featured in several of Jane's novels...which Lilith has presumably read."

"Indeed. But you can be certain that Lilith and her companions don't think that they've borrowed anything from Jane or any other author of speculative fantasies. In their minds, any inspiration flows the other way: all historical authors, going all the way back to Homer, are merely obtaining snatches of distorted remembrance of things remotely past, which they reshape and misinterpret to their own whim. Like all thinkers of that stripe, Lilith finds numerous recurrent patterns in mythology and literature, and like many others she conflates the story of Jesus with other accounts of uniquely privileged males—Osiris, Krishna, Adonis, and so on. In Lilith's view, of course, male anthropologists identifying the recurrent pattern put too much emphasis on the masculinity of the figure, whereas she endorses the central feature of the recurrence, which is..." She paused for effect.

"That they all die," Paul supplied.

"Exactly. In Lilith's notion of a sapphist utopia, the male of the species is necessary for fecundation, but he can't be a permanent member of the community."

"But in the myths you just cited, the deaths are symbolic, often followed by resurrection. In vulgar terms, all that would be necessary is expulsion, just as any male children born to the legendary amazons weren't simply killed, but had to be expelled at a certain age, to seek their fortune in a wider world."

"Lilith doesn't think in vulgar terms, nor does she think in terms of simple repetition: her notion of imaginary history and prehistory have a built-in component of moral evolution, as other theories of serial reincarnation invariably do. They stopped communicating their supposed discoveries to me some time ago, but so far as I can judge, their dreams of the primal community are violent and cruel, the originality of priestesses practicing human sacrifice...or, to be strictly accurate, male human sacrifice, with sharp knives. Over time, however, those actual sacrifices were replaced by symbolic sacrifices, as in the Old Testament's account of the evolution of the Hebrew religion. On the other hand, symbolic sacrifice can still be brutish and nasty, as witness Jesus and several of the other examples you cited—there are many more."

"So," said Paul, "if, as you clearly imagine, Lilith and her sisters have cast me in a role akin to that of Jesus in the Galilean community, I really am in crude physical danger."

"I certainly don't think you can rule it out. I know nothing for certain, but I've seen the development of fanaticisms before, and I know the pattern. There's always a tendency to extremes of craziness."

"But when I met Lilith his afternoon she didn't give the impression at all of being raving mad. She was a trifle impertinent, but not without charm even when bordering on rudeness—not unlike you, in fact, but more likeable."

"I'll try to take that as a compliment," said Zosima, "in spite of the nasty rider. Yes, she has borrowed a good deal from me, and she makes every effort to capitalize on her natural advantages to seem more likeable—which might make her all the more dangerous. In truth, though, I don't believe that she's malevolent, and specifically, I don't believe that she means you any harm. The problem is that, like me, she might expose you to great danger without any conscious intention to do so. Psychic force is blind and wayward, only marginally responsible to willful direction, if at all. Like me, all Lilith can do is supply the fuel; she can't direct the carriage of dreams. Perhaps you have a degree of willful control, but it's by no means imperious. If you consider the dream that Madame Louvot has just described, and your role in it, I think you'll agree that any power of decision you had was effectively impotent, requiring the intervention of your supposed angel...and also that your angel was limited in her own heroic agency."

"Not a very hopeful observation," Paul observed.

"Which I exactly why we you need to figure out how to make the most of what little hope it contains. And that's what I'm trying to help you to do—belatedly, I admit, but hopefully not too late."

"Very kind of you," said Paul, dryly. "So, putting it crudely, you think Lilith wants me to inseminate one of her sisters—presumably not her, as she's past her peak as breeding stock, even if she had the inclination. Who, then? Sister Monique?"

"I doubt it. In fact, given the kinds of recruits that my communities tend to take in, they leave a lot to be desired—as, in fact, for reasons I've explained, you do yourself..."

"I take your point," said Paul. "In vulgar terms, then, the whole idea is a farce. But Lilith isn't thinking in vulgar terms, you say. What terms is she thinking in, then?"

"That, I don't know precisely. But you named the most likely idea yourself: alchemical marriage: an exercise in mystical symbolism. The formation of a magical bond: the kind of bond you've already demonstrated your ability to form...the kind that even survives death, in the cases of Juliette and Jane de La Vaudère."

"A bond with whom? Lilith?"

"Possibly, but I suspect not. She sees herself as a mastermind, not an instrument."

"Clémence Sancerre?"

"A more likely possibility; Lilith has certainly been interested in Clémence for a long time, as in much the same distant fashion as she's taken an interest in you. She considers her to be a true Marian, and an intuitive painter—but to mention that you and she already seem to have an appropriately peculiar bond of sorts, which might only need a hypnotic nudge to make it...something more."

"But in sum, you think that she wants to hypnotize me in order to direct my erotic attention toward some target of her selection...in spite of what she knows about the post-hypnotic suggestion that, according to you, has put on a curse on all my sexual relationships?"

177

"Vulgar terms again. Whatever she wants, it's much more than that. It's precisely because of the alleged post-hypnotic suggestion and its apparent effects that you seem to her to be marked out as someone special, perhaps unique, but that's only one component of your uniqueness. You're the painter of the spirits of the dead, and the person who can form mystical bonds under the power of magnetization. The role that she has in mind for you might not have anything to do with physical fecundation—it surely can't, if Clémence Sancerre is involved, given that she's only slightly younger than Lilith, already nearing the limit when pregnancy would be safe. I suspect that she's thinking in terms of psychic heredity rather than physical heredity."

"But that, in her view, is essentially a female matter, the potential to remember past lives only being handed down from mothers to children, not from fathers?"

"Did Monique tell you that?"

"No, it was Gaston—but it's true, isn't it, that you and your sisters only work with female clients, and only enable them to remember female incarnations?"

"Yes, it's true. We regard females as the true humankind, and men as mere suppliers of gross hereditary material—exactly contrary to animal breeders who give priority to the hereditary contributions of stallions, bulls and so on. A number of biologists, including Hugo de Vries, have already produced evidence that the contributions to physical heredity by both parents are equal, but we believe that even in physical terms the egg makes a greater contribution than the sperm, and that in terms of psychic heredity, the line of female descent is of cardinal importance."

"So, if your sisters are using terms like alchemical marriage, they're surely thinking in terms of psychic heredity, not physical heredity: a marriage of minds...the formation of a bond like the ones your magnetism enabled me to form with Talia, Juliette and Jane?"

"Yes."

"And as we've just discussed at length, the bonds in question are more far-reaching than simple couplings...not only have they linked me with more than one person at a time, but they also seem to have formed links, at least in some instances, between those other individuals...between Jane and Madame Louvot, for example. You think they want me to function as a psychic catalyst, not so much to bond with a target female, but more importantly, to enable two—or more—target females to bond with one another?"

"Very good," said Zosima. "I would have explained it, but since you've got there on your own, so much the better. Yes, although I'm not privy to the detail of Lilith's scheme—and there might be details she hasn't even confided to Justine and Salome—I strongly suspect that she wants to hypnotize you, in the hope and expectation of provoking a collective vision that will bind together a select band of initiates, including supposed biological descendants of one or more of the three Maries."

"One or more?"

"Probably all three. We all have two grandmothers, remember, and the number doubles every generation. Lilith and her sisters believe that here's something magical—or at least mystical—about their trio, which reproduces previous triplets, echoing numerous such triplets in ancient mythology, reflecting the tripartite nature of the primal Triple Goddess herself. In all probability, the alchemical marriage they want to achieve is their own, and they've probably been trying to achieve it all their lives, but have never succeeded to their own satisfaction, so they've convinced themselves that it can't be achieved without the appropriate catalyst, or catalysts—to wit, you, and perhaps Clémence Sancerre."

"And you think that might pose a danger to me?"

"Don't you, given what you and Madame Louvot have just described about the nature of the vision induced by Baron de Rochemure's quest for redemption?"

"A highly idiosyncratic quest, to associate himself with the victim of a brutal murder. Surely that isn't what Lilith and her sisters have in mind?"

"I don't know—but I do know that the history of the Christian community on the shore of Galilee ended in Calvary and Crucifixion, not of the three Maries but their chief male collaborator, and I know, too, that it doesn't require the misandry of some of my sisters to impel mortal violence. Even the meekest and most virtuous of women"—she looked at Madame Louvot with obvious intention—"is capable of stabbing a man in the back without compunction if the occasion seems to warrant it."

Madame Louvot was already so pale that there was no further margin for blanching, but she maintained a rigid silence.

"But it's all complete nonsense," Paul put in, swiftly. "Whatever Lilith and her sisters want to achieve, it's all just a product of their imagination—pure fantasy."

"You're being deliberately obtuse again," Zosima said, a trifle waspishly. "*Everything* that we've just been talking about was a product of the imagination: a combination of imaginations. It was, as Madame Louvot said, *just a dream*...but it was a dream that was dreamed by several people simultaneously, which none of them could direct or control, and which left most of its participants feeling desperately helpless. Of course Lilith can't procure anything, in her own mind or anyone else's, but products of the imagination. But products of the imagination can provide at least the illusion of salvation, or the illusion of damnation—and what more is necessary to constitute salvation or damnation, at a personal level? Products of the imagination can save or destroy people, and they can have effects far beyond the imagination in which they're initiated. World conquests begin as dreams of world conquest, mass murders as dreams of extirpation, and we have no idea of the extent or effects of telepathic contagion in respect of such dreams, because such contagion is by definition, unconscious.

"Thus far, Paul, you've been fortunate in the particular stimulations of your unconscious mind by magnetization, and the consequent telepathic contagions, but the evidence I've heard here tonight confirms my existing fears about the danger posed by such experiments in hypnotism and telepathy. I already have Talia's death on my conscience, as you know, and hers isn't the only one. Yours, to tell the truth, wouldn't add that much to the total burden...but even so, I feel an obligation, a sense of duty, to prevent it if I can, or at the very least to warn you. That's why I'm here. That's why I've been trying to get a clearer picture of the situation—and, as a matter of particular relevance, to discover who or what the guardian angel was that seemingly saved you from disaster and damnation at Baron de Rochemure's séance."

"And are you any closer to that discovery now than you were this morning?"

"Perhaps—but without further confirmation, it remains just a hypothesis."

"Would you care to share the hypothesis?"

"If you wish, although, as before, I think the answer would do you more good if it came from your own deductions. The first principle of psychoanalysis is that the therapist can only be a catalyst; the understanding has to come from within. The only true discovery is self-discovery."

"That's just wordplay."

"So it is—but as your angelic Voice pointed out to you, it's the only game in time. Whether your rescuer swooped down from the sky, as Madame Louvot imagined, or was present with you in your symbolic carriage, as Jane believed that she saw, we can be almost certain of one thing, which is that none of the active participants in the telepathic nexus were able to supply the necessary help. It came from outside—which is to say, inside. In one sense, the angel had to be you, and in another, it had to be one of the dead who haunt you. I'm convinced now that it wasn't Talia and it wasn't Juliette—which, in my calculation of probability, leaves only three possible candidates. Take your pick."

"Amélie and Martine Lambrunet?" Paul had no difficulty guessing.

"Evidently," Zosima agreed. "And the third?"

"My sister," Paul guessed.

"That's it. You're getting the hang of it now. If you can decide between them, do so, because you might need that help, and it will be psychologically convenient, at least, to know where to direct your prayer if and when the time comes."

"You're sure it's coming, then?"

"I'm sure it's nigh."

"But it might all be hot air. And let's not forget that all that actually happened to me at Passy was that I fell asleep, and woke up perfectly fit and well, as I did after the two earlier occasions when you hypnotized me. When Henri Lemastur did it, I didn't even blink. Even if Lilith were to succeed in hypnotizing me somehow, by stealth and cunning, why should I presume that the result would be any different?"

"You can certainly pin your future to that hope," Zosima conceded, readily, "but I wouldn't if I were you, once I'd reflected thoroughly on what Amélie Lambrunet had done to me more than twenty years ago and the effect it had had on my life."

"I'm still not convinced that it had any effect at all," Paul said, stubbornly. "Even if Amélie really did try to hypnotize me, and even if she persuaded herself that she had succeeded, I don't believe that it had the kind of wide-ranging effects on my psychology and my life that you've proposed."

"Again, you can certainly pin your future on that hope— but if you don't trust me, or yourself, trust Jane. She told you that if you ever allowed yourself to be hypnotized again, you'd be in grave danger. I resented that judgment at the time, but now—all the more especially after our discussion tonight—I believe that she was right, and I shall never attempt to magnetize you again, unless it's absolutely necessary."

"And what would constitute absolute necessity?"

"I don't know—but if ever you need me in your nightmares, call. Even if I'm on the far side of the world, I believe that I'd hear you. Whether I'd be able to do anything in response is, of course, another matter. Talia was no angel, but I'm even less suited to the role. If I can, though, I'll help. I owe you that."

"As a matter of interest," Paul said, "who do you remember when you venture into your own past lives?"

"No one," said Zosima. "I'm an original: a brand new soul, with my primal magnetism undiminished. I have no psychic ancestry."

"And is that how the Three Witches have cast you in their legendary epic?"

"Of course not. But as I've never allowed myself to be hypnotized, by them or anyone else, I've conserved my essential mystery, and hence my power of intimidation. Otherwise, they'd have stabbed me in the back—metaphorically, at least—long before today. If I'd stayed away from you, they'd probably have been content to let me be, but now I've told you what I know, it's open warfare. You needn't worry about that, though—concentrate on looking after yourself. Although, having said that, if I do need to call on you for help, I hope I can rely on you to try, even if you prove to be impotent."

"I'm not impotent," Paul told her. "Whatever Amélie Lambrunet might have told her five-o'clock friends and soirée sisters that she's tried to do to me, it didn't render me impotent. I don't believe that it had any effect at all, but if it did, it certainly didn't render me helpless. I believe that I'm the way I am because that's simply the way I am, and it's *not* a kind of impotence. Call me timid, or respectful, or whatever you want, but don't think that I've been permanently crippled in some way by some amateur hypnotist playing a practical joke. That's absurd."

"Agreed," said Zosima, equably. "Almost as absurd as thinking that you murdered your twin sister in the womb because there wasn't enough nourishing blood for the two of you. At least, your sister obviously doesn't believe that, if she's your guardian angel. If you want to call me crazy, at least check your entitlement to cast the first stone."

"It was a stupid joke," Paul said, not for the first time. "I never believed that it was true."

"Not consciously," Zosima countered. It was not the first time Paul had met that response either, and he knew that there was no answer to it, so he didn't try to find one.

"Do you have any more bombshells to hurl?" he asked, or have we finally reached the end?"

"I'm sorry that you see it as a matter of hurling bombs," said Zosima. "I had no intention of injuring you with psychic shrapnel. You could at least be grateful for the fact that you're no longer in the dark about things that even your dearest friends and lovers have been reluctant to tell you."

That, Paul had to concede, was true.

"Sorry," he said. "Too much food for thought can give you indigestion, I suppose—and the liqueur really didn't help. I'll feel better in the morning, I hope—and I'll seek further clarification, within and without. Thank you, Madame...and good luck in your contest to keep control of your brainchild. I infer that the lease on the convent isn't in your name?"

"Of course not. My organization is a collective of equals. The lease on the mountain domain is held by the collective, but for legal purposes, there have to be responsible nominees, and there has to be a network of conduits through which money flows. In the past, I've had control of those matters, but my control always depended on the consent of my sisters, and once a majority of them could be persuaded to exclude me from the process, that's what happened."

"And even though I don't have a vote in your ideal Republic, you want me to be on your side in the contest...or, at least, not to side with the opposition."

"Yes. It's necessary that all Lilith's schemes fall apart, nipped in the bud if possible."

"Necessary to you, that is," Paul amended.

"And to you, although I seem to be having difficulty persuading you of the fact."

"Indeed," Paul agreed.

Zosima turned to Madame Louvot, who was still listening in silence, her face as white as a flag of surrender. "And what's your opinion, Madame?"

"My opinion," declared the housekeeper, "is that Paul would be well advised to steer clear of all of you, as he has been doing very successfully for some years. Until a few days ago, he seemed to be safe enough here, with you in Paris and the ladies of the convent ignoring him, but that has evidently changed, and it might be better for us to go elsewhere—far away."

"Physical distance and psychic distance are not identical," Zosima said, "and whatever force is keeping Paul here will not be easy to evade."

"It's a choice, not a force," Paul put in.

"Consciously," Zosima told him, "you're bound to think that—but I won't argue the point. The important thing is to be on your guard, and to continue exploring your own resources. And whatever frustrations the full account of the Passy dream might have left behind, it certainly offers scope for optimism, Enigmatic as she is, there appears to be an angel of sorts watching over you, Paul...and the more help you can give her in her protective task, the better. Now, though, I had better return to the convent. I still have a lot of work to do there if I'm to preserve and build on what influence I still have. You had best get some sleep—tomorrow might be an eventful day, and your hand might want to draw. *Au revoir*."

Polite, as ever, Paul escorted her to the gate, and watched her disappear into the darkness. Then he returned to Madame Louvot.

"I'm sorry," she said. "I should have told you...everything."

"It doesn't matter," he told her. "In sum, there wasn't really a great deal to tell—nothing very substantial, at any rate. It's probably wise of you not to pass on idle gossip, of which I suppose you hear a good deal when you go to the village in search of food. That, I suppose, is where you first heard of

Lilith, and picked up whispers about her exploits in Toulouse?"

"No—well, yes, I do pick up little bits of gossip there, but I knew of her existence before, in Paris, via the baron's occult connections, and Madame Jane mentioned her too. Everything up at the convent is secret, of course, but keeping secrets only stimulates curiosity, and the sisters who call at our back door and shop for supplies in the village let things slip. Things leak out, even without blabbermouths like the slut who sprained her ankle. If you ask me, they're all mad...but not all madwomen are harmless, as you know full well."

Paul didn't bother to add a verbal agreement to that observation, contenting himself with helping Angélique clear the table and wash the dishes, pensively.

And Zosima was right; his hand, that night, did want to draw.

CHAPTER X

The next morning, Paul found yet another blurred image of a fetus on his sketch-pad. Its eyes were closed, in seeming mockery. For all his speculation, he had not the slightest idea what it symbolized—except, of course, life, death, immortality and reincarnation, in an appropriately vague fashion.

In the hope that exercise and fresh air might help to clear his head, and at least put him in a suitable frame of mind to finish his painting of Jane before saddling his horse and riding into Toulouse to see Clémence Sancerre, to see what information she could give him about the mysterious Lilith and her bizarre machinations, he went for a walk in the woods. As usual, he headed away from the slope overlooked by the grounds of the convent, and went instead toward the Great Cleft, curious to see whether the climbing equipment was still in place, indicating a probable resumption of the exploration now that the sides of the fissure had presumably had time to become a little drier, with no substantial leakage of water through the lateral cracks.

He was surprised, when he arrived within sight of the cleft, to see that, even at a very early hour, there was someone there. He was even more surprised to see that the person in question was wearing the habit of the fake nuns of the convent, with the cowl raised so that her face was invisible. She appeared to be peering into the fissure pensively, but without getting too close to the edge—a wise precaution.

His first hypothesis was that the lone stray must be Lilith, who might be waiting for him, brought to the location by some premonition of his movements. As he approached, however, the woman turned in his direction, and he was able to see enough of her face to be sure that it was not Lilith.

The expression of surprise in her dark eyes revealed clearly enough that she had had no presentiment of his arrival, and had not expected to see him. There was a moment of hesitation, when she almost turned and ran into the forest, but she steeled herself and held her position; there was an evident curiosity in her manner. Her olive complexion was smooth, and she seemed significantly younger than Lilith, although he knew that she must be the nearly the same age.

Warily, she watched him approach.

Tired of being a pawn in everyone else's game, Paul decided to take a gamble, and said: "Salut, Salome."

Her eyes widened in surprise. "You know me!" she exclaimed.

"Of course," he said, as casually as he could. "Not from Toulouse, of course, but from long before then, when you stood on that same spot centuries ago...and from long before then, in Massalia...and from long before that."

Shock and confusion were manifest in her expression, and she seemed to regret not having obeyed her first impulse to run away. "That's not possible," she blurted.

"Who told you that?" Paul followed up, immediately, pausing a few feet away lest excessive proximity trigger a flight reaction, or a perilous fit of vertigo. "Zosima? Lilith? Like physical heredity, psychic heredity has its complications and its mysteries. Men can't remember ever having been men in previous lives, but they're born of mothers, from the same wombs that yield daughters, and sometimes...you have heard my story, I suppose?"

Her jaw almost dropped in astonishment. Yes, she had heard his story. Everybody in Zosima's phalanstery had heard his story

"It is rare," he said, without waiting for a verbal response, "for children of opposite sexes to share the same womb, and even rarer for one to die and her nascent soul to pass into the other, to fuse there with its twin, and thus form a psychic androgyne, but it happens, and in the course of the centuries, it even happens repeatedly. I've experienced more than one magical marriage, Marie Salome—as you have, in your own different fashion."

Plainly, she had no clear idea of what he was implying—which was only reasonable, as he had no idea himself—but she did not dare to draw the conclusion that he was deliberately talking nonsense. "How do you know?" she demanded, retaining enough presence of mind to continue challenging him, in the hope of obtaining more information while revealing none.

"I know many things now," Paul assured her, not entirely falsely, although he was well aware that his ignorance was still enormous. "For a long time, I didn't remember it, and it lay dormant within my being, but I've received the transformative breath, and now, it's only a matter of time before I remember everything, and am able savor the ecstasy of the long metamorphosis. Then, my dear, I might be able to help you and your sisters attain the oblivion you seek."

Uneasily, she replied: "Who told you that we seek oblivion? It isn't true."

He hadn't supposed for a moment that it was, but he had his next move prepared. "Consciously, perhaps not," he said, "but if you study the pattern of your past lives carefully I think you'll be able to glimpse the pattern. The ways of destiny are strange, but not incomprehensible, when you understand what death is, and what life is not."

Under other circumstance he would have been tempted to call himself a pompous fool, but for the moment, he thought that pomposity in mystery might be a sound strategy, at least to keep his interlocutor off balance. He could see that he had not misjudged his audience. She was deeply uncertain about the significance of what he was saying, but too curious about what he might mean simply to dismiss it as nonsense. He decided to continue with the game, estimating that he had nothing to lose, and confident that he could improvise rapidly enough to keep it moving.

"I assume that Justine has accompanied Lilith on the journey to Toulouse, in order to see the notary who has custody of the lease of the convent," he said. "And you came here because you feared being alone with Zosima, knowing as you do what knell of doom is tolling for her ambitions. You've stolen her holy grail! But I don't need to advise you to beware of her magnetism, because you know full well that eternal ecstasy isn't the only fate that might await you in oblivion. Was it really wise to come here, knowing as you do what lurks at the bottom of the cleft, and what might emerge from it if the nightmare comes true? Yesterday, before I saw Lilith, I drew a dragon in my trance...but last night, I drew my sister: my other self, the darker fraction of my soul. Is that an omen, do you suppose? A presage? There was a time when it might have alarmed me, but not anymore. I'm at peace with myself now. Are you?"

The force of his suggestion had drawn her eyes automatically to the dark slit cutting through the forest. Still determined not to approach the dangerous edge too closely, she could only look into it obliquely, and she certainly could not plumb its depths with her gaze, but that did not prevent the fantasy that Paul was concocting from taking effect.

"How many nascent souls, do you think, are lost there?" Paul asked her. "How many children were cast into the depths when the pit was still imagined to be bottomless, having barely opened their eyes?"

She turned her head again to look at Paul sharply. "What do you mean?" she demanded, bluntly.

"You know full well what I mean, Marie Salome," Paul hazarded. "You have stood on that very spot yourself, more than once, in other lives, and cast the fruits of your womb and others into that pit, because the offspring were born male. Have you not lived as a daughter of Artemis the huntress, and before that, as a sacrificer priestess of the Triple Goddess, a wielder of the Sacred Knife? Have you not been a bacchante of the Androgyne Dionysus? Have you not been an amazon of the tribe of Penthesilea? And are those previous selves not within you still, fused in your soul with the buried memories of the mother of John of the Apocalypse? I know you, Marie Salome. I know that once, as a child, you danced for Herod the Great, for the prize of a man's head. You repented of that, and

190

joined the Children of Galilee, but there are some sins that can never be forgiven in the tribunal of the soul, no matter how hard you might seek forgiveness. We are not all redeemable, are we?"

Finally, she managed to defend herself more robustly. "You're lying," she said. "You're trying to confuse me."

"Am I?" Paul countered. "Well, perhaps I am—but it's so easy, isn't it? So easy to lie, so easy to sow fear and confusion in fertile psychic ground. But the world is a fearful place, and we can't begin to understand it, can we, without being frightened and confused? We're reluctant to admit it, obviously, but secretly, we know how little we know and how little we understand. That's how charlatans like you and your sisters operate—but exploiting that secret anxiety, that gulf of incomprehension."

"We're not charlatans!" Salome retorted.

"As every charlatan says, and many believe; but charlatans always run the danger of falling prey to their own charlatanry. In working so hard to convince others, they convince themselves. It's easy enough in isolation, but when three conspire, that's when the possibilities open up for real mutual delusion. But I believe in your sincerity, and I even understand it. Anyone who cultivates an atom of wisdom and isn't terrified of what they can see and what they can't is stupid or insane, and you're neither. You're merely living in fear, as are we all, and making what mental adjustments you can to keep the fear at bay. And it works...as long as you don't let the doubts insinuate themselves through the cracks in your certainty."

But he had taken a false route, adopting an argument that was too subtle. He could see that she was beginning to relax, to look at him with a sharper, more confident curiosity. Philosophical rambling about fear was no substitute for actually scaring her, and even though she was standing on the edge of an abyss with a man she did not know, she was not in fear of any violence on his part. He was almost insulted by that. He was a man, after all, taller and stronger than she was, with all

191

the brutal instinct of the species. The way she was staring at him, nevertheless, suggested that she was simply waiting, now, to hear what else he had to say, skeptical but interested.

He carried on. What else could he do?

"There are a thousand ways to make peace with the fear," he said. "Ours is just one of them, and not necessarily the best. But it does work, if you persist. It's just a matter of going further, of stripping back more layers of memory. We haven't always been human, you and I. In our time—or, rather, in our eternity—we've been truly innocent. We aren't now and we never shall be again, but the past is one thing that can't be taken away from us, which always lies in the utmost depths of our bottomless darkness. In the very center of our being, there is an absolute and eternal peace, an ecstasy or a nirvana, a psychic paradise—but the road of descent is hot and hard."

That was better. There was enough bait on that hook to catch her attention.

"Is it?" she countered, inviting another move.

"Yes," Paul said, still improvising at full tilt. "Do you see those pitons hammered into the stone shelf above the rim of the cleft? Today, or tomorrow, the searchers from the university will be back, with more pitons, more ropes and more lanterns, in order to lower themselves into the depths, in the hope of getting down further than anyone has ever been before, and living to tell the tale, but they won't find anything. Even if they were able to go beyond the emptiness, they wouldn't find a solid bottom. At best they'd find a slow river of glutinous mud flowing slowly but surely downwards to the blackest of seas, black in its mire and black in its sin, where multitudinous worms and protozoans are wriggling, which feed on the living matter washed into the cleft by the storms. It's a long time, I think, since they had the kind of feast that you once fed them: the succulent flesh of newborns. What a delicacy an innocent brain must be, unexposed to the assault of any but the quietest of sensations!"

He saw her wince slightly at that. The idea that the corpses of unwanted children might once have been thrown into the cleft had struck a chord; it was not an unfamiliar notion. She was capable of believing that women like her really had stood where she was standing, in times past, and committed infanticide for reasons not entirely alien to her own way of thinking and being...and that the culpability of such acts might still be lurking in her own soul.

"But nothing endures down there," Paul went on, keeping the argument flowing, slowly but surely, toward some as-yet-unglimpsed goal. "If the scientists were able to get down that far, and then to dam the flow and drain the ditch—ludicrously expensive in time and effort as that would be—what could they find? Nothing. Everything precious that was ever down there has already flowed away, drawn down into the ultimate oubliette, in the bowels of which is the central fire, the fragment of the sun that that forms the kernel within the nutshell of the Earth's crust. You and I are fortunate, however, are we not? We can descend further into ourselves, into our primeval psychic slime, than any mere human furnished with a rope will ever be able to descend into a slight crack in the earth's rugged crust.

"You and I are the blessed, Marie Salome; we know the way to heaven and hell, and believe that we have the power to choose between them. We've seen monsters, you and I, the beasts of your son's Revelation, but we've also seen angels...or at least, we know that the angels have seen us. The dead have no voices but they have sight, and a hypnotic power of suggestion. Be careful of the dead, though, Marie Salome; they're not all as loving as the ones who have so far haunted you or me. And beware of chemical weddings of every sort, for their hymeneal nights are sometimes more than trivially bloody."

Paul stopped then, although he could have carried on, almost indefinitely. He was no stranger to fantastic monologues, although he normally pronounced them silently, while painting.

He tried to imagine Salome as a painting, something subject to his whim, but there was too much solidity in her. Paintings could only give the illusion of depth, in faces there were as thin as shadows, albeit brighter. Sister Salome was not a painting; she was human, and a distiller of intoxications.

She laughed—which was not the reaction that Paul had been expecting, or hoping for.

Even so, he was quick to say: "That's right. There is no saner reaction to the absurdity of existence than laughter."

"My laughter is far more prosaic, I fear, Monsieur Furneret," she said. "I was recalling that when we interrogated Sister Monique about the impressions she had formed when her accident threw her into your arms, she said that you were just a man, like any other, but that you were obviously the victim of a spell that armored you against your own desire. She said that your lust had all been transmuted into mere kindness, like gold decayed into lead, and probably impotent. I think you disappointed her."

And that enabled you to laugh? Paul thought. *A strange sense of humor.* He supposed it as understandable, however, that he might not be able to see the joke, of which he was the victim. And as he had told Zosima the previous evening, he was definitely not impotent, even though he would not need all the fingers of one hand to count the witnesses to the contrary, and the majority of those were dead.

"Perhaps I did disappoint her," he said, aloud, "but it wasn't really me she wanted. I'd have been a poor substitute, I fear, for her long-lost Fabien. As she said, I'm just a man like any other, and what woman wants a man—or a woman, for that matter—like any other? The fortunate, of course, never meet any other kind, but for those who have once made contact with the extraordinary, the ordinary will always be a disappointment. You, Justine and Lilith must understand that far better than poor Monique, with all those lives to remember...even though you still have one another."

"We are extraordinary," said Salome, flatly.

"Of course you are, but are you extraordinary enough?"

"Yes," she replied, without hesitation—but Paul was sure that she could not be confident. In that, at least, he had sown a seed of doubt; but it was the cheapest of victories, and he was beginning to feel the pressure of time. He had a painting to finish, and an excursion to Toulouse to undertake. It would be a busy day, with more than one nettle that would have to be grasped firmly if he were not to be stung.

"I'm glad to hear it," he said, "and I truly wish you every success in all your projects, Mademoiselle. It was a privilege to meet you again, Marie Salome, and I'm sure that it won't be the last time we meet, now that your previous rule has been rudely shattered by its maker. I need to go home now, but I'll be going to Toulouse later, to talk to Clémence Sancerre about chemical weddings, and perhaps to receive a commission to paint a lovely Englishwoman. If I cross paths with Justine and Lilith on their way back, should I give them your regards?"

"Of course, Monsieur Furneret," she said. "And if they return without having seen you, should I give them yours?"

"Certainly. *Au revoir*, neighbor."

She did not return the *au revoir*, but nor did she say *adieu*. Her gaze went back to the cleft, and she resumed the reverie that Paul had interrupted, seemingly serene again after a momentary surprise.

When he reached to the cottage, however, intending to go into the studio, he saw Victor Marvaud's automobile stationed outside the gate, and its owner inspecting the small landslide that had carried away a section of its far edge. He felt a sudden sinking feeling, knowing that he had lost control of his schedule and that the tide of circumstance was about to bear him away—but he was not entirely sorry to see his friend, with whom he had a bone or two to pick.

"Not good, that, my dear," Victor opined, nodding toward the crumbling ledge. "A sign of worse to come. Fortunately, Gaston has plenty of connections. I'll mention it to him before we set forth for Paris, so that he can set things in motion. The repairs will take time, though, and the expense might make your English landowner flinch."

"Gaston and Armande aren't with you?" Paul asked.

"No. Their honeymoon voyage may be officially over, but when I'm with them I still feel like the third person in a small Parisian fiacre. In any case, Gaston's making more obligatory family visits today, and although I like Lambrunets well enough, everything becomes unbearably tedious in profusion. I thought I'd come out for an early-morning spin, and perhaps take you for a ride in the old girl. I don't suppose you've ever been in an automobile?"

"No, I haven't," Paul admitted.

"Disgraceful," Victor observed. "It's 1909, damn it. But at least you'll be starting with the best. You only have to climb aboard."

Paul knew that he had the option of saying that he absolutely must finish his portrait of Jane, but he knew full well that the relentlessly tactless Victor would not hesitate to remind him that she was dead, and could wait.

"Madame Louvot says that you're planning to go into Toulouse today anyhow," Victor added, evidently having made enquiries. "I'll be happy to take you there, by a suitably scenic route. It's a good opportunity—you might not have another for some time if you don't come back to Paris with me. I know you live here, but believe me, you haven't really seen the country until you've seen it from the passenger seat of a Panhard. What do you say?"

"I say that's very kind of you," Paul replied, surrendering to the hand of fate. "Yes, of course. Just give me a couple of minutes."

He went into the cottage to make hasty preparations for the sudden change of plan. By the time he returned to the road, Victor had turned the automobile around, and the engine was throbbing in a manner that did not seem too cacophonous. Paul climbed in.

He waited until they were well under way before saying: "By the way, do you remember Monique?"

Victor peered at him through his goggles with evident surprise and a hint of suspicion. "Which Monique?" he asked, warily.

"The one you knew in Toulouse—one of your early conquests—and then met again in Paris. One of Juliette's friends."

"Yes," said Victor, his voice still carefully neutral. "I remember her. Why?"

"She's in the convent. She was responsible for the landslide you were just admiring, when the cart she was driving broke a wheel in a storm and spilled its load. She hurt her foot and had to spend the night in the cottage."

Victor's eyes widened behind the goggles. "She spent the night?"

Paul suspected that there might be a hint of jealous resentment in his amazement, absurd as that would be. "On the sofa," he added. "We had a long chat, though."

"Oh. How is she—apart from the bad foot?"

"Surprisingly cheerful, considering her situation. She saw us climbing the mountain the day before and considered slipping out to say hello, but she didn't want to risk embarrassing you in the company of your friends."

Paul thought he heard a slight sigh of relief, but it might have been his imagination. When Victor spoke again, it was to say: "She doesn't hate me, then?"

"No—her memories of you seemed reasonably fond. Why would she hate you?"

"You'd be surprised how many do, after liaisons come to an end. I always retain fond memories of them, but they're not reciprocated as often as one would like. I would never have picked her out as a likely recruit for Zosima's cult, though."

"I think it was a case of desperation rather than choice. She offered to come and work as my housekeeper if I cared to sack Madame Louvot, so you can measure the extent of her desperation from that. I don't think she took it too personally when I declined. But then, she's probably heard the same rumor that everybody in the world except me seems to have heard."

Victor looked at him obliquely. "I suspect there are a lot of those," he said. "You'll have to narrow it down."

"The rumor that after we climbed the mountain the first time, with Martine, Amélie Lambrunet hypnotized me and commanded me to keep my hands off...an instruction that subsequently blighted all my relationships with women."

"Oh, that old joke. Wasn't worth mentioning—too ludicrous for words. And you're not the only person in the world who hasn't heard it—for God's sake don't mention it to Gaston. It's for his sake rather than yours that I've always kept a tight lid on it. You and I know that it's utterly ridiculous, but it might still be a sore point for him. He won't ever let anyone say anything against his mother, and he hates being reminded that she was once a little too close to the lunatic fringe of the sororities for comfort. Monique never could keep her mouth shut."

"Actually, it wasn't Monique who told me; it was Zosima. Monique probably adopted the same attitude as you—that it was ridiculous and not worth mentioning. Zosima, on the other hand, believes it."

"Does she? Well, as a magnetizer herself, and someone not really aware of how things work in Toulouse, she probably would. But she didn't know Amélie and she didn't know you, so she can't see how stupid the suggestion is. I suppose she wants to hypnotize you again, in order to remove the imaginary hex?"

"Actually no, she just wants me to steer clear of a rival who's trying to take over her cult, or at last the Toulousan branch."

"Lilith? The linchpin of the old Three Maries?"

"That's right. I just had a chat with another one, Salome? Do you remember her?"

"Only vaguely, from Toulouse. She knew my mother slightly as well as Gaston's—they all did, although Amélie wasn't all that far out in sorority mysticism in those days, and my mother never was."

"How well, exactly, did Lilith knew Amélie?"

"How should I know? But it would just have been sorority stuff, five o'clock teas, not black masses, mostly before you or I was able to walk and talk, as the Three Maries seemed to be detached even from the lunatic fringe by the time I was old enough to take notice of their existence. I ran into them a few times in Paris, but I kept my distance. Not my type, as you can imagine, my mother's generation rather than mine, and very much on the periphery of my social orbit, broad as it is. Salome's the dark one, as I remember, prettier than Lilith when they were younger but under her thumb in spite of it. How did she seem?"

"Confused—but that's not entirely surprising, as I put some effort into confusing her, just in case what Zosima said about their plans for me has a grain of crazy truth in it.

"What plans?"

"She was a trifle vague about it, but according to Zosima, when the three of them have got rid of her for good they want to arrange some sort of psychic wedding ceremony involving me and Clémence—not for our benefit, but for theirs. It doesn't make much sense, but the straw they appear to be clutching at is the idea that under the effects of psychic magnetism I can forge telepathic links, not merely between myself and others but between those other parties. According to Zosima, Lilith wants to hypnotize me in order to leech my secret power and turn it to her own ends."

"Well, they're probably crazy enough to believe it. What was Salome doing out of her cage, though? I thought the sisters weren't allowed to talk to you."

"That's over. Monique's accident broke the ice. Zosima took me aside when she and her minions came to collect her, and that prompted Lilith to put in an appearance. Then Zosima came back to make her pitch. She's built an entire biography for me on the foundation of the idea that Amélie was responsible for screwing up my relationships with women."

"The bitch. Let's hope she doesn't talk to Gaston. But why? What does she want from you?"

"According to her, she wants to protect me. She says that she wouldn't dream of magnetizing me again, but she's probably lying, hoping that I'll beg her to defend me against Lilith's supposed machinations, on the principle of better the devil you know than the one you don't. As I was just suggesting to Salome, though, charlatans are notoriously prone to fall for their own theories. The last time Zosima hypnotized me, supposedly on Rochemure's behalf, she tried to induce me to summon the spirit of Talia Cadelan. I suspect that, like her clients, she feels a need for forgiveness. She's told me more than once that she feels direly responsible for Talia's premature death, and I think that she really did love her, even though she exploited Talia's love for her instead of reciprocating it as Talia would have wished."

"It's a crazy world," was Victor's only comment in response to that.

"It must be nice to be as carefree as you are," Paul said. "You and Gaston have never put a foot wrong in life, have you? Everything has gone exactly to plan, whereas I...what's the matter?"

Victor was frowning deeply. "Is that really what you think?" he said. "Gaston thinks the same, I think. Stupid, isn't it, that I've always envied him while he was envying me? Not that I haven't tried with all my might to make myself seem enviable—but I never thought I was fooling you. I always thought that you knew what a hollow sham I was...am. And now you've met Monique. How you must despise me!"

Paul was astounded. "Why would I despise you?" he said. "I already told you that she didn't say a word against you. Yes, of course I've always known that you put on an act, just as we all do, that you're not really the dashing playboy you pretend to be, but that never made you any less enviable, in my eyes. It's over now, anyway, and you're marrying Clorinde. Who wouldn't envy you that? Or has something happened between you?"

"No," he said, his hands gripping the steering-wheel tightly and his eyes on the road ahead. "Not yet."

"Not yet? Is something going to happen then? Apart from your enjoying a pleasant honeymoon, like Gaston and Armande, and then living happily ever after in domestic bliss?"

"Don't be so bloody sarcastic. It's bad enough watching Gaston and Armande without you adding your snide commentary. You, of all people know that I'm not cut out for it, that I'm not Gaston. Oh, I can play the fiancé—everybody can play the fiancé, it's such an easy script. But the husband? That's a very different role. And I don't want to let her down. I can tolerate your being able to see through me, but her...I don't think I could stand that."

"I wasn't being sarcastic," Paul said, feebly. "If I sounded as if I were, I'm truly sorry. As for seeing through you...well, yes, you've always been a bit of a poseur, but that's just the way you are. It doesn't make you any less likeable, or admirable. I've always appreciated the bonhomie, and never minded in the least that it was a little bit forced—I always thought that it was very good of you to make the effort, even for people of no real consequence, like me."

"The false modesty has never been one of your better points," Victor retorted, but seemed to repent of it immediately. "You're serious, aren't you?" he said. "But you still couldn't wait to throw it in my face that you knew about Monique, could you?"

"I didn't think of it as throwing it in your face," Paul said. "But I suppose you're right—no, I couldn't wait. It was amusing...I didn't think..."

"Big news!" Victor remarked. "Paul Furneret didn't think! That's something that's never happened before! But it's all part of his charm...no, cancel all that. How can I snap at you for being sarcastic and then go on like that? How can I complain that you might despise me and then go out of my way to make myself despicable? I'm sorry. You touched a nerve, that's all...and not deliberately. She really doesn't hate me?"

"She gave no indication of it to me."

There was a brief silence. Paul looked sideways at the sloping vineyard alongside which they were passing, beyond the poplars that lines the road. As promised, Victor was taking the scenic route back to Toulouse, but like the proverbial Rome, the city was where all the local roads eventually led, and its steeples and outskirts were already visible whenever the automobile topped a rise.

"She should," opined Victor, eventually. "I treated her very badly, first in Toulouse, and then, again in Paris. I felt guilty then about the part I'd played in what she'd become, but it didn't stop me exploiting what she'd become. I never loved her, even though I told her I did in the beginning—everybody does, you know, except you—but even when the truth was manifest...well, when I could have her just by paying her, I still wanted her...occasionally. You have no idea how scared I was, when you asked Juliette to model for you, that she would be sure to tell you about me and Monique."

"I doubt that she even knew," Paul observed, "but if she did, she wouldn't have considered it a matter of consequence, anything worth mentioning. She can't have been the only one of her friends that you paid, and she had no reason to think that Monique was any different from the others."

"Don't rub it in," said Victor. "You're right, obviously. And what difference would it have made if you'd known? But it seemed to me that it might. It seemed to me that you might despise me...especially when you didn't want to touch Juliette at first, and only slept with her in the end out of kindness. And then, you stuck with her, all the way. I couldn't have done that. Nobody could, I'm sure, except you. I thought you were an utter idiot...but I admired you for it."

"You did mention, I believe, more than once, that you thought I was a idiot...you didn't mention the second part, though."

"Well, I wouldn't, would I? Victor Marvaud admit that someone was a better man than him...even his closest friend? Impossible. But you are, in spite of not knowing what's good for you...and so is Gaston, because he knows exactly what's good for him."

"But we're still the best of friends," Paul reminded him, albeit without the perfect confidence he would once have put into the observation. "Do you think the Three Maries are any freer than we are from those kinds of suspicions and feelings?"

"Who can tell?" Victor said, probably glad to catch sight of neutral ground. "But they must be doing something right, as they've stuck it out for twelve to fifteen years longer than we have. They're old enough to be our mothers, just about. I'd love to know what my mother really thought of them—too late to ask her now of course. They were all orphaned too, I expect, long before they reached our age, but can they really love one another? Of a couple, I could believe it...but three of them? That really would be a magical marriage."

You know what they say about three in a fiacre, Paul though, remembering the occasion when he had first heard the saying, outside Juvisy railway station.

"Yes," he said. "I suppose it would."

But that can't be what all this is about, he thought. *They're in their forties, for God's sake. If they've come this far, and made such progress, surely they must be confident of one another by now. But what was Salome really doing at the cleft? If she was simply trying to put distance between herself and Zosima, why go there?*

"Well," said Victor, as they came into the outskirts of Toulouse. "That didn't go as planned. It's all your fault, you know. You had to go and bring up Monique. If you had just kept quiet, the way I have for the last ten years...and then that old joke about Amélie. They're all mad, you know. You really ought to come back to Paris. It's not too late to find you a Clorinde of your own. It would do you the world of good. You can see that, can't you?"

"I can see it," Paul admitted. "But that doesn't mean that I can do it. I'm not like you and Gaston; I never have been. I know you have my best interests at heart, and I'm grateful, but

I can only do what I can do...and mostly, that's paint. And it seems that I can only do that, much of the time, while semi-entranced. Perhaps it's curable...but what would I be if I were cured, and no longer a painter? With all due respect to you and Gaston, I wouldn't want any job that either of you was willing and able to give me. I'm the painter of the dead, and I honestly don't think that I could ever have been anything else."

"I believe you," Victor said "Do you want me to drop you at the ancestral manse of the Sancerres, now a shrine to *trouvère* art, or at Jean-Bénigne Lambrunet's similar ruin-in-waiting?"

"The former. Why would I want you to take me to Jean-Bénigne Lambrunet's house?"

"Didn't Gaston tell you that he wanted to see you next time you were in Toulouse? I'm sure he did—and he's repeated the insistence since we last saw you. I should have mentioned it, I suppose, but we got sidetracked. Anyway, the old boy obviously can't get around much anymore, and was relying on us to persuade you to drop in. It would be a kindness to do that, when you've seen Clémence...and, I suppose, the English couple, if you still have business with them."

"I have," Paul confirmed, wondering whether he had any chance now of getting back to the cottage while there was still a chance of completing the portrait of Jane today.

The car had stopped, and Paul made as if to climb out.

"Just a second," Victor said. "If you need me to take you back, you know where to find me. I'll be glad to do it, although I might have to drop you in the village rather than risk that final stretch again." He hesitated visibly.

"And?" Paul prompted.

"Just a thought," Victor said, in a low voice. "Monique knew Scarab...Juliette. She was with her that night when you were at Antoine Cros's house, and she saw her while she was helping you to fend off reporters wanting to keep the lifeboat story alive, didn't she?"

"That's right," Paul confirmed.

"Well, if I know her—and I did—she'll be back. She knows that you have SOFT TOUCH written on your forehead in letters of fire. Try not to be too kind to her, will you?"

"For my sake, or yours?"

"Yours, obviously."

Obviously, Paul thought, a trifle sarcastically. Aloud, as he climbed out of the Panhard, he said: "Don't worry—she'll never get past the guard-dog."

CHAPTER XI

When Paul had traversed the courtyard of what Victor had termed "the ancestral manse of the Sancerres" he thought about ringing the doorbell, even though he did not usually bother, having long ago received *carte blanche* to go in and out as he pleased without being formally introduced and announced, but after a momentary pause he opened the unlocked door and he strode through the corridor to the artist's studio. There again he thought about knocking, but again he simply opened the door and went in. At that hour of the morning the artist was almost always alone and working, and hated having to interrupt herself in order to get up and answer the door.

Today, however was an exception. The studio, enormous as it was, almost seemed crowded, qualitatively if not quantitatively. Clémence was not at her easel; she was in the process of moving round the perimeter of her huge workshop, showing off the works that she retained there, as advertisements for her talents or for personal reasons. She was indicating them, one by one, to four visitors: Richard and Ellen Megister, and two women in capacious nunnish habits. One of the latter was Sister Lilith; the other was shorter and stouter, and her hood was up, hiding her face, but Paul knew that he would not have recognized it anyway. Evidently, Lilith and Justine had not been long delayed in the notary's office settling the "technical details" that would make triumvirate—provisionally, at least—the legal mistresses of their Temple of the Triple Goddess.

Clémence hardly had time to salute him, and he only contrived to exchange a nod of the head with Richard Megister before Lilith excused herself from the guided tour, saying that she needed a brief but important word with Paul. She drew him into a remote corner of the room with imperious urgency.

"I apologize for my rudeness and my selfishness," she said, "but I'm very anxious to know what impression Zosima made on you last night with the demolition of my character that she must have attempted. She is not a good loser, I fear— the legacy, no doubt, of spending her formative years in Cairo and Naples."

"In fact," said Paul, guardedly, "she came to talk about old times, mostly about me. She's been kind enough to take an interest in my art and my career, and we have been out of touch for some time. She did mention that there were internal disagreements within her Order, but only to say that they were no concern of mine and would be of no interest to me."

"Indeed?" said Lilith, skeptically. "I'm delighted to hear it. Now that the rules of the convent can be relaxed considerably, and communication with wider society will become much easier, I would like us to be good neighbors, and I would not want that opportunity to be spoiled by idle gossip."

Paul tried to recall what he had said to Marie Salome, and to wonder what she might have understood by it. Perhaps nothing, given that it was all fantasy and hasty improvisation, akin in some ways to his entranced drawing, except that the contribution of the unconscious had all been filtered through his consciousness, reformed and sculpted. Nevertheless, he thought, the conversation might not have been very conducive to good neighborly relations between himself and the convent, and was definitely at odds with the defensive strategy he had automatically adopted in replying to Lilith's question about Zosima.

All is confusion, he said to himself, philosophically, *but in that confusion, there are glittering flecks on meaning, which merely have to be filtered, cleaned and fused to make ingots of truth. But I really must try to save that poetic streak for my art. What's got into me lately?*

"Have no fear, Madame Lilith" he said to his interlocutor. "I had a long chat this morning with Sister Salome, and although she proved slightly taciturn, I think we might have laid the foundations for an understanding."

If Lilith was annoyed by that revelation, she was careful not to show it. "That's good," she said rather slowly, while she paused for thought. "Was she by any chance, standing by the Great Cleft?"

"Yes she was," Paul confirmed, surprised by the question. "How did you guess?"

"She has always been fascinated by it. I suspected that as soon as the restriction was lifted, she might go to peer into it. The bounds of the convent's terrain once extended far enough to contain it, and I hope they might again one day—but you need not have any fear for your home, which will remain sacrosanct."

"In spite of the polluting effect of a male presence within your domain?"

"There are some pollutions of which the world will only be cleansed with great difficulty—but everyone to whom I speak assures me that you are less of a stain on human nature than most."

"I believe that's the greatest compliment I've been paid in quite some time," Paul retorted, assuming that he was matching sarcasm with sarcasm.

"I know that's not true," Lilith replied, serenely. "I have paid you better ones myself, and I know that you have received even more flattering ones from Mademoiselle Ellen over there, who is longing to have you paint her portrait. I think, one way or another, that she will get her way. But you must be eager to speak to Madame Sancerre, and I ought to keep my rudeness to a minimum. I need to speak to you about an important matter. Would it be convenient for me to come to your cottage this evening?"

"What important matter?" Paul hedged.

Lilith hesitated, glancing at the party studying one of Clémence's many depictions of Clémence Isaure, elaborately attended by symbolic flowers. Ellen Megister seemed to be showing a genuine interest, but Richard was not bothering to conceal his ennui, and Justine also seemed voluntarily isolated. Although it was difficult to tell while she was swathed in the loose robe with the capacious hood, her stance seemed distinctly uncomfortable.

"It's a personal matter," Lilith said, eventually.

"Really?" said Paul. "How can you and I have any personal matters to discuss?"

He realized immediately that he had provided her with exactly the cue that she wanted.

"I was with your mother when she died," the would-be magicienne said, with a devastating casualness. "I—and I alone—received her last request."

If that was a brazen lie, Paul thought, then it was an exceedingly bold one. But he knew that it was not impossible. If the three Maries had known Amélie Lambrunet, then they had surely known his mother, who had been a close friend of Amélie's. And although the three strange friends must have been young when he was born—not yet twenty—they would only have been a few years younger than his mother. Amélie must have recently give birth herself when his mother had given birth, and would still have been confined. It would have been perfectly normal for their sorority to lend support to the midwives in such circumstances, tokenistic unless something went wrong...as it had in his mother's case.

"I see," he said, as calmly as he could, remembering that he had drawn his mother during the night only a few days ago, and Amélie Lambrunet only a few days after that, as if in anticipation of their return to his conscious concern. "Yes, in that case, I'll be glad to speak with you later today. I need to speak with the Megisters as well as Clémence, and while I'm in the city I ought to call in on Jean-Bénigne Lambrunet, who is apparently not in good enough health to make the journey to the mountain, but after that, Victor Marvaud has offered to drive me home in his auto. Would you like me to ask him to take you and Sister Justine back too?"

"No, thank you," Sister Lilith replied. "But I will come to see you this evening, if I may."

"Of course."

She nodded, satisfied. "In that case," she said, "Sister Justine and I will leave you to your important discussions."

As they turned in order to return to the group in front of Clémence Isaure, however, Richard Megister, who had evidently been waiting for their conversation to end, immediately detached himself from the three women and strode across the room purposively.

"Excuse me," he said, brusquely, to Lilith, in English, "but if you've finished, I need a private word with Monsieur Furneret myself."

"Of course," said Lilith, granting the permission with a queenly condescension—and she too traversed the room, with a shorter stride, but with a grace that still exhibited, even within her unflattering brown robe, the legacy of distant lessons in deportment. Paul remained where he was.

Richard Megister waited until she was out of earshot before saying, in a low voice: "Is that woman mad, do you think?"

"I don't know her well enough to make a judgment," Paul said, judiciously.

"She seems to have taken over the convent in some kind of palace coup, and she's talking about expanding its grounds, although I can't think why, and diverting springs with concrete dams. Almost as bizarre as those fellows from the university—they're going back today, apparently, with a larger crew and a lot more rope. Monsieur Lambrunet says that they're wasting their time, risking a fatal fall for no possible reward, but they seem determined. The notary assures me that I have no liability, but I'm regretting having granted that permission. In fact, I'm beginning to wish that I'd stayed at home."

"I'm sorry you feel that way," said Paul, equably. "I'm sure that we're all doing our best to be hospitable."

"That's the problem" the Englishman muttered. "Between you and that weird woman, you've put it into Ellen's head that she simply has to have her portrait by you. I even suggested, as a last resort, that she get Madame Sancerre to do it instead, but she only weighed with the rest of them in recommending you. Ellen simply won't take no for an answer, so I'll have to give in—but I have conditions."

"What are they?" Paul enquired.

"Well, I've thought it over, and I'd rather you painted the picture in your own studio than here. I can give you three days, no more, starting tomorrow. I'll come with her in the car and bring her back after the sitting. If you don't want me to watch I'll take a stroll in your woods. Everyone assures me that Ellen will be perfectly safe with you, that you're a man of unimpeachable honor, and that your housekeeper is a perfectly adequate chaperone, but one can't be too careful with a sister's reputation. There are people back home who think that crossing the Channel is practically a compromise in itself. And I won't pay a penny more than two hundred guineas. I can get it done for that in London by a Royal Academician."

Paul seriously doubted the last assertion, but he had no interest in haggling or arguing.

"That's all fine," he said. "I'll expect you tomorrow morning—and thank you very much for the commission."

"You're welcome," Megister said, with blatant insincerity. "I can't think what's got into the girl. She's almost of age, I know, but it doesn't do in London society for an unmarried woman to get a reputation for being headstrong. She's already turned down two perfectly reasonable requests that I've had for her, saying that she's not ready for marriage yet. I've told her that there's a fine line between not being ready yet and being on the shelf, but she doesn't listen. The bluestockings have a lot to answer for—corrupting an entire generation. Do you have bluestockings in France?"

"We do," Paul confirmed. "We even take leave to think that we had them before you did, although our ancestors called them *femmes savantes*."

"Wise women? I thought they were midwives—or witches?"

"No, that's *sage-femmes*—but I fear that we're being rather rude, although I'm sure your sister is perfectly safe in the care of the good sisters and Clémence."

Richard Megister looked at him sharply, evidently wondering whether he was being sarcastic, having probably formed his own judgment as to how safe his sister would be in such company, and immediately began to cross the room again.

When Richard had told Ellen that an agreement had been reached, the young woman performed a little skip, which might have been a respectable Englishwoman's version of jumping for joy. "That's so kind of you," she said to Paul. "You didn't have to agree to Richard's absurd conditions, I assure you, but I'm so glad that you have, because it saves us from further discord. It will make this entire trip worthwhile— which I'm sure in spite of Richard's assurances, Nice and Monte Carlo wouldn't have been able to do."

"Only too true, I fear," Clémence put in. "They're terrible dens of vice nowadays, full of Var nobility and other fortune-hunters. Biarritz is no better, alas. I hear that automobile races along the Corniche have become very popular, though, in spite of all the dreadful crashes. Do you race your automobile, Monsieur Megister?"

"No," replied Richard, shortly. "It's strictly utilitarian."

"How very practical," said Clémence, with a slight contrived sigh. "But you've always admired English practicality, haven't you, Paul? You'd be a stern utilitarian yourself if it weren't for the spur of your Muse."

Paul declined to respond to that gibe, which gave Sister Lilith the opportunity to intervene and take her leave on behalf or herself and the taciturn Sister Justine, who seemed to Paul to be more than a little uncomfortable, perhaps because her obesity was unused to as much activity as the excursion had forced upon it. Richard Megister was quick to drag Ellen away thereafter, although the young woman gave the impression very strongly that she would rather have continued her discussions with Clémence regarding her namesake, the ancient troubadours, and the importance of the annual floral games.

Left alone with Clémence, Paul attempted to collect his thoughts before broaching the matters that he wanted to discuss with her.

"Your landlord seems a trifle upset," Clémence observed., "I assume that it's not your fault—that you just happened to provide a convenient pretext for the young lady to rebel against what she presumably perceives as unjust oppression?"

"That seems to be the case," Paul agreed. "Perhaps I should have turned down the commission."

"Absolutely not. When dragged into a dispute reluctantly, it's merely a matter of taking the right side. Lilith dragged them here after completing her takeover bid for the convent at the notary's étude. It took the gentleman all of five minutes to decide, on observing that Lilith and I were old acquaintances, that his sister would be in more moral danger here than in your cottage, in spite of the fact that the Lesbian Empire is within walking distance of your cottage and that I'm not, as he would probably put it, 'that way inclined.' I gather that he's been trying to marry her off in London, without much success."

"So it seems," said Paul, "but as you say, it's probably just rebellion against oppression; she probably wants to choose her own husband, if she can escape the surveillance long enough to search for one."

"She's already found you," Clémence pointed out.

"I doubt that she's that desperate," said Paul. "How old is your acquaintance with Lilith?"

"It goes way back, albeit is a relative slight fashion. Amélie Lambrunet introduced us when I first got the vocation, back in my teens. We had common interests for a while, but we lost touch when she went to Paris. When she came back she was virtually confined to the convent for a while, but recently, she and Salome have been coming to town quite regularly. And yes, before you ask, she has asked me lots of questions about you, and no, I don't know why, and I hope that I haven't been indiscreet in what I've told her. I've been as evasive as I could, but I didn't think that you had any secrets—none that I know about, anyhow."

"Amélie Lambrunet introduced you, you say? So you knew Amélie well, then?"

"Fairly well. You knew that—I told you ages ago, when we first met. You didn't seem interested—just a sorority acquaintance, you thought, quite rightly.

"And she and Lilith were friends?"

"Not close friends, but amicable. I was too young to keep track of the way things developed, but I gather that Amélie stuck by her when she, Salome and Justine were eased out of the social circuit. To begin with, as you can imagine, the three of them were regarded as good friends, but as the realization grew that they were more than just friends, the barriers began to form. Knowing how the circuit works, I presume that no formal anathema was ever pronounced, but they were gradually excluded from one salon after another, and edged out even of the organization of the games. But Amélie refused to treat them as pariahs, and did what she could to protect them. You know what she was like, having benefited from the same instinct."

"Yes, I do," Paul agreed. "She was a remarkably kind person."

"She was good to me too. Of course, she and Lilith had interests in common...unorthodox genealogy, I suppose you could call it."

"How can genealogy be unorthodox?"

"Easily. Orthodox genealogy, preoccupied with the inheritance of titles and surnames, calculates relationships through the male line; family trees are compiled primarily by linking fathers to sons. Women come into the tree from outside, their status within it primarily determined by their fathers and forefathers. Amélie and Lilith were interested in compiling trees in which priority was given to female lines of descent, paying no attention to titles—at least, not to titles in the orthodox sense."

"You mean that they were ardent Occitan Marians, trying to calculate lines of descent that led back to supposed descendants of the legendary three Maries?"

"Obviously. Why do you think Lilith, Salome and Justine started calling themselves the Three Maries?"

"Because there were three of them?"

"Well, that, obviously, but they wanted the number to be more than just a number. You know how things are in these parts—there was no shortage of theories about the identity of the mythical Maries, and Lilith simply had to chose the one than suited her best. Naturally, she picked one that allowed the original three Maries to be bisexual, lovers as well as carriers of the holy seed. Having chosen one they simply tailored and elaborated it to their own liking. They figured in unorthodox genealogy first, and then began developing more fanciful ides of heredity, including the idea that only women could pass memories of past generations down to their descendants, because such memories were stored in ova, not in sperm. Recent developments in science seems to have encouraged them greatly in that—natural science as well as occult science."

"And Amélie Lambrunet believed all that?"

"Well, not all of it, because some of the refinements are recent, and belief might be too strong a word, but she was certainly interested in it, and she had the key resource by which it could be elaborated."

"Uncle Jean-Bénigne."

"Exactly. He was sitting in a mountain of documents, including a considerable number filched from the city archives—not by him, I hasten to add, and his grandfather or great-grandfather probably didn't think of it as filching. One way or another, though, he had a lot of documents, which were only interested in titles and family names, but which nevertheless enabled some calculations to be made regarding lines of maternal descent. It's just a game, of course. If you go back a sufficient number of generations you'd probably find that everyone is related to everyone, but Amélie certainly believed that she had identified a number of what she called true

Marians—including her and Lilith, naturally, Salome and Justine—and me, as it happens."

"And my mother?" Paul queried.

"I wouldn't know about that—I was only ten when you mother died and I didn't become acquainted with Amélie until some years afterwards—but it wouldn't surprise me in the least. She always talked about her fondly, in connection with you."

"She didn't happen to mention, I suppose who was present at my mother's deathbed?"

"No, why would she? How could she even have known, given your mother died in childbirth and Gaston is only a couple of weeks older than you. She couldn't have been present herself. Why ask such a strange question?"

"Because Lilith just told me that she was there, and implied very forcefully that my mother gave her some secret instruction which she has been carefully keeping from me for the more than thirty years, but is now prepared to reveal."

"Really? Well, I'd take it with a pinch of salt, if I were you. She's a friend, I suppose, but she really does have bats in her belfry, which ring some very strange carillons. She and the truth lost meaningful contact a long time ago."

"So I gather. And one of those carillons, I've been told—admittedly from a not very reliable source—concerns you, me and an alchemical wedding."

Clémence laughed, but Paul thought that the laughter seemed a trifle forced.

"She hasn't said anything to you about any such thing?"

"No. She has been very curious about our relationship, but I thought her hidden agenda there was trying to ascertain that we weren't together, rather than that we were or might be. I conceived the idea long ago that Lilith's sexual appetites weren't entirely slaked by her relationship with her weird sisters. Recently, she's been quite openly trying to recruit me to her company of fellow travelers—souls sympathetic to the ideal of the convent without actually wanting to live in poverty and pretend to be heretic nuns—but that's understandable.

She's been casting her tentative net quite widely, and if she's made a mistake about my inclinations she wouldn't be the first, by any means. Nor would she be the first to be puzzled about our relationship and provoked to make up fanciful explanations for it."

"Why does it need any explanation?" Paul asked. "We're fellow artists, with technical and thematic interests in common. Why wouldn't we be friends?"

"Why indeed? And six years ago, we had more in common than that. My husband died within weeks of your mistress. It seemed only natural to the local gossips that we sympathized with one another—pooling our grief, as it were. Naturally, the rumor spread that we were probably pooling more than our grief, and further developments were awaited. I'm ten years older than you, so nobody seriously expected wedding bells, but they did expect...well, more than there actually is. You have to remember that people who aren't artists can't imagine that you could come to my studio regularly just to watch me paint, and talk about what I'm doing and how, and exchange advice and opinions about what we paint and how. In their minds, man plus woman adds up to fornication. It was just a low level puzzle of no interest of course, until the Lambrunet cousins started stirring the pot with a healthy seasoning of malice. I won't say that it's become ugly since then, but it's certainly become more grotesque."

"You mean the three cousins that Gaston introduced me to, one after another? But nothing happened."

"Exactly. The first one probably wasn't that interested, at first, but nobody likes being rejected. Being a man, poor Gaston doesn't really understand the logic of these situations, any more than you do, so, having tried once and failed, he simply tried again. That introduced an element of competition into the matter. The cousins love one another, of course, but that doesn't diminish the appetite to best one another. So the second was even more disappointed than the first when nothing came of it. But when you rejected the third as well...perhaps you've heard the saying that once is happenstance, twice is coincidence but three times is something fishy going on. They started looking for explanations. Naturally, one possibility that sprung to mind was that you weren't interested in them—the cream of what Toulouse had to offer in terms of female marriage fodder—because you were pining after me, which prompted the corollary question of why, if you were pining after me, I was rejecting you, given that I was a widow whose period of decent mourning was surely over. Hence suspicions about my inclinations as well as yours. As you scrupulously pointed out, nothing has happened, between us or between either of us and anyone else...but can't you see how suspicious that nothing seems, especially to three competitive cousins formally offered and carelessly spurned?"

"I hadn't thought about it," Paul admitted.

"I know. But your not thinking about it doesn't compel others not think about it, even though it's none of their business. Compared with Paris, upper bourgeois society in Toulouse is a small world, which doesn't have a great many topics of conversation, and you're famous, in an odd way. You've won medals in the Paris salon. Your spirit paintings were on the front pages of newspapers sold all over France...and you're practically an adoptive son of the Lambrunets. You might think that living way out there on your mountain, with your equally mysterious housekeeper, isolates you from the world, but that's not the way society works in the city. It just makes you more enigmatic. Nobody knows what to make of you, and that annoys them. Perhaps it shouldn't but it does,"

Paul shook his head. "But you understand?" he said more tentatively than he could have wished.

"Do I? I know that in the last five years, when you might plausibly have made advances to me if you actually had been interested in me in that way, you've never made a move, but I don't know why. Naturally, I'm reluctant to think that I'm ugly, or that I lack charm, so I tend to fall back on my age, but the way you talk about your late author friend, without ever saying anything explicit, certainly led me to think that your feelings for her weren't deterred by her age, which was ten years in advance of mine, and that you were far more distressed by the fact that she was married. Then again, perhaps it isn't a matter of competing with the living but with the dead. I've been in your dining room; I've seen Juliette on your wall, and I've never been convinced for one second by your relentless insistence that you never loved her. So, although I can see possibilities, I really don't know what to think, and I have to admit that I don't really understand you at all."

"That makes two of us," said Paul, sullenly. "And if I've never said anything or one anything to indicate that kind of interest, nor have you."

"The situations aren't parallel, Paul. It's not a woman's prerogative. But you're right—it would be unjust to put all the responsibility in you. If I'd ever wanted to take our relationship further, I could have maneuvered you into an admission or declaration, even at the expense of my pride in having to resort to it. But I've been perfectly content with the way things are. If you had made a move, I probably wouldn't have said no, any more than I said no to my husband and might possibly not say no if someone else were to come along who had a avid interest, but I'm not avid myself. I've tried it, done the whole thing, beginning to end, and I don't feel any particular need to repeat the experiment. I know what I'm missing, so I have no curiosity any more. And if I had expressed an interest explicitly, how would you have reacted?"

After a pause for thought, Paul said: "I probably wouldn't have said no."

"Well, that's a relief, albeit not much of a compliment. But on the whole, you're grateful that I never did?"

Instead of answering that question, Paul said "Ten years or so ago, did you know a local girl named Monique, about my age or a year or two older—a friend of Victor's?"

"One of the coquettes that your friend Victor chased so relentlessly, you mean? I don't think so, although the name does ring a bell. Why not ask Victor? If I remember rightly, he caught most of them in the end, and then threw them back, typically. Why that particular way of changing the subject?"

"She's in the convent now. She was hurt when the vege-table cart she was driving broke a wheel in the storm a couple of nights ago. I didn't remember her at all, but she remembered me, from both Toulouse and Paris. She knew Juliette."

"Ah. And you've mortally offended her by not remembering her? She thought she was ignoring you, and it turns out that you were oblivious to her existence. How humiliating."

"That's what she said. She was the one who told me that Lilith has plans that involve you, me and an alchemical marriage. It was something she overheard."

"Really? People who listen at keyholes never get the full story, and you can be sure that if here's a stick to be grasped, they'll get hold of the wrong end of it."

"I suppose so—but Lilith does seem to have a plan of some sort. Did Amélie Lambrunet ever tell you that she had hypnotized me when I was fifteen or thereabouts, in order to plant a post-hypnotic suggestion?"

"Yes—to keep your newly-lecherous hands of her darling daughter. She seemed rather proud of the fact that it seemed to have worked. Nobody believed her, of course—that it had worked, that is. Everybody knew how shy you were. They were ready enough to believe that she had tried, but they thought that she was just trying to claim credit for nature. Surely you don't think that's why you've never made advances to me? You were living with Juliette when I first met you, remember, and you didn't seem to have had any difficulty making advances to her."

Paul did not correct the misapprehension. "Zosima is convinced that Amélie succeeded, more extravagantly than she had hoped."

"And you believe her?"

"No—but it was food for thought. If you've known about Amélie's claim all these years, why have you never mentioned it?"

"Because it would have been in rank bad taste to do so. Somebody must have mentioned it to you, though—you can't possibly have been unaware of it all these years."

"No, they didn't, and yes, I have. But that's not the point—the point is that if Zosima believes it, Lilith might be believe it too."

"I doubt it. She knew Amélie, and wouldn't have taken her seriously on that matter. If she's the one who told Zosima, though, she might have misrepresented her opinion deliberately. I gather that she doesn't like Zosima very much, perhaps because they have so much in common, and she's had no compunction about deposing her from her position of authority in the convent—which must have been easy enough, I suppose, in a community where there isn't supposed to be any authority. Do you care?"

"About that, no—about what lies behind it, perhaps."

"You think one or other of them is going to try to magnetize you again, with or without your consent?"

"I'm certain of it. But why? What do they think I can do?"

"Raise the dead, if only within illusions."

"Perhaps so. And perhaps, in Zosima's case, the dead person she would like me to raise—if only in illusion—is Talia. But who does Lilith want me to raise?

"I don't know. Clémence Isaure? Marie Magdalen? Artemis? Does it matter? You can always say no. The more important question, surely, is: now that you have a fuller understanding what you can do than you had eight years ago, who do *you* want to raise, if you don't want to say no. From what you've told me, you didn't have a choice before."

"According to Talia, mediums never have a choice—and they're far more likely to provoke visions they don't want to see that those they do."

"And Talia is worthy of belief because...?"

"Fair point. She was generalizing from her own experience, which might not have been typical, for many different reasons."

"So, if she was wrong, answer my question. Who do you want to invoke? Amélie Lambrunet? Your mother?"

221

"I already have," Paul murmured. "Not to mention Juliette, Jane and a thousand more, most of them unidentifiable, most of them chimerical, some of them fetal and a few purely insectile. And I have no idea why."

"Poor Paul. I'm sorry I can't help, but you know full well that I have difficulty decoding my own symbolism, let alone yours—and mine, as you've occasionally pointed out, albeit while diplomatically beating around the bush, is all hackneyed, standardized stuff, the constant imagistic apparatus of the floral games, inherited from Medieval romance: hearts, flowers and the holy grail. At least you have a fertile imagination...perhaps even as much as Lilith, although I wouldn't care to bet on that."

"It has occurred to me that what she might want me to do is to help her to forge a more intimate psychic bond between her, Justine and Salome: to contrive a true psychic fusion between them, in which I wouldn't be involved at all, except as a catalyst."

"I wouldn't put it past her. In fact, given what your scrupulous informant told you it wouldn't surprise me entirely if that's where she might like to fit me in to her crazy scheme. Not everyone, it seems, is as immune to my charms as you are, faded as they are nowadays...but if Lilith thinks that she's get much sapphic joy out of a psychic fusion with me, she might be deeply disappointed...and confused. There are some things to which, if offered, I might not say no, but that's not one of them. And unless I'm much mistaken, she's not going to get much joy out of the little Englishwoman ether. You might, if you can be bothered, but not Lilith."

"You think Lilith has designs on Ellen Megister?"

"I think Lilith probably has designs on every pretty young woman she meets. If I can read a tight lip accurately, Justine thinks so too, although I suppose she might simply have been uncomfortable. Lilith certainly seemed to want Ellen to insist on your painting her portrait, and I don't think it was for your benefit. She probably thinks that you're not a significant rival."

"Richard won't let Lilith anywhere near his sister."

"If Ellen were willing, he wouldn't be able to stop her...but as I say, I can't imagine that she is. You, on the other hand..."

"Yes, you've made your point, but I have no intention of doing anything untoward. Even if I wanted to, what would be the point? In three days, she'll be gone, forever."

"O ye of little faith. If you wanted to, in three days she could be yours, forever. But believe me, she isn't worth it. Let her go, just like all the rest. You'll doubtless get your reward in Heaven, as you seem so utterly determined not to collect it here, but don't blame Amélie Lambrunet for that. The fault is not in your forgotten post-hypnotic suggestions, but in yourself. I can tell you that, because I'm your friend, and because I know that you'll always forgive me, even though you'll never love me."

"Because I have the words SOFT TOUCH branded on my forehead?"

"If you have," said Clémence, quietly. "It's false advertising."

"That's not what everyone else says."

"I know," she said, looking up at Clémence Isaure, who was smiling benignly at her creator, "but they don't know you as well as I do. They only know your diffident social persona, but I know the painter. They know the shell, but I know the soul."

"I wish I did," he said. "I met Salome this morning, for the first time, beside the Great Cleft. I was in a bad mood...or maybe just a strange mood. I told her that I'd seen her there before, in previous lives, and when she said that was impossible—I knew why because Gaston, Monique and Zosima had all told me about women being the only ones capable of remembering past lives—I told her that I was a psychic androgyne, because I'd absorbed my sister's soul in the womb when she died."

"And did she believe you?"

"I don't know; but looking back, I wonder whether her reaction might simply have been one of surprise—surprise that I knew. You don't believe it, then, given that you know my soul so well?"

Clémence laughed, but Paul thought the laughter slightly forced. "It's one way of looking at it," she said. "You've always been haunted by the idea of your twin having died in the womb, and there's at least a metaphorical sense in which you've taken her aboard, in the depths of your own soul. That's not what I meant when I said that I knew your soul, but it might just be a different way to expressing the same insight. The point is that you're not always a soft touch, n spite of your inclination to generosity. When the occasion warrants it, you're as hard as nails, and resilient.

"I didn't know you very well back then, but I know you looked after Juliette, almost unaided, out in that stupid cottage, while she took months to die horribly. That wasn't being a soft touch. I don't know whether it was heroism, or love, or something else, but there was nothing soft about it. And when you're painting, or drawing, you're utterly focused, relentless in your attention. Even when you're simply watching me paint, you're intent, concentrated...but it doesn't make me uncomfortable, strangely enough, because I know that it's sympathetic. You've never loved me, but you do love my painting, and you always seem to understand it better than I do."

Paul scanned the nearest wall with a sweeping gaze, taking in the faces, the flowers, the armored knights, the occasional dragon, the beautiful, glorious, wistful women, and the auroled jeweled cups: the symbolic grails. Clémence, he knew, did not think deeply or intensely about the symbolism of the various motifs; she simply painted the images that came to mind. He could not do that. He had to interrogate even the simplest images. By virtue of analyzing her art work, he had sometimes been able to explain her work—and hence her self—to Clémence, but he had never been convinced that he was doing her a favor by so doing. He knew that there was no point in asking her for a similar analysis of his own work, because that was not the way she operated—but still, she felt that she did know him, because she had an empathic understanding of his work, and she felt that she probably knew him better than anyone else. Perhaps she was right.

"Do you think I'm mad, Clémence?" he asked, thinking that she would probably gave him an honest answer, or at least a plausible one.

"Of course you are, my dear," she said "But what does it matter? You're an artist. You're mad to live in that ridiculous cottage on the mountain, between Lilith's sapphist colony and the Great Cleft—abundant symbolism there—and you're mad to have turned down all three of the Lambrunet cousins, even though they're just silly young women. You're probably as mad as me, and perhaps even as mad as Lilith. But while you have the spirits of the dead, and can paint them, what need have you of sanity?"

CHAPTER XII

"Thank you so much for calling, Monsieur Furneret," said Jean-Bénigne Lambrunet. "I've wanted to meet you for some time, but the thought of making the journey has always put me off. The last time I visited the mountain, some eight years ago, the after-effects informed me in no uncertain terms that I was no longer a young man, and I've only grown frailer since. Had I known twenty years ago what I know now, I could have undertaken some very interesting excavations, with the aid of a handful of laborers, but all the interesting sites are leased now."

"Except for the Great Cleft," Paul said, casually, while sipping the tea that the old man's maidservant had just poured for him.

"Well, I certainly wouldn't have wanted to try to go down there, at any age. Better men than me have tried, and never reached the bottom. The National Assembly commissioned a serious expedition in 1791, but it cost the lives of three men and they didn't get with sight of any bottom, solid or liquid. We have better equipment nowadays, of course, but if those professors from the university who asked Monsieur Megister for permission to make a descent get out safely, they'll come back empty-handed, I'm sure of it. I don't say that their geology is faulty, but I suspect very strongly that even if the National Assembly expedition's relay pitons are still in place or can easily be substituted by better steel, they won't find anything more than their predecessors. I have a copy of their report—the only surviving copy, I suspect, as the one they sent to Paris probably didn't arrive there until the Assembly had collapsed and the Convention had taken over the reins of government, bringing a very different philosophical atmosphere."

Paul had never heard the Terror described as a "philosophical atmosphere" before, but he made no comment on the idiosyncratic discretion. "Why did the National Assembly commission the descent?" he asked.

"Chasing a myth—foolishly, in my opinion."

"The myth of the Holy Grail? Why on earth would the Revolutionaries have sent men on a wild goose chase like that?"

"They were chasing wild geese of a very different myth species. When the National Assembly seized church property and started expelling recalcitrant monks and nuns from their convents by force there was an outcry, and a brief propaganda war. It may seem absurd today, but one of the key items of anti-clerical propaganda at the time was that dissolute nuns used to discard the bodies of their new-born bastard children in wells or oubliettes, where their tiny bones accumulated. Unfortunately for them, the anti-clerical brigade had great difficulty finding any evidence to support the claim. Local rumor had long suggested that the nuns of the Cistercian Abbey on the mountain had been throwing the bodies of babies into the Cleft, but in my opinion, the legend was an adaptation of a much older story—much as the convent itself was an adaptation of a sacred site whose occupation and use went back more than two thousand years, to a temple built by emigrants or refugees from Massalia, and probably to an earlier temple dedicated to a goddess whose name has been lost."

"You mean that the story of babies being thrown into the Cleft might date from pagan times—like tales of Druid human sacrifices?"

"Similar, especially in being formulated in much the same sprit as slanderous propaganda. I don't believe, personally, that such accusations are worth any more than the loathsomely lurid propaganda that Roman persecutors employed against early Christians, or that Christian persecutors have repeatedly employed against Jews. In my opinion, the persistence of such tales over centuries, or millennia, is not evidence that anyone ever threw any babies into the Great Cleft. Such stories owe their grip on the human imagination to their element of horror, not to any kernel of truth."

What Paul had said to Salome on the edge of the cleft—an improvisation inspired on the spot with the aid of the Muse—returned to his mind, with a slight twinge of embarrassment. Why, he wondered, had he done that? Had the poor woman ever done him any harm? Why had he attacked her in that sly manner? He took what comfort he could from the fact that Salome had seemed to weather the strange assault serenely enough.

"The fervent anti-clerical National Assembly members had no difficulty in believing in infanticidal nuns," Jean-Bénigne went on, "but as good rationalists, they didn't believe that the Cleft could really be bottomless, and probably took some slight exception to that myth too. At any rate, they dispatched orders from Paris to Toulouse to send men down to explore. As I said, three died—presumably, since no bodies were recovered—and no solid or liquid bottom was discovered. That was the last serious expedition. The sludge accessible at the bottom of the other two clefts led people to hypothesize that something similar must lie at the bottom of the great cleft, albeit at a greater depth, but no one knows for sure. Logically, of course the fissures must end somewhere in solid rock, probably with deep water above that bed, but that doesn't mean that reaching the bed in question will ever be practical for human beings."

"Especially if the fissure is the shaft of an extinct volcano, with the central fire still lurking beneath it," Paul suggested.

"The so-called central fire is another myth," Jean-Bénigne said, shaking his head skeptically, "but as I say, I don't dispute the geologists at the university. Their latest theory is that the mountain isn't volcanic in the sense that it ever spouted clouds of steam and dust and streams of molten rock in an explosive fashion, but that events far below the surface elevated a section of the crust like a blister, and caused the rock to split along a number of innate fault-lines. Even the lesser clefts haven't been filled up in, as solid matter accumulates beneath the variable liquid surfaces, hence the hypothesis of subterranean flows of mud ferrying the descended material away. But events far below the surface are of very little significance to us. I'm far more interested in the figuration of mountain in local legend, and more particularly in the refiguration of legend that has taken place within my lifetime. You knew my cousin Amélie quite well, I believe?"

"Not as well as I thought," Paul observed, wryly. "She was kind to me when I was a child, and I was very grateful for her kindness, but I didn't really know her. I knew nothing about her interest in unorthodox genealogy until Clémence Sancerre told me about it a little while ago—a trifle belatedly, it seems to me, as I've known her for six years without her saying a word about it."

"You can't blame her for that. Sorority secrets aren't kept very closely, but they tend to leak rather selectively. I'm not supposed to know anything about it either, but there was no way that Amélie could obtain the information she wanted from me without my knowing what she was looking for, and without my figuring out why. I come from a long line of antiquarians, as you probably know, and three generations of my forefathers have been interested in the genealogy of various Toulousan families—especially, obviously, the Lambrunets. That interest, like the name, has been handed down from father to son, that being the way that inheritance is organized in our society. When we search the past we look for male ancestors, regarding women as mere bit-part players in history. Amélie, as what the English call a bluestocking, or a feminist in more modern jargon, was primarily interested in ancestresses, and in tracing lines of decent from mother to daughter."

"Because she had a mystical theory about the heredity of ancestral memories and certain psychic abilities only being transmissible across the generations via ova and not via sperm," Paul supplied.

"Clémence told you about that too?

229

"I've heard it from more than one source. Could it be true, do you think?"

"Who am I to say? I'll leave that decision to the development of natural science. But the genealogical data, once sorted out in the unusual manner that Amélie and her associates wished, was certainly interesting..."

"Associates?" Paul queried. "Would they have included my mother, by any chance?"

"Certainly. She and Amélie were quite close—but I suspect that the real fount of ideas was an older woman, Mireille Fargeaud."

"I've never heard mention of her."

"No, she died a long time ago—almost my generation, although I only knew her very slightly. You might have encountered her daughter, Lilith, though. She's at the old convent now, and we've been in correspondence for some time about the same matters. She and her two associates seem to be taking over where the previous trio left off, although the two groups aren't really similar. Lilith and her two friends are all much the same age and...celibate, whereas Mireille was older than Amélie and Jeanne, and all three of them had children. They'd be very disappointed, I think, to know that none of their own daughters have had children, Martine and Virginie having died and Lilith being...celibate."

"Virginie?" Paul queried.

"That's what Amélie said that Jeanne would have called your sister, had she lived to be born."

Paul suppressed a laugh. "My mother intended to call her two children Paul and Virginie?" he queried.

"No. As I understand it, she had no idea that she was pregnant with twins; she was only expecting one child, was convinced that it would be a daughter, and intended to call her Virginie."

"So, when I arrived instead, her immediate improvisation was to call me Paul?"

Jean-Bénigne now looked more than slightly uncomfortable. "All this is news to you?" he said. "Amélie never told you?"

"The things that Amélie never told me appear to be almost infinite," Paul remarked, dryly.

"Oh. Well, I wasn't there, obviously, and neither was Amélie, who had only recently given birth herself—also to a boy—and it's possible that her second-hand understanding was flawed, but Amélie gave me the impression, on the basis of what she had been told, that your mother never knew before she died that she had actually given birth to a boy and that her daughter was still...trapped inside her. I don't know who named you Paul, but I can understand how the name might have come readily to the mind of anyone who knew that your mother intended to call her daughter Virginie, even if they had never read Bernardin de Saint-Pierre. Thanks to him, the names are forever linked in French consciousness."

"Yes, of course," Paul agreed, unable to help remembering that in the famous novel, in which Paul and Virginie are raised as brother and sister, although secretly destined by their widowed mothers to be married, Paul dies of grief when Virginie dies in a shipwreck.

"I'm surprised that Amélie never told you that," Jean-Bénigne said, his discomfort increasingly evident.

"I'm not," said Paul. "I'm beginning to see the pattern—and I think I'll get the final piece of the puzzle before the day is out. Let's get back to the unorthodox genealogy. Given that there can't be any records going back to the epoch of the legendary three Maries, how far were you able to go back?"

"No further than the twelfth century, even with the aristocracy, with any degree of reliability, except for the descendants of Charlemagne and his nobles, who were obsessed with their own ancestry—calculated, of course, through the male lines. The documentation is very thin, though, and although several families of the twelfth century constructed genealogies tracing their own descent back to Roman times, their authenticity must be reckoned dubious. Tracking the female lines would be even more dubious. Amélie, however, was particularly interested in a number of women alive in the twelfth century whom she identified—speculatively, in my opinion—as what she called 'true Marians': descendants through the female line of one of the legendary three Maries."

"Marie Salome—the repentant daughter of Herodias who became the mother of Saint John?"

""Well, that particular link is dubious in the extreme, in my opinion—it's reading a great deal into a coincidence of names, and the required chronological reconstruction is quite absurd—but yes, Mireille Fargeaud seems to have believed that the Marie Salome whom Joseph of Arimathea brought to the part of Gaul that had previously been Massalia was, in fact, the same Salome who had danced for Herod, and was indeed the mother of the supposed prophet of Patmos. The fact that her belief appears to have been based on her own ancestral memories, reproduced in visions, makes it even less plausible, in my opinion—but not, obviously, in the opinion of anyone who shares those beliefs."

"Indeed." Again Paul could not help remembering the story he had spun for Salome on the lip of the great cleft, and wondered again why he had suddenly come out with all that, and where he had obtained it. He had been fully conscious to the time, definitely not entranced...but that did not mean that the imagery that had sprung to his mind had not come from the same source as the imagery of his drawings...

"Initially, of course," Jean-Bénigne went on, "Amélie was intent on finding proof—or at least evidence sufficient to convince her, that she, Jeanne and Mireille were all 'true Marians,' all descended from the supposed saint who had lived on your mountain, perhaps on the site of your cottage, or that of the convent. Unsurprisingly, given that she was looking with what scholars call 'the eye of faith,' she found it...and equally unsurprisingly, she then began looking around for other true Marians—sisters under the skin, as it were, albeit only seen as distant relatives by the calculations of orthodox genealogy.

She didn't find very many, but she identified a few among the prolific Lambrunet family, and a handful of others."

"Including Clémence Sancerre," Paul suggested, "and a young woman named Monique, nicknamed Monique Magdalen?"

"Yes, both of those. It's not only women, of course—you and I are both Marian descendants, in Amélie's reckoning, but unlike Clémence, and Martine if she had lived, we can't pass it on to our offspring. Even if we were married to true Marians, our daughters would only inherit their Marian characteristics from their mother. In terms of the kind of psychic heredity in which Amélie believed, male Marians are essentially sterile."

"Except," said Paul, repeating what he had told Salome, "that there might be complications and mysteries in psychic heredity of which Mireille Fargeaud had not dreamed."

"Well, perhaps," Jean-Bénigne sounded uncertain.

"But it can't have been entirely surprising to Amélie when she detected visionary capacities in me," Paul ventured. "Given that I am, in her view, a Marian, I could inherit such psychic capacities—I simply couldn't pass them on to any offspring I might have. I can see, though, why she was interested in my art and my trances, and why she made every effort to encourage them...including the use of hypnotism. Planting a post-hypnotic suggestion instructing me to keep my potentially lecherous hands off Martine was really only a subsidiary issue, and it was only supposed to be temporary, anyway."

"She told you about that, then?" Jean-Bénigne inquired.

"Not a word," Paul told him. "But in the last few days people have been queuing up to inform me of the details they know—including you, it seems. Gaston says that you'd like to see my sketches. I assume that's because your interest in Amélie's, or Mireille's, ideas about psychic heredity has recently been reawakened by your correspondence with Lilith. You think they're absurd, from a rational point of view, but as an antiquarian, and a collector of local legend and folklore, you think that they might constitute interesting data?"

"Yes," said Jean-Bénigne, "That's correct. I've seen your paintings of Amélie and Martine in Gaston's house, of course, and one or two of your other paintings that were said to be based on sketches, but that only whetted my appetite to see the originals, if I might use that term. May I?"

"Of course. I'll bring a selection next time I come to Toulouse; I'll be interested to hear what you think of them. Is it the depictions of the alleged spirits of the dead that interest you, or the chimeras?"

"Both, evidently...and Gaston mentioned one that he had seen of a female martyr, probably one of the several allegedly crucified by the Romans."

"I know the sketch he means...but it's not a Christian martyr. Did you describe it as such to Lilith?"

"I did mention it. Perhaps it was indiscreet, and we shouldn't have been discussing you at all...but she did bring the subject up, and I saw no harm in telling her what I knew about you. I hope you can forgive me."

"Of course. Lilith is coming to see me at the cottage to-night—doubtless she'll ask to see the sketch."

"Lilith is coming to see you? I thought her superior had forbidden her acolytes to speak to you."

"Lilith no longer recognizes Zosima as her superior— and neither, apparently, does the law. A new rule is coming into force at the convent. She'll doubtless be calling on you in person very soon, to view your collection and examine your documents. Given that you have no son of your own, I wouldn't be in the least surprised if she offered to become their future custodian."

"She'd be wasting her time. I might be a Marian in her eyes, but in mine I'm a Lambrunet. Gaston is my designated heir; I know that his scholarly interests, such as his business dealings leave him time for them, are scientific rather than antiquarian, but he has a fine and sensitive mind, and I trust him to serve the collection and find an appropriate curator for it. He knows the younger generation far better that I do. But that needn't concern you. There is one point of information

I've recently discovered that might interest you, however, although it didn't seem to interest Monsieur Megister in the least."

"Let me guess," said Paul. "The associate of Simon de Montfort who was gifted the domain that includes the mountain in the division of the spoils of the Albigensian crusade married a local noblewoman—a noblewoman strongly suspected of Cathar sympathies, for whom the marriage provided a necessary protection...and she, in Mireille Fargeaud's reckoning, was a true Marian. And without there being any legally-defined incest in the family, there have been sufficient cousin marriages to determine that Richard and Ellen are descended from the Cathar lady through a female line of descent as well as Simon de Montfort's crony through the orthodox genealogy."

"That's very good," said Jean-Bénigne. "Almost uncanny, in fact."

"Not really," Paul confessed. "You had obviously communicated the discovery to Lilith, and it has had an effect on her actions, from which the datum was deducible by entirely rational means, with the aid of a little modest conclusion-jumping. Ellen Megister is coming to the cottage tomorrow, in order that I can paint her portrait. Richard has only give me three days...but that's plenty for Lilith to drop in, now that she's operating under new rules, and for her to increase her acquaintance with her new...sister under the skin. Richard won't like that at all, but in Lilith's scenario, as you also put it, he's only a bit-part player, of no real consequence. In the eyes of society, on the other hand, he has all the authority, and I can't help thinking that Lilith is overestimating her own capacities."

"She certainly doesn't give the impression in her letters of any conspicuous modesty," Jean-Bénigne observed, judiciously. "I'm no judge of such matters, but did you get the impression that Mademoiselle Megister might have...inclinations similar to Lilith's?"

"I'm no judge of such matters either," Paul admitted, "and I doubt that three days spent painting her portrait will enable me to form a reliable impression, but whatever her inclinations are, it won't do Lilith any harm to make an impression on her, if her long-term ambition is to assume effective control of the whole mountain, as a sacred site, or simply as a more extensive farm and vineyard."

"That does appear to be her ambition," Jean-Bénigne agreed. "If it is, your presence there will presumably become an embarrassment...unless she can accommodate you within her plan somehow."

"Which must be exactly what she is thinking...a dilemma perhaps all the sharper because of my history with Zosima, who certainly seems to be thinking of me as a potential ally in her quest to regain hegemony within the Toulousan branch of her Order. But in Lilith's thinking of course, I'm a Marian descendant first and foremost, and a visionary as well: not only a natural ally, but an ally of some potential significance as a collaborator. The alchemical wedding of which Monique heard oblique mention is presumably, as its name suggests, an essentially mystical relationship. Her first choice will likely be to convert me to her way of thinking, to bring me aboard, but if she finds that it can't be done...well, Gaston and Victor Marvaud are both absolutely convinced that I'd be better off in Paris, and they might be right."

"Gaston has said as much to me," Jean-Bénigne told him. "He seems to think that he has a better chance of persuading you to return now than before...and his three female cousins, who were previously keen for you to stay and join the family, appear to have lost their enthusiasm...although I suspect that you could reignite it, if you wished, simply by making a choice between them...if circumstances permit it."

Paul deduced that Gaston had told Jean-Bénigne more that discretion permitted the old man to admit, at least without due circumspection.

"Circumstances are complicated," he said, simply. "I have yet to make up my mind what my long-term plans ought to be, or even in which direction I want to go. Pressure seems to be building up that might force a decision soon, but my immediate reaction, perhaps inevitably, is to try to slow things down, to give me time to think."

"Very sensible, I suppose," said Jean-Bénigne, "although I have spent my life doing the same thing, and I'm no advertisement for the strategy. Now, alas, I have no time left. I'm in no position to give anyone advice, but...sometimes I can't help thinking that I might have done better to grasp one or other of various nettles that were offered to me over the years, instead of always holding back because of the risk of being stung. One of the reasons that I admire Gaston so much is his decisiveness. May I ask you what you think of his new wife?"

"She's adorable; I think she'll make him very happy."

"So does he," the aged uncle replied, without much conviction. "I hope that he's right."

"You don't like her?"

"On the contrary—I find her infinitely likeable. So, I fear, will everyone else. To be infinitely likeable is a terrible trial of constancy. I cast no aspersions on her character, but she's very young, as has a long future ahead of her. But as I say, I admire Gaston for electing to take the risk, knowing what a risk it is. He's not a natural gambler, like his friend Victor. Victor knows how to lose and bounce back. Gaston, I fear, might not. But I'm just an old cynic, who regrets having been a young coward. Gaston is right to be bold, and I'm sure that he'll take full advantage of his happiness for as long as it lasts...and if it ends some day, well, so will the world, and there's nothing that a rational man can do except enjoy it while it lasts. I have not been a rational man in that regard, although I am the most rational man I know in others. We are paradoxical creatures, are we not, Monsieur Furneret?"

Paul suspected that the old man might be indulging in a little special pleading on behalf of his nieces, but there was certainly nothing insistent about it, and it might even be reckoned discreet; he did not resent it. "Your extensive knowledge of local legend and folklore," he said, judiciously, "must have made you aware of other visionaries, within and without the alleged Marian line of descent. What became of them?"

"You're an educated and intelligent man, Monsieur Furneret," Jean-Bénigne replied. "You must know very well what verdict the lore of legend passes on visionaries, everywhere and everywhen. Eventually, they fall or are driven over the edge of ordinary social life into a cleft, where they are lost, either coming to a sticky end, or vanishing into oblivion. To be different from one's fellow men, even in a moderate fashion, is a kind of martyrdom in itself...but you have your art, like thousands before you. If you examine visionaries from the viewpoint of a historian, you will have great difficulty finding the few that had happy lives...but no difficulty at all in finding many who were compensated for that lack of happiness with the fruits of their genius. I am, as I say, in no position to give advice to anyone, but if I were, I think the advice I would give to someone like you would be: *Paint, my son, and damn the rest.* Leave the quest for happiness to vulgar souls like Gaston and Victor Marvaud, and pity them if they fail. Yours, in my opinion, is a higher calling—but I'm just a crazy old man, whose judgment can't be trusted."

"I'll bring you the sketches next time I come to Toulouse," Paul told him. "Perhaps you'll be able to see something in them that Camille Flammarion couldn't, given your greater knowledge of their context."

"Don't be too hopeful," Jean-Bénigne replied. "My reason for wanting to see them is pure idle curiosity. As a good rationalist I have never believed that there are things man was not meant to know—but if I've learned anything in my long life, it is that reality is far too complex to allow the hope that any individual can ever hope to comprehend it, with the sole aid of a feeble human brain."

CHAPTER XIII

Paul found Victor, as expected, at Gaston's house, in conversation with Gaston and Armande.

"There's no need to disturb yourself," he said to his friend. "I can easily make my way back to the mountain in a hired carriage."

"Nonsense," said Victor, as Paul had known full well that he would. "I've topped up the fuel tank, and checked the engine. If the old girl had hooves instead of wheels she'd be pawing the ground impatiently. Gaston and Armande are coming along for the ride, as it's such a lovely afternoon, without a cloud in sight, and the artificial breeze of traveling and twenty-two kilometers an hour is exactly what's needed to take the edge off the heat. We were just waiting for you. Have you had a profitable day?"

"On balance, I suppose I have," Paul admitted. "I haven't finished my painting of Jane, as I had planned, but I have obtained a commission to do a rapid portrait of Ellen Megister, and Sister Lilith has promised to drop round to the cottage this evening to tell me—a trifle belatedly, I feel—what my mother's last words were."

"And how would she know that?" Victor said, not sure whether or not to laugh.

"Because she was by her side when she died, apparently, substituting for Gaston's mother, who couldn't be there because she was still recovering from the effort of having giving birth to him."

"Really?" said Gaston. "I never knew that. And Lilith has waited more than thirty years to pass on the message?"

"It isn't a message," Paul said. "Not for me, at any rate. According to Jean-Bénigne, my mother never even knew that I existed. She died thinking that she'd given birth to a girl named Virginie. Apparently, Lilith and her sisters were as

239

economical in giving people information then as they are now."

The four of them climbed into the car. Gaston and Armande got into the back seat, leaving the seat beside the driver for Paul.

"How on earth would Jean-Bénigne know? Gaston asked. "He can't have been there."

"No," said Paul; "he got the information third-hand, via your mother, who presumably got it from Lilith—which, he admitted, as the scrupulous scholar he is, casts something of a shadow over its reliability."

"You've been to see Jean-Bénigne this morning, then," Gaston deduced, effortlessly. "How is the old boy feeling to-day?"

"Old and frail, to judge by appearances, but still razor-sharp mentally, and full of useful information. I've promised to bring him my sketches, which he wants to see, next time I'm in Toulouse."

"Don't leave it too long," Gaston advised. "The word in the family is that he might not have much time left. Mind you, he's always on top form when I drop in—sharp intelligence, as you say, and always glad to see me. He didn't like Richard Megister, but he thinks the sister is adorable. Mind you, he always has had a keen eye for young ladies. I can't imagine how he managed never to get married."

"He is an antiquarian," Victor observed, adjusting his goggles. "I can't imagine that he was much of a Romeo, even in his youth. I know they like to fix these things up in your family, but you don't use force, do you?"

Gaston, ever sensitive to family honor, and probably having received some criticism for having stubbornly made his own arrangements in the wicked city of Paris, refused to reply to that.

"Is Ellen Megister very pretty?" Armande asked.

"Tolerably, I suppose," Paul supplied, gallantly, "but not as pretty as you."

"And you won't have to rush your portrait of me," Armande observed, accepting the compliment with casual ease. "Take all the time you need—just make sure that it's a masterpiece."

"But no more effort than you put into Clorinde's, when the time comes," Victor put in. "There mustn't be any cause for jealousy between our wives. You can be as slapdash as you like with Ellen Megister—she's English, so she won't know the difference."

"She's only English by the calculations of orthodox genealogy," Paul said. "According to Jean-Bénigne, she's as much a Marian as Gaston and me—more so, given that she's female. She's allegedly a direct descendant of Marie Salome on the distaff side, a distant relative of the dreamer of the Apocalypse, with a talent for dancing in her feet."

"That's ridiculous," opined Gaston, briefly.

"Is it?" said Paul. "Apparently, your mother wouldn't have thought so. Didn't she ever mention to you that she was a true Marian?"

"Of course she did," said Gaston. "Everyone has their little idiosyncrasies, which it's polite to ignore...except, you say that Lilith was substituting for my mother at your mother's childbed. How so? I mean I knew that your mother and mine were close, and would naturally have been in attendance at one another's births if the two events hadn't happened within days of one another, but Lilith? The Three Witches? An odd choice of substitutes. They were practically outcasts long before they went to Paris."

"Not at that time, apparently, when they were young and everyone was prepared to believe that they were just friends— and even later, according to Clémence, your mother's natural kindness and generosity ensured that she treated Lilith and her friends better than the rest of their social set."

"Oh," said Gaston. "Yes, I remember that, and it makes sense. She certainly wasn't one to go along with popular intolerance and bigotry. When she thought the Three Witches were being badly treated, she did go out of her way to be nice to them."

"I wish I could have met her," said Armande,

"So do I," said Gaston, and fell silent again.

"So, if your mother didn't leave a message for you, because she didn't know you existed," Victor said curiously, "what could Lilith possibly have to tell you?"

"I have no idea," Paul said. "Perhaps it's just an act of kindness, to tell me something I didn't know. Or maybe she just wanted a pretext to call at the cottage without Madame Louvot refusing her entry. She knows that Zosima gave me a long lecture last night, and probably wants to counter any accusations she suspects might have been laid against her. Not that it matters—I have no intention of taking sides in their little civil war, and there's nothing I could do to help either of them if I wanted to."

"That's not true," Victor objected. "You keep forgetting that you're quietly famous, regarded almost with awe by a substantial fraction of the city's elite. Maybe nothing you said would have any effect in the convent, but it would have an impact in Toulouse. If Lilith could get you and Clémence Sancerre on side, it might make a big difference to her standing and influence in the city, especially if Zosima is going to kick up a fuss about her entitlement to control the finances of the convent. That's presumably what this is really all about, isn't it? The money?"

"I don't think so. I don't believe this has ever been about money. Zosima didn't establish the Parisian refuge in order to extract an income from it, and the Toulousan phalanstery has always been an experimentation of her utopian ideas—at least, until this morning. Zosima really does think of herself as a true Fourierist, whereas Lilith, Salome and Justine think of themselves as true Marians. Zosima thinks of her hypnotically-assisted illusory memories of past lives as a practical way of helping downtrodden women feel better about themselves. Lilith and her associates think that they really are discovering the lost secrets of Marian descent, including a magical component, of which I—somewhat to their chagrin, I suspect—appear to be an outstanding, albeit peculiar and problematic, example. I don't think that it's my hypothetical influence on opinion in Toulousan society that Lilith wants to recruit; it's my supposed ability to conjure the spirits of the dead and build telepathic bridges...an ability that she probably takes even more literally and more seriously than Zosima. And I might have done something very stupid this morning in yielding to a sudden whim to tease Salome by pretending to knowledge I don't actually have, which she is probably reporting to Lilith and Justine as we speak."

"Why did you do that?" Gaston asked.

"Sheer pique at the way people keep telling me things that I ought to have known and didn't. I just wanted to get a little of my own back. Stupid, as I say—but things have been happening so fast that I simply lost my bearings. I'd grown used to quietude and stability. Now, it's turmoil."

"Well, I'm sure we're sorry," said Victor.

"Oh, it's not you. If it had only been you three, it would have been a welcome break, a pure pleasure. The turmoil started with Monique, and then went from bad to worse as Zosima and Lilith both weighed in. Clémence and Jean-Bénigne have only tried to help, but they've been tossing their contributions into a whirlpool, where they've simply joined the swirl. I wish I could ignore it all, but as more and more information is added to the mix, I'm finally beginning to get a clearer picture of why I might be the way I am, and although it doesn't make much sense yet, I want to clarify it as far as possible. Hopefully, once Lilith has delivered her final contribution, I'll be able to settle down to painting again tomorrow, and concentrate fully on rendering a acceptable, if somewhat hurried, likeness of Ellen Megister, albeit for a minimal fee.

"You should have referred him to me, as your agent," Victor said. "Whatever he's paying you. I'd have got you twice as much. It's just a matter of knowing how to negotiate.

243

"Actually," Paul said, "I think he was hoping that I would turn him down, in order to give him a means of blaming me for the non-execution of the commission."

"Why didn't you," Victor demanded, "if doing it is only going to cause you trouble?"

"I didn't want to let Ellen down. I'm her excuse for standing up to her brother."

"She must be very pretty," observed Armande.

"Oh, you needn't make that assumption," Victor said. "Paul would do as much for an ugly girl. He..."

"...might as well have SOFT TOUCH tattooed on my forehead," Paul furnished for him. "You can give it a rest now, Victor. Everyone knows the chorus. And you're probably right; I'd do the same for anyone in her situation. But she is very pretty, although..."

"...not as pretty as Armande," Victor interjected, playing tit for tat. "We know.

Gaston suddenly broke his pensive silence. "They're blaming it on my mother, aren't they?" he said.

"Who?" said Victor. "What?"

"Everybody—Paul's trances, and what he draws. They're saying that it was my mother's doing, because she used to hypnotize him as a kid?"

After a brief pause, remembering what Victor had said about Gaston's sensitivity regarding his mother's involvement in sorority occultism, Paul said: "In a nutshell, yes, that does seem to be a common opinion—but I don't believe it. Yes, she probably did try to hypnotize me, but that doesn't mean that it had any effect, let alone that the effect has lasted all this time."

"Don't be ridiculous, Paul," Gaston retorted. "I wasn't there on any of the occasions when Zosima hypnotized you, and nor was Victor, but we both saw the pictures in the papers—even Armande saw those, even though she was just a kid at the time. We know how badly hypnotism affects you, and we know that after the séance in Passy you swore off it forever and went into hiding. Are you seriously telling me that now you know what my mother tried to do when you were a child, you haven't connected the dots and put the blame on her?"

"Whatever your mother did," Paul said, "I'm absolutely certain that she did it for the best of reasons, for my benefit. She was extremely kind to me, and never did me anything but good."

"That's a matter of opinion," said Gaston, glumly.

"It's mine, and it's yours," said Paul. "Nobody else matters."

"Easy for you to say," Gaston opined, with blatant inaccuracy. "You don't have to listen to my cousins. I should never have introduced you to them—or at least, I should have stopped at one. It was bad enough when they thought it was my fault for giving them false expectations, but now they've got it into their heads that you were ruined because of some stupid joke my mother made in one of her secret salons...I'll be glad to get back to Paris."

"Nobody's said anything to me," Armande observed. "Everybody's been perfectly sweet."

"Of course they have," said Gaston. "That's the way it works...everything covert, always saving appearances. You really let me down there, Paul. You had a choice of three, all perfectly marriageable. What on earth is wrong with you?"

"Gaston!" said Armande "Is that why you married me—because I was perfectly marriageable and because we were introduced with...covert expectations?"

"No," said Gaston, "of course not."

"Well, then, why should you expect anything less of Paul than waiting to find someone he loves?"

Paul was looking round, and he saw Gaston's mouth open, and then close again like a steel trap as he thought better of his retort.

The car drew to a halt. "I won't go any further, if you don't mind, Paul," Victor said. "I'll go straight through the village and on rather than coming up to the cottage. You're very welcome to come with us, of course. We can find a picturesque spot from which to watch the sunset, and we could drop you off on the way back to Toulouse."

"No, that's all right," said Paul, exiting the car. "Thanks for bringing me back. You will all call again before you head back to Paris, won't you?"

Armande put out her hand palm down, which Paul took and kissed lightly, and then he walked around the vehicle in order to shake hands with Gaston and give Victor an affectionate tap on the shoulder. Gaston's handshake was firm, constituting an apology of sorts. Then, after a chorus of adieux, Victor pulled away again and the Panhard sped into the distance.

Paul turned up the hill and walked the last kilometer to the cottage, thinking that he might, perhaps, be able to finish the portrait of Jane before dusk.

Lilith, however, being either less patient or less melodramatic that Zosima, had not waited for nightfall to come to the cottage. She was already there, ensconced in an armchair in earnest discussion with Madame Louvot. Both women stood up as Paul came in and stopped dead.

"I'm sorry if I'm unexpectedly early," Lilith said, smoothly, "But I had the carriage drop me here on the way up the hill rather than go all the way up to the convent and then have to come back down on foot. Madame Louvot has been kind enough to keep me company. Might I be so bold as to ask to see your studio? The pictures in here, especially the one of Juliette, have awakened a keen interest to see more."

"Of course," said Paul, unenthusiastically. He exchanged a glance with Madame Louvot as he showed his guest to the studio, but the housekeeper's expression was unreadable, as if continual surprises had left her bereft of the ability to form an opinion.

In the studio, Paul's enigmatic visitor spent several minutes studying the unfinished portrait of Jane and a handful of other oil paintings. Her only comment was directed at the image of Jane.

"You have still to put the final touches to the face," she observed. "To the gaze, that is...and also to the voice?"

"It's a painting," Paul said, in a neutral tone. "It doesn't have a voice."

"Of course it has," Lilith replied. "At least, it will when it's finished. Silent voices are often the most eloquent, don't you find?"

Paul saw no point in repeating a negation in which he did not believe. Instead, he said: "Do you have many paintings at the convent?"

"Some," she said, "but only a few of them speak. We have other images as well, which I hope you'll be able to see very soon."

"You're relaxing the rule about allowing admission to men?" Paul queried, taken by surprise.

"No, but I'm prepared to make an exception in your case, the circumstance being so very exceptional. Indeed, I hope that you'll accept my invitation. That's part of the reason that I'm here."

"Only part?" Paul queried—but she made no immediate response.

She had paused in front of the tall chest of shallow drawers in which the bulk of his sketches were housed. "May I?" she asked—and before he had a chance to reply, she began opening the drawers, starting at the top. Each one contained between three and a dozen sketches, and there were forty drawers in all.

While Paul watched her commence opening them, methodically, one after another, in order to inspect the contents, she said: "I believe that you saw Sister Salome this morning, at the Great Cleft?"

"That's right," said Paul. "How do you know, if you haven't been back to the convent?" He was aware, as he voiced the question, that he was being impolite, and wished that he had phrased the question more diplomatically, in order to conserve some moral high ground in the conversation, but he could not help being disconcerted, and impatient.

"She followed you into Toulouse," Lilith explained. "At a slower pace than the automobile, obviously, but as rapidly as she could, because she thought that it might be urgent for her to inform me of what you had said."

"I'm sorry," Paul said insincerely. "I didn't mean to alarm her."

"You didn't; you merely surprised her. If her account of what you said is accurate, it surprises me, too—but I'm glad, because it will lighten the burden of my explanation. I congratulate you; I've been underestimating you all your life, it seems, and I would never have believed that you could have made such rapid progress in understanding in two days, when you didn't have the fundamental information before then."

She was still opening and closing the drawers, pausing briefly over images of faces and images of chimeras; but she did not stop dead, as Baron de Rochemure de Harvanges had, when he had come across an image of particular personal significance. It was as if what she was seeing—thus far, at least—was only confirming what she already knew.

Paul felt his head begin to spin, as he tried to calculate what Lilith might have read into Salome's reportage of his flight of fancy; hastily, he tried to anchor himself. "If you had given me that *fundamental information* four years ago," he said, "I would doubtless have made even faster progress."

"I didn't have it then myself," she replied, with perfect equanimity. "Not enough of it, at any rate. Have you seen Jean-Bénigne?"

"Yes."

"And he told you about my mother's research into the female descendants of alleged Medieval Marians?"

"Yes."

"Good. Did he mention the Great Cleft, by any chance?"

"Yes he did—he told me that the myth concerning dissolute nuns throwing unwanted babies into the cleft as just a myth, and always had been. Did Sister Salome tell you that I had accused her past selves of something similar?"

"She did. Jean-Bénigne is correct; our past selves were not guilty of that particular crime. That was...a misunderstanding."

"I'm glad to hear it. Please apologize to Salome on my behalf."

"I will," Lilith promised. She made a slightly longer pause, and then held up a sketch of a woman's face. To judge by the position in the stack from which he had extracted it, it must have been several years old. Paul had no idea who it was.

"My mother," said Lilith, laconically. "A trifle flattering, I fear, but perfectly recognizable. But you never knew her, because she was on her deathbed when you were being born, else I would not be standing here. Did you ever see a portrait of her?"

"Not to my knowledge, but quite possibly, given that Amélie Lambrunet knew her very well, and I spent a lot of time in Amélie's house as a child. It's perfectly possible that the sketch is a product of cryptomnesia." He could almost see the spirit of Antoine Cros nodding in approval.

"I suppose it is," Lilith conceded, readily enough. Then she held up another sketch, of a blurred embryo. "This is one of many, I believe?"

"Yes," Paul admitted. It was no secret that he had drawn multiple variations of the image.

"Have you ever done one in oils?"

That was a more surprising question, but Paul simply said: "Yes."

Sister Lilith paused, probably for effect rather than for thought, in Paul's judgment, and then she said: "And does it have its eyes open?"

"Yes," said Paul, blandly. There had been numerous witnesses to the drawings he had made in Passy, at the time and afterwards. There were several ways in which Lilith could have discovered that he sometimes drew fetuses with open eyes.

"Good. Can I presume that Zosima has already given you a full account of her interpretation of your life story?"

"*Full* would be a drastic overestimate, but she has certainly given me an account."

"And she questioned you intensely about the collective vision that you, Jane de La Vaudère and Madame Louvot had at Passy?"

"Yes."

"Well then, that is presumably something about which she now knows far more than I do, although I believe that I know the significance of one datum that she might not. Perhaps I will ask you to give me the details of it at some stage, but I'm not here to interrogate you about your intimate nightmares, nor to strike bargains. In addition to having an invitation to issue—or a commission, if you would rather look at it that way—I've come here to give you some information that you will need, and an apology for waiting so long to pass it on. I have no excuse except that it touches matters of great secrecy, which I was...and am...forbidden to reveal to any man. I think, now, that I can break that secrecy in your case—and, indeed that I need to do so—but it is a serious matter, for me, and I need you to recognize that."

"And you want me to swear to keep the secret?"

"I do."

"And you trust me to do so, even though I'm a man—albeit a true Marian, thanks to my mother?"

"I do." She said it simply, in spite of the hint of mockery in his query.

"All right," he said. "I swear by the memory of my mother that I won't reveal whatever it is that you have to tell me about my birth to anyone else."

Although she was trying hard to maintain her magisterial indifference, he thought that she perceived a genuine relief in her gaze—which meant, among other things, that she was prepared to believe him, and to trust him, already making the assumption that he was not Zosima's pawn, and that when she had told him whatever she had to tell him, he would take her side, like the true Marian she believed him to be.

He was not so sure—but he intended to keep his promise, at least to the letter.

"I also kept quiet," Lilith said, "because I didn't realize how important you might be to my own understanding until very recently. If only Amélie hadn't died in that stupid accident, I would have had far better guidance, and if Martine hadn't died, so might you. Everything would have been so much easier. And then, if your mother hadn't died trying to give birth to your dead sister...but then you wouldn't be the person you are, and that might be reckoned a truly tragic loss. It's not a reckoning I could have made until very recently, but I fear that I've been distracted, and Zosima has been...well, to call it uncooperative would be putting it mildly."

The speaker was still going through the shallow drawers of the cabinet one by one, but she was now only glancing very briefly at the drawings they contained. She seemed to be gathering herself for an effort. Paul simply waited for her to continue, which she did, a trifle hesitantly.

"You don't trust me and there's no reason why you should. You can't even begin to trust me until I tell you what I know—but everything I am about to tell you is true. The fact is that I should never have been at your mother's beside. My mother should have been supervising the birth, with the aid of the midwife. When my mother fell ill—terminally, as it transpired—Amélie Lambrunet should have substituted for her, but your mother went into labor early, while Madame Lambrunet's own labor had been protracted and arduous. Had the midwife been more competent, we might have known that your mother was pregnant with twins, and that one of them had died in the womb, but we had no idea. Your birth was very difficult, and then things went from bad to worse. Your mother only contrived to deliver the dead fetus after suffering a nasty hemorrhage. She was delirious by then. I don't believe that she knew that she had delivered two...children...and she had no idea that the one who had been delivered alive was a boy. In a final brief period of semi-lucidity, however, she begged me to conduct a certain rite with respect to her daughter's umbilical cord, which I promised to do, by way of granting her last request."

"Her umbilical cord?" Paul echoed, incredulously.

"Yes. It's..."

"I know what it is. I can even understand the symbolism it might have for...unorthodox genealogists. Go on."

"Without going into unnecessary detail, the ritual disposal of the umbilical cord that my mother's ancestors had been practicing for generations involved throwing it into the Great Cleft...presumably, garbled accounts of the rite helped give rise to the slanderous myth about the destruction of unwanted children."

"Unless the rite is a residuum of something nastier," Paul suggested.

"No," Lilith retorted. "I don't believe that. It's a very ancient rite, and perhaps a strange one, but as you say, the symbolism is easy enough to decode, and it has the weight of tradition behind it. It's local to the region; Zosima knows nothing about it. At any rate, the circumstances of your birth were very unusual; even Mother would have been unaware of any precedent. I had to improvise. After some hesitation, I bound the two severed umbilical cords together and I disposed of them in accordance with the rite. Whether that action had any causal effect, I can't tell for sure, but I think not; my belief is that the unconscious impulse that dictated it was simply a symbolic representation of a circumstance that already existed, something that had already happened."

"What?"

"I'll get to that. On a mundane level, your sister was buried with your mother. Your grandmother had already taken custody of you, at your father's request, by the time Amélie was out of bed again, and Amélie had enough to do taking care of Gaston, but she did what she could as you grew older—woefully neglected at home, I fear, before and after your father's death—to provide a little quasi-maternal care. Amélie did everything she could to foster your artistic abilities, in spite of her anxieties regarding your periodic entrancements, with which your talent and activity seemed inexorably bound. She had no substantial assistance, your mother and mine both being dead, the three of them having previously made up a trinity of sorts. My involvement had virtually ceased, and I was involved in the formation and cementation of a trinity of my own—not an isosceles trinity like the one of which your mother had been a part, with a dominant leader, but an equilateral trinity of similar individuals—very similar, and, it seemed to us, very exceptional.

"The members of my mother's trinity were all married and they all had children. They also loved one another. The members of my own trinity could, I suppose, have married and had children while continuing to make love in their own way, but it did not seem to be an attractive proposition to any of us. The fact that we were a trinity rather than a couple, however, created problems for us within the wider community of our own unorthodox kind. Even in ultra-liberal Paris, we were something of an anomaly, looked at askance, even though there is no necessary asymmetry in three women of our kind making love to one another simultaneously, as there is in any heterosexual trinity. Our example provided an extra impetus to Amélie Lambrunet's genealogical research, via which she attempted to identify other trinitarian relationships akin to mine as well as her own."

"And naturally," Paul suggested, "she found some...or invented some, with the aid of fanciful speculation."

Lilith ignored the skeptical sarcasm; her persistence had now become dogged. The sun was low in the sky now; although its disk was not directly visible through either of the windows in the studio, the effects of its oblique light were modifying the variegated tints of the crowns of the trees further down the slope. The world outside was beginning to seem mellow, in advance of becoming gradually somber.

"The attraction of the legend of the three Maries to Amélie is obvious," Lilith went on, "especially when she had connected it, hypothetically, to the ancient worship of Artemis in Massalia and the Albigensian heresy. Jean-Bénigne

Lambrunet's research was invaluable to my mother, but her own enquiry was tragically interrupted by her sudden death. I was not in a position to take up the reins immediately, but when Justine, Salome and I joined Zosima's organization, and were able to help in founding the colony here, we were finally able to realize the crucial relevance of Jean-Bénigne's research to the history and prehistory of the community that we—meaning myself, Salome and Justine—wanted to build. Zosima, who was initially sympathetic to our notions, which were accommodated easily enough within her broad church, became increasingly hostile to us as our ambitions grew. By the time she decided that we could not be brought into line, however, we could not be ousted, and it was only a matter of time before we wrested control of the colony away from her notional control.

"When we first settled on the mountain, we regarded you as something of in irrelevance, even though you were a child of my mother's trinity. You seemed to be a kind of private hobby-horse of Zosima's, on which she had imposed a kind of proscription. As further rumor reached us, however, of what you had done in the first three séances held in Paris, and then in the fourth held in Passy, I realized that you might be far more relevant to our endeavors than we had initially imagined. More detailed information was difficult to gather, because Zosima was not as communicative as we could have wished, but by means of assiduous research we were able to piece together sufficient information to make the crucial deduction— the one that Zosima, so far as we can tell, has never made."

She paused again, probably more for dramatic effect than to draw breath, but Paul, having grown increasingly impatient with her apparent prevarication, did not bother to supply a prompt inviting her to continue. Eventually, she condescended to explain what she meant by her teasing suggestion.

"Zosima does not appear to have noticed that in both the séance in Juvisy and the one in Passy, crucial trinities were formed, in the former instance between you, Talia Cadelan and Jane de La Vaudère and in the latter between you, Madame de La Vaudère and Madame Louvot. The situation at Antoine Cros's house reproduced the trinity formed at Juvisy. In each instance there was another individual present whose relation to the trinity was probably significant—a significance represented by the inclusion of a fourth individual in the compound sketches you have sometimes made while entranced. At Juvisy you included Antoine Cros's brother in the sketch you made, and the fourth individual completing the psychic tetrahedron at Passy was obviously Baron de Rochemure. I don't know exactly what happened at Cros's house, but it's possible that the tetrahedron was completed there by Camille Flammarion, although the focal point of its energy appears to have been Juliette Scarran. At any rate it is a group of four that is repeated over and over again in the sketches in these drawers, just as it had been produced for the first time at Juvisy."

"Except that the image of the fetus is substituted for me," Paul pointed out.

"Indeed," said Lilith. "In fact, that's the whole point of what I'm saying."

"You man the fetus is my symbolic representation of myself."

"Not exactly. In fact, I mean precisely what you just said: the fetus is *substituted* for you."

"I don't know what that's supposed to mean."

"That's because the words aren't equipped to make the situation clear. It means, in essence, that you have a kind of dual personality. If you wish, you can call it having two souls. The most colorful way to put it would be to suggest, as you did this morning when preaching to Salome, that when your sister died in the womb, her soul passed into your embryo and fused with yours—the psychic equivalent of a entanglement of your umbilical cords—but that's just an analogy. The point is that while you're entranced, the personality that draws the sketches isn't the same one that that operates in your mundane everyday thoughts—except that the two are never really separate, and they routinely collaborate, as they do when you paint consciously, especially when you make paintings based on

255

sketches. Although your two souls can operate independently, they very often overlap and combine their efforts—and the best of your art work is the product of that collaboration.

"Perhaps, in other circumstances, the two souls would have fused completely and become one, but in order to be able to form a functioning trinity, you need your second soul to be essentially female—to become your sister once again, at the point of the initial fusion of the two souls. Her soul needs, therefore, to remain separable, able to function in isolation. You can call all of that an illusion rather than an objective reality if you wish, or you can call it insanity, as many others undoubtedly would, but such labeling makes no practical difference. Whether you really have two souls or whether you only imagine unconsciously that you have, it comes to the same thing in terms of the activity of your mind. When you sketch unconsciously, it's actually your sister-self that is making the sketches, but while you paint consciously, it's mostly the other...mostly, but not entirely, and sometimes, I assume, more so than others."

"That's utterly bizarre!"

"Of course it is. You're a bizarre phenomenon, Paul, who requires a bizarre explanation. The point is not whether the hypothesis is bizarre, but whether it fits the facts better than any other. Only you can tell me whether it does, because I don't have the full set of facts. Nor did you, until just now. But you had enough this morning to declare, in so many words, to Sister Salome, that you were a psychic androgyne, having absorbed your sister's soul at the moment of her death. That, in my opinion is exactly what you are...and when your second soul is able to collaborate seamlessly with your first, you even know that you are. Test the hypothesis. Take some unexplained circumstance of your experience that hasn't yielded to any other hypothesis, and ask yourself whether this one can explain it."

That, Paul realized, was easy. Zosima had needled him only a short time before by bringing one particular enigma to the forefront of his mind: who or what was the "angel" that had snatched him from the jaws of disaster dung the vision at Passy? He had already concluded that, in some strange fashion, it had to be himself...but from the viewpoint of Lilith's hypothesis, it was not his usual self, but his other self, his sister-self. He had been saved by the spirit of his dead twin, which was contained, or at least replicated, in the hidden coverts of his own strange mind.

"It's ingenious," he admitted, aloud. "Perhaps it might turn out to be a´helpful interpretation—but does it have any practical consequences?"

"Well, does it, Paul? Unless I'm much mistaken, Zosima suggested to you yesterday that your relationships with women had been permanently affected by the unintended after-effects of Amélie Lambrunet's post-hypnotic suggestion instructing you to let her daughter alone, at least for a while. I'm suggesting to you that, if that suggestion had any effect at all, it had exactly the effect it as intended to have, and nothing more. If your relationships with women have been rendered problematic, the roots of that problem were embedded long before then, in the womb, two months before you were born—and the effects are still continuing, because of your dual personality, because you're a psychic androgyne. But that isn't an illness or a disability; it's just a modification. It has practical consequences, but it needn't be regarded as something blighting your life. If my judgment is accurate, you've had at least one, and perhaps two, relationships with women that you can estimate retrospectively as having been rewarding; there's no reason why you shouldn't have more in future—perhaps even the one that, for a few fortunate people, substitutes adequately for all others...probably, but not necessarily, a coupling."

Paul considered that argument for a moment or two, before saying: "And why, exactly, have you decided to tell me all this, in spite of your instinct and rule of secrecy?"

Lilith's laughter was a little forced. "Firstly," she said, "because I thought you had a right to know. Secondly, because, if my account of your nature is correct, its configuration has a curious aspect, which I had never considered before in relation to my own trinity but which might be relevant to it. When your mind appears to function psychically, it seems to do so as part of a tetrahedron. When you do multiple drawings rather than single ones you tend to draw four figures rather than three, and they usually have the pattern of one male, two females and a fetus. Perhaps that's an essential feature of the tetrahedral relationship, but perhaps it's simply the way your inner fetus tends to imagine it. At any rate, it doesn't take much imagination to look back at the original three Maries and to suggest that they too were part of a tetrahedron whose fourth component was initially Jesus, subsequently replaced by Joseph of Arimathea. I had always regarded my trinity as a perfect equilateral triangle, possessed of perfect symmetry...but ours is a freethinking organization, thanks to Zosima. Perhaps we can only function optimally with the addition of a fourth reference-point."

"You mean Zosima?" suggested Paul, knowing full well that that was not what she was implying.

"I mean you," said Lilith.

"And how, exactly would that work?" Paul asked. "Am I supposed to serve as a stallion to make you all pregnant with wonder-children?"

This time, Lilith did not laugh, even forcedly. "That won't be necessary," she said.

"So what am I supposed to do if I accept your invitation to visit the convent?"

"Paint, of course. We—Justine, Salome and myself—would like to commission you to make a portrait of the three of us. Ideally, but not necessarily, we'd like you to work simultaneously with another artist, Clémence Sancerre. We think the psychic collaboration might be fruitful."

"Because it completes a tetrahedron."

"No. We'd like you to paint the portrait in one of the convent's chapels. The fourth component of the tetrahedron we'd like to construct for you will only be present in spirit and in image."

Yet again, the bizarre woman paused, for dramatic effect—but this time, she expected Paul to figure out what she meant.

"You mean that you want me to paint the three of you in front of a crucifix. You want me to try to forge a psychic link between your little trinity and Jesus...the son of God."

"Even in Scripture, he represents himself as the Son of Man," said Lilith, mildly—but that's the representation of orthodox genealogy. Even in the Roman Church's version of Marianism, he is, quintessentially, the Son of Woman—more than that, the son of the Virgin, and tripartite himself, the third component being the paraclete. And isn't the psychic link that we want you to forge for us exactly what countless Christian mystics have been attempting to forge for centuries. What else is the hypnotic effect of Christian Art supposed to conceive?"

Paul was stunned. "And naturally," he said, "You want to hypnotize me before I do the painting"

"No," she said. "This isn't one of Zosima's parlor tricks. We don't want to put you to sleep in order to release Virginie. We want all of your artistry, conscious and unconscious. We want a collaboration that you're probably only now able to achieve. Insofar as you're hypnotized, we want you to be hypnotized by yourself, by your painting, and by the Son of Woman."

Paul had to stop himself blurting "Why"—or, even more stupidly: "What's in it for you?" For her, the purpose was self-evident, and had no crass motive. She wanted to link herself with the divinity because that was a goal in itself...and also, if it turned out to be achievable, a endorsement of the holiness of her own exotic trinity, regarded as aberrant by almost all of her peers. In her own way, like every other client of spiritists in quest of contacts with the dead, she wanted forgiveness...but in her case, even more so than in the case of Baron de Rochemure de Harvanges, she wanted far more than tokenistic absolution for some imaginary sin. She wanted supernatural proof that she was right and that all the prejudices of the world were wrong.

Nor, he realized, was there any point in asking what was in it for him, or haggling over the fee that he would receive for executing the commission. She expected, now that she had "explained" to him exactly who and what he was, that he would want to do it, that he would be eager to do it, that he would be just as avid for the communion that she wanted him to contrive as she was. Not to put too fine a point on it, she thought that now that he knew the truth—her version of it, that is—he would be as crazy as she was.

Am I? he wondered—and the mere fact that he could even pose the question to himself surely implied the possibility.

She had finally reached the bottom drawer in the cabinet. She closed it carefully, and then looked at him, with a hint of accusation. He knew why. Gaston had seen the sketch he had done of the crucified Jane de La Vaudère, although he had not known who the crucified woman was. Gaston had mentioned it to Jean-Bénigne Lambrunet and Jean-Bénigne had mentioned it to Lilith—in all innocence. She had interpreted the symbolism of what she had been told in the light of her own ideas. She had also interpreted the fact that the sketch was not in the cabinet in that context.

"You've given me a lot to think about, Sister," Paul said, his voice scrupulously level. "It might take me some time, I fear. I'll give you a decision when I can."

His visitor accepted that procrastination with perfect equanimity. She did not appear to have any doubt as to what the decision would eventually be.

"Of course," she said. "Take all the time you need. You have a painting still to finish and a portrait of Ellen Megister to paint. We're perfectly prepared to wait our turn."

It occurred to Paul that he had also agreed to paint Armande Lambrunet, and Victor's Clorinde, but he did not suppose that those commissions would be contiguous with those immediately in hand, and might not provide a pretext for delay. As a matter of curiosity, he asked: "Have you mentioned this commission to Clémence?"

"Only vaguely," Lilith replied, "and she's hesitant—but if you agree, I'm certain that she will. As I said, her collaboration is not a necessary condition...but we think it might be helpful."

In her thinking, he would have to be part of a trinity, Paul supposed. If Clémence's participation were not a necessary condition, who could be substituted for her? Zosima? Madame Louvot? Sister Monique? As he had said, he needed time to think, and probably ought to start that thinking at a much earlier point in the pattern of insanity.

"Thank you for the information you've given me, Sister Lilith," he said, with scrupulously overemphasized politeness. "The sun is setting, I fear, and if you're going to get back to the convent before darkness falls, you have no time to waste, so I'll bid you *au revoir*."

She did not seem displeased by the dismissal, perhaps because he had not said *adieu*. He escorted her to the gate, and watched her set off up the hill, at a measured pace. Then he went back into the cottage, where Madame Louvot was waiting for him, standing beneath Juliette's portrait.

"That woman," she opined, curtly, "is mad."

Paul presumed that she was making the judgment based on whatever conversation the two women had had before he arrived rather than any eavesdropping she might have contrived through the closed door of the studio. "Quite possibly," he said. "But more relevantly, she's a damn nuisance. Ellen Megister will be here in the morning to have her portrait painted, and I need to finish my work in progress before then, although I'll have to do it by lamplight now. I'm going back into the studio right away, and I am absolutely not to be disturbed for any reason whatsoever—do you hear? If, or when, Zosima comes back, tell her to go away or to wait, but don't disturb me. If the world ends and we're summoned to Judgment, you'll just have to go without me and make my apologies to God. Understood?"

She hesitated, perhaps wondering whether she had time to ask about dinner, but evidently decided that she had not. "Understood," she said

Paul sighed as he turned away, and wished that he could say the same.

CHAPTER XIV

When he was alone with Jane, with the door closed and bolted, Paul took up his palette and his prepared colors, and set to work. As Sister Lilith had observed, the face—or, more specifically, the gaze—was not yet complete. The painting still lacked a soul; but that did not affect the fact that Jane, being dead, was present, silent but attentive.

"Well," he said to her, "you heard all that. "Now you know as much as I do, or possibly even more, given that you always had secrets of your own while you were alive, and kept them preciously. But I trusted you then and I trust you now. You had your reasons, or thought you had. You didn't understand them, but you had them. That's the human condition. You'd still like to protect me, if you could, but you probably can't, being dead...not that you could, in any really effective sense, while you were alive. But your presence made a difference then, even at a distance of six hundred and eighty kilometers, give or take a few, and it makes a difference now, even at a greater separation.

"I have no idea whether I loved you, or whether you loved me, or whether the supernatural bond that was somehow formed between us is something entirely different from carnal concupiscence—can you hear Zosima laughing?—but whatever it was and is, it's important to me. Perhaps it's just an element of my self-hypnosis, or the curious fragmentation of my personality, but it really doesn't matter what labels we stick on it. It was what it was and is what it is, and for the moment, I need to be alone with it in order to think...or, to be strictly accurate, in order not to think. For the moment, I need to work. I need to be whatever it is that I am when I'm working. I need to be engrossed...not in the sense that I'm pregnant...or perhaps, on reflection, in exactly that metaphorical sense...but in the sense that I'm abstracted from the pressure and the stress, so that I can have a breathing space...or perhaps not in any sense at all, but in the particular nonsense that underlies all magic and all true creation.

"Because what I'm doing, right now, is magic, and it's creation. I'm painting the dead, and although I can't give you a voice, because that's not the way death works, I can give you a gaze, and I can give that gaze power: not just the illusory gift of being able passively to follow people around a room, but the more potent gift of captivating, the gift of fascinating, the gift of looking into souls and stirring them. And it's important that you have that, just as Juliette has it and just as Virginie has it, because I need the particular vision and the particular agitation that only you can provide.

"Perhaps, in other circumstances, someone else might have been able to provide that vision and stimulation. It's not unimaginable that another could have taken your place, in a purely material sense. Perhaps Antoine Cros could have given someone else an escort to Juvisy that night, or perhaps he could have gone alone, and I would never even have met you, but I don't believe that anyone but you could have played the role in my consciousness that you've played. You became a crucial piece in the jigsaw of my life, fitting a gap precisely, and the picture would be quite different, and crucially incomplete, without you.

"I'm not going to ask your advice as to what to do about Lilith and her bizarre proposition, because we both know that your advice would be to have nothing to do with her, and we both know that I can't take that advice. We both know that this might have a kind of inevitability to it, and that perhaps even Zosima, with all the traction of her psychic magnetism, couldn't stop it if she wanted to—which she probably doesn't, for covert reasons that even she might not fully understand. We both know, now, that her function in all of this, like mine, has been only ever been catalytic. In hypnotizing me, she was only helping me to hypnotize myself, and she had no more control over the result than I did.

"At Passy, Zosima tried to cheat, wanting me to induce me to summon Talia's spirit as well as, or instead of, Yvaine de Rochemure's, but it didn't work. Talia had already told her that mediums can't choose—consciously, at least—and that whatever comes, comes haphazardly...I won't say *of its own accord*, because we both know full well that the dead have no more will and purpose than they have a voice, and I won't mention the hand of Fate, because we both know full well that Fate doesn't have hands any more than it has a brain, but maybe I shouldn't say *haphazardly* either, because it's surely not random, but merely, at least in the strictest sense, uncontrollable.

"So, no advice, no guidance, no active support...but I still need you to be there, just as I need you to be here. In fact, I need you to *be*, period; and that's why I'm creating you, shaping you giving you a gaze, and a soul. I need you, urgently. I need Juliette too, and Virginie: the entire trinity. Because this is going to be dangerous, I don't know exactly how or why, but you've always felt that, intensely and urgently, just as Talia did, and just as Juliette did, without being able to perceive where the danger was coming from. Lilith doesn't mean me any harm, any more than anyone else who has become involved in this terrible tangle has ever meant me any harm, but the harm will arrive anyway, because it's there, innate in the configuration of illusion and reality, even in the absence of human malevolence...although that, of course, magnifies it a hundredfold whenever it interferes.

"Where is the human malevolence? I don't know. Richard Megister? A viper in the flower-bed. Madame Louvot might say, but he's not. He's harmless—no poison at all. And Ellen surely can't be a viper; she's sweet. No, any malevolence that enters into this configuration of absurdities surely comes from beyond the human world, from the realm of the dead. But who, among the dead could have anything against me? Have I not been as charitable to the dead as to the living, with the possible exception of a handful of murder victims who deserved to be victims of revenge?

"For what can I possibly I need forgiveness? I've asked myself that question before, of course, without being able to find an answer, even knowing that the conscience is a corrupt judge, and that feeling I need forgiveness isn't the same thing as having actually committed a serious crime or a sin. And I have, of course, committed sins, even though all the ones of note were sins of omission: primarily, the sin of being unable to love. I couldn't love Juliette, and, although I certainly came very close to it with you. I'm still not entirely certain, and certainly didn't provide much physical evidence, in terms of frequent proximity, for reasons that any objective observer would be bound to call cowardice...

"I don't even count the trivial cases, of course like Gaston' trinity of cousins, but I know that others do, and perhaps they're right...and even if they're not, in some ultimate calculus of morality, perhaps I still need forgiveness, because, after all, even if a person only needs to forgive himself, his assessment of that need, let alone his judgment of whether the forgiveness has been granted, requires some sort of endorsement. We need to see ourselves as others see us in order to weigh ourselves accurately in the scales of justice. But how can I expect to see myself as others see me when people are perpetually hiding things from me, keeping secrets?

"Is it my fault that, even after today's revelations, I still have little or no idea of how people see me, and what they think of what they see? It's not that I don't have good and loyal friends. No one could ask for anyone better than Gaston and Victor. But how do they really see me? What do they really think of me? I don't know. I've always been fortunate, to, in that the company of the dead has always been affectionate. If Gaston and Victor are the best of living friends, you and Juliette are surely the best of haunters. And Virginie? More problematic, I suppose, uncertain and confusing, but what can one expect of a fetus who died innocent of thought if not of feeling...if that's what she really is?

"I'm sorry to bother you with all this, but you were always such a good listener; even while you were alive I told

266

you things I could never have told anyone else, and I always thought you understood. Perhaps that was an illusion, but if so, it was a precious one. I never had to say to you 'Don't look at me like that,' because you never did. You always looked at me like this, with sympathy and with genuine interest, with compassion, but not with pity. You always looked at me with...gladness—and believe me, there's no more precious gift that a gaze can have. And I truly hope that I've captured it, and preserved it, because it's something I need..."

While Paul was painting, he was quite conscious, still aware of the world around him, beyond the edge of the canvas to which his attention was committed, but his consciousness was modified—not necessarily abnormal, given that he was a painter, but different from its neutral state, when his concentration was not absolute. He heard the bell at the gate ring on two separate occasions, although he could not have calculated what the interval of time was that had elapsed between him bolting the studio door and the first carillon, or between the two carillons, or between the second clamor for attention and the moment when he finally set down his palette and his brushes.

Eventually, when he had done that, he stood back in order to look Jane's spirit in the face, and meet her consummated gaze, and to agree with her that they were united now, properly and completely, in the only sense that could really matter, now that death had parted her from her husband in accordance with the letter of their pious contract.

After that, his mind changed gear, and his consciousness returned to the condition that it had when he was not really himself, when he was merely an actor in the world of everyday objects and other human beings, and a soft touch.

By that time, it was pitch dark outside, but Paul could not have said exactly when he had lit the lamps in the studio or positioned them in such a way as to illuminate his work appropriately. Lamplight was sometimes propitious for painting the dead, just as it was sometimes propitious for painting chimeras. At the moment, it was propitious for seeing the dead, and for enabling the dead to see him. He studied Jane, and her painted eyes, still not quite dry, studied him.

But one thing that his consciousness had not yet recorded, one thing of which it had refused to take note even while winding down from his temporary mesmerism, although it could have done had the unconscious part of his mind permitted it to do so, was that someone in the room beyond the bolted door was sobbing. That fact only caught his attention suddenly, and belatedly, when he took his eyes off the painting.

When it did catch his attention, he drew the bolt on the door and went through into the other room, where only the light of a single lamp kept the darkness at bay, and where the portrait of Juliette was looking at him with a hint of disapproval, because of the failure of his kindness—an unintentional failure, but a failure, a sin of omission, nevertheless.

Madame Louvot was sitting on the sofa with Zosima, who was trying her best, ineffectually, to console her in her uncontrollable distress. The housekeeper was clutching a crumpled telegram. Even the mountain was not out of the range of twentieth-century communications, and the messengers who worked for the Post Office were nowadays equipped with racing bicycles. The arrival of the telegram explained the second carillon of the bell at the gate.

"What's wrong?" Paul asked, although he knew already that there was only one thing that could have provoked such a reaction in his voluntary housekeeper.

"It's Fabien," Madame Louvot interrupted her sobbing to say. "He's been shot."

Paul's first impulse was to say: "We're not at war," but he knew that contingents of the Republican Guard were called out routinely in Paris—almost on a daily basis at the moment—to suppress "civil unrest" and although he had not paused to read a newspaper while he was in Toulouse, the cries of the vendors and glimpses of headlines had made him aware that recent calls to for the government to resign had been accompanied by riots in the ironically-named Place de la Concorde. Usually, the mere presence of a picket of soldiers was sufficient to calm hot heads, but the firing of revolver shots when a certainly level of popular anger and confusion was reached was all too common.

"Is he dead?" he asked.

It was Zosima who answered. "No—hit in the knee, but..." She extracted the telegram from Madame Louvot's hand and showed it to Paul, indicating the crucial words: *Leg amputated.*

"I have a carriage outside," Zosima added. "I was on my way into Toulouse to catch the overnight express that leaves at ten-thirty, and stopped to obtain news of Lilith's latest move in your regard. I've packed a traveling bag for Madame Louvot so that I can take her with me. I'll go with her to the Invalides in the morning. She can stay at the refuge until we can sort out what can be done and what needs to be done. It's safe to say that she won't be back for some time, if at all, but she has money, thanks to the baron. Whatever needs to be done for her nephew, she can do."

"I should go with her," Paul protested, very weakly.

"No," said Madame Louvot, pausing again in her sobbing. "Stay here. I'll come back, if I can—but Fabien will need me, I'm all he has."

"Of course," Paul agreed, before Zosima, who had risen to her feet, and was presumably feeling the pressure of time, drew him away from the sofa and said, unceremoniously: "What does Lilith want from you?"

"She wants me to paint her—and Justine and Salome, naturally."

Zosima frowned. "She thinks she can hypnotize you while you're painting," she opined.

"According to her, that won't be necessary; I'll do it to myself without any external help, to the extent that it can and needs to be done, while I'm painting consciously. I believe her. She wants Clémence Sancerre to be present—and, I suspect, she'll supply a third true Marian in order to complete what she calls a trinity."

"I know about that. It makes sense—to her, at least. But what's her end-game? Did she give you any idea?"

"Oh yes. She wants to make contact with Jesus—the Son of Woman, the Virgin—and the paraclete. She wants his mother's blessing and protection for the community she's intent on establishing here, as an example to the people of Toulouse: your phalanstery, with her distinctive heretical twist."

"There isn't any heresy in my philosophy," Zosima muttered, "except intolerance. She's serious, isn't she? She really does want to create a Marianized version of the Daughters of Artemis. How far does she think the psychic influence of your endeavor will extend?"

"I don't know, and nor does she. She'll gladly settle, I think for me casting a spell on the convent, and probably won't be entirely disappointed if it doesn't extend much further than fuelling a blissful hallucination for her own little trinity."

"Which you can't deliver," Zosima reminded him. "Not to order, anyhow. Remember Talia's judgment of the essential perversity of the work of the seer."

"I do," Paul told her.

Zosima looked at him sharply, her eyes catching the lamplight although she had pulled Paul into the penumbra beyond the pool of clarity around the sofa. "You're thinking of doing it, aren't you? In spite of Jane's prohibition, and your own common sense you're actually thinking of doing what the crazy bitch wants." She did not seem entirely displeased with the prospect, as Jane had been. She was interested, already making calculations as to how she might contrive to be involved, even though she knew that Lilith was determined to exclude her, as a potentially disruptive presence. For the moment, though, time was short. "When does she want it done?" she added.

"Not for the next three days—but once I've consented formally, if I do, she'll probably want to move rapidly."

"*If* you do?"

270

"I haven't agreed. I honestly haven't made up my mind. But I can't deny a certain curiosity—and I really can't see where any malevolence will enter into the equation."

"Malevolence might not be needed—except for the malevolence of Fate."

"I know. That's why I'm still in doubt."

"What did she say to make you even consider the possibility, after all I said to you?"

"I can't tell you that. She swore me to secrecy."

"Of course she did. So much for the rule, though. Not only inviting a man into the sanctuary but letting him in on the secrets of the Sisterhood!"

"Not so much a man," Paul told her, wryly, "as a psychic androgyne. I had a revelation of sorts this morning, although I didn't realize at the time that it was a revelation. I met Salome on the edge of the Great Cleft, and the Holy Spirit, or the Imp of the Perverse, moved me to speak in tongues. I revealed myself to be a chimera, mentally, at least. It's only an illusion, which has been lurking in the back of my mind all my life, but it's clearer now than ever before. I can even put a name to my other part. The name of the embryo with whom I've been obsessed in spirit, I learned from Jean-Bénigne Lambrunet today, is named Virginie."

"Paul and Virginie?" said Zosima, incredulously.

"Precisely. Her unformed body died in the womb but her soul lives on within me, at least in my unconscious imagination, constituting a fraction, and perhaps far more than half when circumstances are propitious, of my talent."

There were probably dozens of question that she wanted to ask, but time was limited. "You do know how the story of Paul and Virginie ends?" she observed, dryly.

"Tragically. Even people who haven't read the book know that."

"But you aren't taking that was a warning?"

"It wasn't intended as a warning, Calling me Paul was some joker's idea of propriety, improvised on the spur of the moment. It wasn't a prophecy. There is no prophecy, just experimentation."

As a professional prophet of sorts, she knew that. "You also know what happens to rabbits and guinea pigs at the Institut Pasteur," she said—but the resistance was so lukewarm as to be almost tokenistic.

"Yes—but this time, if I agree, and for the first time, I'd be going into the experiment with my own eyes open as well as Virginie's, although I wouldn't have control, but I would have consciousness. Perhaps I'm ready."

"In that case, come back to Paris with me, now. We'll go to see Flammarion, and this time, we won't let anyone else usurp the séance. It will be just you, me and the astronomer, with the whole universe at our visionary beck and call."

"No," said Paul, "I can't do that."

"*No?* After all I've done for you, you'd rather play lapdog to a crazy traitress? Don't you think that you owe me—or at least that you owe Talia—more than a cursory *I can't*—especially as you clearly can?"

"I probably do owe you something," Paul conceded, although his moral calculation suggested that any unsettled debt was the other way round, "but I suspect that I also owe something to my mother, and to Amélie Lambrunet, and perhaps to the entirety of my Marian ancestry, all the way back to Salome and the Daughters of Artemis, and beyond."

"None of that is true," she told him. "It's all just fantasy, made up to help downtrodden women feel better about the raw deal than Nature handed them. It's been around for centuries, so I can't claim credit for making it up, but who do you think brought it all to the surface in those three little refugees? Who do you think gave them the psychic energy and enterprise to allow them to stop being pariahs and to become high priestesses instead? They all owe me, and so do you. Even my unorthodox genealogy is better than theirs: it goes back all the way to the Egyptian Isis and the Sumerian Inanna, and the Triple Goddess at the dawn of civilization. It's *my* game, damn it." She did not add, although Paul was in no doubt that she thought it, that he was her pawn, and that he should not have allowed himself to be captured by her opponent.

"You should be proud of your achievement," Paul told her. "Wasn't the whole point of your new crusade to make your clients better, to give them confidence and strength? Well, you succeeded with Lilith, and perhaps you even succeeded with me. Keep up the good work. And please look after Madame Louvot, who also owes her recent life and purpose to the side-effects of your psychic energy. Be kind. And don't linger any longer, if you want to get to Toulouse in time to catch the overnight express."

So saying, and without waiting for a response, he went back to the sofa and took Madame Louvot's hands. "I'm truly sorry about Fabien," he said. "I'll be coming to Paris before long, to paint Armande and attend Victor's wedding. I'll come to see you then, wherever you are. Don't worry about me. I can look after myself, and I have my ghosts to help me."

He helped her to her feet. Then he picked up the traveling bag that Zosima had prepared for her and deposited at her feet.

"There's hardly anything in it," she observed.

"I'll pack the rest of your clothes and linen," he assured her. "I'll ask Victor to bring a parcel to Paris in the automobile, if he has space in the trunk, or send it by train if not. For now, let's get you settled in Zosima's carriage. You can trust her. Behind that brusque exterior, she has a heart of gold."

He walked her out of the front door and along the path, and then helped her to climb up into the two-seater carriage that was parked outside the gate. It had no driver—unsurprisingly, as it had doubtless come from the convent; Zosima evidently intended to conduct it herself.

As she settled into the seat, Madame Louvot muttered: "It's a punishment." Although she was pretending to say it to herself, she obviously intended him to overhear.

"It's not," he told her. "There are no divine punishments, and if there were, you wouldn't warrant one. Believe me, if

God ever starts handing them out, there'll be millions in the queue in front of you."

"Maybe not for killing the bastard," she muttered, still audibly, "but for only ever feeling remorse because I hadn't done it soon enough."

"You don't need forgiveness for that either," he assured her. "Look after Fabien. I'll see you soon."

Zosima, meanwhile, had illuminated the lanterns fixed to the front of the shafts, in order to light her way down the treacherous hill; the moonlight and starlight were clearly not up to the task unaided. Now she climbed up on the other side of the carriage and picked up the reins and the whip.

"Trust me," she said to Paul. "Think it over, and then come back to Paris with your friend Victor. That's where your future is. Think of Flammarion, and compare his dreams with Lilith's." She was earnest and sincere, but she did not sound confident.

"*Au revoir*," said Paul, and then went back into the cottage, hoping that the vehicle would not come to grief before it reached the better road that ran through the village.

The house seemed strangely empty without Madame Louvot in it, and no evening meal had been prepared. Fortunately, there was still bread left over from the morning, as well as convent eggs and milk in the larder. He made himself an omelet, and sat down on the sofa in order to eat it, so that he could talk to Juliette. He also took the bottle of convent brandy, which still had a couple of mouthfuls left in the bottom

"There's no need to be jealous of Jane," he told Juliette, although he knew that the plea would fall on deaf ears. Juliette was jealous by nature—and so, for that matter, was Jane. Rationally, they had both known that they were not in competition, but that had not quelled the feelings welling up from the unconscious, and he had no reason to suppose that the dead were any more rational than the living, in spite of Camille Flammarion's optimistic reports of happy afterlives on other planets, augmented by those of "Hélène Smith" and numerous other mediums.

The common supposition among spiritist believers in interplanetary reincarnation, Paul knew, was that other worlds had to be happier than the corrupt Earth. That was natural, because it was difficult for them to believe in God's benevolence otherwise. No one, since Voltaire had punctured the delusion with such surgical acuity, could seriously believe that ours was the best of all possible worlds; it was far easier to believe that it might be very nearly the worst.

"Your fate did nothing to deny that, alas," he said to Juliette. "No matter what people might think who consider the profession into which you were forced by circumstance to be inherently evil, you were an entirely virtuous person, who suffered nothing but affliction in consequence, and my kindness was a poor compensation for that, no matter how valuable it seemed to you in the circumstances. And no matter what Zosima or Lilith might think, it can't be Virginie who prevented me from loving you; it was only me who failed you. If Virginie really does exist within me in some way or form—and I can't say that I'm entirely convinced of that, by any means—I don't think she would want to stop me loving anyone. Why would she?

"In fact, now I come to think about it—belatedly, because I was too distracted to think of it before—I don't believe that, when I told Sister Salome that I was a psychic androgyne, I was thinking about Virginie specifically. I was simply employing her symbolically, as I had when I lectured Armande during dinner, extrapolating on the basis of an idea of reincarnation in which I wasn't restricted to female ancestors, or human ancestors. I was thinking of being a fragment of a collective soul of humankind that necessarily partakes of both male and female identities, as well as retaining the legacy of animal identities, and an imagination capable of mingling them.

"I say *mingling* and not *confusing* because I'm sure that it's a misconception to think of a chimera as a result of some kind of imaginative error. In fact, it's anything but that; it's an exercise in deliberate creation, a kind of discovery, a defiance of the straitjacket of happenstance. And I do mean a straitjacket, of the kind they use in lunatic asylums, to stop people hurting themselves and others. That's what reality does, after all; like consciousness, it's a form of protection, a restriction for the sake of preservation from madness—but whatever benefits we get from that kind of protective custody, it's a not a good thing to lose sight of the idea of freedom and the dream of freedom, within the relatively safe space of the imagination. Chimeras remind us of that; they remind us of our true selves, as opposed to our merely real selves.

"Do you remember when Jane first came to my studio in Montmartre? Of course you do, because you loathed her at first sight, albeit unjustly. She looked around my paintings and she picked out, without hesitation, one of my mermaids—the one that one of us characterized as the wistful mermaid. She saw herself in that: a creature of two social elements, able to exist in both but fully adapted to neither, condemned never to belong. That was the way she felt: unable to belong either to the social milieu into which she had be born, and in which a marriage had been arranged for her, or to the milieu of art, literature and amour, into which her intelligence, imagination and creativity strayed incessantly and obsessively. Later, I gave her a sphinx, because that was the way I symbolized her, as a beautiful enigma, an insoluble puzzle. But I never gave you any presents, did I? I never gave you a painting, even though I put you in several, in disguise. I sketched you several times after you were dead, and perhaps I also symbolized you then, but if I did, it was probably on the basis of the careless pun that produced your nickname.

"I sketched a beetle once, which might have been a scarab of sorts, although it had horns, which most symbolic scarabs don't have. According to antiquarians, the reason that the ancient Egyptians considered scarabs to be sacred is because they saw an analogy between scarab beetles rolling up balls of dung in which to lay their eggs, so that their larvae would hatch out surrounded by food, and the sun-god Ra making is daily circular tour of the universe, transforming and regenerating bodies and souls by means of his kindly radiation. Personally, I think that's utter nonsense. I think the Egyptians carved oval amulets to look like beetles because there aren't very many things that such amulets can be carved to resemble, and because black beetles with hard, shiny elytra have a certain unique somber beauty and elegance. Either way, though, I never saw you as a beetle any more than I saw you as a chimera. I saw you as Jeanne d'Arc, a heroine and martyr, cruelly mistreated by the world, which added insult to injury in your persecution.

"I'm truly sorry that I didn't love you while you were alive, and that whatever I feel for you in retrospect, it can't do you any good now that you're dead. And I'm truly grateful to you for the fact that, although you don't love me either, you did your best to protect me, shielding me as best you could from importunity—perhaps a little excessively, sometimes, but with good intentions. The important thing is that we've both forgiven one another for our various failings and ourselves, and we've done that without the aid of any medium or psychic catalysts. It was a close run thing, I know, whatever story we choose to believe about the real reason why you jumped off the Pont Neuf, but the important thing is that you were able to get past that and die in a much more dignified and satisfactory fashion. It wasn't comfortable for me, sitting by your bedside for weeks and months, watching you coughing blood and dying by degrees, but it did me good, I think, and it helped me to straighten out my head, which was direly confused at the time.

"I won't ask you for advice, any more than I asked Jane, because I know what your advice would be. Go back to Paris, you'd say. Don't get involved in all this Marian nonsense. Zosima is right about one thing, you'd say: it's all nonsense, all fake, all stupid self-aggrandizement, and in all probability, it won't work. Whatever the three would-be Maries are expecting to get out of their adventure in illusion, they'll be disappointed. The baron was a special case, because what he wanted was so strange, so inherently perverse that the inherent perversity of the universe couldn't thwart him. Lilith isn't like

277

that; Lilith, in her fashion, is quite banal, even if her particular concupiscence leads her to design equilateral triangles rather than binary couplings. That's not genuinely perverse, it's just a matter of taste; it doesn't even startle Sister Monique, or you, let alone provoke a horrified reaction.

"Obviously, I agree with you: It won't work. But that's precisely why it's interesting. Because no matter how fearful the perversity of the universe makes you—quite rationally—there is a certain artistry in it, a certain charming irony. If one were to characterize the essence of universal nastiness, it isn't so much cruelty as black comedy—or so it seems to me, at any rate. Bad things happen, and they don't happen in any discernible moral context, by way of punishing evil—quite the reverse, in fact. There is no Hell, where moral account books can be settled, any more than there's a Paradise where the virtuous, if such creatures actually exist, could receive any reward beyond virtue itself. But the world isn't simply evil; indeed, its evil is surprisingly complex, not devoid of subtlety and flair even in its basest brutality, even in terms of four drunken soldiers smashing the child in a pregnant woman's belly with rifle butts after they'd finished raping her, for no reason at all.

"You probably think I'm just rambling, and you'd probably be right. You probably think that I've hypnotized myself finishing Jane's portrait by lamplight, that I'm not quite in my Paul mind at the moment, and you'd be right again. The Other is breaking the surface again, and we have to bear in mind the fantasy that she isn't really Virginie at all, or at least not all the time, that there are worse things lurking in wombs than loving little sisters. We have to consider the possibility that it's really her that finds the prospect that Lilith is holding out to us attractive; that it's not the Paul you know—mild, kind, slightly bewildered, soft touch Paul—but his evil dead twin. But you mustn't worry. I'll be going to bed very soon, under Virginie's watchful eye...will it seem even more watchful, do you think, now that she has a name?...and the probability is that I'll slip into a trance. Then she...or the Other...can relieve her straitjacketed frustrations by drawing something horrible and violent, as she does on occasion, so that the real Paul can wake up refreshed and surprised, as he does fairly often, and the world will seem more-or-less equilibrated again.

"And let's not forget that tomorrow is another day, when we have another painting to do, of Ellen Megister, who really and honestly isn't quite as pretty as Armande Lambrunet—because she can't be expected to contrive, given her present situation, anything akin to Armande's aura of healthy honeymoon self-satisfaction—but is nevertheless very pretty, and a lure for any man's dormant concupiscence. It's necessary to do a truly hypnotic painting of her, so that her eyes can follow her brother around wherever he hangs her up, and can criticize him silently for his tyranny in trying to dictate her life to her, however normal that might be. With a little artistry, even working at a fast pace, I ought to be able to produce something so truly beautiful that it will be uncomfortable for him to look at it, a permanent remonstration for his flaws of character. You can approve of that, can't you? That's a kind of artistry that you understand, and practice."

Juliette inevitably, made no verbal reply—but she did look at him, with her usual sympathy and her unquestioning approval...not because she loved him, but because she was making the best of a bad predicament.

What else could she do?

CHAPTER XV

Paul went down to the village at dawn in order to buy bread and other comestible supplies. There was nothing particularly unusual about that, but the messenger's bicycle had been seen going through the village, and so had Zosima's carriage, in spite of the darkness. The sun had hardly cleared the horizon, but the bakery was already the center of a web of rumor. Paul had to explain formally that Madame Louvot had been summoned to Paris by a family emergency, even though the baker's clients knew that already, and to confirm that he did not know when she would be able to return. He promised to pass on any news as soon as he received it, although he suspected that the baker and his loyal clientele would almost certainly intercept it before it reached him.

When Richard and Ellen Megister arrived, by contrast, it was in a state of complete ignorance. They were not connected to any gossip pipeline. Richard Megister did not seem pleased to hear the news that Madame Louvot would not be in residence during the three days that he had given Paul to complete the painting, even though the actual sittings would not take up more than a few hours in total, all in broad daylight, while Bernard, the Megisters' chauffeur could sit in the other room even if Richard elected not to be there himself. On the other hand, Richard did not seem to be pleased by anything, and Paul deduced that his tour of France was not going well, in spite of the glamour of being a genuine seigneur.

The brother and sister both came into the studio, and while Paul was posing Ellen for the initial sketches Richard positioned himself in front of the recently completed painting of Jane de La Vaudère, which he studied with a gaze that was clearly not poised to admire and marvel. In fact, as Paul placed the first tentative strokes of charcoal on the canvas, he distinctly heard Richard mutter, probably more loudly than he intended: "Disgusting."

Paul was startled by his own reaction, the reflex of a raw nerve. "What did you say?" he retorted, sharply.

Richard Megister turned round, not blushing but clearly confused. "Not the painting," he said, swiftly. I didn't mean the painting, I meant..." He stopped, evidently realizing that Paul would probably be just as displeased by an insult aimed at his model as his artistry. He tried to rescue the situation by blurting: "Not her personally...her books..."

Paul had regained control of himself, but that did not stop in saying in any icy tone: "Have you read her books, Monsieur Megister?" knowing full well that he Englishman, whose command of French was distinctly mediocre, would never have attempted to read a book in French.

"No," the Englishman admitted, "But..." He stopped again, and this time he did blush slightly.

"But you've seen the pictures in *Les Prêtresses de Mylitta*," Paul concluded. "Monsieur Méricant, the publisher of that particular volume, is embarked upon a crusade at present to establish nude photography as an art-form parallel to the painting of nudes. He has begun using such photographs as illustrations for books by those of his authors who sympathize with his point of principle. The story, on the other hand—the text for which the lady in the picture is responsible—is set against the background of the Biblical book of Daniel, concluding with the episode known in English as Belshazzar's Feast and the writing of the wall prophesying the imminent fall of Babylon—an account of divine justice exercised against tyranny and cruelty. Does that disgust you, Monsieur Megister?"

Megister's lip curled, this time with anger, and Ellen was quick to intervene. "Don't you think, Richard," she said, "that Monsieur Furneret would be able to make more rapid and efficient progress if you were to sit in the other room? If you get bored, by all means go for a walk. I shall be perfectly safe."

For a moment, it seemed that the Englishman might argue, but his sister's stare was so censorious in its studied mildness, and so challenging in its implication that no reasonable objection could possibly be raised to what she was saying, that he capitulated almost immediately.

"I'll leave you to it, then," he said, and did not even favor Paul with a venomous glace as he withdrew.

"Is it all right if I talk?" Ellen asked, when the door had closed, "or do I have to be silent as well as still."

"Yes, you can talk," said Paul. "In fact, it would probably be as well, if it helps you to relax. There's a difference between stillness and stiffness, and for the moment, you're erring a little in the later direction."

"I'm sorry," she said. "I'm a little tense. Don't blame Richard too much—he's...out of his element. I don't know what he expected in coming here, but not what he's found. You know I suppose, the rumors that are running around Toulouse regarding the convent?"

"Vaguely," Paul agreed, cautiously.

"Are they true? Is it really a hotbed of unnatural vice?"

"Popular imagination always exaggerates. It's an unorthodox convent to be sure, but it's certainly not a den of Satanism. You've met the new superior, so you know that she's an intelligent and reasonable woman who simply observes a slightly unorthodox dress code." Silently, he awarded himself full marks for diplomatic understatement.

"That's partly the problem. What little Richard saw of her, he saw in the context of what he'd already been told by...people whose social importance in the city is probably no guarantee of their reliability. There are people there who...well, you'll probably understand if I say that they're almost worthy of having been born English. They seem to have horrified themselves with the lurid fantasies of their own imagination, and they seem to think that because Richard is the landowner, it's his responsibility to put stop to all the things they think are going on, and of which they disapprove.

It's absurd, of course, but Richard...well, he doesn't really understand..."

Paul remembered what Armande Lambrunet had said at dinner about the logic of the situation of closeting female adolescents in boarding schools and convents. England was not a Catholic country, but he assumed that the schools in which the daughters of the upper classes were routinely isolated were not so very different from those in France, that Ellen probably knew a good deal more about certain unmentionable subjects than Richard suspected, and that she probably had a very different attitude to them.

"Toulouse is a city with its own idiosyncratic divisions," he said, "which have deep historical roots. It might seem absurd to you, but the Albigensian crusade still has social and psychological repercussions even after seven hundred years, and they become entangled with entirely modern conflicts regarding religion and feminism. The bigots in the city who have taken the opportunity to harass your brother's ears aren't representative of general opinion in the city, which is essentially liberal and tolerant as well was reasonable and intelligent. The convent might seem to some individuals afflicted by moral panic to be a threat to conservative religious and moral values, but it's perfectly harmless. I know its previous superior, Sister Zosima, quite well, and I know that her intentions have always been virtuous, although her fervent attachment to feminist causes hasn't endeared her to agents of male tyranny, in the church and elsewhere."

Ellen laughed. "Very neat," she said. "Unfortunately, as you've doubtless observed, Richard is unduly sympathetic to what you call agents of male tyranny and alarmed by feminist causes, especially in their more fervent manifestations. And he's very suspicious of artists, too. In spite of everything he's been told about your stern moral probity by reliable sources, he's also been told by others that you're a degenerate who used to live with a prostitute who modeled at Jeanne d'Arc for you, and that you've had other suspect relationships that have caused you to reject perfectly respectable alliances with young women in the city whose hearts you've broken casually. All wildly exaggerated, I'm sure, but Richard...well, he thinks I'm only insisting on sitting for my portrait here in order to annoy him. He's angry with me because I refuse to see things as he sees them, and so he's also angry with you."

"That's a pity," said Paul, neutrally.

"Yes it is. It's all been rather frustrating. He's alarmed by the imminent end of my legal minority, although he'll still have financial control of almost everything, so my freedom will be purely technical...but it's a pity, as you say, that my problems have been reflected on to you. I'm sorry."

"No apology is necessary," Paul assured her. "I'm delighted that you think highly enough of my artistry to risk displeasing your brother."

"I do," she said, but added: "Although I wouldn't be honest if I didn't admit that I take a certain pleasure in annoying him. I'm strongly tempted, in fact, to accept Sister Lilith's invitation to visit the convent, precisely because they wouldn't allow him to accompany me—but that might be a step too far."

"Perhaps it would," Paul agreed, although he had a strong suspicion that meek agreement was not what she was fishing for. "Would you like to look at the sketch before I proceed?"

She seemed startled by that. "I thought artists never showed sitters their work until it was finished?" she said.

"Some do have that idiosyncrasy," Paul agreed, "but when working from life, I prefer to get a measure of approval as I go along. If the drawing displeases you, it's easy enough at present to try a different stance, or for you to adopt a different expression—although I'd rather you didn't strive to adopt an attitude or expression that isn't entirely natural, because artificiality is hard to maintain."

She came to study the drawing. "Is that really what I look like?" she asked, genuinely hesitant.

"Yes," he told her. "Your face is very symmetrical, so it should be very similar to what you see in your mirror, but the angle is one that you can't replicate to the gaze in reflection, and when you look in a mirror you don't pay attention in the same way. Then too, there's a certain subjectivity in sight, which ensures that painters are often told that they haven't captured a likeness, because they haven't captured the particular likeness that appears to a specific observer. Trust me, this is you."

"You will make me beautiful, though?"

"I don't have to. You're already beautiful; all I have to do is copy it."

"Flatterer," she said, resuming her pose, while he prepared to add preliminary colors to the charcoal outline. "Is this right?"

"Perfect."

"Can I still talk?"

"By all means. I'll let you know if I need you to stop and hold absolutely still momentarily. But please don't be offended if don't reply to you while I'm concentrating. It's not that I'm not listening."

"That's all right. Richard says that most of the time, I just drivel on, and he often stops paying attention. He should listen to himself sometimes. I think he might ask the land agent to put the estate up for sale before we go on to the Riviera, although he's already been told that there's little prospect of finding a buyer, unless Sister Lilith or Sister Zosima can raise the capital somehow, in which case either one of them would be only too glad to take it off his hands. That would be a pity, I think. I like the place. I wouldn't mind living here, if I could...not actually on the mountain, but in Toulouse. Society there seems much more interesting and amusing than at home.

"I'd have to improve my French, obviously...but Richard wouldn't hear of it, obviously. I'd have to be married, and there's very little possibility of my having any choice in that while Richard continues to maintain illusions about finding me a husband he considers suitable, and keeps me in a straitjacket in the meantime. There's always the convent, I suppose, but I really can't imagine that, for all sorts of reasons, even though it would horrify Richard so much it would probably give him a heart attack. He's thinking of getting married himself, although he's still a bit young—he was shopping around before we came away, but hasn't had much luck. He sets his sights a little too high, if you ask me...not that anyone does.

"I wish he would marry, because tyrannizing a wife wouldn't leave him nearly as much time to tyrannize a sister, and if I were lucky, he might find one who would tyrannize him—although perhaps it wouldn't be lucky if she wanted to tyrannize me as well. Not that he seems vulnerable to that sort of thing—he's not by any means as cold as the proverbial fish, but he doesn't seem to be a man to go in for grand amour. I'm sure he loves his automobile more than he could ever love a woman, even though it's noisy, smelly and keeps breaking down...not unlike some of the floozies he gawps at when he thinks I'm not looking...and he has the nerve to call your friend disgusting.

"For a moment there, I thought you were going to hit him, and I was wondering which of you to cheer for if there was a fight...but that's silly, isn't it? Sometimes, I wonder about myself, and whether I ought to have some of the thoughts I have—Richard would say no, obviously, but his isn't an opinion I'm prepared to trust any longer—and to be honest, one of the reasons why I want to have my portrait painted, and painted by you, is so that I can look at myself from outside, as it were, and see the portrait looking back, so that I can read what I think in the portrait's gaze. Is that absurd? Probably, but that's why, when I saw that picture hanging in the other room, I thought that I wanted to be painted by the man who could do that.

"With all due respect to your friend Clémence, who I'm sure is a fine painter, I wouldn't want her to paint me, all pastel and profile, with all those flowers and everything Medieval. No, I wanted the man who could do those eyes. I wanted to have eyes like those—and I don't care about what Richard says about her only having that gaze because she was a brazen whore, because he's absolutely no judge, and I could tell that there was love in those eyes, and love in the way they were painted, and even though you don't love me, nor I you, I knew that you could do justice to my face, to my gaze.

"Maybe, as Richard says, it's just learned technique, but if it is, why don't more people learn it and use it? That's a rhetorical question, by the way, although I know you weren't thinking of answering it, because I know that you're not really listening, and that's good. I want you to concentrate. I want you to be absorbed in what you're doing. I want you to focus on me so intensely that you aren't any longer aware of anything in the world except me, because it's the first time that anything like that has ever happened, and it will likely be the last, at least once the sittings are over and the painting is finished. Just once, just for the moment, I'd like to be the center of everything, to think that my presence has the power to hypnotize..."

Paul woke up with a start, not knowing where he was. He remembered listening to the voice, but suddenly, that seemed to have happened a long time ago. He was not aware of any time having elapsed since then, but he knew that there had been a gap of sorts, and he did not know how wide that gap might have been.

He opened his eyes, lifted his head, and met a stare. It was a strangely disturbing stare, all the more so because now, for the first time, he could put a name to it.

Virginie.

The stare—the impossible stare of the seven-month fetus—belonged to Virginie...whose imaginary story, as related by Bernardin de Saint-Pierre, had not ended well, and which had not ended well in reality, either, where she had not even survived long enough to be born.

Unless...

A hand touched his arm, and he looked away from the painting that was hanging on his bedroom wall, at the person sitting on the chair beside the bed.

The situation was familiar. It had happened before. He had once woken up to find Jane de La Vaudère keeping vigil over him, and on another occasion, Madame Louvot. This time, however, the dim daylight filtering through a gap in the closed curtains outlined the hooded face of Sister Monique, who was gazing at him with infinitely more embarrassment than Virginie, but also more concern.

"Thank God" she said. "They said that you were only asleep, that you'd wake up in your own good time, but I wasn't at all convinced that they knew what they were talking about."

"What are you doing here?" he asked, a trifle rudely. A swift palpation of his body assured him that he was still fully dressed, apart from the smock in which he had been painting; he had evidently been laid down on top of the bed by persons unknown, without overmuch ceremony.

"I volunteered," she said. "Madame Louvot's not here. Poor Faby's been shot, it appears, by some crazy anarchist, and has lost his leg. You'd think you'd be safe in the Place de La Concorde, wouldn't you, surrounded by fifty of your mates with bayonets fitted? He should never have joined the Guard, poor lamb. Didn't he take a lesson from what happened to the Baron?"

Losing his patience slightly, Paul said: "How long have I been unconscious?"

"Ages," she replied. "I don't know exactly. I've been here for two hours, but I don't know how long it was before that when they picked you up of the studio floor, or how long before that you'd been out on your feet, painting like an automaton. The English girl was hysterical—they couldn't get much sense out of her."

"Ellen was hysterical? Because I collapsed?"

"Don't flatter yourself. So far as I can gather, she hadn't even noticed that you were away with the fays. She was still posing when they bought her the bad news. She's gone now, in the auto, with the chauffeur."

"What bad news?" Paul demanded—although, to judge by the sinking sensation in his stomach, a part of him already knew, by some superhuman means.

"Her brother. He went out for a walk. There was a crowd at the Great Cleft, where those idiots from the university were getting their students, or laborers, or whatever, to rig up more ropes and pulleys and God knows what. Sister Salome was there—the trinity alone knows why. The Englishman went to watch. One way or another, he went over the edge. He must be somewhere in the center of the Earth by now. Salome ran to the convent, the professors sent someone to the cottage, the girl became hysterical, and you collapsed. Chaos all round. That's it."

Paul absorbed the information. Then he said: "What do you mean, *one way or another*?"

"I wasn't there," Monique said. "According to the men that were there when I arrived, the idiot got too close to the edge while trying to peer over, had an attack of vertigo, and fell."

"And who says something different?"

"Nobody with any sense, probably—but when Salome arrived at the convent she said that he'd been pushed."

"By whom?"

"That's why I added the rider about anyone with any sense. She said that there was nobody within five meters of him, behind or sideways, but she still insisted that he was pushed—that she couldn't see what pushed him, but she could see the reaction to the thrust in his body. Mind you, she believes in ghosts, even at midday. They all do. I'm the only sane one up there. But you paint dead people, so you can probably believe her. There's going to be a hell of a fuss—he was the landowner, after all. If it had been some village kid, nobody would care, but the seigneur...even if he was English...that's different. A hell of a fuss, with the Mairie, the parquet, the gendarmes and God only knows who sticking their noses in. An international diplomatic incident, I shouldn't wonder. Anyway, in the circumstances, nobody cared much about you when you collapsed...except me. So I volunteered to sit with you until you woke up. And here we are."

"Except you?" Paul queried.

"Well, maybe not just me. The Englishwoman wasn't in any condition to care, but Lilith was concerned. If I hadn't volunteered to sit with you, she'd have ordered someone else to do it—she'd probably have done it herself if she hadn't been determined to go in the auto with the girl, and she'd left Justine in bed up at the convent. Anyway you've hardly met Justine, whereas you know me, even though you used to look right through me when Scarab was around—which I'm prepared to overlook, in the circumstances, insulting though it was."

"I take it that your foot's better," Paul commented, dryly.

"Better than it was. I can limp, sort of. I came down in the cart, though, with Lilith and the others. Tigany took the others back in it. I told them that it would be all right."

Paul swung his legs over the bed and stood up, glad to find that his head didn't reel. As before, in parallel circumstances, he felt fine. Without any further ado, he went out, traversed the corridor and the dining room, and went into the studio. Someone had hung his paint-stained smock on a hook, and replaced his palette on the table. The canvas was still on the easel.

The painting seemed well advanced for a single session, but he knew how fast his hands could move while he was entranced. The picture seemed promising. He had not yet copied all of Ellen's beauty, by any means, but he had made a good beginning. The eyes were just faint charcoal blurs, barely indicated, but suggestive. Even though part of the sitting had gone to waste, he thought that he might still be able to finish in a further two days—except that he no longer had a deadline because he no longer had a mission, because his patron had fallen into the Great Cleft, or had been pushed by invisible hands, and was now deeper within the Earth's crust than anyone else had ever contrived to go...nobody, at least, who had returned to tell the tale.

Would the body ever be recovered? He had no idea. Even if the incentive to search was sufficiently great, given the importance of the victim, would it be possible, finally, to reach the bottom of the cleft? And if it were, would the body still be there, or would it have been borne away by some underground river of sludge, to the place where all ritually discarded umbilical cords and fake holy grails ended up?

Why? he wondered, although the question only made sense if Richard Megister had not, in fact, simply fallen, because he had lost his footing. Why would anyone, dead or alive, have wanted him out of the way sufficiently to contrive a shift in the laws of material reality? He could not think of anyone who had a plausible motive...not a conscious motive, at any rate.

I had no reason, he told himself. *It couldn't have been me. Just because he called Jane disgusting? Just because Ellen has accumulated a light baggage of petty resentments? No, surely not. If it had been Virginie, surely she'd at least have waited until we'd finished the painting. Although, I suppose, there's no real reason why it shouldn't be finished, now that Ellen is free, and presumably owns the mountain, cottage, convent and all...*

"Thanks a lot," said Monique, catching up with him. "When I said I could limp along, I didn't necessarily mean that you could just run off and leave me. It still hurts, you know."

"I'm sorry," Paul said. "Let me help you to the sofa in the other room."

He did that, and stood looking down at her. She had pushed back her cowl, and she was staring at the portrait on the wall.

"Thanks, Paul," she said. "Look, I don't know how long I've got before somebody comes back, looking for you or looking for me, so I'll spit it out. Can I stay, at last until Madame Louvot gets back?"

"You seem to have ensured that you won't be able to get back until they send a cart for you," he observed, looking down at her with a certain irritation.

"Lilith ordered me to stay," she said, defensively, before adding, quickly: "But I volunteered. I had to. It's was bad enough up the hill when Zosima was still in charge, but now the unholy trinity is running everything, the craziness is going to get out of hand. It's lonely being the only sane one, believe me. I can't give you anything much in return. I can't look at you the way Scarab did, and I won't be much use for cooking and cleaning until my foot gets better, but I promise I won't be a hindrance. Just for a while. I've no entitlement, I know, but if you could just give me just a tiny fraction of the kindness you showed Scarab..."

Lilith had ordered her to stay with him. Had she also ordered the rest of the speech? Had she brought Monique from the convent precisely in order to intrude her into the cottage? In order to do that she would have had to know that Madame Louvot was no longer here, but that was by no means improbable, given that the entire village must be aware by now.

Monique's judgment that she might not have much time proved correct before she had even finished her plea, which was interrupted by the roar of an automobile coming up the hill effortfully, followed by a screech of brakes.

Paul went to the door, threw it open and advanced toward the gate, although he did not go through it.

The automobile, unsurprisingly, was Victor's Panhard. He was carrying two passengers: Armande Lambrunet and Clémence Sancerre.

It was Armande who reached him first, while the other two were still climbing out of the vehicle. "You're alive!" she exclaimed, unashamedly stating the obvious. "They said you collapsed when you heard what had happened. Gaston was furious with that English chauffeur for not bringing you back, but the fellow just babbled about his mistress and the old nun said that she's left one of the sisters to look after you."

"I'm fine," Paul assured her. "Is Ellen all right?"

"Of course she is, apart from the blubbing. The nun's with her at the hotel, and Gaston's running around, the way he always does, making arrangements—informing the relevant agencies, as he puts it. The parquet will have to be involved, and notaries, and Heaven only knows who else—Heaven and Gaston, that is."

"There'll have to be an investigation, obviously," Victor supplemented. "Do you know what hap—?" He broke off abruptly as Monique arrived on the doorstep, a few meters behind Paul, but added: "What's she doing here?"

"Bonjour, Victor," Monique called, with a false joviality. "Nice to see you again, after all these years." The entire party was now on the path, moving toward her, and she scanned them all in a glance. "And you must be Armande, my dear? Gaston's a lucky man. And you're Clémence Sancerre, of course. You probably don't remember me—it's been a long time."

Armande looked at Victor, seemingly in expectation of an introduction that was not forthcoming from that direction. Clémence Sancerre looked at Paul, quizzically

"This is Sister Monique," Paul supplied. "Victor and I used to know her in Toulouse ten years ago, and we met again briefly in Paris. She knows Gaston as well. Sister Lilith asked her to sit with me until I recovered consciousness"

Armande seemed slightly uncertain as to how to react to the limping mock-nun.

"Paul, dear," said Monique. "Could you possibly help me back go the sofa? I'd ask Victor, but I'm afraid he might pick me up and drop me—again."

Victor winced at the double entendre.

Paul helped Monique back to the sofa, followed by the three new arrivals. As soon as she was seated she patted the seat beside her and said to Armande: "Sit with me, my dear, and I'll tell you all about Gaston, Victor and Paul when they were adolescents. What a trio!"

Obediently, Armande sat down. Clémence seized Paul by the arm and drew him sideways. "What happened?" she demanded, completing Victor's question in a low voice, but with a different object in mind.

"I was painting," said Paul, tersely. "I was entranced. Then I collapsed." He knew, though, that that would not be enough. Clémence was more familiar with the long story of Paul's entrancements than anyone else. He had told her about previous losses of consciousness, and the circumstances associated with them—enough for her to know that they were sometimes associated with seemingly supernatural occurrences, including Juliette's leap from the Pont Neuf as well as uncanny drawings.

"And Richard Megister fell into the Cleft?" she said, incredulously. "He seemed perfectly steady on his feet when I saw him."

"According to the witnesses," Paul told her, "there was no one within five meters of him when he slipped. The ground had dried out after the rain the other day, but the leaves are full of sap. He's unfamiliar with the local vegetation. He must have put his foot down carelessly and it skidded. He was too close to the edge and couldn't regain his balance."

"He wasn't bitten by a snake, then?" she said, a trifle sarcastically.

"I don't think so. Perhaps he was stung, though—a bee, a wasp or a scorpion, disturbed by all the activity." That, he knew, was possible, and might even explain why Salome had seen the victim's body react to an unseen stimulus. He made a mental note to make the suggestion to the examining magistrate. Clémence clearly did not believe it, but she had no rational objection to raise to the hypothesis.

Meanwhile, Monique had already launched into her own explanation of the fatal accident, very similar to the account she had given Paul. She was addressing herself directly to Armande, but Paul had no doubt that she was watching Victor from the corner of her eye. The latter, on the other hand, turned away from her deliberately as soon as she paused—when she finally ran out of breath—in order to say to Paul: "Where's Madame Louvot?"

"She had to return to Paris last night," Paul said. "Her adoptive son was shot during a riot, and the surgeons were apparently forced to amputate his leg. He's in the hospital at Les Invalides, for the time being"

294

"But it's all right," Monique was quick to add. "I can serve as Paul's housekeeper until she gets back...if she ever does."

Victor stared at Paul, wide-eyed. "You can't possibly...," he began.

Paul made a dismissive gesture. "Sister Monique is getting ahead of herself," he said. "If I were to ask Sister Lilith to lend me one of her flock for a while, I'm sure she'd oblige, but it might be better if it weren't Sister Monique, given that she can hardly walk."

That statement startled everyone "You think Sister Lilith would lend you one of her lesbian nuns to cook and clean for you?" said Victor, skeptically.

"I think so," Paul said, equably. "We're on good terms now, after our conference last night. I've even been invited to the convent, now that the rule has been relaxed, in company with Clémence. Lilith wants us both to paint her triumphant triumvirate."

"And you agreed?" said Victor, incredulously.

"I agreed to consider the proposal. We didn't discuss terms, but it would be an interesting experiment, in artistic terms. Is there any reason why we shouldn't reach an agreement?"

When neither Victor nor Clémence replied, Monique, apparently having taken offence at Paul's failure to welcome her own generous offer, was quick to put in: "You mean apart from the fact that she's a crazy bitch who thinks that, because you paint dead people, you can also act as a middleman for the advent of the new Messiah?"

Everyone looked at her, their astonishment continuing. "The *new* Messiah?" Paul queried, warily.

Monique shrugged her shoulders. "I'm not supposed to know," she said, "and I'm certainly not supposed to tell—but what the hell. The rule book has been torn up and burned. I can't be absolutely sure, given that I'm the pariah nobody talks to confidentially, but from what I can gather, the alchemical wedding between you and Clémence is supposed to help bring down the Holy Spirit from Heaven, incarnate as Sophia, or Ennoia, or whatever: the Wisdom of the Goddess, Jesus in a skirt. A bit late if you ask me, as Justine must be at least six months pregnant, if she's a day, under that loose robe, but what do I know?"

It was interesting, Paul thought, that Lilith had left out that particular item of information—if it were not simply a product of Monique's imagination—in spite of the opportunity she had had to mention it when he had made his joke about perhaps being requested to serve the Trinity as a stallion. He knew that all three Maries must be in their forties, but how old would Mary Salome have been when Joseph of Arimathea supposedly brought her to Provence, if the allegation were true that she was the mother of the prophet of Patmos. On the other hand, if the rationally incompatible allegation that she was the same Salome that had danced for Herod as a child before the death of John the Baptist were true, she would have been much younger...

He derailed that fruitless train of thought in order to wonder whether, when Lilith had asked him if he had done an oil painting of a fetus with its eyes open—which Monique now knew for certain that he had—she might not have been thinking about Virginie at all, but about another fetus entirely.

He realized that Monique was looking at him as if to say: *You'll have to let me stay now*, although her grounds for thinking that were extremely weak, to say the least. Was she really being flagrantly disloyal to Lilith in revealing secrets, or had she been instructed to do it?

"You really don't want to get mixed up with that sort of nonsense, Paul," Victor opined, feigning the voice of reason. "I've only been back in Toulouse for a few days, and it's a long time since my finger was firmly on the pulse of local rumor, but I can tell that a backlash is building up in certain sectors of the city against the so-called abomination of the convent. Lilith might think that the opposition will die down now that its governance has passed to native Toulousans, but she really ought to remember the reputation that the Three

Witches had before they decamped for Paris. It's only a matter of time before the priests start preaching from the pulpit. Things could get ugly. Even if you're still determined not to come back to Paris for good, you really ought to come back with me when I take the Panhard back, at least for a while. Paint Armande, paint Clorinde, stay for the wedding, and don't come back here until all this has blown over. If the word goes round in Toulouse that you're collaborating actively with Lilith's black magic, your reputation in respectable quarters will fall from a height into thick mud."

"I can go to Paris with you," said Monique, hopefully. It was not entirely clear whether she was addressing Paul or Victor, and Paul wondered whether she was sure herself.

"If you'll forgive me saying so, Sister," said Armande to her companion on the sofa, "you're the least likely nun I've ever encountered."

"Thank you," Monique replied. "That's the nicest compliment I've had in years. I can hardly remember that last time Victor told me I was pretty, and Paul didn't even see me when I was standing next to his beloved Scarab."

"I remember you now," Clémence put in, apparently speaking sincerely rather than making a joke. "You're the girl they used to call Monique Madgalen."

"That's right," Monique replied, serenely. "A prophetic nickname. Jesus never got to wash my feet, but Paul did, which is the next best thing—at least, I thought so until a few minutes ago."

"Apparently, Lilith thinks something similar," said Clémence, slowly.

"Apparently, she does," Paul agreed, but pouring sarcasm into his tone in order to imply that he was not speaking seriously, "and she seems to have cast you as one of a new trinity of three true Marians. But who does she have in mind to play the others?"

"Anyone you like," suggested Monique. "It's impossible to throw a stone up there without hiring a supposed true Marian. I'd volunteer myself, if I didn't think I'd already spoiled my chances. But if alchemical weddings only involve mumbo jumbo and no actual screwing, I'm probably better off out of it."

She turned to Armande. "You must think you've just walked into a madhouse, you poor dear. That's my fault. I always did let my mouth run away with me. But you've got the sanest of the lot back in Toulouse, with Gaston. He's a rock. Treasure him, and forgive him his friends...no, cancel that; he doesn't need forgiveness. I'm just annoyed with Paul because he never wanted me, and Victor because he's ashamed of having had me, which probably warrants your approval in both cases. And if you have any credit with Paul, which you undoubtedly do, if he's going to paint you, you might want to lend your support to Victor in urging him to get away. Since it seems that I've nothing to gain, I might as well be altruistic. It won't do him any good at all to get mixed up with Lilith now that her iron whim is law up at the asylum."

As she finished speaking she looked round at the door, as if she almost expected to see Lilith standing there, but the door was closed and their conclave was still secret.

Paul looked at Clémence. "How much do you know about what Lilith has planned?" he asked her.

"Nothing detailed," she replied. "She sounded me out about the possibility of my coming to the convent to paint her and her cronies, and I hedged. She said that she might make the same offer to you, but I assumed that the three of them would come here if you agreed to paint them. I noticed that Justine seemed a trifle stout, but it didn't even occur to me to wonder whether she might be pregnant. Obviously, I've heard plenty of Marian fantasy over the years, illustrated a fair amount of it, and taken part in some of the mummery, for the sake of curiosity, so I know how rich the legendry is, and how contradictory. I've always found it fascinating, but never believed any of it. I knew that Lilith takes it seriously, so when she brought the Megisters to see me, after she'd seen the notary to confirm her formal control of the convent, I inferred that she must be planning something to celebrate the takeover, but

I couldn't even make an educated guess as to what it might be. I'm not an initiate, even in the sorority, just an interested fellow traveler."

"And now?" Paul queried. "If she makes a firm proposal, will you accept it?"

"I don't know," she parried. "Will you?"

"I don't know," he replied. "I certainly can't deny that I'm curious, and rationally, I can't see any harm in it."

"I've just told you, very rationally, what harm there is in it," Victor reminded him.

"But that's not the point, Victor, is it?" Armande put in. "I don't know Paul very well, but I've seen his paintings. He doesn't seem to me to be the kind of painter who's overly concerned about what a bunch of high society bigots in Toulouse think of him. As Sister Monique says, I've got the cream of the Toulousan crop in Gaston, and some of his family members are lovely people...but some aren't, and for what it may be worth, I think it would be unworthy of Paul to shelve his curiosity just because people like that might disapprove of him. If I have any credit, Paul, my advice is to do what you want and damn the naysayers—as long as you come to Paris to paint me when you think the time is right."

"Bravo," said Monique. "I've changed my mind—I'm with her. You don't want a lame chambermaid, Madame, by any chance?"

"No," said Victor, swiftly, "she doesn't. Not that you have any more chance of seducing Gaston now than you had when you settled for me instead—much less, in fact."

"Ouch," said Monique. "Ingrate."

The bell at the gate rang at that moment and Paul ran to answer it, thinking that it might be news. It was: a hasty note from Gaston sent by bicycle messenger. It reported that the parquet intended to appoint an examining magistrate to investigate the accident that had occurred at the Cleft and that Paul should expect to be consulted, albeit merely as a formality, as a witness to the surrounding circumstances. Gaston also reported that Ellen had recovered from her initial distress, and that Sister Lilith was staying with her in order to support her in her grief and assist with formalities, which she would undoubtedly find daunting without the help of an interpreter. The British Consulate had been informed of the tragic death of their citizen, and they would make sure that the authorities in England were kept abreast of developments.

Paul relayed all that information to his guests, who reacted to it in various ways without their commentary adding anything further to what he already knew.

"Come back to Toulouse with us, Paul," Victor said, when the inevitable discussion had run its course. "You shouldn't stay out here on your own."

"He isn't on his own," Monique put in.

"You can stay with me, if you like," Clémence offered.

"That's very kind," Paul said, "but to be honest, I'd rather stay here for the moment."

"With *her?*" Victor said, incredulously.

"She's not in any moral danger, Victor," Paul told him, sharply, "and neither am I. Sister Lilith has instructed her to stay with me, and she's be failing in her duty if she didn't. Even with a limp, she might be able to make herself useful—and it wouldn't be kind to throw her out, would it? Juliette would never forgive me."

Monique, who had known Juliette, cast a rather incredulous glance at the portrait on the wall, but kept her mouth shut, apparently trying to repress the expression of the satisfaction she undoubtedly felt at Paul's decision.

"Thank you all for coming to make sure that I'm all right," Paul went on, "but as you can see, I'm fine. Gaston probably needs more help than I do, back in Toulouse, and I'm sure that Armande is anxious to get back to him. Clémence, we'll talk another time about Lilith's plans, but my opinion now is we both need more information from her about her intentions and expectations before we can think about them seriously. Armande, thank you for what you said; you do have credit, and I'll certainly take note of your opinion. Give my thanks to Gaston, for his usual quick action—he's a godsend to us all."

While he was speaking he was already ushering his guests toward the door. They went slowly, offering opinions and advice all the way. He finally contrived to conduct them to the automobile, where the ritual *au revoirs* were exchanged, and he watched Victor turn the vehicle around, carefully avoiding the section of the road that had crumbled away, the gap of which was increasing because of the further erosion of the edge. Then he went back into the cottage.

Monique was sitting on the sofa, holding the note from Gaston.

"She's hypnotizing her," she said, bluntly.

"Obviously," said Paul. "It might help her to cope with the shock and the loss."

"It might—but that isn't why she's doing it. What do you suppose she wants from Miss Megister?"

"As much as she can obtain," Paul judged "now that Ellen is presumably the legal owner of the estate, and who knows what else in England—or will be, once the death can be officially certified, which might take time in the absence of a body, and Ellen reaches the official age of majority."

"It's lucky I don't believe in magic or ghosts," said Monique, "or else I might be willing to think that the brother really was pushed."

"I have no option but to believe in both," Paul admitted, with a sigh, "and I have a strong suspicion that he might have been. The problem is that I don't know by whom. I have an awful suspicion that I might well have been an unwitting catalyst, but if so, I have no idea on whose behalf I was acting."

"Well," she said, "I, for one, am glad you're crazy, because if you were in your right mind you'd probably have asked your friends to take me back to the convent before returning to Toulouse. I'm not a great cook, but I can limp round a kitchen and I'll do my best. I'm praying that you have plenty of wine in the cellar, and maybe even some of that rotgut that

Salome distils up at the madhouse, strictly for the initiates and you."

"Enough," Paul assured her.

"Good." She looked up at Juliette, ostentatiously, and said: "Honest to God, Scarab, I'll behave. I won't do anything you wouldn't do." She didn't laugh, perhaps not even having realized that it might qualify as a joke. But as she made the sign of the cross, she muttered: "Poor Faby. If only I could be there and your wicked stepmother could be here"—a touch of ingratitude for which Paul forgave her.

CHAPTER XVI

When Paul woke up the next morning, later than usual, the drawing pad beside the bed was blank, for the second day running. Given the duration of the previous day's blackout, he was not surprised. Monique was already up and about, and she made coffee before Paul went down to the village in order to stock up on supplies. Many questions were asked of him there to which he did not know the answers, and his own questions were no more fruitful.

He was climbing the hill again, toiling slightly with the heavy basket, when he heard the sound of an automobile behind him. He stopped and turned, expecting to see the Panhard again. In fact, it was the Megisters' Sunbeam, driven by the ever-reliable Bernard. It was carrying two black-clad passengers: Sister Lilith in her quasi-monastic habit, and Ellen Megister, clad in mourning. Bernard dawdled deliberately, so that he would arrive at the gate of the cottage simultaneously with Paul.

Sister Lilith got out first. "Perhaps you weren't expecting Mademoiselle Megister to keep her appointment for the sitting," she said, "but I advised her to come. In my opinion, posing is exactly what is required of her, for the moment, and for some time to come, and once your friend Gaston had assured her that she could liberate herself from the formalities for a while, he agreed that it might be as well for her to leave Toulouse and spend a few hours in quietude."

Paul did not bother to point out that his model was not wearing the same clothing as the day before and could hardly be expected to reproduce the same facial expression. Instead, as soon as the chauffer had helped his mistress out of the vehicle he went to her and said: "My deepest condolences, Mademoiselle, and my sincere apologies for being unable to lend you my support when you heard the news."

Lilith had moved with him and was by his side. "I've explained to Mademoiselle Megister that you have had such episodes before at moments of great stress," she said. "I am the one that should apologize, for not having been able to offer both of you my assistance. Monsieur Lambrunet criticized me for not bringing you back with us to Toulouse, but you'll understand, I think, that it really wasn't practicable to put you in the automobile while you were unconscious. It seemed more sensible to allow Sister Monique to repay the favor that you had done her, as she was so eager to do that; but if I can be of any assistance now, please ask."

Paul was still looking at Ellen Megister, not entirely surprised to find her serene and composed. "I'm glad that you've recovered, Paul," she said. "Please don't worry if you're not able to resume work on the portrait, or if you think that I've altered too much to allow you simply to continue, at present. I shall have to remain in the vicinity for some time, it seems, while your men of law conduct an investigation into the accident, which might take days, or even weeks, I really did feel that I had to get out of the city for a while. Sister Lilith has been an enormous help."

Paul escorted Ellen and Lilith into the cottage. He offered them breakfast, but Ellen had no appetite. He invited her to sit on the sofa, while Lilith remained standing. Monique offered them coffee, which was similarly refused

"I feel bad," Ellen said, "about the things I was saying yesterday about Richard while you were painting. You weren't saying anything, and I felt a little nervous, so I was just saying things that came into my head. I let out certain...frustrations— but I really did love my brother, dearly, and since mother and father died, he's had a lot of responsibility to bear. He was doing his very best, and I shouldn't have criticized him."

"Of course," Paul said. "To be honest, although I was listening to what you were saying, I wasn't really taking it in. Although I can understand spoken English, and hold reasonably fluent conversations in the language, it's not my native tongue, and it's tends to turn into raw noise when I'm not concentrating intently. When I focus on my painting, I tend to become totally absorbed, almost as if I were in a hypnotic trance, so if you said anything about your brother that you regret, it probably fell on deaf ears."

Ellen contrived a wry smile, evidently unconvinced.

"Monsieur Furneret is being honest," Lilith assured her. "I'm unfamiliar with his case, obviously, although I've heard intriguing second-hand reports, but as I told you last night, I've been interested in the phenomena of hypnotism for many years, and have practiced it intensively. Artists who produce alternative state of consciousness when they work—writers and painters especially—often do become oblivious to what is being said to them, and things that are happening around them—especially if what's being said is in a foreign language."

"But when you hypnotized me last night," the English-woman said, "I didn't fall unconscious. It wasn't like going to sleep—in fact, you told me it wouldn't be, that it would just be helping me to relax, to be calm."

"The old idea that the hypnotism is a kind of artificial sleep—although that's what its name implies—is oversimplified," Lilith told her. "Its phenomena of suggestion are much more varied—as they have to be, if artists are to employ them productively. Monsieur Furneret is unusual, and perhaps unfortunate, in being able to make sketches while asleep, but when he's painting, especially when making portraits with a model, he has to retain a modicum of consciousness that is variable in degree. In the same way, the effects I endeavor to induce are variable, from a simple suggestion that is hardly noticeable to the consciousness of the subject, all the way to an exertion of psychic force that plunge them into complete unconsciousness, provided that they consent. In your case, as you say, I was merely helping you to calm your distress; I had no need to send you to sleep, and it was far better for you to remain fully conscious."

"Not that you would be aware of it now," Paul put in, "if she had put you to sleep."

Ellen reacted to that suggestion with slight alarm.

"Don't be unkind, Paul," said Lilith, mildly. "You mustn't make me out to be some kind of Svengali...or a Zosima." Addressing Ellen, she went on: "My former associate, the founder of the colony, was a very accomplished magnetizer—to use her term—but she was the victim of her own strength, to some extent, able to induce a profound somnambulism with apparent ease but less adept at more delicate forms of suggestion. Paul also seems to be able to plunge himself into a deep trance, perhaps far more frequently that he would wish, but he is also capable of maintaining a much lighter and productive mental balance, crucial to the production of such works of genius at the one in front of you." She gestured at the portrait of Juliette.

"Which is easy when I'm painting the dead," Paul said, "whose mental presence is more easily controllable, but not so easy when painting the living—as evidenced by my sudden loss of consciousness yesterday. I've been trying for years—all my life, in fact—to get the balance right. Sister Lilith would like me to paint her and her associates, in the convent, but I fear that the likelihood of my being able to strike the right balance in such circumstances is extremely remote."

"Your lack of self-confidence is understandable," said Lilith, serenely, "given your history, but I wonder whether you might be underestimating your ability. Your experiences with Zosima have evidently deterred you from seeking assistance, but you have never stopped trying to refine your talent by means of your own efforts. The shock you suffered yesterday was due to an exceptional disturbance, and the work you did on the portrait before collapsing seems first-rate to me. I think the time might be right for a bolder experiment."

"Why is the time right?" said Paul, bluntly. "Because Justine will shortly be seven months pregnant?"

He had hoped to jolt Lilith out of her complacency, but the challenge had no such effect. She did not even turn to glance at Monique, who was hovering in the curtained doorway to the kitchen. "That is a factor," she said, calmly. "There are others—the stars are right, as common parlance has it, and the omens propitious. And let's not be melodramatic. What I have offered you is simply a commission for a portrait, like many others you have accepted and completed. What harm can possibly come of it?"

Paul thought that he could have asked himself exactly the same question twenty-four hours ago—he knew that it would be utterly absurd to think that his setting out to pant Ellen Megister's portrait had anything to do with Richard's catastrophic fall into the abyss. There could be no rational grounds for any such suspicion. Nor were there any rational grounds for suspecting that the fall was anything but a bizarre accident, in spite of what Sister Salome had said.

"And when, exactly, do the stars require the portrait to be made?" he asked.

"The stars are majestically patient in their courses," she riposted, "and a portrait is not something that can be completed in a day, let alone an hour—not normally, at any rate. But as you've just pointed out, Sister Justine's condition imposes temporal considerations of its own."

"And hazards of its own," Paul said. "Not too long ago, a pregnancy at her age would have been regarded as a virtual death sentence, and the risk to the mother and child alike must be estimated to be severe. Your trinity might not survive the summer."

At last he had fired a shot that struck home. For the first time, Lilith was visibly disturbed by that suggestion—but Paul was not at all sure that he ought to feel proud of the achievement.

"I'm sorry," he said. "I shouldn't have said that—but the idea of mothers dying in childbirth has always been a sensitive issue for me, for reasons that you understand."

Ellen Megister was visibly confused.

"Being English, my dear," Sister Lilith said, after a slight pause, "you evidently can't know, but Paul was once notorious in Paris for admitting, in jest, to having murdered his twin sister in the womb, and thus, indirectly, causing the death of his mother in childbirth. Needless to say, he is entirely innocent of any wrongdoing, but he has never quite been able to convince himself of that innocence, so the sudden discovery that Sister Justine is pregnant, at a dangerously advanced age, struck a nerve."

"Oh," said the Englishwoman, still somewhat mystified. "I'm sorry."

"There's no need to apologize, my dear," Lilith told her, "But your sympathy isn't inapt. Whether the experience was traumatic in itself or not, it has had a profound effect on Paul's condition, and the deaths of his sister and his mother before he even acquired consciousness of himself is probably responsible for his becoming what popular gossip calls the painter of the dead. As he is the first to admit, he is a haunted man, if only by the figments of his own unconscious. That is why the news you received yesterday of your brother's accident had such a dramatic repercussion on him. However absurd it might be, in rational terms, he cannot help feeling that he might somehow have had a partial responsibility for the accident."

For the moment, Paul couldn't help feeling that the tables had been turned, and that Lilith had riposted very effectively to the blow that he had struck.

"I think, perhaps, that we should go into the studio now," he said. "If you feel capable of posing, Mademoiselle Megister, I think it might be good for both of us to proceed with the painting."

Ellen seemed a trifle surprised by the change of subject, but all she said in reply, naively, was: "But will you still be able to make me beautiful, when I'm so sad?"

"Sadness," he said, "does not destroy or hinder beauty. The timing, I agree, is far from ideal, and the omens are far from propitious, but you came here today because you thought that sitting for the portrait might help you remain calm in your grief, and if I can be of any help with that...the worst that can happen now is that I do a bad portrait. It wouldn't be the first time, and, if necessary, I can always start over."

"May I watch?" Lilith asked.

"I'd rather you didn't," Paul told her, curtly. "You're welcome to stay here, if you wish. Sister Monique can keep you company."

That did not seem to be a prospect that delighted Sister Monique, but it was hardly a matter that permitted her to show evident displeasure, and she made no protest.

When they were alone in the studio and Ellen sat down in order to pose, she said: "Thank you for that. The Sister has been extremely kind, but...I can't help finding her presence a trifle oppressive and intimidating, knowing...what she is."

Paul assumed that she did not mean a fake nun, but he did not want to pursue the point.

"I hope that my presence will be more tolerable," he remarked, "in spite of what you've just heard."

"Oh, it is," she assured him. "I'm an orphan myself, and although my mother didn't die in childbirth, I've always had an irrational feeling that if I'd been better behaved, she wouldn't have gone away. Richard never felt that, I know, but he was hit hard when Father died, leaving him the notional head of the family while he was little more than a child. These things are disturbing" After a pause, she added: "But I don't understand how that nun we met yesterday can be pregnant, if she's...what she is...and at her age. She's surely over forty."

"I find it hard to believe too," Paul admitted. "Which is to say, I can understand how, but not why. The sisters have some strange ideas, though, which no one from outside the region can fully understand, so intertwined are they with old legends and old superstitions."

"Oh, I know all about the legend of the three Maries now, and the notion of true Marians descended from them through the female line, although I don't find it at all plausible that I might be one, just because a twelfth- or thirteenth-century ancestor married a Frenchwoman while he was fighting in the Albigensian crusade."

"It does require a certain stretch of the imagination," Paul conceded, "but there are plenty of people in the vicinity whose imaginations stretch that far and further. Lilith is far from being the only one, and it seems that she's her mother's daughter, just as my mother and Gaston Lambrunet's mother were her mother's protégés. Gaston has never been let in on the secrets of the sorority, because he's a man, but Lilith seems to have constructed a special case for me."

"Because she wants you to paint her?"

"In crude terms, yes—but she takes the notion that I'm the painter of the dead far more seriously than most people who quote the phrase. She believes that I really can summon spirits, not just from my own unconscious mind but from the beyond. Other people have believed that, and have been satisfied that I've done it, but their views have been confined to the routine concerns that drive people to consult spiritists—the desire to consult dead relatives. Lilith's ambitions apparently go far beyond that. It seems, if Monique hasn't misinterpreted what she's overheard, that she wants me to help her summon *the* Spirit: the paraclete—or, more likely, in Gnostic terms, Sophia or Ennoia: the wisdom of God conceived symbolically as female."

"And she wants you to aid its incarnation in Sister Justine's baby?"

"Apparently, but I've only pieced the story together from hearsay, accidentally or deliberately revealed. I might be wrong."

Paul was prepared to leave it at that, but Ellen Megister's curiosity had been piqued. "Do you think the pregnancy was contrived specifically for that purpose?" she asked.

"Possibly. On the other hand, maybe it was an unexpected accident, for which the trinity felt compelled to find an explanation—not a biological explanation, with would presumably be simple enough, but a supplementary supernatural explanation: something that fits into their notion of who and what they are. Perhaps Justine has never been able to bring herself to explain to her sisters how it happened...and perhaps there's a third possibility."

"Which is?"

"That she isn't really pregnant at all: that it's what modern medical jargon calls hysterical pregnancy, or pseudocyesis. It's a condition from which even queens of the realm have be known to suffer in England, but which is more common in France in nuns preoccupied with the idea of virgin birth."

"Yes, I've heard of that...you mean Queen Mary—Bloody Mary."

"She's the most famous example—but whether that's the case here, I have no idea...and it's quite possible that they have no idea themselves."

"But Sister Lilith seems such a reasonable person, intelligent and controlled."

"So do I," said Paul, a trifle grimly. "It doesn't stop me drawing dead people in my sleep, or painting them and talking to them, even though they can't talk back. In spite of that, I think I'm perfectly sane, and some very intelligent and discriminating people have kindly help to shore up that belief."

"Including Sister Lilith?"

"I only met her for the first time a couple of days ago, when you were present, and I'm certainly not convinced that she qualifies as discriminating, or that she has any interest in shoring up my convictions of sanity. I was thinking of Camille Flammarion and the lady over there, whom your brother called disgusting, but who was actually anything but."

"Forgive him for that," she said. "He inherited my father's prejudices as well as his estate. I was partly spared, precisely because one of those prejudices was that I'm a weak-minded girl, a daughter of Eve. I suppose I have to hope now that they're wrong, as the Megister wealth will soon be all mine, to do with as I wish... or what my husband wishes. I presume that eager suitors will already be forming a queue back home, now that wireless telegraphy has brought them the news in dots and dashes."

"Inevitably," Paul agreed.

"Lilith says that she can help me with that. She says that she can enable me to remember past incarnations of the perpetually-replicated ovum that produced me, in order to draw upon the experience of numerous strong, independent women, strung out over generations going all the way back to the Massalian Daughters of Artemis—amazons of a sort. Some favored subjects, she says, can remember lives even more remote, from the dawn of human consciousness and the origins of religion, when humans were much more fearful of the forces of nature and all deities were terrible. She says that we've made great psychological progress since then, and that some of us might be closer to the terminus of enlightenment than we assume"

"I believe that Lilith makes something of a specialty of enabling women to remember—or invent—remote past lives," Paul said, carefully refraining from passing judgment on what Ellen had just related to him. "Zosima is certain that such psychic adventures help enormously to give women a better image of themselves, and to help them feel stronger."

"By turning them into lesbians? Demon-spawn, as Richard would probably have put it."

"I genuinely don't think that that's her primary purpose, or even a hidden agenda. Zosima, it has always seemed to me, had genuinely altruistic motives in founding her organization, and she certainly didn't make lesbianism compulsory within her cult, although Monique does seem to have found a certain tacit moral pressure uncomfortable. Tolerance was always Zosima's watchword, although I don't know whether that will subsist now that Lilith's in charge."

"So you don't think that Lilith is trying to...convert me?"

"If she is, her primary objective is undoubtedly to convert you to her eccentric species of Marianism. Whether that necessarily entails lesbian practices, I wouldn't know."

"And can hypnotism do that?"

"Again, I wouldn't know exactly what hypnotism can achieve and what it can't. I expect it varies from person to person, and I'd hesitate to generalize from my own idiosyncratic case even if I were sure of the effects it has allegedly had."

"What do you mean?"

Paul hesitated, but eventually shrugged his shoulders—metaphorically, given that he was making every effort to hold his hand perfectly steady in order to apply paint in the precise manner that he wished.

"When I was a child I was hypnotized by Amélie Lambrunet. According to Zosima, a hypnotic suggestion she planted has had a profound effect on my personality and conduct in adult life. Lilith, who has more direct knowledge of what Amélie did and why, denies that it had the effect that Zosima attributed to it, speculatively, but claims that it had a considerable effect in the development my artistry...or my curse."

"Why call it a curse? Surely it's a gift?"

"That is one way of looking at it—perhaps the reasonable way."

"And what's the unreasonable way?"

Again, Paul hesitated. Then he countered the question with a question: "Why did you want me to paint your portrait, with sufficient determination to defy your brother, who clearly didn't want me to do it."

"Partly for that very reason," she said. "It was something in which I could oppose him, to make a stand against his petty tyranny. He was being unreasonable, thinking that you might try to seduce me—or, more seriously, that I might try to seduce you. And also because you're famous, in a way that isn't banal. Isn't that perfectly reasonable?"

"Perfectly. And if asked, Armande Lambrunet would presumably say something very similar, and that would be perfectly reasonable too. And I'd believe it, just as I believe you—because it would be absurd, wouldn't it, to think that my portrait of Juliette had hypnotized you both."

"You can't believe that!"

"Indeed I can't. As I said, it would be ludicrous. Just as ludicrous as thinking that a picture of that I once painted of Juliette, costumed as Jeanne d'Arc, nearly killed her by hypnotizing her into hallucinating that she was burning to death, and that when she survived, I felt obliged to spend the rest of her life trying to atone for it. Nobody could believe that seriously, any more than they could believe that I was responsible for Talia Cadelan's death, also from tuberculosis, even though she started vomiting blood while I was under hypnosis, or that the portrait I did of Talia could have provoked Baron de Rochemure's cancer, or that I was responsible for your brother's death yesterday while I was here, in a trance, painting. All of that is utterly absurd. From a reasonable viewpoint, my artistic talent is a gift, not a curse, and neither I nor my paintings have the affliction of the evil eye. And what Lilith suggested to me two nights ago about my sister's soul still being alive in mine, whether in a real or illusory fashion, because when I killed her in the womb, by means of the hereditary telepathic link between our nascent brains, I sucked her identity into mine, is just a fantasy, and I'm right not to believe a word of it. But irrational guilt feelings can be surprisingly tenacious, can't they?"

She thought about that for a moment or two, and then said: "Do you think everyone has them?"

"If they do," Paul said, sourly, "they certainly don't let on. If I had to guess, I'd say that most people are fairly successful at suppressing them—more so than me, at any rate."

"And that's what Lilith was trying to do for me last night? Suppress my irrational guilt feelings about Richard—feelings I had because of what I was saying about him before he fell, which you say you didn't hear?"

"Probably," Paul agreed.

After a pause, she said: "I don't think it's working."

"Give it time," Paul advised. "If there's one thing I've learned in life—and there aren't many others, alas—it's that it isn't easy being reasonable, but that you have to try. You really do have to try. There's no rational alternative."

"So," she countered, perhaps not quite ready to try as yet, "if it turns out that my portrait has the hypnotic eyes I wanted, you don't think I need to lock it away in a cupboard, in case it starts killing people—because that would be absurd?"

314

"It would," Paul agreed.

"And even in the realms of absurdity, that portrait in the other room only makes impressionable young women want to have their own portraits painted, which is hardly a serious crime?"

"That's good," said Paul. "Turn it into a game, a joke. That's what I do."

"But just in case, you haven't painted any more martyrdoms since your model was hallucinated?"

That gave Paul slight pause. "Not consciously," he said. "I did do a second Jeanne d'Arc, but that was a deliberate reparation, to show her with sword in hand, inspired by her saints to fight adversity."

"And unconsciously?"

"Unconsciously, yes, I've sketched more martyrdoms. That is rather the problem," he said. "I have no control, you see. I can't pick and choose what my telepathy does while I'm not conscious. But I'm in control now; I went at it too hard yesterday; this is better. The dialogue helps."

"I think it's helping me too. Do you think I ought to stay away from Lilith, and refuse to let her hypnotize me again?"

"I honestly don't know. Similar advice has certainly been given to me, by people who had my best interests at heart. Jane forbade me to have anything more to do with Zosima for as long as she was alive, and if she knew that Lilith was now taking an interest in me, she'd probably repeat the advice."

"She forbade you?"

"That was just her way of making the point forcefully. She knew that she didn't have any power actually to forbid me. Zosima's face when she did it was a sight to behold, though. She couldn't believe that I didn't object. She told me, however, that she'd come to understand, later."

"So you did have more to do with her in spite of the prohibition."

"Not while Jane was alive. I stuck to the letter of the contract. And Zosima, in all fairness, didn't try to push very hard, even to spite Lilith. She simply invited me to continue my experiments in hypnotism with her and Camille Flammarion at Juvisy rather than playing Marian games with Lilith—but I don't think she knows exactly what Lilith has planned. If she did, she might have pushed a little harder, because she believes, in spite of the irrationality, that what I do...or what my unconscious mind can do when it's let off the leash, really is dangerous."

"And when she hears what happened to Richard, will she be even more convinced?"

"I don't know. Richard simply lost his footing and fell, remember. It would be absurd to think otherwise."

"That's not what Sister Salome told Sister Lilith."

"Well, I'm not at all sure than Lilith had any right to repeat that to you, even if she believed it herself. But as you're here, and seem to find my presence more reassuring than hers, I assume that she didn't accuse me of administering the phantom push?"

"No, and she didn't accuse me, either. She said that she only told me what Salome had said because she was afraid I might hear it from someone else, and she wanted me to know that Salome had something of a fixation about the Great Cleft being haunted, and thinks that it has a hunger that sometimes draws people into it. She said that it was something that came out of more than one of the anterior lives she remembered—Salome, that is—because so many of those lives had been spent on or near the mountain, including some on the site of this cottage. She said that Salome was frightened for you, because you'd been drawn to the cleft yourself only a day or two before, and might easily have fallen victim to it yourself."

"It's kind of her to be concerned," Paul said, unable to help feeling a slight chill, "but I've lived here for nearly eight years, and I've walked past the cleft many a time without feeling any supernatural attraction to it or any force impelling me toward the rim. It's not the only pothole in the south of France that has that reputation—there are dozens of caves that have the reputation of being the lairs of undines, empusas or other seductive monsters. It's the fantasy itself that's tempting. And people do go down them, looking for imaginary treasures or just out of curiosity, and some of them don't come back, because they're dangerous places. Other caves have paintings in them, which probably go back to Mousterian or Magdalenian time, with probably had some magical function—again, simply because caves and supposedly bottomless pits exert an inherent fascination on the human imagination. I don't doubt for a moment that the professors from the university who have been rigging up all that equipment for several days really do have serious geological investigations to pursue, but that's not the whole reason why they want to go down into the cleft, and one doesn't need the interpretation that Doctor Freud would undoubtedly impose of the symbolism of the feature to explain that."

"Who's Doctor Freud?"

"A Viennese psychoanalyst. He published a book on the interpretation of dreams a few years ago."

"Oh, yes. I think Richard might have mentioned it. *Poppycock*, think, was his verdict—but he didn't read it."

"A judgment that Dr, Freud would doubtless have analyzed in his own fashion. But let's not lose sight of simple likelihood. Richard went for a walk because he was bored. He saw the men working at the lip of the cleft and sent to watch, idly. He wasn't concentrating, went too close to the edge, and slipped on treacherous vegetation—or perhaps he was stung by a bee or a scorpion disturbed by the workmen. It was an accident. Sister Salome probably won't be the only unorthodox thinker to read something more into it; she just happened to be close enough, drawn by her own fascination, to misinterpret what she saw—but it can't alter the fact that it was just an accident."

He could not help remembering, however, that in Sigmund Freud's view of the world, as well Salome's, there were no accidents. He met Jane's gaze, across the studio, briefly, glad to find no criticism therein, and breathed in the sickly emanations of the colors on his palette. Then he stepped back momentarily to study his handiwork. Again, he was making rapid progress, even though he had not lost consciousness for a single instant.

Ellen took advantage of his pause to say: "Can I take a break? My neck is getting stiff."

"Of course," Paul said. "Take as long as you need."

She immediately went to stand in front of the portrait of Jane, and studied it carefully. After a few minutes, she said: "Where are you going to hang it?"

"I don't know," Paul admitted. "I can't hang her in the dining room, because Juliette might be jealous, and I can't hang her in the bedroom, because Virginie might be jealous. Perhaps I'll hang her in here permanently, so she can preside over my work. She played a major part in launching my career, by buying one of my early paintings and commissioning me to do a portrait of her—the first important commission I received after I won my first minor medal in the Salon."

"And where's that one now?" Ellen asked, innocently.

"I don't know," Paul admitted. "For a long time, it was in her boudoir in Paris. I assume that her husband has it, or perhaps her son."

She turned to look at him, but said nothing until she broke the silence by saying, half to herself. "I must try again to read one of her books, although I'm not that much better at reading French than Richard is—was." Then she added: "Which is the one he would have disapproved of most and would have forbidden me even to open?"

"I can't be sure," Paul said, equably, "but *Le Mystère de Kama* is probably the most notorious. It's certainly not likely to be translated into English any time soon."

"But it's not disgusting?"

"Well, yes, in a way it is, and deliberately so. It's a horror story about the exploitation and oppression of women by men, and the manner in which women are led by their treacherous emotions not merely to endure it but to collaborate with it, because it's impossible to fight it."

"It doesn't have a happy ending then?"

"Not in the conventional sense of the hero and heroine achieving a loving marriage and economic security. Few of Jane's books do end that way. She was always reluctant to pander to popular demand in that regard. She thought that kind of happy ending extremely rare in real life, perhaps impossible."

"And you agree with her?"

Paul considered that question carefully before saying: "Not entirely. I'd certainly like to think otherwise, for Gaston and Armande, for instance, and for Victor and Clorinde...and for you."

"But not for yourself?"

"I haven't given up hope of that either."

"But you think it unlikely?"

"I'm not a businessman like Gaston or Victor. I'm a painter. For me, that kind of happiness isn't the primary goal of life."

"You think you need to suffer for your art?"

"No—and on the whole, I'd rather not. In fact, I think suffering is mainly injurious to study and creativity, whatever popular mythology says. But I also think that a career as a painter, or a writer, is injurious to the kind of happiness that a contented marriage and children are supposed to provide for...well, for the orthodox. And in my particular case...I don't think any sane woman could be happy with me. I can't provide what she would need."

"That's sad," she said, after a moment. "But don't lose heart—there are always the insane...or the sick."

"I know—and it's something of a comfort to me."

She walked around the easel then, in order to study her own portrait.

"You haven't copied my mourning," she said.

"No. The costume you were wearing yesterday is already in place, and I saw no necessity to paint over it. I've mostly been working on the hair and the face."

"But not the eyes. I can't possibly look as sad in reality as I do in your picture, with only dark blurs for eyes."

"It isn't finished. There's a lot more work to do. Things have to be done in order, and it isn't simply a matter of letting some patches dry before you apply adjacent colors. Eyes take time. Some painters prefer to work on them first, but I can't get them right in isolation. I need the rest of the face in place before I can begin to make sense of the eyes. It's an idiosyncrasy, I suppose. There are an infinite number of ways to construct a face on canvas; I have mine, as others have theirs. Copying reality is difficult; capturing its essence is very difficult, reproducing its beauty...that's the holy grail. Nobody ever succeeds entirely, because beauty is a living, dynamic thing, and you can only produce the illusion of it on canvas, but artists are privileged, I think, because they can at least search for it, and appreciate it when they find it. It seems to me that most people can't, and that a surprising number are far more able to perceive it in the illusion on canvas than in the reality. *That*'s sad. But I shouldn't praise myself; all my best paintings are paintings of the dead, reproducing beauty that I couldn't perceive fully while the people were alive. I'm hoping that this one might be one of the rare exceptions...the true grail, an almost-accurate reproduction of living beauty."

"For the derisory fee that Richard offered you, hoping that you'd turn it down?"

"No, for the challenge, for the quest. But I won't know whether I've succeeded until I've finished—and if I fail, the derisory fee will be all it's worth, and I won't feel cheated in accepting it."

"And if you succeed?"

"Oh, then you could have it for nothing, because I'd already have had the reward—but I'll take the fee anyway. A man has to eat."

"If you succeed," she said, "I'll more than double it."

"That would be very kind. Not unprecedented, I'm glad to say, but very kind."

"And if you do decide to paint Lilith, Salome and Justine, will you be able to find any beauty in their faces, the way you did with her?" She flicked a finger in the direction of the portrait of Jane de La Vaudère."

"I certainly hope so," Paul said. "What would be the point of doing it, otherwise?"

"To see the Wisdom of God?"

"Oh, I won't see the Wisdom of their Goddess, even if I enable them to see it. I'll fall unconscious. The best I can hope for is that when I look at what I've done, I won't be appalled, and might be glad, and that if the other people present report any hallucinations they might have had, they won't have seen horrors—or, if they have, that they've also seen angels. There can't be any guarantees, but there's always hope isn't there?"

"I don't know," she said. "Is there?"

He thought about the little he knew about the witnesses who were likely be recruited to share any telepathic visions he was able to catalyze, if he accepted Lilith's commission: Lilith, Salome, Justine, Clémence, perhaps Monique, or at least some other true Marian of similar ilk and fallibility.

Is there? he asked himself. *Who can tell?* But the reasonable thing to do, surely, would be to refuse the commission, if that were any longer possible.

"We should get back to work," he said, "if you're rested. I can't do much more today, but what I can do, I should."

"There isn't a deadline anymore," she said.

"Yes there is," he said. "The toils of official procedure will snatch you up very shortly, and might keep you in Toulouse for days. Respites like this one might not be easy to obtain in future."

"It might be a terrible thing to say," she said, "but finishing the painting is my top propriety, more important than anything else. If Richard can hear me, from the bottom of his abyss, he'll probably never forgive me, but he's dead and I'm alive, and I want you to finish, and to succeed. The hell with mourning, the hell with grief, and the hell with Hell. But please don't tell anyone else I said so."

"I won't," Paul promised.

CHAPTER XVII

As the Sunbeam finally pulled away, heading for the convent, still carrying two black-clad passengers, Richard turned back to the cottage thoughtfully. Sister Monique was standing in the doorway.

"It should go past again in a few minutes," she observed, "heading in the opposite direction, with only one passenger." She sounded skeptical.

"It will," Paul said, confidently. "Whatever post-hypnotic suggestions Lilith might have planted in Ellen's mind won't take effect until all the legal formalities are tidied away. And I can't believe that Lilith wants her to join the colony. She just wants distant sympathy."

"Don't be too sure of that," Monique said. "She might think that all her ambitions are focused on the Holy Spirit, but when you dig deep down in anyone's motivations, you usually find vulgar lust in fancy dress."

"I don't think Ellen's that way inclined," said Paul, as they went back into the cottage.

"No? Well, you're the one who's been locked away with the little flirt for hours on end, so you obviously know her much better than I do—but don't underestimate Lilith. She old now, but she still knows how to work the magic. I'm not *that way inclined* myself, but she's had me. Then again, who hasn't? Except you, obviously."

While she was speaking she slumped down on the sofa.

"Juliette would never forgive me," Paul observed, dryly.

"Juliette's dead. It was bad enough letting her push you around with her little girl act while she was alive, but letting her do it now is just stupid. And if you're just using her as an excuse, that's even worse...unless, I suppose, you're hankering after the English girl yourself. She does look rather sweet in mourning, and grief sometimes makes women do crazy things, so you're probably in with a chance if you care to try."

"I never make improper advances to my sitters," Paul said. "I wouldn't want to ruin my reputation."

"If you think that a reputation like yours could suffer any further ruination, you're living in Cloudcuckooland."

"The accusation has been made before. Is this the way it's going to be, now you seem to have settled in for the duration? A constant stream of abuse and insults?"

She seemed slightly startled by the remark, as if she had not realized that she might have said anything offensive. After a pause for thought she said: "Sorry. Lilith rattled me a bit. As you can imagine, the chat we were having in here was less pleasant for me than the one you were having in there probably was for you. I tried to pretend that I was being a good little pawn, but she wasn't convinced, and I was a little offended that she didn't really seem to care. She obviously thinks that you're well and truly hooked, and that nothing I could say can unhook you. She's probably right. Why would I want to, anyway? It's not as if you'd whisk me off to Paris, is it? I'm in the convent for good, aren't I?"

"Probably," Paul agreed, blithely. "I don't suppose it'll get any worse without Zosima, even if I can't summon the Holy Ghost for Justine's child...assuming that there really is a child."

"I think you can take that for granted. Lilith took her into Toulouse yesterday to see a doctor—a real doctor, not some so-called wise woman."

"How on earth did it happen, then? Not at the convent, I assume?"

"Probably not. More likely some lusty lad from the village, although Justine doesn't go to market—that's strictly for the penitents, like me, and personally, I draw the line at quick fumbles in a pig sty for a few copper coins. It's a puzzle."

"It must have involved more planning than that," Paul mused. "And if Lilith planned it, she would have wanted...oh!"

"Oh what?"

Paul went to the larder, and came back with a bottle of convent brandy.

"Thank the goddess," said Monique. "I thought you'd never volunteer, and I was already weighing up the risk of being thrown out if you caught me swigging it on the sly."

"You're not allowed to drink this stuff in the convent?" he asked.

"No, of course not. Strictly a commercial venture, for re-sale in Toulouse, so far as I know—except for you and old Louvot. You're privileged—unless Salome's just using you as a poison taster to make sure...oh! I see what you mean. Do you really think...?"

"That they slipped us a drugged bottle seven months ago, so that Justine could take advantage of me while I was unconscious and Madame Louvot was fast asleep? No, it's absurd—but then, absurd is the normal in these parts. But they do know perfectly well that if they can catch me in the process of somnifabrication, I wouldn't remember a thing afterwards. A cupful of semen, a rapid donkey-ride up to the convent and a syringe...it's bizarre, but not impossible...and I'm not only a true Marian, in their estimation, but a psychic androgyne...the perfect candidate, at that end of the process as well as the other..."

Monique laughed. When she saw the way that Paul was looking at her, she stopped, but said: "Well, it if that's actually what happened, it really is funny. Do you honestly think they could be that crazy?"

"I can hardly rule it out...but on the whole, I think some secret escapade in Toulouse is the likelier explanation." He went into the studio them in order to add a few touches to the painting and tidy up. At least half an hour went by before he was drawn to the window because he heard an automobile making its way down the hill, slowing down in order to pass carefully around the subsidence opposite the gate.

He went back into the main room, where Monique was still sprawled on the sofa, staring at Juliette. She didn't bother to get up, but simply waited for him to say: "One passenger, dressed in mourning. Lilith must have given her a short guided tour of the sanctuary."

Monique shrugged, and then said: "While we're not ruling things out, do you think what happened to her husband really was an accident, or did Lilith give him a magical push?"

"If it had been Lilith," Paul said, thoughtfully, "Salome would hardly have made a fuss about him being pushed, given that nobody else did. No, I don't think that was the Three Witches, any more than Fabien getting shot was anything to do with them. They might dream about being huntresses and amazons in past lives, but they're polite and civilized now. They surely aren't murderous. If Richard had help going into the cleft..." He stopped.

Monique had sat up straight in order to take the bottle of liqueur from his hand. She removed the stopper, and took a swig directly from the bottleneck. Then she pulled a face, and said: "Goddess, that's awful!"

"It's an acquired taste," Paul said, absent-mindedly.

She took another swig, and then shrugged her shoulders. "Well, I suppose I could acquire it. Go on, then."

"Go on with what?"

"Go on telling me who did do it, if it wasn't the Three Witches. Who gave Richard Megister the supernatural push? Surely not his sister?"

"No," said Paul, "definitely not his sister—but I'm not so sure about mine."

"Yours?"

"You've seen her picture in the bedroom. She's been dead for a long time...but if Zosima and Lilith can be trusted, that hasn't stopped her drawing. And it wouldn't be the first time that a psychic force born of my entrancement had driven someone to make a fatal leap."

"Scarab? But that doesn't make sense. You didn't love her then, I know, but you had nothing against her. And if Lilith's polite and civilized, you're positively meek and mild. Murderous, you certainly aren't."

"No," Paul agreed. "I'm certainly not, but..."

"But what?"

"As I said, I'm not so sure about my sister."

"You're crazy."

"I think we've already established that. The question is, how crazy...and how dangerous?"

"You're just trying to put the wind up me—to scare me off."

"No, I think I'm trying to put the wind up myself...and I think I'm succeeding."

She held out the bottle. "Have a drink!"

"And you think that will make me feel better, after the fantasy I just cooked up regarding Justine's mysterious pregnancy?"

"It always used to work for me," she said, taking a third swig. "And you're right—once the alcohol kicks in, the taste almost becomes tolerable. They're never going to make a fortune out to it, though, unless they improve it vastly. Anyway, stop being so ridiculous. Even I can think of killers much more likely than the ghost of your dead sister, if there really was a supernatural push."

"For instance?"

"The goddess."

"Artemis, you mean?"

"No. Artemis came before the Virgin of the Maries and the Cathars, but she wasn't the beginning of the series. I mean the primal goddess"

"The hypothetical primal goddess" Paul rectified. "The Parisian Occultists who call her the Triple Goddess didn't even make up a name for her, in order to add that extra touch of mystery. Or has Lilith discovered one in someone's dreams?"

"Not as far as I know. But the sisters who mention her generally add a little shudder. Those were the days of actual human sacrifice, they say—the sacrifice of males, at any rate."

"It's a fantasy," Paul asserted, confidently. "If the anterior lives of the true Marians only went back as far as the first three Maries and the Sea of Galilee, they'd be more than a little tedious—mostly sufferings and martyrdoms, in much the same spirit as the Church's legends of the saints; hence the invocation of Artemis, the active huntress, much more useful for Zosima's psychotherapy, and the amazons. The theory is that you and others like you have to explore your strength in fantasies before you can begin to develop it is reality."

"Your theory, not theirs," said Monique. "It's all secret, obviously, but the initiates are proud of being able to recover deeper memories that only the gifted and the privileged can access. There's status attached to it, and a competition of sorts—a competition to rediscover lives that are a lot more fun: less praying and suffering, more action and violence."

"I can understand that," Paul said, nodding his head. "The wives, daughters and sisters of Toulouse and Paris must build up an abundant supply of resentment against the men who rule their lives, just as Ellen did against Richard, which diplomacy forces them to suppress. It must be much worse for...well, the likes of you and Juliette. Zosima's hypnosis, when she first started the Paris refuge, was a means of establishing a space where those resentments could be expressed, not only in fantasies of imaginary societies from which men were excluded or reduced to powerlessness, but fantasies of violent revenge."

Fantasies, he thought, that sometimes couldn't be contained. When Ignatz Fell had raped Angélique, she had repressed her anger, but when he had raped her sister she had been furious with herself for not having acted before, for having allowed it to happen...and the baron had understood that, and he had protected her from the law, not because she was his lover, but because he approved of the murder.

"And it's not just the goddess," Monique added. "There are monsters too. Everybody dreams about monsters, I suppose—but most people are scared by them, in nightmares. The initiates are proud of turning the tables. They're supposed to keep it secret, but it's common knowledge up there that the initiates dream of *being* monsters. The sirens of the Clefts are favorites, apparently: empusas, lamias, nixies or whatever, part woman and part animal...snake, worm or scorpion, take your pick. Maybe it wasn't a push that took Richard Megister into the Cleft, but a pull."

That too was understandable, Paul thought, in terms of what little he knew of Zosima's hypnotic therapy. It was not simply a matter of helping the weak imagine themselves as strong, but of enabling the intimidated to imagine that they could be intimidating, the haunted to imagine that they were haunters, the terrified to imagine that they were administrators rather victims of terror.

Aloud, he said: "You can't believe that there are monsters of the Cleft." His voice was skeptical, but he knew that Monique, like Lilith and Salome, was Toulousan by birth. She had grown up with all the local legends and horror stories. As a child, they might well have terrified her, if not entirely consciously....

"Of course I can't," she replied. "But there are people up the hill who can...and I have my doubts about you."

Not unreasonably, Paul thought. The monsters of that kind in which he believed were, of course only figments of his unconscious mind...but they surfaced repeatedly in his somnifabrications, perhaps emerging from a symbolic dream-equivalent of the Great Cleft, and he had never understood why.

"On the other hand," Monique added. "The arrogant pig might just have thought that, being a big bold Englishman, he ought to show the local Frenchies what a fine, devil-may care fellow he was, immune to such weaknesses as vertigo—so he deliberately went too close to the edge, and then found that his immunity wasn't as secure as he thought. It happens, especially to men who buy fancy automobiles and ride them all the way to the south of France in order to show off to the peasants what fine fellows they are. Believe me, having been a whore in Montmartre, I know the type."

"And what Salome saw?" Paul queried.

"What *only* Salome saw, you mean: the Salome notorious in the convent for having dreams about the Great Cleft—who was only there because she has dreams about it. You've met her. Is she your idea of a reliable witness?"

"No," Paul admitted, immediately having mental recourse once again to the hypothetical sting that had made the English man start with shock, administered by a sly wasp, or a scorpion disturbed in the undergrowth, which had climbed up his leg.

But Monique was only fantasizing herself, letting her tongue run away with her in order to make conversation. She didn't believe in the primal goddess, or chimerical monsters. She retired with the utmost facility behind the ramparts of her own particular consciousness.

"If you don't want a drink," she said, "I know another way to bring you down to earth. We could put a dust-cloth over your sister if you don't want her to watch."

"No, thank you."

"Because Scarab would never forgive you?" There was more contempt in her voice than disappointment, but that might have been a sham born of resentment.

"No," said Paul, tersely. "Just because."

She opened her mouth, perhaps to argue or protest, but she was cut off by the bell at the gate. She did not get up from the sofa.

Paul went to answer the summons.

The two men waiting at the gate, having descended from an old-fashioned cabriolet pulled by a chestnut mare, were clad in black and possessed of the formal stiffness and varnish that years of bureaucratic formality are required to hone and polish. They were far out of their element on the mountain, and seemed well aware of it. Their self-introduction revealed, unsurprisingly, that they were an examining magistrate and his clerk, calling on their way back from visiting the Great Cleft, in order to collect Paul's official statement: a pure technicality, given that he had not actually witnessed the accident.

He invited them in, and confirmed formally that he had, in fact, been in the cottage at the time of the incident, with Ellen Megister. He also gave them a selective and somewhat censored account of what he had been able to observe of Richard Megister's character, and his state of mind on the day of the catastrophe. He also mentioned the possibility that the unaccustomed activity around the rim of the cleft might have stirred up the local wildlife, long used to peace and quiet, and provoked a surreptitious bite or sting. The examining magistrate seemed to like that hypothesis, and asked his clerk to make a careful note of it. He even shuddered slightly as he looked down at his trousers, wondering whether anything might have climbed up his own leg in the course of his investigation of the scene of the incident.

Monique, who had consented to stand up but had not let go of the bottle of liqueur, confirmed with equal formality that she had been present in the cottage too, in the other room, with Sister Lilith. She did not mention dreams of Artemis or any other goddess, amazons or any other warrior women, empusas or any other monsters.

As a matter of excessive scrupulousness, the magistrate asked to see the studio, where Paul showed him the recently-completed picture of Jane de La Vaudère as well as the portrait in progress. The officer of the law admired the portrait of Jane silently, but did not ask the name of the model. He paid the artist a single token compliment, taking in both paintings in an insultingly casual fashion, and glanced again at the portrait of Juliette as they returned to the main room. Then he left, with his dutiful clerk in tow. There seemed to be absolutely no doubt in his mind that the death had been an unfortunate accident, only troublesome because it would require some bureaucratic dealings with the English consulate. How could it be otherwise?

Dusk was falling as the magistrate's cabriolet made its way carefully down to the village, but it was a clear night, and the twilight was adequate to allow them to make the journey safely, even without the aid of a lantern.

When they were alone again, Monique consented to limp into the kitchen in order to demonstrate the expertise in the culinary arts that she had cultivated during her years in Zosima's organization. The expertise in question, when it was eventually displayed, was not up to Madame Louvot's standard, but it was perfectly adequate. The wine that Paul and Monique drank with the meal did not come from the convent, and the repast was not concluded by a glass of liqueur—not, at least, in the dining room. Monique did not make any further indecent suggestions, and she retired meekly to Madame Louvot's room when Paul decided that he wanted to go to bed.

The relative abstinence of the meal and its aftermath did not seem to have provided Paul with any protection from the hallucinatory effects of a strange day. There were too many hypothetical questions floating in his head. Might he really be due to become the father, via drug-assisted artificial insemination, of Lilith's Ennoia, an imaginary incarnation of divine wisdom? What if the child turned out to be a boy? Either way, what might be expected of him afterwards, in the increasingly unlikely event that he had painted the Three Witches, and they had hurled the newborn's umbilical cord into the bottomless pit? Would it not be wiser by far for him to finish the portrait of Ellen Megister, and then throw his baggage into the trunk of Victor's Panhard, in order to head for Paris as fast as the vehicle could carry him, there to paint Armande and Clorinde, to serve as a witness at Victor's wedding, and to allow Victor to find him a studio in Montparnasse, where he could set lures for American heiresses and the native nouveau riche, with a view to building the careful commercial career that Auguste Chazelle had always wanted him to adopt, while Victor shopped around on his behalf for a Clorinde of his own, more romantically inclined than the original, who might be able to tolerate the eccentricities of an artist who made incomprehensible drawings in his sleep...?

After all, he thought, what was keeping him here, now that his presence in Paris could no longer be an embarrassment to anyone, whereas his presence on the mountain would inevitably become an increasing embarrassment to himself.

What, indeed?

As to the reply to that, like so much else, it was a mystery. And yet...he still felt that this was his home. Why? Because he had been hypnotized into that sensation in the distant past of his childhood or early adolescence, and had never been able to get away from it even while resident in Montmartre? Or simply because the "angel" that had allegedly saved him from a fatal plunge in the dream he had catalyzed in Passy had told him to "go home"? Or because he really was a true Marian, substituting for the daughter that his mother had desired, and to whom she believed, briefly, that she had actually given birth? Or because he was simply psychically captive in a cottage allegedly built on a site where the mother of John of the Apocalypse had once lived, delivered to her custody like John the Baptist's head on a platter, in spite of the blatant anachronism that prevented the imaginary Salome from having danced for Herod as a child and being the mother of Jesus's favorite ephebe only a few years later. One did not need to go back beyond Artemis to find legendary instances of the terrible Triple Goddess surfacing momentarily within her milder avatars.

None of the possible answers to those questions made any sense, of course. He could not make sense of himself, and had never been able to do so, even with the aid of expert counsel. He was, in essence, a chimerical creature: a bizarre compound incapable of actual life; a product of the inventiveness of the collective imagination. *But isn't everyone?* he thought. *Isn't everyone a hybrid product of the unconscious and the conscious aspects of mind*

Where on earth, in fact, was the soul not subject to the vagaries of dreaming and the surreptitious pressures of repressed feelings? Some people were more prone to it than others, hence the existence of artists and visionaries, but who was immune? Certainly no one that he had ever known. The challenge was not to avoid failing to make sense, but to find a means to live with it—and, if possible, to draw upon one's own nonsensicality, to mine it for seams of inspiration...in spite of the dangers that all miners faced, whether working in actual or metaphorical pits.

That was what he had been doing all his life, simultaneously aided and menaced by the processes of his self-hypnosis. Perhaps he had been further aided in that, as a child, by Amélie Lambrunet's deliberate experiments in hypnosis, but his vulnerability to hypnosis, to the induction of alternative states of consciousness whenever his normal state of consciousness relaxed and surrendered its control, was surely innate, an accident of fate, like most of the determining features of human souls in general. Again, the challenge had always been, not to avoid it or rid himself of it, but to find a way to live with it and employ it, to turn it to his advantage...which he had.

Or had he?

Superficially, yes. He had build a career as a painter, a métier in which many aspirants failed, and although, as Victor had reminded him, he owed a good deal of his success to his friend's urging and tireless promotion, he was the one who had actually done the painting. He was the painter of the dead, the unique and intriguing seer of spirits. He had exploited the natural mine of his unconscious, drawing imagery from it, with an enormous ingenuity, making a real connection with the collective soul of the species, and on occasion, building bridges to and between other minds.

But it had not been without cost. Those advantages had been compensated by disadvantages. If he had built exceptional quasi-supernatural bridges to other minds, he had also failed to build run-of-the-mill natural ones. His day-to-day human relationships had been, if not abnormal, at least stunted in their growth; they had not been unrewarding, but could he possibly claim that he had ever had anything to compare with Gaston's relationship with Armande, or even Victor's many brief relationships with his temporary lovers?

And as well as that cost, had there not been a progression, or regression, by which the solid and safe domination of his everyday consciousness, his sanity, had been gradually eroded over the years of his adult life, by which the nonsensical component of his self had gained ground, unsteadily but inexorably, gradually consuming his soul? Was he not now approaching a critical point in that process, a point at which a precarious balance would finally tip? It might, of course, have tipped long ago, with the provocation of the external magnetism that he had avoided so scrupulously, but in sum, the avoidance of such force had only been a holding measure. Lilith was surely correct in her judgment; he did not need, any longer, the intervention of someone like Henri Lemastur or Zosima to push him over the edge of the bottomless abyss; he was perfectly capable of doing that himself, in the right conditions, merely by doing what he did, merely by painting, and letting psychic vertigo do the rest.

Lilith had seen that. Perhaps she had seen and understood it long before he had even become aware of her existence, perhaps as much as seven months ago, and perhaps several years, without him once catching a glimpse of her face. She had observed him, secretly, and measured him. She had gathered and collated information, and because she knew him better than Zosima did, because she understood him better than Zosima could, she had been able to formulate a plan to make use of his peculiar abilities: a plan that might well break him, but might, in her eccentric view of the world and its opportunities, allow him to achieve something unprecedented even as he broke: a sacrifice, but a productive one.

Except, of course, that Lilith was crazy—even crazier than he was. What, then, was the likelihood of her plan working? Probably zero, even in terms of her mad but hopeful imagination. Perhaps, like poor Rochemure, she would somehow be able to persuade herself that the spell had worked, but Rochemure had only been delving into the remote past, trying to make his peace with his own failures and lift the burden on his own conscience. It had only required a psychological conjuration. Lilith evidently wanted far more than that. And the seven-month fetus that she had apparently provided, in order

334

to satisfy the esthetics of coincidence and to assist in summoning the spirit of his sister, was evidently supposed to come to term, to become a living human being as well than a manipulable symbol, a literal incarnation of the Wisdom of the Goddess. But which Goddess? The merciful and loving Virgin revered by the Cathars and the original three Maries, or the primal goddess whose avatars were Isis and Inanna, and the huntress Artemis?

Did the fetus in question even exist? Everything he knew, or supposed, about Justine's pregnancy had originated from a single source: Monique—who, by her own admission, was at least pretending to be "a good little pawn." Did Lilith need Justine actually to be pregnant, in order to manipulate, bamboozle and hypnotize him, or did she only need to put the idea into his head? What if it were not even a phantom pregnancy, but a simple sham? What if the story about incarnating Ennoia, the Wisdom of the Goddess, were mere moonshine, and the endeavor that Lilith actually wanted him to catalyze was something else entirely, something undisclosed?

Absurd, again. But what was not? The point was not to try and solve a puzzle that might be largely illusory but to focus on himself and his own psychological survival. That question was surely capable of simplification, and the means had been offered to him on a platter. All he had to do was accept Victor's invitation of a seat in the automobile and a new life in Paris. It was so simple. But would a mere geographical displacement enable him to avoid the psychological crisis? Could he flee a disintegration that was, in essence, internal?

In all probability, he thought, some kind of crisis was probably inevitable, because the time was nigh. Zosima's deposal, Lilith's schemes and the unexpected death of Richard Megister were incidental, and fantasies about drugged liqueurs and possible pregnancies were elaborations largely supplied by his own runaway imagination. The problem—and hence the answer, if an answer could be found—was in his head, in his soul, in his own absurdity. Running away from the mountain would certainly avoid any scheme that Lilith might have in mind for him, however simple or complicated it might be, but it could not avoid the particular personal crisis that was shaping up within him. Perhaps it might contrive a postponement, but perhaps not even that.

On the other hand, what alternative was there? If he were able to shape the coming cataclysm, or even determine its timing, that might improve his chances of surviving it, but one principle that had been hammered into his head time and time again was that seers could not choose what they saw—and if poor Talia was right, fate could generally be relied upon to confront them with exactly what they did not want to see.

Talia was only a poor, uneducated, unhappy, unhealthy girl, perhaps the most unreliable imaginable expert witness, but she *was* a seer; she knew whereof she spoke, at least in her own experience. Was his own really so very different?

Unable to keep his eyes closed, Paul opened them. The room was very gloomy, but not entirely dark. He did not have a night-light burning, but he had not closed the curtains over his window, and outside, the starlight was as bright as only Provençal starlight could be, in an age when the north of France was blighted by industrial air pollution as well as natural cloud. Dark as it was in the room, he could see the vague outline of Virginie's head, and her open eyes caught and concentrated what little light there was, in order to fix themselves upon him, to stare at him, and to observe him from the world beyond, from the world of the imagination where the dead accumulated, and from which they returned to haunt the living.

"We can't go on like this," Paul told her. "We've come too far, and we can't go back, but we can't go on. We need a reckoning. We need to change. We need to reconstitute our lives."

She did not reply, obviously. She had no voice. She was a painting. But she had eyes, mysterious in the almost-darkness, and those eyes had an expression. They were not hypnotic eyes, like Juliette's. They were not loving eyes, like Jane's. They were, he realized, questioning eyes. He had not contrived that effect consciously. He had not even realized previously that he had contrived it; but there was no doubt about it. Virginie had a questioning expression. She wanted to know what to do. She wanted to know what she could do. She wanted to know what she ought to do. She wanted to know what she was, symbolically, and therefore in reality, because she was a painting, who existed in a world of imagery, in which all was ambiguity and symbolism, because it could not be otherwise.

"The problem," Paul told her, "is that there are too many ambiguities. We need to simplify things, if we can; clarify them, if possible. The story I gave Armande, Gaston and Victor at dinner the other night is obviously true: you really are a symbol of life and death, immortality and reincarnation, and the great continuity of the soul of the species, the soul of life itself. But then, what isn't? I can't live with you on those terms, not because you're a horror, as Victor alleges—Armande was right to argue that horror is an inappropriate reaction to thoughts of that order—but because living with you requires something more down-to-earth than that, less abstract. For practical purposes, we need to be pragmatic.

"The thing is, Virginie, that the time has come to sort out our relationship, once and for all, if we can. Whether the answer lies in fusion, or separation, or some third alternative, I don't know—yet—but we have to figure it out. If we don't...well, we know how the story of Paul and Virginie always ends, and it isn't happily.

"You know, don't you, that I love you—that I've always loved you, just as you loved me? On one level of course, that's an absurdity. How can two fetuses love one another, and how can they continue loving one another when one grows to adulthood and the other remains a figment of his imagination? But it would be foolish, would it not, to represent love as something entirely confined to consciousness, entirely a product of thinking, when that's never the way it's experienced, if rumor can be trusted. Do you remember what Baron de Rochemure told us about his relationship with his daughter—

how there's a kind of spontaneous, unreflective love of which, he claimed, only little children are capable, which predates interest, and even awareness, and is all the purer for it?

"I'm hardly an expert on the matter, never having been successful in loving anyone as an adult, and having been orphaned at an early age, but nor have I been entirely without love. I loved Martine, and Amélie, and Gaston and Victor too, initially with a kind of spontaneity and an impetus that didn't come from the intellect, but surged like a spring from the mysterious entrails of mountainous being. How far back can that sort of spontaneous emotion go? All the way to birth, as soon as open eyes begin to pour information into a avid brain? Surely. All the way to conception? Probably not. But somewhere in between, a fetus acquires that avid brain, and rudimentary sensory perceptions, and even though it can't see and can't think, it can feel. It isn't consciously aware of where it is, or what it is, but the elements of unconscious mentality, the psychic foundation-stones on which consciousness and intellect will gradually be edified, are already in place.

"You and I didn't know one another consciously in the limited time when we were both alive in the same womb, but our brains weren't inactive—indeed, they had a great deal of work to do to prepare for birth. They couldn't think, but the precursors of thought were there; instincts were already forming. Our bodies were capable of reacting to one another, and so were the precursory elements of our minds. And I believe—I feel, strongly—that those reactions, on your part and mine, were not hostile. I believe that they were loving. I did not murder you in the womb. Had I been capable of mourning, I would have mourned your death. Had I been capable of keeping vigil, I would have kept you company while you died. Had I been capable of holding your hand, I would have held your hand. I know that for certain, because that much I have done, even for someone I didn't love, with whom I merely happened to share a bed, for the sake of convenience. You, I loved, and I believe that you loved me. You, I have always loved, and I believe that you have always loved me...or would have, if you hadn't died.

"Why did you die? I don't know. I doubt that an autopsy would have been able to identify a cause, if any had been carried out. It was an accident of fate. Everyone dies, some sooner and some later, mostly sooner, although it's only the later who ever become conscious and get to tell the story. In purely statistical terms, more humans must die before birth than after, in multitudinous ways. Most such deaths must be unknown, only involving microscopic bundles of cells, and others are unheeded, only constituting mere bloodstains in the eyes of beholders, but some are mourned; some are not merely perceived but perceived as tragedies...and some as crimes, or horrors. Some leave a mark on beholders, and in some cases, that mark is indelible, lasting throughout the lives of those who bear the stigmata: Talia, Baron de Rochemure, and me, to name a tiny few.

"The stigmata in question are always hidden, and usually darkly secret, often carried to the grave by those whose blood they shed in intermittent trickles, unknown to those around them. Even in the deepest secrecy, however, there is a kinship of sorts between the stigmatized, tangible, at least unconsciously to the psychically sighted, with or without magnetic aid. And that, in general, is a good thing. Empathy, sympathy and commiseration are, on the whole, good things, partly because they can't and don't need to be voiced, because they function more unconsciously than consciously, even when conscious and deliberate. But there are costs, overt and covert. You know about some instances of those costs as well as I do—Talia, Baron de Rochemure—and others are just as much a mystery to you as they are to me, no matter what suspicions we might have, so we have the same understanding, don't we? We have the same resources on which to draw, in order to find a way out of our own predicament.

"Because, let's face it, our situation has become a predicament. It always has been, but we haven't always realized the fact. It's often the way, apparently, that people don't realize that they have a problem until it becomes acute, and the acuity in question sometimes creeps up on them. It has crept up on us. This farcical contest between Zosima and Lilith to shape the ideology of the convent might have helped precipitate it, but it wasn't the beginning. Perhaps it's unnecessary, and foolish, even to look for a beginning in something that really originated before either of us was ever conceived, but if we're analyzing the present crisis, I think it began when we were climbing the mountain and Armande took my arm, exactly as Martine had half a lifetime before. It was such a little, insignificant thing, but it brought the past back out of a drawer where it had been filed away and sealed up. It shook us up, didn't it? And then, when she demanded to see you, when you looked her in the eye...not that you actually saw her, of course, because your eyes are just paint on canvas, an optical illusion...but I knew—I wasn't even there, because I deliberately stayed the table—but I knew that she'd seen your eyes, and that they had hypnotized her, and since then...the questions have simply kept coming, yearning for answers.

"Well, Virginie, I'm not sure there are any answers, let alone what they might be, but we have to do what we can, and we have to be pragmatic. The simple fact is that we can't go on as we are. Tomorrow, or the next day, or next week, things have to change. As I said, I don't know whether the answer lies in fusion or in separation, in alchemical marriage or alchemical divorce, or some third alternative, but we have to find another way, something less costly to my sanity than intermittent unconscious somnifabrication. I can't go on being a psychic chimera; the contradictions are becoming too blatant, and too disturbing. Perhaps, given that I'm already cracked, there's no other destination possible than breaking, perhaps even shattering, but even if that's the case, I don't want to go without making a effort, without trying to understand.

"I know that I have the option of asking Zosima to magnetize me again, in Juvisy, and asking for her to use hypnotic suggestion to open my mind. I know that I also have the option of simply going along with Lilith and letting her open my mind, in the hope and expectation that while she's following her own weird agenda, I can follow mine. But I'd rather do it a different way, and I need your help. I want *you* to hypnotize me instead of them. I want *you* to open my mind...our mind...and show me where it is that we go when you take over my hand and my brain, and become my body's pilot.

"I know what you'd say if you had a voice. You'd say that there's a reason why I forget what happens to me while I draw in a trance. You'd say that the forgetfulness in question is a protection, a defense, an essential component of the rampart surrounding consciousness, which defends my sanity against the dangerous siege of the collective unconscious. You'd say that you only exclude me from an aspect of my own creativity because you love me, and want me to be safe. I know all that. But I have to know more than that. I need to know the whole substance of my dream-self, and not just fragments. At this point in time, you see, that's what matters. It's not the only thing that matters, but it's a hurdle that I need to get over if I'm still to be in the race.

"I'm not asking for immediate action, here and now, but what I am requesting—or at last suggesting—is that the next time you take over my body and my mind, by night or by day, that we go together, as brother and sister, as comrades in arms, and as lovers. Perhaps that's something you've always wanted, and all you ever needed was my permission—but I don't think so. It's more likely, I think, that you believe that you can only exist in the interstices of my existence, that if you granted me what I've just requested of you, it would be a kind of death for you: that you'd be lost, dissolved in the alkahest of living consciousness. Well, perhaps you would—what do I know? But you can see—can't you?—that we have to take the risk, because if we don't, the risk will soon take us. It's surely better if we make the first move, if we try to seize the initiative.

"I don't suppose that it will be easy. It's unknown territory for both of us, perhaps for anyone. Just because it seems simple doesn't mean that it is. But the important thing, surely, is that the relationship we have is a loving one. I won't try and fool you with a specious argument that it isn't carnal, because we both know that it's entirely carnal, because when it began, neither of us had an intellect. It is, quintessentially, a relationship of the flesh, even though it's now located entirely in the imagination. Is it incestuous? I suppose so, but my feeling is that it's way beyond conventional definitions and prejudices, and that the terms can have no reasonable relevance to our situation. Anyway, that doesn't matter. It is what it is, and given our initial situation, it couldn't have been anything else. We all begin life in an incestuous vampiric sharing of blood with our mothers, half of the human race, of necessity, in homosexual incest; all that matters is what we do later.

"At any rate, the essential point is that our relationship is loving—and that love, I insist on believing, is a good thing, infinitely better than if it were hateful, than if there really had been a battle between us for survival in the womb, which could only result in murder. We were in this together at the beginning, and we still are. Perhaps we can even get out of it together—but not in the way we have been operating. That way leads to fracture, to disintegration, either sooner or later. If there is another way, we need to find it, and the only chance we have of doing that is by facing the future together. Your eyes are open now; I need to open mine, fully. We need to dream a dream—*the* dream—in order to find out who and what we are, and what we might become.

"I don't expect an answer now, and I don't suppose that you can give me one. Your eyes are still full of questions, I can see that. I don't even know whether you can give me a sign...or, for that matter, whether you've been giving me signs all my life that I haven't been able to read. But I'd like to think that I might be capable, now, of reading a sign that I wasn't capable of reading in the past, so I'd like you to try again, if you can. And then...well, that will be up to you, at last at the outset. First, you have to let me into your dream. Once I'm there, I'll try to take a hand, but even if I can't...and the nature of dreams suggests strongly that I might not be able to do it consciously...I'll be there, and the dream won't be the same as it would have been if I weren't. With luck, it might be better.

"Is that a laugh? Probably not—but I get the point. If you could believe that the dream would be better if you let me share it more fully, you'd have tried it years ago. But the limitations of your imagination aren't an argument. Just because you can't believe something, it doesn't mean than it isn't possible. You have to remember that I'm the one with the intellect, the one with the power of reason. Another laugh? The hilarity of fate? Well, yes, I expect that I do sound anything but reasonable at present, but in fact, the opposite is true. It's when logic leads to strange conclusions that it's most powerful, and most reasonable...provided, of course, that it's methodical and accurate. What can I say? *Trust me? What have we got to lose?* Neither of those, obviously. But still, we have to try. Doing nothing is only a prelude to disaster."

After which, he fell asleep.

When he woke up, his first action was to check his drawing pad, praying that it wouldn't be blank.

It wasn't. It bore a depiction of a manticore—one of several chimerical creatures that he drew routinely. Like others he had drawn, it had a scorpion's tail equipped with a gigantic sting, a lion's body and the face of a woman. As usual, he did not recognize the face, but as often happened, he felt that he detected a family resemblance therein—this time, to another face on his bedroom wall, the only one that was the work of another artist.

The most remarkable thing about the drawing, however, was its conformity with mythology. The leonine body was red.

More than once, since the first fateful occasion at Antoine Cros's house, Paul had put colored crayons on his bedside table as well as charcoal, and had sometimes used them in his trance, but last night, he had not.

The manticore's body was not red because it had been scrawled in red wax, but because it had been daubed in blood.

CHAPTER XVIII

Paul went outside as soon as he heard the sound of the Sunbeam's engine toiling up the hill, and he opened the gate, ready to receive his sitter. She dismounted from the automobile with an admirable grace, and came to meet Paul while Bernard went to the trunk in order to extract his tools and perform the rituals that had already become a standard part of automobile worship in England, in France, and all over the world. All that Paul knew about them was that, like many church rituals, they tended to involve oil. So far as he was concerned, the rest was mystery.

"I'll be able to finish the painting today, I think," Paul told her, "as I promised your brother I would."

"I've already told you that the deadline doesn't apply anymore," she said.

"I know, but I made a promise, and one ought to keep one's promises if one can, even to the dead—perhaps especially to the dead."

They made their way into the studio, observed by Monique from the doorway to the kitchen. The studio was tidy; Paul had put the bloody manticore away in a drawer, so that it would not be visible. Also invisible to his client was the cut in his breast, above the heart, from which he had apparently drawn the blood with which he had colored the creature's body. Although the wound had not hurt to begin with, it was stinging a little now in contact with his chemise, gently pressured by the mass of his smock.

"Did Lilith come back to see you yesterday, after I'd gone?" Ellen asked, as she took up her position on the divan, still moving with a fluent grace that seemed more natural than her trained deportment of previous days.

"No," said Paul, warily. "Why would she?"

"She asked me questions about the sitting—about whether you had fallen into a trance as you had the day before. I said no, obviously, but I'm not sure that she believed me. She seems to be very curious about you—rather anxious, in fact, presumably because of your fainting fit. I know that she's offered you a commission to paint her and her associates, but I believe that you haven't told her yet whether you'll do it?"

"That's correct," Paul confirmed, putting colors on to his palette and selecting a brush.

She waited to see whether he would say any more before prompting him. "Are you going to do it?"

"I don't think so," he said.

"Why not?" She seemed surprised.

"Because I suspect that Lilith has unreasonable expectations of what I can achieve. She has mentioned the possibility of Clémence Sancerre doing a similar group portrait, perhaps simultaneously. Clémence might be better qualified for the task, and it might be best for me to leave it to her."

"Lilith will be disappointed."

"Perhaps so, but I have another commission, to paint the newlywed Madame Lambrunet, which I shall have to do in her new home, just outside Paris. I'll probably go in Victor Marvaud's automobile, with Gaston and Armande, if he can fit us all in, with our hand-luggage. The trunks will go by rail, of course."

"It will be to cramped," opined the Englishwoman. "The Panhard's trunk isn't large enough to take four lots of traveling bags, including a young woman's. You'd be more comfortable with us, in the Sunbeam. Perhaps the two automobiles can travel together, in convoy."

Paul raised his eyebrows. "You're going to Paris?" he queried.

"One can hardly help passing through it, en route for England," she confirmed. "As you can imagine, I need to return home as soon as possible, in order to sort things out there. There can't be a proper funeral, obviously, with no body, but there will be all kinds of formalities and complications. To tell the truth, I'd be quite glad of company on the journey, at least as far as Paris. Bernard...well, to be honest, traveling alone with him on a journey that will be spread over several days, including the wretched Channel crossing, would be another complication."

"I'm sure that Gaston could find you a traveling companion or a chambermaid in Toulouse," Paul suggested. "His family is legion, their domestics multitudinous."

"He has offered, and I'll probably accept, but I'm not sure that a lady companion or a chambermaid would constitute company of the kind of which I feel the need."

"Wouldn't my presence seem even more compromising to malevolent eyes than Bernard's?"

"Probably, if you were alone in the back of the automobile with me, and certainly, if it were to continue any further than Paris, but if the two automobiles were traveling together, and Armande were present, with her husband..."

"You wouldn't need me at all." Paul pointed out.

That objection clearly did not fit in with the wandering train of her thought. "It's the first phase of the journey that troubles me most," she continued, "given that I'm in a foreign country, and Bernard doesn't even speak the kind of elementary French that I do. It's just a suggestion, though—and I suspect that Lilith would never forgive me, if she thought I'd collaborated in your escape from her design, whatever it is. She's been very kind to me, and I don't like to seem ungrateful, but she intimidates me, and she has some strange ideas, with which I find it difficult to sympathize."

"I know the feeling," said Paul, dryly.

"Do you? I had assumed that you must have at least some sympathy with all the legends that Monsieur Lambrunet told us about, or you wouldn't have chosen to live here."

"It wasn't the legends that made the place seem attractive when I selected the spot eight years ago," Paul told her. "It was more a matter of childhood memories. Gaston was eager to help me, I think, for the same reason. The legend of the three Maries is everywhere in these parts; you can't get away from it; so that connection didn't seem striking to me as it probably does to you. The convent was just a ruin then, of course; things have changed out of all recognition in the last few years. I would never have believed it possible if I hadn't been living alongside it. Its presence has changed the mythological and symbolic landscape as well as the physical one, and now that Lilith has dethroned Zosima and taken sole change of it, that will doubtless change even more."

"I suppose so. While she was keeping me company yesterday, and trying to console me, she was also trying...well, I won't say to convert me, because that would be putting it too strongly, but at least to recruit my sympathy. Obviously, I don't have the same attitude as Richard had...devil's spawn, he called them, along with some even less polite terms, but I'm not sure I can give them the degree of...do you call it protection in France?...that she'd like me to accord them."

Again, Paul was tempted to observe that he knew the feeling, but he was already intent on his work, and his level of concentration was reaching the point at which it would be difficult, if not impossible, for him to maintain a conversation. When he did not reply immediately she realized that that was the case.

"That's all right," she said. "Concentrate on the painting. I'll just talk, as I did before, if you don't mind, in order to relax. Don't bother to listen, if it's distracting—it's only English, after all. Do you remember what Richard said, when we visited the cottage the other day, about the temple that used to be where the convent is now? He asked me the name of the goddess that Monsieur Lambrunet had mentioned: Artemis. Well, piecing together what Lilith told me before and after yesterday's sitting, it seems that Lilith's nuns have recovered memories—Richard would have thought that they were just made-up fantasies, but I'm not so sure—about the society that was established here by refugees from the Phocean colony of Massalia hundreds of years before Christ, whose members worshiped Artemis.

"According to Lilith, the refugees fled the colony because they were considered outcasts, for the same reasons that she and her followers are considered outcasts. They were herders and hunters—or huntresses—rather than planters, and they thrived for more than a century before being wiped out by marauding nomadic tribesmen. They took refuge behind some sort of defensive wall on the mountain-top, but they couldn't withstand a long siege because they ran out of water. Their society wasn't entirely female—they had a few male slaves, but they controlled their numbers rigorously, throwing unwanted male babies and many men they captured into the Great Cleft. They didn't mate with their slaves, apparently, that being taboo, but they had rituals in which they intoxicated them, milked them—her term, not mine—and inseminated themselves.

"The Massalians weren't the first, though, according to Lilith, they were reflecting an even earlier society, whose name has been lost, and the name of their goddess has been forgotten, although Lilith says that she was certainly part of a trinity, as Artemis was with Hera and Athene. They too were exterminated, but they didn't go down without a fight, and the anger of their defeat still echoes in all the later replications of their utopian quest, ever more deeply buried.

"Six hundred years after the fall of the Massalian splinter, Lilith says, the descendants of the three Maries who had come from Galilee established a similar society, but pacifist in its inclinations, preaching the message of the Sermon on the Mount, as dictated to Jesus by the Virgin. It didn't last as long as either of its predecessors before it was wiped out by a cohort of Roman soldiers. Later still, in the twelfth century, a company of female Cathar perfecti established another reclusive community here, which was also pacifist as well as feminist; it lasted for half a century before being slaughtered by a contingent of Simon de Montfort's troops—again the women took refuge in a fort on the summit, but they ran out of water.

"According to Lilith, at least thirty of the women currently in the colony are reincarnations of women who lived in all four of the earlier communities, as seeresses, whose talents were dependent on their being organized in what she calls trinities, and on the binding of the trinities by what some people call animal magnetism, although she doesn't like the term—too polluted, she says. With the aid of genealogies compiled with the aid of Monsieur Lambrunet, she has identified a number of other women who might be reincarnates of the original daughters of the Triple Goddess, who, she says, are potentially more useful outside the community than within it, but would become a great deal more useful if they could formulate trinities and cement their bonds.

"Obviously, Lilith was suggesting, not very subtly, that I might be one of these reincarnated daughters of the goddess, but I can't believe it. She wants to hypnotize me in order to enable me to recover memories of past lives and identify the other members of my trinity, but I don't want to do it. I don't want to get involved with that sort of thing—absolutely not—and I suspect that she only wants to involve me so that I'll collaborate with her plans for the future. Exactly what they are, I'm not sure, except that I know that she hopes to be able to lease more land on the mountain, eventually, as and when she can raise the money, because she wants to dig more wells and perhaps divert some underwater streams, in order to increase the colony's water supplies, which are already limiting its agricultural activities.

"I don't know how she intends to raise money, other than by donations and hypnotic therapeutics, but she seems to have high hopes of a liqueur that one of her associates is distilling from the rather meager vines they grow. They would need to increase production considerably, though, and improve the quality markedly, in order to make it into a commercially viable operation. She was obviously angling for me to make a financial investment, but I'm not sure that I'd be in a position to provide it even when Richard's estate is settled, which might take some time, and I'm certain that it wouldn't be a sensible thing to do. England isn't like France, you see; it the news ever got around in London that I own land on which a notorious colony of lesbian anarchists has been established, let alone that I lent it any financial support, I'd be ruined in Society..."

Paul had lost track of time—and, for that matter, space—and his attention was focused with complete intensity on the face that he was painting, with an uncannily rapid hand, focused most particularly on the eyes, which he would normally have left until the very last phase of the detail, but which he was presently filling with an unusual urgency, because it felt that it was the right time to do it, esthetically. He was meeting their brazen stare with unflinching fortitude, but had no sense of being in a conventional staring march, because he was striving to evaluate the synthesized eyes, to read what was behind them, to penetrate their mystery...

Those eyes, he thought, were commanding eyes. They were hostile eyes. They were the eyes of a goddess: a goddess much older than Artemis, and more violent, in complete contrast to the mild and merciful goddesses of later eras, the Virgin of the Christians and the Cathar perfecti. This was a goddess from a deeper layer of the psyche, a goddess not of orderly, quasi-Fourierist anarchism but of chaotic anarchism, of bloodlust and fury.

The goddess was staring at Paul, from beyond the eyes that he had gifted to his portrait of Ellen Megister—which were a veritable representation of Ellen's actual eyes, although their power and purpose were far too deeply buried in her psyche for her to be consciously aware of it—but she did not speak. Like the human dead, he knew, dead deities had no voice. The goddess merely stared, because that was her gift, her means, her ambiguous existence beyond life and outside time.

His gaze switched, then, from the paining to the model, and he saw that Ellen Megister was still sitting in the same relaxed posture, still talking garrulously, in order not to be alone with her thoughts, in order not to be entirely contained by the walls of her consciousness. She was still exactly what she had been before: a demure, naïve, lonely Englishwoman in a foreign land, abruptly dispossessed of her guardian—a guardian who had been a tyrant but had kept her safe—and left to cast about, rather helplessly, in search of alternative support, and alternative guidance. And her eyes had nothing hateful about them at all...on the surface, where her consciousness operated and lived. That consciousness was completely civilized, polite and pleasant; Ellen Megister had no idea what she was or might be, in the unconscious depths and coverts of her own identity, and no idea of what she wanted to be...except, of course, that she wanted to be loved.

Paul felt every sympathy for her in that regard, but he was not sure why. He was not sure, in fact, that it was his own sympathy...or, if it was, why it felt slightly wrong, strangely out of joint. After all, he and Ellen were not devoid of things in common, in spite of the stark differences in their social status, nationality and sex. They had each lost a sibling, and they each had presences lurking deep in their psyche, hidden, ambiguous and perhaps menacing, of which their consciousness was only liminally aware, at best...

As Paul's right hand—which might not have been entirely his right hand at that particular moment—drew the brush he was using away from the canvas, in order that he could look the goddess in the eyes, the tip of the brush's slender handle jabbed him in the breast, to the left of the center. Even through the coarse cloth of his smock and the fine cloth of his chemise he felt the jab sharply, as if it were a knife stabbing him, aiming for the heart, although not intending to go that deep...not, at least, materially.

Where was the knife? Paul wondered—and then wondered why he had not wondered before.

Where was the knife with which he had drawn the blood that he had used to color the manticore? Where he had got it from, and where had he put it afterwards? It had not been on the table with the drawing pad, either before or after he had gone to bed. Had he got up and gone into the kitchen, not once but twice, in a somnambulistic trance? Or had someone else come into the bedroom while he was in the process of somnifabrication, and stabbed him symbolically in the heart?

If someone had, it had to be Monique, but why would she do such a thing? How much of the convent liqueur had she had to drink? And to what extent had she acquired a taste for it?

Then, Paul knew that he was dreaming. And with the intuition that sometimes comes with dreams, and sometimes enables the most absurd ideas to take on, at least temporarily, the force of conviction that underlies the sensation of revelation, he perceived the trinity relative to which he was the tetrahedral addendum: the trinity composed of Ellen, Monique and Virginie, but which constituted the goddess older than Artemis, echoed in legend as the Triple Goddess; the goddess older than the Biblical Lilith, the accursed First Woman, older than any human echo, let alone any human worship: the condensation of the soul that predated human being, and predated the dawn of consciousness; the primal soul; the source.

Antoine Cros, he remembered, had once suggested to him that the magnetic analogy was not the only one by which the fumbling modern mind might try to represent psychic force; he had used the analogy of psychic gravity, in order to be able to make reference to psychic orbits. It was just a slight variant in the mental quest for crutches to shore up limping thought, but it served as a reminder that such ideas were, indeed, just makeshift crutches, which should not be mistaken for psychic reality. Except that, vague as his scientific knowledge was—Gaston would undoubtedly have been able to give him a fuller explanation—he knew that the Newtonian theory of gravity gave rise to something called "the three-body problem," which was to do with the difficulty of calculating the eventual stabilization of the movement of three bodies extracting a mutual gravitational attraction, given their initial positions and velocities.

And, absurd as it was, Paul wondered whether there might be a psychic equivalent of the three-body problem, which affected patterns of reincarnation and recapitulation, and the recurrence and reformation of the trinities required for the deployment and control of psychic force. Perhaps those equations, too, had no unique solution. How, in fact, could it be otherwise, given all the complexities and ambiguities inherent in human thought and language?

Then the wound in his chest opened up again, and began to bleed, and the symbolic knife went deeper, completing the little thrust that Monique had made, plunging all the way into the heart—the heart that was symbolic itself, of the soul. That renewed thrust was mortal, killing him—at least symbolically.

There was blood everywhere, which might have been illusory, but was certainly red.

Then the manticore came—although "came" was something of an understatement, given that it did not simply arrive, through the door or the window, like any normal monster, but crawled out of the wound in his chest, with a wriggle and a slither that must have been exceedingly ingenious, given that the manticore was so much larger and more massive than the fleshy envelope that had contained it.

That's not surprising, Paul thought. *The flesh is weak but the spirit is willing. The body is just a microcosm, an agglomeration of vulgar minuscule atoms, but the soul is a macrocosm, which contains worlds and infinities.*

The surprising thing, surely, was that the manticore was only a moderate giant, albeit still capable of seizing him in her red feline claw and fixing him with her unfeeling stare.

Her eyes were not cat's eyes, because her face was not a cat's face. Her eyes were blue, like Paul's...like his mother's. They were loving eyes. The manticore had a mouth, too, and lungs. The manticore also had a voice, because the manticore was not dead. She had not spoken, yet, but he knew, intuitively, that she had a voice, and that when she was ready to speak, she would use it.

Virginie was not dead! Not only had he not murdered her in the womb, more than thirty years ago, but she had not even died there, of natural or supernatural causes.

How could that be? It was absurd. Nevertheless, it was true. There were more ambiguities in heaven and earth than were dreamt of in Paul's previous philosophy. He had to adapt.

Virginie the manticore—or, since the voice in the background was speaking English, the womanticore—carried him away. How did she get through the door to the studio and the door of the cottage? He couldn't tell, but her expertise in slithering obviously went far beyond the apparent capabilities of her leonine and arachnid body-parts. She had something of the snake about her, too, like so many of the other chimeras that his entranced hand was fond of drawing. She had Protean capabilities.

She could also move very rapidly, scuttling like a scorpion rather than bounding like a lioness...or perhaps, given her human head, a sphinge. She had other arachnid capabilities too, because when she reached the edge of the Great Cleft, ignoring the complex apparatus that the men from the university were still in the process of setting up in order to lower themselves down, she simply went straight over the edge and ran down the side of the bottomless precipice, into the darkness.

Paul did not have to ask where they were going, or why. They were not going anywhere is particular, yet; for the time being, they were just running away, into the deepest darkness available, following an instinct far older than the human species and its collective soul. They were running away from the other elements of Virginie's temporary trinity, from the Triple Goddess and the Sacred Knife, from the monsters lurking in the utmost depths of the unconscious minds of Ellen Megister and Sister Monique, and her own. And the pursuit, the threat, was his fault; he was the catalyst that had permitted the ramparts of consciousness to crack, for the possibility of emergence to occur; that was his curse, his fate. He could not help it, and he could not choose...but he and the manticore could run away, for now. And they were running as fast as Virginie's protean pseudomechanical apparatus could carry them in the hope of preventing the emergence culminating in a fatal psychic catastrophe.

That crack in the ramparts of consciousness, of course, was exactly what Lilith had wanted to Paul to contrive, not merely for the benefit—was it really a benefit, or a disaster?—of her own makeshift trinity but for others she had identified, or thought there might be a chance of improvising. She had thought such a fusion of mentalities, with the access of psychic force that it would permit, was an intrinsically good thing. She had an apostolate, gifted by revelation. She was not the first, and would not be the last. Nor was she culpable; certainly, she knew not what she was doing, but did anyone? Could anyone? In order to think rationally about such matters, one needed axioms on which the construct logical edifices, and in that matter, human consciousness was in the dark.

Paul, meanwhile, was literally in the dark. Any thin sliver of light that might have been behind him when his marvelous sister had first scuttled over the rim of the Cleft had shrunk and disappeared. Everything now, was black. Nor could he feel the perpendicular wall down which the monster was running, slithering or abseiling, perhaps on a thread of arachnid silk thousands of times stronger than steel, which could be paid out far more extensively than any cable woven by human hands.

Everything was black. Not a comfortable situation, he thought, for a painter, a dealer in color and light. But it was his own fault. He had asked for it, quite literally. He had asked Virginie to permit him to retain consciousness, in a situation where consciousness did not belong. And he had been allowed to do it, because he had asked someone who could grant his wish. Nobody else, he was convinced, could have done that, if they had wanted to, because no one else as possessed of his magic, his ambiguity. But his wish had been granted, and now he had to live—or die—with the consequences.

So where would they end up, if and when they reached the paradoxical bottom of the bottomless pit? Would there be a covert in which to hide, or a terrain in which to duel? And what would happen if the entity they were fleeing caught up with them before they could reach a place of relative safety, or were cornered and had to fight?

When he had first learned to speak and read English, Paul's teachers had employed poetry as a mnemonic device, that being standard practice, and one of the poems that had been employed as means of introducing him to the language, its rhythm and its esthetics had been "The Hound of Heaven," by the mystic and opium addict Francis Thompson, in which the narrative voice had fled the eponymous pursuer through nights and days, through the arches of the years, through the labyrinthine ways of his own mind, in a mist of tears...but Paul could not remember where the voice had ended up, and what sentence of judgment had been passed on him. He had paid too much attention to the language and not enough to the meaning.

He struggled, because he thought that if he could remember more of the words of the poem, they might give him imagery to which to cling, to populate the horrid darkness with ideas, if not with sensations. But his memory was not up to the task; the hound of Heaven was lost. He could only remember scattered fragments of the first book of Milton's *Paradise Lost*, when Lucifer, the morning star, the angel of light metamorphosed into Satan, had been plunged into a realm where there was no light, but only darkness visible discovering sights of woe, where peace and rest could never dwell and hope never came...

And for an instant, those ideas almost possessed him, and almost condemned him to Hell...but he fought back. His pride fought back, and he refused the condemnation.

The hell with paradise lost, he thought. *The hell with the hound of heaven and the mists of tears; the sights I discover in darkness visible aren't woeful or vengeful shades, but loving ones. I'm not alone. There might be no room in the manticore's claw for all my traveling luggage, and Gaston's, Victor's and Armande's, let alone for my paintings, but there's room for Jane and for Juliette. They're here, and they don't*

356

have to jostle for room or grapple for attention. Nor are they
helpless, crucified or not. The hound of heaven and the wrath
of god have missed their chance. I'm strong now, because I've
painted my dead, and I have their gaze. They're not helpless,
and nor am I. I'm not alone, and nor are they. We can survive
this, Virginie. I don't say that we can win, but we needn't lose.
So run, my lovely, darling monster, run like Hell.

It wasn't a great speech, he knew. It was absurd, without
even being particularly poetic, in spite of its noble models, but
it was good enough. It set out the agenda. It tore through the
confusion, and made things simple...not easy, by any means,
but simple. It focused the attention, defined the target.

It was still dark: limitlessly, terrifyingly dark—
unsurprisingly, as they were scuttling down a vertical face of
cold, damp rock, heading for a bottom that no one had ever
seen, and which only consisted, in all probability, of icy, glutinous, cloying mud, oozing slowly down to an invisible sea.
He remembered, though, that there was a Voice, as there had
been the last time he had been able to capture fragments of a
nightmare that he had catalyzed. According to all logic, there
should not have been a Voice, or an Angel to snatch him from
the death into which Baron de Rochemure de Harvanges had
very nearly dragged him, but there had been a Voice nevertheless, and now he knew why.

Virginie was not dead.

He knew that, but could not quite believe it yet. "But you
must be dead," he said to Virginie, as they fled the labyrinthine ways of the collective unconscious. "This is impossible.
You're impossible. I'm impossible." He knew as he spoke,
though, that he was playing Devil's Advocate, inviting and
hoping for contradiction, and confident, now, that he would
receive it.

"There are more things in Heaven and Earth," Virginie
told him, finally speaking her mind, "but that's about as far as
poetry can go, written and remembered in fragments. Science,
alas, can't go much further, as yet, and it has the handicap of
prosaicism. But in material terms, I'm not impossible, only

357

very rare, and not so very odd, in terms of the reach of the Platonic imagination. There are chimeras in nature, of various kinds, hybrids and mosaics. Call them monsters if you wish, but they don't all deserve that stigmatization, in my estimation...although you could argue that I'm biased..."

Virginie's Voice, Paul realized, was not that of a naïve fetus. In fact, it was something of a pedant. But he loved her anyway. She was his sister...in a manner of speaking.

Wordplay, he remembered, was the only game in time. The Voice had told him that. There was no other with which to gamble.

"It's not unusual," Virginie told him, preaching from the pulpit of the limitless darkness while the invisible monster of the primal deity pursued her, but could not snap at her heels because that particular anatomical feature had been omitted from her complexion, "for human ovaries to deliver more than one ovule into the womb simultaneously, accessible to fertilization, nor for two fertilized ova to develop there.

"Twins are a familiar phenomenon, whether non-identical twins resulting from the separate fertilization of two ovules, or identical twins, resulting from the division of a single fertilized ovum into two individuals. What are less familiar, because their development is more problematic and they usually die before birth, are individuals resulting from the fusion of two ova shortly after fertilization, resulting in a compound blastula. Sometimes, when such compound embryos do succeed in coming to term, it isn't obvious that they're unusual, because the two individuals that have fused and become one are the same sex, so that the individual is simply male or female, and it isn't obvious, physically, that they're hybrids. Even when the compound individual is a hermaphrodite, or an androgyne, it isn't necessarily obvious physically, either at birth or later in life. It's actually unusual—if we haven't moved beyond the scope of that term—for real androgynes to have two sets of manifest sex organs, or even for their outwardly visible sex organs to fall outside the range of normal variation.

"It's probably not so very exceptional for compound ova to divide, to produce identical twins—compound ova are probably more likely to undergo such division than normal ova—but it's much more exceptional for either of the embryos to survive long enough to develop even for a few days, let alone months. In most cases, they don't even survive long enough to miscarry, but are simply reabsorbed into the maternal womb, devoured by their mother, nature tacitly disapproving of their abnormality. Technically, the twins thus produced are 'identical,' but in this instance it doesn't mean that their embryological development will be similar. It's perfectly possible for one of the androgynous embryos to develop as an apparent male and for the other to develop as an apparent female, and for one of the two to have greater viability, to be able to survive until birth while the other dies.

"You didn't have to absorb my soul when your twin died, Paul, as Zosima and Lilith both suggested; you already had it. You were already an androgyne, already both male and female, physically as well as psychically, although the body that developed only had male secondary sexual characteristics. In a sense, you know all this, because if you hadn't read Augustin Cabanès and other pioneering investigators of medical mysteries, I wouldn't have been able to piece the argument together. But you didn't pay conscious attention to the same aspects of your reading as I did. You came to the study of anatomy primarily as a painter, interested in appearances, and your curiosity didn't probe much deeper—but you saw much more than you can remember consciously, and although you couldn't be aware of it, the unconscious sector of your mind remained ambivalent.

"While your conscious mind developed, learning, changing and maturing, your unconscious mind developed too, including its ambivalence. Your mind isn't divided in any simple sense—you don't have what psychologists are beginning to call a double, or a split personality, but what you do have is a chimerical personality, capable of protean metamorphoses, the abilities of which are invoked when you draw or paint, at least when you become absorbed in your vision. It's probably a much more common phenomenon than anyone realizes, but it generally goes unnoticed and unheeded, perceived as a relatively minor eccentricity; it's more obvious in your case because you're a physiological and psychic androgyne, beneath your masculine appearance.

"You can't be unique, of course, however unusual you might be, and there must be counterparts as well: androgynes who only have female secondary sexual characteristics, and although it's difficult for such things to run in families, because of the increased frequency of inviability in compound ova and the reduced fertility of the adult individuals, logic suggests that over time, ancestral lines capable of producing such anomalous individuals will produce more of them, and such individuals, in the course of history, will be concentrated historically in certain human lines of descent—as mapped, obviously, by unorthodox genealogy. Logic also suggests that such anomalies are likely to be associated with others, in terms of both physical and psychic heredity, which are evidently associated as well, albeit in ways still mysterious at present."

"What you're implying," Paul put in, "is that the bizarre aspects of Lilith's Marian mythology aren't entirely nonsensical: that, although the phenomena are doubtless grossly distorted by the imagination, they have some kind of material hereditary basis?"

"That's exactly what I'm asserting. Would we be here otherwise?"

"I don't know. Are we here? It's very dark. Is there even a *here* for us to be?"

The blackness was, indeed, oppressive and suggestive of a void that was more than mere emptiness: something devoid of space, devoid of time, and devoid of meaning.

"Perhaps not," Virginie told him, sternly, "but believe me, there's definitely a *here* where we don't want to be, if we want to get out of this alive, and that *here* is trying to find us. The ramparts of your consciousness couldn't protect us any longer, the siege had worn you down and you were dying of metaphorical thirst. You had no alternative but to risk this sortie, but whether we can actually get away, I don't know. Nobody knows what lies at the bottom of the Cleft, physically or psychically, because nobody's ever reached it. We're in the dark here, as you've noticed. But we're not alone. The dead are with us, and they're not with the enemy. They can only lend us moral support, but let's not underestimate the value of that. Not that you ever have; you might never have been able to describe what Juliette and Jane meant to you, but you painted it. You gave them hypnotic power, psychic force, and you can draw upon it now. Their eyes are out there, in the visible darkness, and there isn't an atom of hatred or resentment in their gaze: only yearning. Yes, Paul, there's a *here* for us to be. Together, we can see to that."

"But there's a sense, too," Paul objected, "in which we're somewhere else entirely. My actual body is still standing in my studio in front of my easel and my canvas, unconscious but unfallen, with a palette in my left hand and a brush in my right. And Ellen Megister is there too, sitting on the divan, perhaps asleep but holding her pose. And Monique is still on the sofa in the other room, under Juliette's watchful eye, or perhaps in the kitchen, perhaps even moving around, but part of the trinity nevertheless. Whatever is pursuing us is only reaching out psychically from our unconscious minds, in symbolic guise. In principle, we could all simply wake up again, and carry on with our conscious lives. Monique could go back to the convent, Bernard could drive Ellen all the way back to London in the Sunbeam, and I could go to Paris in the Panhard to paint Armande. Or I could simply drop dead, or fall asleep and never wake up."

"It's not as simple as that, Paul, and you know it. If matter is the possibility of perception, then the manticore is material, and so are you within its claw, and so are Juliette and Jane, even though they're shades. More to the point, the other two aspects of our putative trinity are material too, and so is the stupid, primitive goddess that's impelling them, a creature of instinct and blind terror, helpless in her reflexive rage.

361

"If they catch us, there's going to be a confrontation: a physical confrontation. I don't know exactly what form it will take, but one thing I do know—and which you know too, having drawn it time and time again, albeit reluctantly, is that it could be violent, horrible and fatal. But it's a mistake to think that it can't be beaten, or that there's no help anyone else can offer. If Zosima was correct in saying that if you scream for help, she'll hear you, there's no reason to think that she won't do as she said, and lend you her moral, and hence her material, support. And we can be certain, because you already are, that your other would-be protectors, dead or alive, can help you materially, in spite of their own sensations of helplessness, simply by being here. And most of all you have me—all of me, because I'm part of you; we're the androgyne."

"And you've got me out of similar situations before, more than once."

"No, I've got you out of dissimilar situations. This is the first time you've encountered the reincarnate goddess and her sacrificer, the first time the physical proximity of the trinity has enabled the most fundamental of all psychic bonds to form, with the aid of your catalysis. This is uncharted territory: here be dragons—but where there are dragons, there are heroes, and here there are heroes, there are people willing them to succeed. Lilith is mistaken to think that forming such bonds is necessarily a good thing—potentially, a source of enlightenment and power, a summoning of divine wisdom—but she's not entirely wrong; she's just underestimating the dangers, and overestimating the rewards that enlightenment and divine wisdom can bring. It's understandable, given her personal history, that she's trying so hard to solidify her own trinity and to promote and contrive others—but she's asking too much of enlightenment, which is a not only a grail that's very difficult to find, but a grail from which it's direly disappointing to drink, unless you can acquire a taste for it."

After all, Paul thought, *if Joseph of Arimathea really had brought to Gaul a cupful of the blood of a victim of crucifixion, what would it actually have tasted like?*

Aloud, he said: "That's the problem with seeking divine wisdom, via science or mystical vision; no one has the slightest idea what the enlightenment they seek will produce. They can't choose, and statistically, they're more likely to find what they don't want than what they do. Millions, or even billions, of years of natural selection have enabled humans to evolve in the contrary direction: gradually to build the ramparts of consciousness that keep psychic force at bay. Perhaps those fortifications are follies that can't endure for long, but if the humans who are equipped with them are the survivors, while the psychically powerful individuals of whose one-time existence legend insistently informs us are almost extinct, might there not be a lesson in that?

"On the other hand, if I've interpreted the beliefs of the multitudinous mystical cults of contemporary Paris correctly, isn't their fundamental assumption that the great initiates, or the great magicians, haven't simply died and become extinct, but that they've achieved some kind of apotheosis—that they've gone on to some higher and preferable phase of being? According to the mystics, life isn't a matter of a Darwinian struggle for existence, in which the fittest have survived and the rest have gone the way of the giant saurians, it's a matter of the ascent of a favored few to a better world, a better state of being? If they're right, then plunging into the Great Cleft, literally or symbolically, is the road to oblivion, whereas the mystical union of the trinity is the route to divinity. If they're right, we're going the wrong way."

He was playing Devil's Advocate again, but with confidence, knowing that it was just a move in the game, a feint. He was holding his own in the phantom pursuit. He felt that the onlookers approved—not merely Juliette and Jane, but Zosima too, wherever she was in physical space, having responded to his call.

"If Lilith is right, then we are going the wrong way," Virginie admitted. "But you've looked into the eyes of the goddess, Paul. You've painted her gaze. You've penetrated her disguise. So tell me: having seen her, having seen the primal creator within her primal creation, do you really think that she loves you? Do you really think that she loves you the way that I do, or the way that Juliette and Jane love you, or even the way Lilith, Salome and Justine love one another? Do you really want me to open my claw, painful as its grip might be, in order to let you fall into her hands—or would you rather we kept on running, until we find terrain on which we can stand and fight, with a chance of winning, or at least of getting out of this in one piece? No apotheosis, no transfiguration to a higher, paradisal plane of being, but just common-or-garden *alive*—at least for a few more years?"

Paul did not have time to give the matter a great deal of thought. He could not hear the Hound of Heaven barking, because she was not the kind of beast to give warning of her approach, but he could sense her close behind the manticore, and getting closer. He could not see her; of all the hypothetical monsters of the abyss, she was the one who could not be drawn; but she was there; she was real; and she was full of hatred, for him, and for his sister manticore. This was personal.

Why?

He did not know; there would be time to think about it later. For now, it was a matter of survival. But there was no hiding place. In the infinite darkness, there was no covert. No matter what was at the bottom of the physical Great Cleft in the earth's crust, in the world of ideas and imagination, no matter how absurd and illogical it might be, the Great Cleft really was bottomless, offering no escape.

Ergo, he had to fight. There was no other option. Wordplay was the only game in time. He had to place his chip. The dye had to be cast.

"No," he said to Virginie, firmly, "don't let me go. Let's run while we can and fight when we can't, and the hell with the higher plains of being. But can you outrun her minions?"

"Me?" said the manticore, his once-silent but now-loquacious sister. "Of course I can't. You know how the lore of legend goes—the monster is always slain, divinity and des-

364

tiny can't be beaten. But if you've got me, I've got you. Together, we have to stand a chance, or all this is pointless. Together, we can live. Where there's a will there's a way."

While deploring his sister's sudden tendency to think and talk in clichés, and hoping that they would not be clichés unless there were some vestige of truth in them, Paul decided that she was right. There was a sense, after all, in which all of this was happening in the realm of the dead, in the myth-laden collective unconscious of the human race, of life itself: a realm to which he, as an artist—as the painter of spirits, a legend in his lifetime—had privileged access. The manticore's sting was only a symbolic weapon, even if it could deliver a deadly dose of a powerful neurotoxin in the strange materialism of the dream. It could only signify; it could not create, as he and the goddess could. Who, at the end of the day, was the better creator? The goddess was evidently more powerful, because that was what being a goddess entailed, but was she more imaginative? Was she more dexterous? Was she more clear-sighted?

The myth of Arachne said no—but the myth of Arachne also said that the cost of proving it was to be struck dead or turned into a spider.

The hell with the myth, Paul thought. *The hell with the ancient Greeks and their pessimism. I'm a skeptic and a philosopher, and it's 1909. The manticore is still a manticore, but she's an art nouveau manticore now, and I'm a painter, a creator of universes, not a member of the Cubist* avant garde, *but free nevertheless to tell my Muse to get back to Parnassus and let me go my own way. If the goddess were half as imaginative as I am, the universe would be a much better place, and it would have no need of artists, nor any scope for their endeavors. As things are, whether or not this is the best of all practicable worlds—and the very existence of the idea of progress proclaims and proves that it isn't—it obviously has abundant scope for artists, and constitutes a virtual vacuum of genius.*

In that kind of contest, it seemed to him, he could win. In spite of the blackness and limitlessness of the bottomless pit, in spite of the intrinsic horror of the visible darkness, because he was not alone in his flight, he could win.

If Jane had had a voice, he felt sure, she would be shouting at him, writhing against the nails of the cross of death: "The hell with forgiveness. Paint."

"Amen," added Virginie.

So he lifted the small, slender delicate brush that he was still clutching, on which the tiny dab of paint had not yet dried, and he thrust with it. He could not paint the universe with a droplet; that was impossible. Nor could he color the infinite dark with a dot; that was inconceivable. But what he could do was to gather a tiny fraction of that ultimate, limitless darkness on the oily tip of his brush, and then redeploy it.

What should I draw? he remembered asking the Voice once before. *Water from a well, it had replied what else is there?* He had known the answer even then: oil—by which he meant oil paint, not the kind that helped automobiles run, or the kind with which priests anointed the credulous.

So he painted.

In order to do that, he had to reach all the way out of the bottomless Great Cleft into the world of green and gray, and insinuate himself, with an exceedingly clever contortion, into the cottage where his body was still standing, still poised, in order to administer a brisk swipe to the canvas on which he was toiling: his complicated work in long progress.

It was merely a gentle dab, impelled by a flick of the wrist and directed by his fingers—but it was a deft thrust, made with all the expertise of his craftsmanship and all the vision of his talent.

And it had the required effect.

Then he turned round, and shivered.

The door of the studio was open. Sister Monique was lying on the floor behind him, suffering horrible convulsions. In her left hand she was clutching a kitchen knife, with which the spasmodic movements of the hand in question had caused her to slash her right hand—which, in dutiful accordance with cliché, did not appear to have known what its counterpart was doing—several times, perhaps while it had been trying to snatch it away.

Paul put down his brush and his palette and knelt down beside the stricken woman. He knew that she was dying, but he did not know how, in physical terms, the poison had been delivered, unless it had come from within. One way or another, though, the manticore had deployed her sting, in the proverbial nick of time

"Why?" he asked, although he was not at all sure that she could answer him. In fact, even though she was foaming at the mouth, Monique's clenched jaws relaxed sufficiently to let the words through.

"I tried to stop it," she said. "Last night, I only scratched you, and couldn't go on. *She* helped me. Today...I nearly couldn't stop it."

Mystified, he could only repeat: "But why?"

"You couldn't even see me," she said, faintly. "I was prettier than Scarab, and healthy too, but you couldn't even see me. All I wanted...all I needed...was for you to show me a fraction of the kindness you showed her. I offered myself to you, twice, and you wouldn't. And when I asked you why, all you said was *just because*. Just because! But I didn't want to do it. I swear. Even so, I didn't want to do it. In the other room, I couldn't have, any more than I could in the bedroom. Scarab would have made me resist, just by looking at me, just as the thing on the bedroom wall forced me to resist...in here, I didn't think I could stop myself, but I couldn't help looking sideways. If I'd kept my eyes on the painting on your easel, you wouldn't have had a chance to spoil it, but I couldn't help looking sideways—thank the Virgin—and *she* wouldn't let me...the other one. But I swear I didn't mean it. It wasn't really me."

She reached out with her right hand—the injured hand, the bleeding hand, the virtuous hand—and grabbed his left wrist. "Can you forgive me?" she asked. Even in extremis, that was what she wanted.

"Yes," he said. "Of course. It wasn't your fault. You were hallucinating. You were hypnotized. And I'm sorry I couldn't see you, before and just now. Can *you* forgive *me*?"

As things had transpired, she couldn't. She was already dead. But he decided to take it for granted that she had.

He only glanced sideways briefly, at the portrait of Jane de La Vaudère—whose eyes, like the eyes of many portraits, were capable of seeming to following an observer around the room—and then he went to Ellen, who was slumped on the divan. For a moment, he thought that she might be dead too, but she was only asleep. She was sleeping peacefully; if she had been dreaming before, she had probably forgotten her dream already; at the most, she would only remember blurred and bewildering fragments.

She opened her eyes. He flinched momentarily, but they were only her own eyes, her disguised eyes, perfectly serene, if slightly puzzled. Then she caught sight of Monique lying on the floor, and the blood that she had shed.

"What happened?" she said.

"She had some kind of epileptic fit. She was holding a knife and gashed her hand, but the cuts are superficial. It was the cerebral disturbance that killed her."

Another gasp. "She's dead?"

"I'm afraid so. Could you possibly ask Bernard to drive you to the convent again, so that you can inform Sister Lilith and ask her to send help? I'm afraid I won't be able to finish the portrait today. My hand slipped and I made a terrible mistake. It's only a small streak, but I've spoiled the gaze of the eyes. I'll have to clean away the paint and do that part of the face again."

Ellen Megister looked at the body lying on the floor, assessing its location. "I'm not surprised your hand slipped," she said. "That must have been quite a shock."

"Yes," Paul admitted. "It was. The poor woman must have staggered in, seeking help, and I was so engrossed that I didn't turn my head until she was right behind me. I was startled...but I should have had better control over my hand. I think I can repair the portrait, though...in fact, I'm sure that I can. I'm sorry."

"It's not your fault," she assured him, both less and more accurately than she knew. Then, showing no overt signs of any effects of shock or horror, she rose to her feet, and went to rouse Bernard from his siesta.

Within two minutes, the Sunbeam roared into life, and set off up the mountain.

CHAPTER XIX

Paul picked up a rag and a bottle of turpentine, and began cleaning the canvas, where the brief sweep of his delicate brush had taken the hatred and the hypnosis out of the eyes of the Triple Goddess with deadly accuracy, striking like a scorpion's sting. Not until he had obliterated every trace of her stare did he step back and ask: "Why?"

He did not expect an answer, nor did he receive one from that source. Nor did any voice from within echo in the secret arena of his own complex mind. But he thought he already knew. It was because, in the primitive way of thinking that was all the goddess had, unalloyed with the moral sophistication acquired by her later avatars, in various phases, he was an abomination, a transgressor of natural boundaries. He was an androgyne, physically as well as psychically, in spite of the superficial disguise of his seemingly-masculine flesh.

Ironically, had he not been what he was, she would not have been able to strike at him. It was the psychic energy of the trinity that he had forged, between Virginie, Monique and Ellen, that had enabled her to cast Richard Megister down into the Great Cleft. That had been easy, but turning the force around, directing it into the heart of the psychic tetrahedron, had been more difficult. Her control over Monique had been weak, and Monique had fought her every step of the way, because, as Zosima had said, whatever she might once have been, Monique was fundamentally honest, fundamentally good. Even the motivation of resentment that he had unwittingly provided for her to strike at him had not given her the might of conviction. She had remained vulnerable to every hypnotic gaze that he had gifted to his paintings. She had had time to stab him before he struck back at the goddess, but she had not done it; she had not been able to do it. She had spared his life, albeit at the cost of her own. In her fashion, if only briefly, she had loved him; hers had been a heroism of love

Even when the goddess had contrived to look him in the face, therefore, and even after he had seen her, and fallen under her spell, he had escaped. Even then, she had not been able to obliterate him. It was not just him who had beaten her—again—but two thousand years of the evolution of humanity, of the development of intellect, of the progress of morality. She had not been destroyed; she was still there, lurking in the depths of the collective unconscious, able to resurface when the circumstances were hospitable...but it was up to him, as it was to everyone else, to make sure that hospitable circumstances did not occur often, if at all, in his own vicinity. She could be beaten. Historically, she already had been, and without the stupid and brutal necessity, any longer, of slaughtering her reincarnate worshipers.

The Sunbeam soon returned, carrying Ellen, Lilith and another Sister, whom he did not know. Nor did Lilith introduce her. Lilith's expression was exceedingly grim, and she was very pale—grimmer and paler had he would have expected, unless Sister Monique had been more precious to her than he had assumed.

Lilith told him, curtly, that a donkey-cart was following them down and would pick up the body to transport it to the convent for eventual burial, after the legal formalities had been completed. She said that she did not foresee any difficulty, once Paul had explained again what he had explained to Ellen Megister, but even as she reassured him, she seemed distracted, as if her mind was elsewhere.

Paul suggested that Ellen should return to Toulouse for now, and come back the following day, if she wanted to proceed with what would certainly be a final sitting.

"Perhaps you should come with me, Monsieur Furneret," Ellen suggested not using his forename because there were other people present and it would have lacked decorum. "I don't think you should stay here on your own. Your friend Gaston could surely find you somewhere to stay in the city."

"Or Clémence Sancerre," Lilith put in, helpfully.

"No," said Paul. "There are things I need to do here, before I return to Paris."

In spite of her evident distress, Lilith's face contrived to registered limited shock and disappointment, but she said nothing.

"You'll come with me in the Sunbeam, then?" Ellen said.

"That wouldn't be a good idea," Paul told her. "Victor would take it as a mortal insult to the Panhard, and would never forgive me. In any case, I don't want to risk compromising you in the ever-malevolent eyes of Parisian gossip. Ask Gaston to provide you with a female companion—there must be at least one of his female cousins who would relish the opportunity to visit Paris, and perhaps even England."

It was Ellen's turn to register surprise and disappointment, but she too said nothing, contenting herself with sustaining a dignified expression of hurt.

When the donkey cart arrived, Paul and Bernard loaded the body into it. The fake nun he did not know departed with it in one direction while the automobile drove off in the other.

When they had all gone, Lilith followed Paul back into the cottage; her expression was, to say the least, thunderous.

"What really happened, Paul?" she demanded.

"Exactly what I reported," Paul told her, with a conviction that he was rarely able to bring to such a blatant lie. "The poor woman suffered a fit, and staggered into the studio in search of help, which I was unfortunately unable to give her. She died. I'm truly sorry. We had formed a bond of sorts, and I shall mourn her death very sincerely. She was a good person."

She didn't believe him. He didn't care.

"Can I assume, given your remark about returning to Paris that you're not going to accept the commission I offered you?" she asked, although she sounded sullen rather than angry, as if she had known even before he had made the remark that he was not going to do the painting, and as if the shock and disappointment she had shown had merely been a reaction to confirmation, not genuine surprise..

"You can," he said, briefly.

"May I ask why?"

"Because I don't want to do it. Two people have died in three days while I was painting in a trace, and I don't want the total to increase any further."

There were countless rational arguments that she might have deployed against that assertion, of which she would doubtless have made use in other circumstances, but—as he had already observed—she had already accepted defeat. "It already has," she retorted, grimly.

That jerked him out of his relative calm. "Who?" he asked.

"Don't you know?" she countered, bitterly.

"No, I don't," he said. "Surely we aren't going to play guessing games." But he could not resist adding: "Is it Salome?" He remembered seeing her in the rim of the Cleft, and knew how dangerous a place that was to stand

"No," was the reply. "Approximately two and a half hours ago—while you were painting, I presume, Sister Justine went into premature labor. Not long thereafter, she delivered a stillborn child."

Not for the first time that day, Paul felt as if he had been stabbed in the heart, but again, it was a hallucination. He sat down on the sofa, facing Juliette, whose expression, seen from that angle, was now one of commiseration.

Lilith studied him, with what appeared to be clinical concern, but she made no comment.

"Justine?" Paul asked weakly.

"Poorly, but alive. We think she'll recover. Salome is with her."

Paul looked her directly in the face. "Was it a boy or a girl?" he asked.

"We're not sure," Lilith replied. "The evidence is...ambiguous."

After a pause, Paul said: "And have you informed the father?"

"We have not," she replied, flatly, evidently knowing what implication Paul would take from that. Had the fantasy he had invented about drugged liqueur and artificial insemination been true, she would surely have said yes. Or would she?

"Who was it?" he asked, bluntly.

"You don't need to know," she told him.

He disagreed, but he let it go. "I'm not your enemy, Sister Lilith," he said, mildly. "I'm truly sorry for Justine's loss. You know that I have a certain...sensitivity about such matters. I truly wish that the child had come to term, and that he or she could have lived up to your hopes."

"I'll pass your condolences on. When do you think you'll return from Paris?"

"I'm not sure," said Paul, "but probably not for some time, and perhaps never. With Gaston and Victor both settled there, and Madame Louvot too, I have more reasons for staying there than returning."

"What about Clémence Sancerre?" Lilith demanded, matching his bluntness.

"Clémence and I have an understanding," he said. "I can understand why you think you have an interest in both of us, but to be brutally honest, it's none of your business."

"Your mother might have thought differently."

"Perhaps—but to be brutally honest, it wouldn't have been any of her business either."

"To be brutally honest, as you seem unduly fond of putting it," Lilith retorted, "you're a true Marian, perhaps a unique Marian. It *is* our business, whether you like it or not, who you might marry, and with whom you might have children."

"If you truly think so," Paul riposted, "you might be disappointed, certainly with regard to Clémence, who is past the age at which she could bear a child safely, and probably with regard to me, for reasons that I don't care to disclose. I'm far from sure that I shall ever marry, but if I do, I doubt that I'm capable of fathering children—not, at least, children capable of being born."

That frank admission startled her. "Why do you think that?" she asked.

"No matter what you might think," he replied, "I repeat that it's none of your business, except insofar as it's a good reason for you to leave me out of any matchmaking plans you might have conceived, in your capacity as the self-appointed leader of the Marians of Toulouse."

"We don't have leaders," she said, semi-automatically, while she considered the substance of what he had said. After a pause, she softened, and said: "To borrow your own phrase...or Zosima's...I'm not your enemy either." She did not add: *you stupid boy*, although he suspected that the implication was there.

"Actually," he said, softening his own tone, "I know that. I believe that you never meant me any harm, and that your motives are fundamentally benevolent, as are mine. But the forces we have been playing with, tentatively, are dangerous. They can kill, and they have. That's more my fault than yours, and insofar as I've been culpable, I'm truly sorry—but I intend to do my best, in future, to make sure that I cannot serve again as a catalyst for malevolence. I think I shall be better able to do that in Paris than here. I do not think that the attraction that has held me here for the past few years is working in my best interests."

"This is where you belong," said Lilith, positively. "You're a true Marian. I was present at your birth, remember; I threw your cord into the Cleft. Whether you like it or not, you're bound to this place."

"You threw the cord into the Cleft, as you say, where whatever secret current runs through the unknown depths of it, no matter how slowly, eventually bore it away to some unknown sea in the bowels of the earth," Paul told her, "or delivered it to the Central Fire for vaporization."

"Which doesn't affect the symbolism at all," Lilith instead.

"Yes it does," Paul contradicted, "profoundly. I have been into the darkness of the bottomless pit in my dreams, Sister Lilith, and I have met its monsters—of which, perhaps, I am one. But I returned from those depths, this time as I have before. I do not want to descend into them again, lest I put anyone else at risk, and in spite of what you believe, I am not bound here. I am not bound to my sister and my ancestry in the way that you imagine."

"And yet," she countered, "you've invited Ellen Megister to return tomorrow in order to finish her portrait. Presumably you're confident that you can do so without danger; I hope you're right. You do realize, I suppose, that with a very slight effort, you might enable her fall in love with you. We've talked at length, and although she is suspicious of me, she definitely has...a romantic turn of mind. If you wanted to, you could surely persuade her to relocate here, to take up residence on what is now her own land, where she belongs."

"Zosima made the same suggestion," Paul told her. "But Ellen isn't sufficiently romantic, is she, for you to enable her to fall in love with you?"

Lilith smiled, wryly and perhaps bitterly. "She has barriers of prejudice that would be difficult to break down," she said, "but they are not insurmountable. Deep down, she's a true Marian. All I'd need is time."

"I doubt that you can believe me, Sister Lilith, but you have no idea what she is, deep down, or, in spite of all your hypnotic delving, what any of your true Marians is—but I truly fear that if you keep on digging, you might find out one day. Because I'm not your enemy, I wouldn't wish that upon you, so all I'll say is: be careful. You've never seen the goddess stripped of all her veils, but I have, if only for an instant. Believe in my sincerity as well as my benevolence when I say that I hope you never will."

She hesitated for half a minute, but he was right; she couldn't believe him. She had too much invested in her own beliefs.

"This isn't over, Monsieur Furneret," she said.

"For me, it is, at least for the moment," he told her, quietly, "as it is for poor Monique and Justine's unborn child. For the world, it goes on—but there is progress, and you and I are both part of that progress, on the same side."

Again, she couldn't believe him. "You can't get away from your sister," she told him, "no matter where you go."

"I know," he said, "and I wouldn't want to, now that I know her, and know myself. We have an understanding now—it isn't perfect, by any means, and probably never will be, but it's viable. I doubt that we can live happily ever after, in any conventional sense, but we can live, I feel sure, without posing any further danger to anyone else."

If she doubted that, she did not voice the doubt. But she still wanted the last word, at whatever cost. When he had escorted her to the gate, while not looking at him, deliberately staring into the space above the cultivated plain extended from the foot of the mountain, almost as if she were talking to herself, she said: "I love Justine, and Salome. I don't say that it's the only true love that exists, but it is love, and it is true."

"I believe you," Paul assured her, "and I wish you all well. Adieu."

"Au revoir," she said, insistently. What alternative did she have?

CHAPTER XX

The Panhard sped northwards, creating a wind that lashed the faces of its four passengers, all of whom were wearing helmets and scarves, although only Victor was sporting huge goggles. Paul, sitting behind him in the front of the vehicle, had to squint. Fortunately, the windscreen intercepted almost all of the dust stirred up by the wheels of the Sunbeam, which was traveling forty meters in front.

"I could overtake him, you know," Victor said. "We ought to be leading the way. We're on French soil, after all, and mine is the superior vehicle."

"It's not a race, Victor," Gaston told him. "Be polite. Remember that Armande's here, and that one of my favorite cousins is traveling with Mademoiselle Megister. We don't want any risk of an accident. There have been too many of those."

"If you'll forgive me for saying so," Victor replied, "I don't think that that Megister fellow was any great loss to the human race, and Monique certainly wasn't. But I take your point. We have a much more precious cargo."

"Actually," Paul felt obliged to say, "I'm not sure that I ought to forgive you for saying so, even though you've said a thousand things just as tactless over the years. Richard Megister wasn't a bad fellow at all, just a trifle English, which he could hardly help. He didn't deserve what happened to him. And Monique certainly didn't. She was a good person, a heroine after her fashion."

"She was a syphilic whore who evidently fell prey to the curse of her profession," Victor opined. "If she'd been in residence for two more nights, she'd have crawled into your bed, one way or another, and infected you. Fate did you a favor."

"That's a cruel thing to say, Victor," Armande objected, "and not very complimentary to Paul."

"That's all right," said Paul. "We're friends—he can say things like that, without being taken seriously. From Gaston, it would be hurtful, but Victor is just Victor. Don't worry about it—when he's married, Clorinde will soon lick him into shape."

Victor made no riposte to that, there being no possible riposte that could not be construed to his disadvantage. He was not, however, the only person in the vehicle with a gift for tactlessness.

"It's kind of you to honor us with your company, Paul," said Armande, "when Mademoiselle Megister would clearly have preferred that you ride in the Sunbeam with her. You must have made quite an impression on her while you were painting her portrait."

"We did form a bond of sorts," Paul admitted, "but you have to remember that the circumstances were highly unusual. In the four days that she was sitting for the portrait, two people died in the vicinity, one of them in the studio itself. A less strong-minded woman might have considered the endeavor cursed...and to tell the truth, it's far from my best work."

"Even so," Armande persisted, "If you'd wanted it, I believe you could have gone all the way to England with her—but I'm glad you didn't. When you paint me, though, it has to be your very best work. I don't care if the city is struck by one of Monsieur Flammarion's wayward comets and half the population is wiped out: the portrait has to be a work of genius, and nothing less." I'm entitled to demand that, aren't I, Gaston?"

Gaston, evidently unsure of that imaginary entitlement, made no reply, but Victor, ever unimpeded by the kind of scruples that anchored his friend's tongue, said: "You won't have to worry about that, my dear. Once Paul is back in Paris, where he belongs, his genius will finally come into full flower. He'll be out of the toxic miasma of local legend...with all due respect to your uncle, Gaston. No matter what people say about Parisian smog and the new menace of gasoline fumes,

I'm sure the air is healthier there than anywhere else in the world."

Nobody contradicted him, although Paul could not believe for an instant that their silence constituted assent.

Instead Gaston said: "Will you be seeing Flammarion again once you're installed in Paris, Paul? I know you were good friends at one time."

"Yes, certainly," Paul replied, knowing perfectly well that it was Flammarion the spiritist rather than the prophet of cometary doom that the other had in mind, "but I won't be participating in any séances at Juvisy."

"That won't stop Zosima seeking you out," Gaston opined. "She'll be eager to know what happened at the convent after she left. There's a lot of malevolent gossip going round Toulouse about one of the Three Maries having had a stillbirth. The story will reach Paris before we do...although Zosima must already have known that the Sister in question was pregnant. Did she say anything about it to you, Paul, when you saw her? "

"It's not the sort of thing she would mention to me," Paul said. dryly. "I might not have known anything at all about it if it hadn't been for Monique—but Lilith was very cut up about it. She had high hopes of the child."

"Why?" asked Victor. "I would have thought it was the last thing she wanted, given that the Three Witches have been proclaiming the superiority and perfection of their kind of love for more than for twenty years. A blot on the escutcheon, surely?"

"Perhaps—but even in Lilith's thinking, the colony is more phalanstery than nunnery. I'm not privy to her future plans, but I don't think they exclude children. Zosima's certainly didn't. She'll be very upset, I think, abut Justine's loss, but I doubt that she'll seek commiseration from me. We're not enemies, though. We can talk, if she wants to."

"I believe that she's helped your former housekeeper to find a small house in a village some way out of the city," Gaston informed him. "It's probably only a short excursion by railway, though, if you want to visit her."

"I know," Paul said. "Angélique has written to me. Fabien's apparently on the road to recovery, insofar as recovery is possible with one leg amputated below the knee. She still has hopes that he might marry, though. He's still as tall and as handsome as before."

"So are you," said Victor, "And we certainly haven't given up hope, have we, Gaston?"

Gaston made no reply, but Paul suspected that it was not because he had given up hope that his matchmaking endeavors might finally bear fruit.

"You're very kind," Paul said, "but let me concentrate on my painting for a while, please. I'm going to need all my creative energy if I'm to do justice to Armande and Clorinde, and the other clients that Chazelle seems to have queued up, in anticipation of my return to the capital. Settling into a new studio is always a challenge. It's almost a new life."

"I should hope so," said Victor. "That's the whole point. No more living with the dead; from now on, it's the living on whom you need to focus your attention and your brushwork."

"Don't demand too much, Victor," Gaston said. "Paul has a reputation to maintain, after all."

"Reputations," Victor replied, "can be renewed. The Sunbeam appears to be stopping at that coaching inn up ahead, but I assume it's for a break rather than engine trouble. Either way, I'll pull in behind him, and we can all have a drink, a bite to eat and stretch our legs."

He did as he had said. The inn, whose garden ran downhill to a stream bordered by trees, was advertised on its sign as Les Saules, with a picture of willows that appeared to be weeping with joy rather than grief. Paul admired that cunning artistry.

The two parties came together briefly, although Bernard and Victor soon absented themselves in order to check the operation of their machines, in partnership or in competition.

Ellen Megister moved to sit next to Paul.

"My traveling companion and I have been talking about you," she said.

Paul sighed very slightly, and said: "That's not entirely surprising." The young woman that Gaston had chosen to accompany the Englishwoman all the way home was one of the cousins to whom he had once introduced Paul, without bothering to inform Paul that he had represented him to her explicitly as a potential suitor—an expectation that he had not fulfilled.

"She seems a trifle annoyed with you, although I can't quite fathom why. We were wondering what drawing you might have made in your sleep last night. I said that it was probably a woman's face; she suggested that it would be a monster: a malevolent dragon or manticore."

"It was neither," Paul told her. "I've given that up. I won't be drawing in my dreams any longer. From now, all my art will be consciously planned and directed."

That surprised her "How could you give it up?" she asked. "I thought you couldn't help it?"

"So did I—but I'm hoping that I was wrong, and that I've now mastered the trick of it. It's a matter of being at peace with oneself, I think. I'm no longer in conflict with my nature. Perhaps it's only a truce, but I hope it might be a genuine treaty."

"Even treaties can be broken," she observed, but was quick to add: "Did I help you to find that peace?"

"Yes," he said, "You did—for which I'm grateful."

She was puzzled, but she did not ask him to elaborate as to how she had helped. Instead, she said: "Why is my companion hostile to you? She doesn't seem to be a malevolent person."

"She isn't," Paul said. "I fear that I disappointed her when Gaston suggested to her, mistakenly, that I might be a suitable husband. It wasn't that she actually wanted me for a husband, but nobody likes to be rejected. I had no intention of annoying her, but the situation was intrinsically annoying, in spite of everyone's good intentions. How do you like her? Will she be a good traveling companion, do you think?"

"Perfectly adequate," she replied, "but she isn't as good a listener as you are, and her English isn't nearly as good as yours when she interrupts or tries to reply, which she does very frequently. I never realized until these past few days what a relief there can be in a series of mostly one-sided but smooth conversations. I could never have talked to Richard the way I talked to you, and I needed to talk. I felt that we formed a real friendship, a real bond, in spite of the harrowing circumstances There'll be criticism, I think, when I get home, that I continued to sit for the portrait, in mourning-dress, after Richard's accident, but, to be honest, your studio was the only place that I felt safe, where I knew that nothing would be asked of me but sitting still, and that I'd be allowed to...let things out a little. I wanted to thank you for that, before we part in Paris."

"You're very welcome," Paul told her, sincerely. "I'm sorry that your visit to Toulouse turned out so badly, and that you never got to see the Riviera. But perhaps you'll come back again some day."

"To France? Quite probably. The Midi, I don't know. May I look you up in Paris, if you're still there?"

"Of course. It will be a delight to see you again."

She looked around to check the situation. Gaston and Armande were deep in conversation with Gaston's cousin; Victor and Bernard were still poring over the Sunbeam's engine. No one was within earshot of a careful whisper.

"I had a dream," said the Englishwoman.

"Last night?" Paul enquired, although he knew full well what she meant.

She frowned slightly. "While I was asleep, on your divan," she said. "I suppose I should have mentioned it sooner, that day or during the last sitting, when I could have rambled in about it at length, but I was...puzzled, and it didn't seem appropriate. I thought it would fade away, as the memory of dreams usually does, but it didn't. I dreamed that you were in danger, and I wanted desperately to help you, but I couldn't. It was very dark. You were in the grip of a horrible monster, which was running down a perpendicular surface, clutching you in a bloody claw. I don't suppose that there was anything I could have done, but I wanted to try, and I couldn't. I couldn't move. What do you think it means?" She asked the final question very tentatively, as if she were trying to defuse its provocative quality.

"I had a similar dream," Paul told her. "I think that our minds might have been linked momentarily by a kind of telepathy. It's happened to me before. I think it was really my dream, but that you were able to catch a glimpse of it. You wanted to help because you're a good person, but you couldn't because you were outside it. It was my predicament, and I had to get out of it myself...or go through it."

"But you weren't alone...or I wasn't. There were other eyes, invisible in the darkness, however absurd that sounds. They were watching you, as I was, willing you to escape. There were a great many of them...but you're a painter. There's a sense in which the eyes of the world are always on your work. That I can understand. *Did* you escape, in the end? I couldn't see."

"Evidently, I did," he replied. "I always do. As I said, similar dreams have visited me before, but thus far, I've always survived. And I think your presence might have helped. It's good in dreams like that to be able to feel that one isn't alone. One can't have too many guardian angels. For what it may be worth, though, the monster—the manticore—wasn't trying to hurt me. She was trying to save me."

"She?"

"Yes. Perhaps it was a womanticore rather than a manticore."

Because the pun only worked in the language they were speaking, she laughed at it, but only politely, because the wordplay was distinctly feeble. "What was she trying to save you from? I didn't see any other monsters."

"No, the worst monsters are always the ones you don't see, the sly ones...the ones that come from the deepest layers of the psyche. But they needn't frighten you. You're strong, and sane."

"So are you," she said, "in spite of what anyone else might say." She darted a glance at Gaston's cousin, who had apparently be casting sly aspersions on either his strength or his sanity, or both. He forgave her for that.

"You must forgive her for that," Paul suggested to his interlocutor. "There was a misunderstanding. Gaston meant well, but he can be a little clumsy sometimes. He has an excellent head for science and business, but not for matchmaking. He definitely meant well; he's been so happy with Armande, ever since they got engaged, that he'd like everyone else to be as happy as him—but he doesn't quite realize that different people need different things in order to be happy."

"And what do you need, Monsieur Furneret?" she asked, point blank, her eyes still on the cousin, perhaps wondering what there was about her that could fail to make a healthy and virile man happy, and using Paul's surname in an attempt to pretend that she was teasing rather than asking a serious question.

"I don't know," he replied, simply. "I wish I could say that I'll know when I find it, but I know myself too well to have that kind of confidence. I'm over thirty, but there's a sense in which my soul is still in embryo, still in the process of being sculpted by the patient chisel of creative death. I'm not sure yet what the final product will be. In the meantime, though, painting fills the gap."

"That's where I'm going wrong, then," she said, with a sigh. "I need to learn to paint. Will you give lessons, in Paris?"

"I don't think I could," he said, ruefully. "I'm too...intuitive. I don't have sufficient awareness of my own technique to teach it. I'm trying to be less self-absorbed, but I don't know whether I'll succeed fully and permanently. Only time will tell."

"I've given you my address in England," she said. "Will you promise to write to me?"

"I already have," he reminded her.

"I know—but I want you to mean it. Will you look me in the eyes now, and promise?"

He did.

"Thank you," she said. "And don't think you've seen the last of me." She stood up, and returned to her new companion, who shot a glance of intense curiosity at Paul, although it was Armande who stood up and came to join him.

"You've made a conquest there," she said. "I suspect that you could have the cousin as well, or instead, if you put your mind to it. They'll be thinking about you all the way to Lincolnshire. Gaston says he's given up on you, that you're a lost cause, but he doesn't mean it."

"No, he's a stubborn one—so is she, I think."

"The cousin?"

"Ellen. She feels a bond, but doesn't know how to evaluate it. It intrigues her."

"And you, of course, will tease her, keeping her interested without ever venturing anything, taking pleasure in the game. You should have been born a woman."

"I know," said Paul. "In a way, I was, beneath this deceptive masculine exterior. I wouldn't be half the painter I am, otherwise."

She looked at him long and hard. "I'm not going to fall half in love with you when you paint me, the way she has," she said, "so don't try it on me. I'm absolutely committed to Gaston. But that doesn't mean that you can give me anything less than your best. You have my permission to become obsessed with me, at least for the duration. If you do, though, I'll probably tease you a little."

"I'd expect no less," Paul assured her.

"That's better," she said. "You're easing up visibly the further away we get from Toulouse—the tension's ebbing away. Victor was right, you know; you really did need to get away from that damned mountain."

"You're probably right," Paul conceded, meekly.

"Can I ask you a personal question?" she said, suddenly.

"You already have a permanent permission," Paul reminded her, "And you seem be taking full advantage of it."

"No, that was just joking. This is serious. When you move into your new premises, are you going to hang the picture of your sister in your bedroom?"

"Yes."

"So that you can talk to her?"

"Yes."

"Good."

Paul arched in eyebrow. "Good?" he queried.

"Yes, good. No matter what Victor, or anyone else might say, good. I'm not saying that I understand, mind, but I think that it's good. You can trust her, I think, probably more than you can trust any woman who got as far as being born. I remember what you said, you see: a symbol of death and life, proof of immortality and reincarnation. Very poetic, for a painter. You'll come to my salon, won't you, every week? You'll allow me to show you off? You can rely on me not to try to fix you up, the way Gaston has—in fact, if anyone makes indecent eyes at you, I'll probably strike her off the guest list. My worshipful painter, in my salon? Absolutely not—forbidden ground. Unless, of course, you put in a request. That would be different. If you fall in love, I expect to be the first living person you tell, and I'll do everything I can to help you out...even if it's the Englishwoman. Gaston is almost your brother, so it shouldn't be difficult to think of me as another sister."

"I already do," he assured her, insincerely.

"Flatterer. Keep it up." Effortlessly, she changed gear. "Victor was wrong about the poor girl who died in your studio, wasn't he? She didn't die of syphilis at all."

"I'm not a physician," Paul said, "but no, I don't believe she did. She suffered an acute internal conflict, which caused her brain to seethe and seize up. She wasn't at fault in any way—quite the reverse."

"So why do you feel guilty about her death?"

"Is it so obvious that I do?"

"Not to everyone, perhaps, but I can tell. So can the Eng-lishwoman. Even Gaston has noticed, although it's not usually his forte to notice things like that."

"Because it was my fault," Paul said, with a slight shrug of the shoulders. "I didn't cause it by any deliberate action, but my presence did."

"Ah. And the Englishman?"

Slightly surprised, Paul shrugged again. "Less so," he said, "but yes, a little. If I hadn't been there..."

"And the baby that was stillborn at the convent?"

This time, Paul was genuinely astonished. But he knew that she had seen the painting of Virginie and even if she had not understood fully, she had sympathized, when no one else could."

"I don't know," he said.

"I do," she said, "and I'm ordering you to stop it. You can't assume the blame for everything that happens around you. It's too much. Look what it did to Jesus. And I have the right to give you the order, because I own you, at least until you finish my portrait. Your obsession is mine, for the time being, and I won't have it compromised. Is that clear?"

"As crystal." He was tempted to force a laugh, but he didn't.

"Good. Older sister, remember: older and wiser sister. I may look like a chit to you, frivolous and flighty, barely out of childhood, but there are some matters on which my judgment is as sound as a bell. This is one."

"I believe you."

"Good," she said, again, and she turned away, in order to return to her cousin by marriage, who was still chatting with Ellen Megister.

Gaston took his turn to leave the trio and come over to Paul.

"Don't mind Armande," he said. "She's in a bubbly mood. She talks a lot of nonsense, sometimes, but it's just natural exuberance. She likes you, in a mother hen sort of way. You seem to bring that out in women of all ages. If you thought like Victor, you could cut a real swathe through them."

"If I thought like Victor," Paul told him, "I wouldn't have that effect. Is the Panhard going to get us all the way to Paris, do you think, or will we end up taking the train?"

"God, I hope the old lady makes it," said Gaston. "She'll break Victor's fragile heart if she doesn't—and if the Panhard were to break down while the Sunbeam made it all the way back to England, it would be the end of the world. But he's waving at us; we'd better load up again.

He half-turned, and then paused. "Are you all right, Paul?" he asked, with an expression of the utmost seriousness, such as only Gaston Lambrunet, who had been his mother's beloved son, could contrive.

Paul stood up and drained his glass.

"Yes, I am," he said. "I am, in fact." He did not add: *for now*. There was no need.

www.ingramcontent.com/pod-product-compliance
Lightning Source LLC
Chambersburg PA
CBHW020256030726
47499CB00001B/218